Henry James was born in 1843 in Washington Place, New York, of Scottish and Irish ancestry. His father was a prominent theologian and philosopher, and his elder brother, William, is also famous as a philosopher. He attended schools in New York and later in London, Paris and Geneva, entering the Law School at Harvard in 1862. In 1864 he began to contribute reviews and short stories to American journals. In 1875, after two prior visits to Europe, he settled for a year in Paris, where he met Flaubert, Turgenev and other literary figures. However, the next year he moved to London, where he became so popular in society that in the winter of 1878–9 he confessed to accepting 107 invitations. In 1898 he left London and went to live at Lamb House, Rye, Sussex. Henry James became naturalized in 1915, was awarded the O.M., and died in 1916.

In addition to many short stories, plays, books of criticism, autobiography and travel he wrote some twenty novels, the first published being *Roderick Hudson* (1875). They include *The Europeans*, *Washington Square*, *The Portrait of a Lady*, *The Bostonians*, *The Princess Casamassima*, *The Tragic Muse*, *The Spoils of Poynton*, *The Awkward Age*, *The Wings of the Dove*, *The Ambassadors* and *The Golden Bowl*.

Roger Gard was educated at Abbotsholme School, Derbyshire, in the Royal Artillery and at Corpus Christi College, Cambridge. He is now Senior Lecturer in English at Queen Mary & Westfield College, University of London. Among his previous publications are books on Henry James, Jane Austen and the teaching of fiction in schools. He has also edited Henry James's *A Landscape Painter and Other Tales* and a selection of his literary criticism, *The Critical Muse*, for Penguin Classics.

HENRY JAMES

THE JOLLY CORNER
and Other Tales

EDITED WITH AN INTRODUCTION AND NOTES BY
ROGER GARD

PENGUIN BOOKS

PENGUIN BOOKS

Published by the Penguin Group
27 Wrights Lane, London W8 5TZ, England
Viking Penguin Inc., 40 West 23rd Street, New York, New York 10010, USA
Penguin Books Australia Ltd, Ringwood, Victoria, Australia
Penguin Books Canada Ltd, 2801 John Street, Markham, Ontario, Canada L3R 1B4
Penguin Books (NZ) Ltd, 182–190 Wairau Road, Auckland 10, New Zealand

Penguin Books Ltd, Registered Offices: Harmondsworth, Middlesex, England

First published 1990
1 3 5 7 9 10 8 6 4 2
Introduction and annotation copyright © Roger Gard, 1990
All rights reserved

The moral right of the editor has been asserted

Filmset in 10 pt Bembo (Lasercomp)

Made and printed in Great Britain by
Richard Clay Ltd, Bungay, Suffolk

CONTENTS

INTRODUCTION

I

THE following stories are a selection from those published in or after 1900 by Henry James, and so offer a substantial sample of the last flowerings of an important side of his genius. They are the contemporaries and successors of the 'late great' three long novels *The Wings of the Dove* (1902), *The Ambassadors* (1903), and *The Golden Bowl* (1904). Reflected in them too are the perceptions and labours associated with his revisit after twenty years to his native America with its specific fruit in his finest travel book and incisive social critique *The American Scene* (1907); and with the production of the massive, luxurious, and doomed 'New York' edition of his works and its celebrated Prefaces (1907–9). At the end the stories seem to be leading into the unfinished novel *The Ivory Tower* (published posthumously in 1917) which bade fair to take on full face, though in James's own idiosyncratic private manner, the savager results for its beneficiaries of high unbridled capitalism. They are thus the side productions, as it were, of an extremely fecund later life, and only occasionally tail off latterly into diffuseness and an elaboration unjustified by its subject. Established with his little household of servants at Lamb House in Rye (of which there is an affectionate portrait, under the characteristic fictional name 'Marr', in 'The Third Person'), and firmly wedded to the compositional practice of dictating to a typewriter, James was perfecting that famous formidable phenomenon which is called, usually with deference though sometimes with alarm, the 'late style'. It is the manner of a writer elegant, witty, distinguished, and the subject of lavish admiration, even adulation, from a small circle; but also lonely, and despairing, after bitter experience, of his still persistent ambition to be appreciated by a larger intelligent public. No magazine, for example, would publish 'The Beast in the Jungle'. It is a manner above all whose difficulty, whether cherished or deplored, was and is its most celebrated feature. It is the first duty of an introducer to do something about this.

II

How difficult are these late stories? Certainly the style is complicated, elaborate, many-tiered and subtle. But if we recognize this explicitly and allow the prose to dictate the manner of its reading there are great rewards.

One of the least attractive and fruitful results of the dignification of the novel since the eighteenth century, of coming to think that prose – the transcribed medium of every day and of M. Jourdain, the vehicle of every kind of factual discourse, of higher journalism, and of chat – is the obvious and familiar means by which high art is mediated, is that we tend to fuse categories and lose the awareness of possible distinctions. We too easily short cut, and require the ease and softness and lucidity offered by some fiction from all of it, and often inappropriately. Decorum is not explicitly attacked, but it is ignored. And this is irrational. Why should everything be so clear, so fast and at the same time so radiant with meaning as, to take the greatest example, Jane Austen? She is unique, extraordinary, and it is stupid as well as lazy to require (albeit unconsciously) similar conveniences from other writers. In extreme cases, it is true, these demands for ease are abashed: we admit an awe part religious, part historical, and part child-like, for the cadences of the Authorized Version; or, with a dinned-in respect for Artistic Experiment, the overlaid mimicries and pastiches of *Ulysses*. But these are not the books one tends generally to think of as a pleasurable discipline, whereas the works of other great writers, including Henry James (to the satisfaction of no parties) somehow – often lamentably – are. Or, to approach from a different angle, we blandly allow that sentences chopped up into lines of verse deserve a special attention based on the expectation that they will yield a special kind of concomitant reward in pleasure and significance. But, while a thoughtful look at most of what passes for contemporary poetry in magazines will dissipate this expectation – indeed it is often rather banal prose more or less pretentiously divided up – we persist at the same time in a demand for mere base readability from the writers of novels and short stories.

There is a simple, commercial principle which will lead out of this *impasse*. The sole, and minimum, relevant demand is that the expenditure of effort on the reader's part should be repaid by the richness, complexity and depth of the results in the mind and sensibility. We get what we, as it were, pay for – a feature in common with most good-quality human transactions, from the purchase of cloth to the conduct of a love affair. And *any* reader of late Henry James (contrary to the common *canard*, no special training or other documentation is required) will be able to feel freshly his wit and profundity and urbane charm so long as it is held initially firmly in mind (as it would be almost automatically with, for example, Milton or Wordsworth) that something extraordinary and worth a little extra attention is being offered. A good useful practical hint suggested by James himself is to read aloud, or as if aloud, and thus slowly, and giving permission for the rhythms to emerge and lead to the appropriate emphases.

The late James manner is not at all inevitably difficult, though it is always distinctive. 'The Birthplace' begins:

> It seemed to them at first, the offer, too good to be true, and their friend's letter, addressed to them to feel, as he said, the ground, to sound them as to inclinations and possibilities, had almost the effect of a brave joke at their expense.

Here the suspension of meaning, sustained by parenthesis within parenthesis between 'It seemed to them' and 'a brave joke', has the effect – besides informing us of the nature, though not the contents, of the letter – of conveying almost by mimicry the essence of the refined, hesitant nature of its recipients, the Gedges – an essential basis of the story. This type of hanging inversion *can* become a (none the less amiable) mannerism in, for example, the opening of 'A Round of Visits' (James's last, humorously disastrous tale, not reprinted here): 'He had been out but once since his arrival, Mark Monteith . . .' – but it is usually the function and result of an expressive purpose. 'The Birthplace' continues in a manner superficially the same, and still in anticipation of what the letter is about:

> Their friend, Mr Grant-Jackson, a highly preponderant, pushing person,

3

great in discussion and arrangement, abrupt in overture, unexpected, if not perverse, in attitude, and almost equally acclaimed and objected to in the wide midland region to which he had taught, as the phrase was, the size of his foot – their friend . . .

But here the space between 'Their friend' and the third repetition of that phrase is occupied by an economical, explosive, alliterative catalogue of characterizing attributes quite the opposite of the Gedges's – but also as perceived by them. What is to note is that reading it is not at all hard – as opposed to provoking and amusing – precisely because its subject matter is, relative to James's more extended effects, simple. In engaging the attention on the side of the Gedges as well as beginning to describe their situation, these sentences are certainly an expansion of the proposition 'The Gedges received an offer in a letter from Grant-Jackson', but an expansion which obviously pays. The manner is an essential, not an obstacle. This can be appreciated on a much larger scale by considering the brilliant country-house opening (itself comparable to the richly humorous treatment of a similar setting in 'Broken Wings') of 'The Beast in the Jungle', where – with an amazing virtuosity entirely subdued to the purpose of expressing a whole range of nuances related to the subtle and inadequate nature of the tragic hero, John Marcher, and his situation, past, place, and appearance – almost six full pages elapse before we find out what the 'speech' mentioned in the fourth word is. Yet there is nothing in it, parts or the whole, to defeat even a normally careful reader. Rather it achieves in a short space the amount of evocation and blocking-in which it would take an ordinary artist chapters to evolve.

Instead of smothering everything under the blanket of difficulty, then, it is a good idea to see what really is so and why. The picture of a seaside resort at evening in 'The Bench of Desolation', though the latest of late James, is quite straightforward:

> The road, the wide terrace beyond, the seats, the eternal sea beyond that, the lighted lamps now flaring in the October night-wind, with the few dispersed people abroad at the tea-hour; these things meeting and melting into the firelit hospitality at his elbow – or was it that portentous amenity that melted into *them*? – seemed to form round him and to put before him, all together, the strangest of circles and the newest of experiences, in which the unforgettable and the unimaginable were confoundingly mixed.

Straightforward to the attentive, anyway. But compare a similar scene infused with a not dissimilar emotion in 'The Velvet Glove':

> *That* was knowing Paris, of a wondrous bland April night; that was hanging over it from the vague consecrated lamp-studded heights and taking in, spread below and afar, the great scroll of all its irresistible story, pricked out, across river and bridge and radiant *place*, and along quays and boulevards and avenues, and around monumental circles and squares, in syllables of fire, and sketched and summarized, further and further, in the dim fire-dust of endless avenues; that was all of the essence of fond and thrilled and throbbing recognition, with a thousand things understood and a flood of response conveyed, a whole familiar possessive feeling appealed to and attested.

Here, by contrast, the reader may at first find the effect both wildly elaborate and dull, and the hero's emotion unsupported and merely stated in rather embarrassing superlatives. It needs re-reading perhaps. It *is* difficult. On re-reading however the difficulty both evaporates and is seen to be justified. The prospect of Paris is specifically that from Montmartre ('consecrated . . . heights'). And that city, like any modern city seen from a height, defines itself at night in its lights. The plan, or record of casually determined evolution, thus revealed in a great capital (London and Rome offer similar prospects) narrates the history of its own growth stage by stage — from the fortress on the Seine to the outer Haussmann boulevards in this case perhaps. And the underlying simile, elaborated with detailed exactitude and of course appropriate to the ironic literary subjects of 'The Velvet Glove' (epic and Romance and modern trumpery) is of the delighted sudden apprehension of an unrolled manuscript — an illuminated manuscript perhaps: the 'great scroll . . . pricked out [*pricked* is a medieval term for written] . . . in syllables of fire . . . and sketched and summarized'. It is on this very precise visual and literary basis that the hero Berridge, here an urban Wordsworth, is overwhelmed by emotion. And the emotion is itself characterized as essentially vague, and probably excessive, as such quasi-numinous vastations tend to be. The pivotal word is 'endless', which belongs to both spheres and is followed by such obviously wide and general terms as 'fond . . . a thousand things . . . a flood . . . a whole familiar possessive feeling'. This mutually validatory running together of precision with a lavish throb in a complicated verbal texture suggests poetry. We could try a common critical trick to discover whether it is possible to see, for example, the beautiful ageing May Bartram in 'The Beast in the Jungle' in this mode:

> She was a sphinx, yet with her white
> Petals and green fronds
> She might have been a lily too –
> Only an artificial lily,
> Wonderfully imitated and constantly kept,
> Without dust or stain,
> Though not exempt from a slight droop
> And a complexity of faint creases,
> Under some clear glass bell.

No: this is not *quite* right – superior as it is, with its fine rhythmic motor and pulse and specificity of image, to a lot of twentieth-century verse. But the pleasantness of the experiment with diction emphasizes the existence of that element in the late James for which 'poetic' really is the best, or only, word. This is not a question of the ornamental, or optional. It involves function, usually the function of various types of metaphor. The lovely sentimentality of Morris Gedge's Shakespearian reverie, where real *Sehnsucht* for lost time fights with humour –

He felt as if a window had opened into a great green woodland, a woodland that had a name, glorious, immortal, that was peopled with vivid figures, each of them renowned, and that gave out a murmur, deep as the sound of the sea, which was the rustle in forest shade of all the poetry, the beauty, the colour of life. It would be prodigious that of this transfigured world *he* should keep the key . . .

– is attractive in itself, but also illustrative of Gedge's sensibility in relation to the main theme of the story – another essential component. The receptiveness of Marcher's mind is at the heart of 'The Beast in the Jungle'. It is characteristically made present to us by chains of imagery. For example, his partially awakening recollection receives celebrated psychological notation through a suggestion of semi-conscious but spreading ignition:

Her face and her voice, all at his service now, worked the miracle – the impression operating like the torch of a lamplighter who touches into flame, one by one, a long row of gas jets.

This idea, exactly like a motif in a Shakespeare play, undergoes ominous restatement and transformation at the climax of the tale:

> The incident of an autumn day had put the match to the train laid from of old by his misery.

And recurs immediately, most bleakly, at the sight of another mourner which:

> ... named to him, as in letters of quick flame, something he had utterly, insanely missed, and what he had missed made these things a train of fire, made them mark themselves in an anguish of inward throbs ... the stranger's face ... still flared for him like a smoky torch ... Now that the illumination had begun ... it blazed to the zenith ...

And this elaborate covert mine of fire and explosive consciousness is of course subsidiary to the dark main image in this story — that of the lurking wild beast itself.

As might be expected, this grand manner fails, like Milton's grand manner and in very much the same way, on those odd occasions — not, really, at all frequent — when it sweeps because of its confident power into areas where something much simpler would be much better. There it provides the germ — sometimes even the reason — for that opinion of the half-read and half-receptive which finds in late James the merely wordy. Berridge's transactions with limousine windows at the end of 'The Velvet Glove' are extremely obscure, even ludicrous. After their erotically charged and tantalizing drive he arrives with the Princess at her *hôtel* and we are anxious to know what, when he orders the chauffeur to pull up, and in view of all this mutual hand kissing, he proposes to do:

> Berridge, as his hand now broke away, felt he had cut his cable; with which, after he had stepped out, he raised again the glass he had lowered and closed, its own already being down, the door that had released him. During these motions he had the sense of his companion, still radiant and splendid, but somehow momentarily suppressed, suspended, silvered over and celestially blurred, even as a summer moon by the loose veil of cloud. So it was he saw her while he leaned for farewell on the open window-ledge ...

Scarcely a vivid series of actions or impressions. S. Gorley Putt (in *A Reader's Guide to Henry James*, London, 1966) justly remarks of a passage immediately previous that 'No conscious parody of the late James would dare go as far as this.' Subtlety is a redundant and damaging habit where subtlety is not required, and an awkward action is put into awkward, tired prose (there are some comparable descents in 'The Bench of Desolation'). But it is, happily, equally and more importantly true that this fault of over-rendering, where the great complex machine of sensibility is misapplied to the simple and commonplace, is rarely felt in these stories. H. G. Wells's well-known and wounding derisions about a leviathan retrieving pebbles or a hippopotamus picking up a pea are crass as well as weakly cruel (one feels that Wells never really recovered even *his* conceit after the stern courtesies of James's letters of rebuke) for the simple reason that James is rarely concerned with the basic physical actions of his protagonists as opposed to the strenuous and delicate operations of their spirit. We have to balance against the trifling occasional lurch into ponderosity the beautiful, sinuous, uniquely expressive rhythms of psychic movement achieved by exactly the same manner when, for example, Marcher mentally encounters the shade of May, again at the end of 'The Beast in the Jungle':

> He did this, from time to time, with such effect that he seemed to wander through the old years with his hand in the arm of a companion who was, in the most extraordinary manner, his other, his younger self; and to wander, which was more extraordinary yet, round and round a third presence – not wandering she, but stationary, still, whose eyes, turning with his revolution, never ceased to follow him . . .

This is much more characteristic. It represents that curious passionate and masculine delicacy of phrase which makes fanatics out of some admirers: 'not wandering she, but stationary, still' – what is poetic power if this is not it? Nor is this touchstone of our prose particularly difficult to read.

Another area which does become genuinely difficult, it can be admitted with admiration, is that in which late James experiments with yet further expressiveness. In places he pushes to new limits the presentation of, or rather the fusion through metaphor of, the perceiving mind and the external (but how external?) world. The question of this relationship is in an obvious, though divinely subtle, way at the centre of the masterpiece among these tales, 'The Jolly Corner'. But it is ubiquitous in the detail of many of them. The passage I have just cited from 'The Beast in the Jungle' actually occurs over a gravestone in a cemetery – but its strange solemn tripartite pacing takes place in another unspecified world which is just as, or more, real to the reader. And this has nothing whatever to do with ghosts – these being in James in any case always psychological and moral indicators, never mere spooks. Similarly in 'Crapy Cornelia', where things the reverse of tragic or grand are being commemorated, there is at moments a deliberate and fruitful melding of inner and outer. White-Mason visits the wealthy and handsome young widow Mrs Worthingham (names are always important in James, nearly as important as in Dickens, and Abel Taker in 'Fordham Castle' is headily joined by Remson Sturch) in her brilliantly chic modern rococo apartment, in brilliantly chic new-money New York. He is contemplating a proposal of marriage to her while vaguely mentally subtracting the slightly jarring presence of another, older and dowdier, visitor. The view on to his fine wish-fulfilment is at once metaphorical and actual (and I have to quote at length):

> Her outlook took form to him suddenly as a great square sunny window that hung in assured fashion over the immensity of life. There rose toward it as from a vast swarming *plaza* a high tide of motion and sound; yet it was at the same time as if even while he looked her light gemmed hand, flashing on him in addition to those other things the perfect polish of the prettiest pink finger-nails in the world, had touched a spring, the most ingenious of recent devices for instant ease, which dropped half across the scene a soft-coloured mechanical blind, a fluttered fringed awning of charmingly toned silk, such as would make a bath of cool shade for the favoured friend leaning with her there – that is for the happy couple itself – on the balcony. The great view would be the prospect and privilege of the very state he coveted – since didn't he covet it? – the state of being so securely at her side; while the wash of privacy, as one might count it, the broad fine brush dipped into clear umber and passed, full and wet, straight across the strong scheme of colour, would represent the security itself, all the uplifted inner elegance, the condition, so ideal, of being shut out from nothing and yet of having, so gaily and breezily aloft, none of the burden or worry of anything. Thus, as I say,

for our friend, the place itself, while his vivid impression lasted, portentously opened and spread, and what was before him took, to his vision,
though indeed at so other a crisis, the form of the 'glimmering square' of
the poet; yet, for a still more remarkable fact, with an incongruous object
usurping at a given instant the privilege of the frame and seeming, even
as he looked, to block the view.

The incongruous object was a woman's head, crowned with a little
sparsely feathered black hat . . .

This, in a story which also incorporates virtuoso effects taken with brisk
up-to-dateness from the then promising new techniques of the cinema (for
what it is worth, there follows a kind of zoom-shot on to the woman's,
Cornelia's, head), is a whole happy metaphorical structure − itself
generating a separate, impressively exact, internal trope about glazing
pigment with umber in painting, as well as a pleasantry about Lord
Tennyson − concerning privilege, modernity, and a rather mindless
amenity. The dazzling view is all inside White-Mason's calculating mind,
but it none the less clearly *derives* from the envisaged external scene, and
at the end, with a jolt to fantasy, really returns to it. In the same manner
Cornelia's head is both a true visual obstacle and an emotional check,
symbolic in the most natural way of an older New York. As he had done
in parts of the later novels − notably *The Golden Bowl* − James is
experimenting with an elision of the barrier between a comparison and
its object, and instead of making something stand for something else,
presents them as different but simultaneous facets of the same thing. Far
from being a mandarin and purely literary grace, this seems to me to press
close on to experience. The fusion of the external with the fluctuating
exercise of mind and feeling is a constant part of perception, which we
have to deny, if we deny, only in the interests of the clarity and
simplification needed for day-to-day survival. James is a modern realist
writer, but genuinely innovative − the opposite of a verbose punter at
word games in the manner of some current 'post-modernists'.

III

This little description, and attempted defence, of the elaborate late
manner has strayed far from the none the less valid advice to read with

deliberation. Now – though an introducer should never spoil the reader's pleasure by rehearsing the plots of what he recommends, suspense being one of the prime virtues of even the most sophisticated fictions – it is time to remark briefly and selectively on the underlying thematic preoccupations of these rather magical tales. Again the reader who presupposes, in accordance with that tired image of Henry James as the master of the ivory tower – which still receives a remarkable admiring sustenance from some of the lesser universities in the States and from Yugoslavia – that we shall have only, or even mainly, to do with the finessed feelings and drawn out discriminations of an implausibly wealthy Edwardian leisured class, is liable to be surprised, possibly disappointed. Fine feelings there are. As to wealth and leisure, they are not only not the point in any of the stories, but many of the protagonists – the Gedges in 'The Birthplace' and Herbert Dodd in 'The Bench of Desolation' in particular – have difficulty in keeping even afloat in the chill, unforgiving ocean of early twentieth-century shabby gentility. Indeed in 'The Bench of Desolation' James conducted one of his periodic excursions into the territory of George Gissing, or the Wells of *Kipps*, with a result that I do not find totally happy (Herbert's lavish concern with himself, his tears, can be embarrassing) though it is so brilliantly done as to demand reprinting.

James's own life is of only tangential relevance here. But, as I have said, it is evident that these stories go with – as of course we would expect – its important events, and by pointing at these we can get closer to the substantial matter of the fiction. Many things lead towards a predominant, melancholy, questioning of choice and possibility. The semi-retirement from the metropolitan glitter to Rye; the revivification of his interest, as a result of his visit to the transformed America of the Gilded Age, in the 'international' contrast between America and Europe/England, which had been his own fairly celebrated means of defining civilization earlier in his career, and had tended to lapse; the preparation of the New York edition with its consequent even further pondering and re-pondering of the nature of art and the artist; the reinforcement of his sense of failure with the public by the dire fate of that edition (many of its pages were to be used as cartridge paper in the soon ensuing War); and – linked especially to this but much more extensive and deeper than it – the periodic despair caused by the sense that life had been wasted, was unfulfilled and was now unfulfillable. This last is the deepest and most generalizable preoccupation. Its manifestation in life is recorded with particular, disconcerting vividness by Edith Wharton's descriptions in letters to her lover and their mutual friend Morton Fullerton, in the first months of 1910, of the 67-year-old James's sudden swings in and out of blackly suicidal crises (see *The Letters of Edith Wharton*, ed. R. W. B. and Nancy Lewis, New York, 1988). And, transmuted into fiction, rendered predominantly in a series of character-istically complex past tenses, and treated in moods and variations from the humorous to the utterly bleak, it seems to stand behind and inform much of the fiction.

The idea is one of contingency. Everybody must feel that something has been missed, because electing one course of life precludes any other. But what in my case has been missed? By what inadvertence, what crime, what wrong step? When? How? Where? Does it matter? Would it have been better? Or different? Or what? – what constitutes loss? Such questions are appropriate to ageing genius – but so they are, I suppose, to every sentient person at almost every stage of life. It is quite feasible at twenty to feel with James the need to project the 'possible other case' (actually his phrase for irony) and to respond even so early to his remark to Hugh Walpole in 1913: 'I only regret, in my chilled age, certain occasions and possibilities I *didn't* embrace.' This itself recalls the famous 'germ' for *The Ambassadors* – 'Live all you can: it's a mistake not to. It doesn't so much matter what you do – but live . . . Don't be stupid . . . Don't, at any rate, make *my* mistake. Live!' (speech in the 1900 *Scenario* for the novel). And does it depend on one's own *virtú* how the passing and declining years are bestridden? Most of us of course must dismiss or suppress such speculation on the past, or cease to function. One of the things James does in these stories is to create, entertain, and fathom it through his art.

The really distinguishing feature of these stories is his tenderness to this subject. It is the tenderness of a high intellect for the battered experience of the ordinary, the modest, the sad, the possible or real failure, and is the great underlying fact of this fiction, present like a geological stratum beneath all the various moods and outcomes. *The Wings of the Dove* and *The Golden Bowl* are big, detailed, baroque structures which constantly involve, even where they do not invoke,

INTRODUCTION

grandeur of position and of motive and experience. They are, or contain, exemplary tragedies and villainies and sacrifices. Princes and princesses, metaphorical and literal, huge fortunes and at least the shade of past empires are present – Venice, Paris, Rome and London are the portentous places of action. The late stories can include a comparable glamour – the Paris of 'The Velvet Glove' is an example – but on the contrary at their centre tends to be a feeling for little mute tragedies or comedies eloquently explored. The cosmopolitan artist and wit is the exponent of the vulnerable, of the lost life, and of the stupidity inherent in mere passivity. Some people will prefer the shorter works because they can be as deep and charming as the novels while never, for obvious reasons, as daunting.

Since every reader can test these generalizations against the stories for themselves, it would be redundant to be more specific here. Nevertheless it is necessary, though late, to add that their tone is nothing like so doom-filled as the foregoing *might* suggest. 'The Third Person', 'The Birthplace', 'The Velvet Glove' and 'Crapy Cornelia' are predominantly comic. And the quasi-religious treatment of Shakespeare in 'The Birthplace' makes one laugh out loud – a rare effect in literature.

IV

Like all selections from a writer of genius, this one leaves much to be desired – at least by the selector. There are many other tales of this period which could have been reprinted with profit. In libraries all the shorter fiction can be found in Leon Edel's *The Complete Tales of Henry James* (London, 1962–4) – and I would particularly recommend to the interested reader 'The Tree of Knowledge' (1900), 'The Two Faces' (1900), 'The Beldonald Holbein' (1901), 'The Papers' (1903) and 'A Round of Visits' (1910). Meanwhile what follows is a substantial taste of James's distinctive art in its latest flower.

London – Rome 1989

NOTE

It is the frequent practice in paperback reprints of James to include his own 'New York' preface to the work when there is one. This often has the curious effect of starting an earlier fiction (often in an unrevised text) with a stretch of James's later critical prose. Here the work is of the same period, but his comment on the four stories which are in that edition is fairly marginal – though it contains some resonant formulations – and I have therefore, and in order to save space, decided not to extract and reprint it from Vols. XVI and XVII. Those interested may consult the edition itself or, most conveniently, the volume entitled 'French Writers, Other European Writers and Prefaces to the New York Edition' in the Library of America *Henry James: Literary Criticism*, ed. Leon Edel and Mark Wilson, New York and Cambridge, 1984 (1241–2; 1250–52; 1256; 1259–60; and 1263–4).

THE THIRD PERSON

WHEN, a few years since, two good ladies, previously not intimate nor indeed more than slightly acquainted, found themselves domiciled together in the small but ancient town of Marr, it was as a result, naturally, of special considerations. They bore the same name and were second cousins; but their paths had not hitherto crossed; there had not been coincidence of age to draw them together; and Miss Frush, the more mature, had spent much of her life abroad. She was a bland, shy, sketching person, whom fate had condemned to a monotony – triumphing over variety – of Swiss and Italian *pensions*; in any one of which, with her well-fastened hat, her gauntlets and her stout boots, her camp-stool, her sketch-book, her Tauchnitz[1] novel, she would have served with peculiar propriety as a frontispiece to the natural history of the English old maid. She would have struck you indeed, poor Miss Frush, as so happy an instance of the type that you would perhaps scarce have been able to equip her with the dignity of the individual. This was what she enjoyed, however, for those brought nearer – a very insistent identity, once even of prettiness, but which now, blanched and bony, timid and inordinately queer, with its utterance all vague interjection and its aspect all eyeglass and teeth, might be acknowledged without inconvenience and deplored without reserve. Miss Amy, her kinswoman, who, ten years her junior, showed a different figure – such as, oddly enough, though formed almost wholly in English air, might have appeared much more to betray a foreign influence – Miss Amy was brown, brisk and expressive: when really young she had even been pronounced showy. She had an innocent vanity on the subject of her foot, a member which she somehow regarded as a guarantee of her wit, or at least of her good taste. Even had it not been pretty she flattered herself it would have been shod: she would never – no, never, like Susan – have given it up. Her bright brown eye was comparatively bold, and she had accepted Susan once for all as a frump. She even thought her, and silently deplored her as, a goose. But she was none the less herself a lamb.

They had benefited, this innocuous pair, under the will of an old aunt, a prodigiously ancient gentlewoman, of whom, in her later time, it had been given them, mainly by the office of others, to see almost nothing; so that the little property they came in for had the happy effect of a windfall. Each, at least, pretended to the other that she had never dreamed – as in truth there had been small encouragement for dreams in the sad character of what they now spoke of as the late lady's 'dreadful *entourage.*' Terrorized and deceived, as they considered, by her own people, Mrs Frush was scantily enough to have been counted on for an act of almost inspired justice. The good luck of her husband's nieces was that she had really outlived, for the most part, their ill-wishers and so, at the very last, had died without the blame of diverting fine Frush property from fine Frush use. Property quite of her own she had done as she liked with; but she had pitied poor expatriated Susan and had remembered poor unhusbanded Amy, though lumping them together perhaps a little roughly in her final provision. Her will directed that, should no other arrangement be more convenient to her executors, the old house at Marr might be sold for their joint advantage. What befell, however, in the event, was that the two legatees, advised in due course, took an early occasion – and quite without concert – to judge their prospects on the spot. They arrived at Marr, each on her own side, and they were so pleased with Marr that they remained. So it was that they met: Miss Amy, accompanied by the office-boy of the local solicitor, presented herself at the door of the house to ask admittance of the caretaker. But when the door opened it offered to sight not the caretaker, but an unexpected, unexpecting lady in a very old waterproof, who held a long-handled eyeglass very much as a child holds a rattle. Miss Susan, already in the field, roaming, prying, meditating in the absence on an errand of the woman in charge, offered herself in this manner as in settled possession; and it was on that idea that, through the eyeglass, the cousins viewed each other with some penetration even before Amy came in. Then at last when Amy did come in it was not, any more than Susan, to go out again.

It would take us too far to imagine what might have happened had Mrs Frush made it a condition of her benevolence that the subjects of it should inhabit, should live at peace together, under the roof she left them; but certain it is that as they stood there they had at the same moment the same unprompted thought. Each became aware on the spot that the dear old house itself was exactly what she, and exactly what the other, wanted; it met in perfection their longing for a quiet harbour and an assured future; each, in short, was willing to take the other in order to get the house. It was therefore not sold; it was made, instead, their own, as it stood, with the dead lady's extremely 'good' old appurtenances not only undisturbed and undivided, but piously reconstructed and infinitely admired, the agents of her testamentary purpose rejoicing meanwhile to see the business so simplified. They might have had their private doubts – or their wives might have; might cynically have predicted the sharpest of quarrels, before three months were out, between the deluded yoke-fellows, and the dissolution of the partnership with every circumstance of recrimination. All that need be said is that such prophets would have prophesied vulgarly. The Misses Frush were not vulgar; they had drunk deep of the cup of singleness and found it prevailingly bitter; they were not unacquainted with solitude and sadness, and they recognized with due humility the supreme opportunity of their lives. By the end of three months, moreover, each knew the worst about the other. Miss Amy took her evening nap before dinner, an hour at which Miss Susan could never sleep – it was so odd; whereby Miss Susan took her's after that meal, just at the hour when Miss Amy was keenest for talk. Miss Susan, erect and unsupported, had feelings as to the way in which, in almost any posture that could pass for a seated one, Miss Amy managed to find a place in the small of her back for two out of the three sofa-cushions – a smaller place, obviously, than they had ever been intended to fit.

But when this was said all was said; they continued to have, on either side, the pleasant consciousness of a personal soil, not devoid of fragmentary ruins, to dig in. They had a theory that their lives had been immensely different, and each appeared now to the other to have conducted her career so perversely only that she should have an un-familiar range of anecdote for her companion's ear. Miss Susan, at foreign *pensions*, had met the Russian, the Polish, the Danish, and even an occasional flower of the English, nobility, as well as many of the most extraordinary Americans, who, as she said, had made everything of her and with whom she had remained, often, in correspondence; while Miss Amy, after all less conventional, at the end of long years of London, abounded in reminiscences of literary, artistic and even – Miss Susan heard it with bated breath – theatrical society, under the influence of which she had written – there, it came out! – a novel that had been anonymously published and a play that had been strikingly type-copied. Not the least charm, clearly, of this picturesque outlook at Marr would be the support that might be drawn from it for getting back, as she hinted, with 'general society' bravely sacrificed, to 'real work.' She had in her head hundreds of plots – with which the future, accordingly, seemed to bristle for Miss Susan. The latter, on her side, was only waiting for the wind to go down to take up again her sketching. The wind at Marr was often high, as was natural in a little old huddled, red-roofed, historic south-coast town which had once been in a manner mistress, as the cousins reminded each other, of the 'Channel,' and from which, high and dry on its hilltop though it might be, the sea had not so far receded as not to give, constantly, a taste of temper. Miss Susan came back to English scenery with a small sigh of fondness to which the consciousness of Alps and Apennines only gave more of a quaver; she had picked out her subjects and, with her head on one side and a sense that they were easier abroad, sat sucking her water-colour brush and nervously – perhaps even a little inconsistently – waiting and hesitating. What had happened was that they had, each for herself, re-discovered the country; only Miss Amy, emergent from Bloomsbury lodgings, spoke of it as primroses and sunsets, and Miss Susan, rebounding from the Arno and the Reuss, called it, with a shy, synthetic pride, simply England.

The country was at any rate in the house with them as well as in the little green girdle and in the big blue belt. It was in the objects and relics that they handled together and wondered over, finding in them a ground for much inferred importance and invoked romance, stuffing large stories into very small openings and every faded bell-rope that might jingle rustily into the past. They were still here in the presence, at all events, of their common ancestors, as to whom, more than ever before, they took only the best for granted. Was not the best, for that matter – the best, that is, of little melancholy, middling, disinherited Marr – seated in every stiff chair of the decent old house and stitched into the patchwork of every quaint old counterpane? Two hundred years of it squared themselves in the brown, panelled parlour, creaked patiently on the wide staircase and bloomed herbaceously in the red-walled garden. There was nothing any one had ever done or been at Marr that a Frush hadn't done it or been it. Yet they wanted more of a picture and talked themselves into the fancy of it; there were portraits – half a dozen, comparatively recent (they called 1800 comparatively recent), and something of a trial to a descendant who had copied Titian at the Pitti; but they were curious of detail and would have liked to people a little more thickly their backward space, to set it up behind their chairs as a screen embossed with figures. They threw off theories and small imaginations, and almost conceived themselves engaged in researches; all of which made for pomp and circumstance. Their desire was to discover something, and, emboldened by the broader sweep of wing of her companion, Miss Susan herself was not afraid of discovering something bad. Miss Amy it was who had first remarked, as a warning, that this was what it might all lead to. It was she, moreover, to whom they owed the formula that, had anything *very* bad ever happened at Marr, they should be sorry if a Frush hadn't been in it. This was the moment at which Miss Susan's spirit had reached its highest point: she had declared, with her odd, breathless laugh, a prolonged, an alarmed or alarming gasp, that she should really be quite ashamed. And so they rested a while; not saying quite how far they were prepared to go in crime – not giving the matter a name. But there would have been little doubt for an observer that each supposed the other to mean that she not only didn't draw the line at murder, but stretched it so as to take in – well, gay deception. If Miss Susan could conceivably have asked whether Don Juan had ever touched at that port, Miss Amy would, to a certainty, have wanted to know by way of answer at what port he had *not* touched. It was only unfortunately true that no one of the portraits of gentlemen looked at all like him and no one of those of ladies suggested one of his victims.

At last, none the less, the cousins had a find, came upon a box of old odds and ends, mainly documentary; partly printed matter, newspaper and pamphlets yellow and grey with time, and, for the rest, epistolary – several packets of letters, faded, scarce decipherable, but clearly sorted for preservation and tied, with sprigged ribbon of a far-away fashion, into little groups. Marr, below ground, is solidly founded – underlaid with great straddling cellars, sound and dry, that are like the groined crypts of churches and that present themselves to the meagre modern conception as the treasure-chambers of stout merchants and bankers in the old bustling days. A recess in the thickness of one of the walls had yielded up, on resolute investigation – that of the local youth employed for odd jobs and who had happened to explore in this direction on his own account – a collection of rusty superfluities among which the small chest in question had been dragged to light. It produced of course an instant impression and figured as a discovery; though indeed as rather a deceptive one on its having, when forced open, nothing better to show, at the best, than a quantity of rather illegible correspondence. The good ladies had naturally had for the moment a fluttered hope of old golden guineas – a miser's hoard; perhaps even of a hatful of those foreign coins of old-fashioned romance, ducats, doubloons, pieces of eight, as are sometimes found to have come to hiding, from over seas, in ancient ports. But they had to accept their disappointment – which they sought to do by making the best of the papers, by agreeing, in other words, to regard them as wonderful. Well, they *were*, doubtless, wonderful; which didn't prevent them, however, from appearing to be, on superficial inspection, also rather a weary labyrinth. Baffling, at any rate, to Miss Susan's unpractised eyes, the little pale-ribboned packets were, for several evenings, round the fire, while she luxuriously dozed, taken in hand by Miss Amy; with the result that on a certain occasion when, toward nine o'clock, Miss Susan woke up, she found her fellow-labourer fast asleep. A slightly irritated confession of ignorance of the Gothic character was the further consequence, and the upshot of this, in turn, was the idea of appeal to Mr Patten. Mr Patten was the vicar and was known to interest himself, as such, in the ancient annals of Marr; in addition to which – and to its being even held a little that his sense of the affairs of the hour was sometimes sacrificed to such inquiries – he was a gentleman with a humour of his own, a flushed face, a bushy eyebrow and a black wideawake worn sociably askew. 'He will tell us,' said Amy Frush, 'if there's anything in them.'

'Yet if it should be,' Susan suggested, 'anything we mayn't like?'

'Well, that's just what I'm thinking of,' returned Miss Amy in her offhand way. 'If it's anything we shouldn't know – '

'We've only to tell him not to tell us? Oh, certainly,' said mild Miss Susan. She took upon herself even to give him that warning when, on the invitation of our friends, Mr Patten came to tea and to talk things over; Miss Amy sitting by and raising no protest, but distinctly promising herself that, whatever there might be to be known, and however objectionable, she would privately get it out of their initiator. She found herself already hoping that it *would* be something too bad for her cousin – too bad for any one else at all – to know, and that it most properly might remain between them. Mr Patten, at sight of the papers, exclaimed, perhaps a trifle ambiguously, and by no means clerically, 'My eye, what a lark!' and retired, after three cups of tea, in an overcoat bulging with his spoil.

II

At ten o'clock that evening the pair separated, as usual, on the upper landing, outside their respective doors, for the night; but Miss Amy had hardly set down her candle on her dressing-table before she was startled by an extraordinary sound, which appeared to proceed not only from her companion's room but from her companion's throat. It was something she would have described, had she ever described it, as between a gurgle and a shriek, and it brought Amy Frush, after an interval of stricken stillness that gave her just time to say to herself 'Some one under her bed!' breathlessly and bravely back to the landing. She had not reached it, however, before her neighbour, bursting in, met her and stayed her.

'There's some one in my room!'

They held each other. 'But who?'

'A man.'

'Under the bed?'

'No — just standing there.'

They continued to hold each other, but they rocked. 'Standing? Where? How?'

'Why, right in the middle — before my dressing-glass.'

Amy's blanched face by this time matched her mate's, but its terror was enhanced by speculation. 'To look at himself?'

'No — with his back to it. To look at *me*,' poor Susan just audibly breathed. 'To keep me off,' she quavered. 'In strange clothes — of another age; with his head on one side.'

Amy wondered. 'On one side?'

'Awfully!' the refugee declared while, clinging together, they sounded each other.

This, somehow, for Miss Amy, was the convincing touch; and on it, after a moment, she was capable of the effort of darting back to close her own door. 'You'll remain then with me.'

'Oh!' Miss Susan wailed with deep assent; quite, as if, had she been a slangy person, she would have ejaculated 'Rather!' So they spent the night together; with the assumption thus marked, from the first, both that it would have been vain to confront their visitor as they didn't even pretend to each other they would have confronted a house-breaker; and that by leaving the place at his mercy nothing worse could happen than had already happened. It was Miss Amy's approaching the door again as with intent ear and after a hush that had represented between them a deep and extraordinary interchange — it was this that put them promptly face to face with the real character of the occurrence. 'Ah,' Miss Susan, still under her breath, portentously exclaimed, 'it isn't any one — !'

'No' — her partner was already able magnificently to take her up. 'It isn't any one — '

'Who can really hurt us' — Miss Susan completed her thought. And Miss Amy, as it proved, had been so indescribably prepared that this thought, before morning, had, in the strangest, finest way, made for itself an admirable place with them. The person the elder of our pair had seen in her room was not – well, just simply was not any one in from outside. He was a different thing altogether. Miss Amy had felt it as soon as she heard her friend's cry and become aware of her commotion; as soon, at all events, as she saw Miss Susan's face. That was all – and there it was. There had been something hitherto wanting, they felt, to their small state and importance; it was present now, and they were as handsomely conscious of it as if they had previously missed it. The element in question, then, was a third person in their association, a hovering presence for the dark hours, a figure that with its head very much – too much – on one side, could be trusted to look at them out of unnatural places; yet only, it doubtless might be assumed, to look at them. They had it at last – had what was to be had in an old house where many, too many, things had happened, where the very walls they touched and floors they trod could have told secrets and named names, where every surface was a blurred mirror of life and death, of the endured, the remembered, the forgotten. Yes; the place was h— but they stopped at sounding the word. And by morning, wonderful to say, they were used to it – had quite lived into it.

Not only this indeed, but they had their prompt theory. There was a connection between the finding of the box in the vault and the appearance in Miss Susan's room. The heavy air of the past had been stirred by the bringing to light of what had so long been hidden. The communication of the papers to Mr Patten had had its effect. They faced each other in the morning at breakfast over the certainty that their queer roused inmate was the sign of the violated secret of these relics. No matter; for the sake of the secret they would put up with his attention; and – this, in them, was most beautiful of all – they must, though he was such an addition to their grandeur, keep him quite to themselves. Other people might hear of what was in the letters, but they should never hear of *him*. They were not afraid that either of the maids should see him – he was not a matter for maids. The question indeed was whether – should he keep it up long – they themselves would find that they could really live with him. Yet perhaps his keeping it up would be just what would make them indifferent. They turned these things over, but spent the next nights together; and on the third day, in the course of their afternoon walk, descried at a distance the vicar, who, as soon as he saw them, waved his arms violently – either as a warning or as a joke – and came more than half-way to meet them. It was in the middle – or what passed for such – of the big, bleak, blank, melancholy square of Marr; a public place, as it were, of such an absurd capacity for a crowd; with the great ivy-mantled choir and stopped transept of the nobly planned church telling of how many centuries ago it had, for its part, given up growing.

'Why, my dear ladies,' cried Mr Patten as he approached, 'do you know what, of all things in the world, I seem to make out for you from your funny old letters?' Then as they waited, extremely on their guard now: 'Neither more nor less, if you please, than that one of your ancestors in the last century – Mr Cuthbert Frush, it would seem, by name – was hanged.'

They never knew afterwards which of the two had first found composure – found even dignity – to respond. 'And pray, Mr Patten, for what?'

'Ah, that's just what I don't yet get hold of. But if you don't mind my digging away' – and the vicar's bushy, jolly brows turned from one of the ladies to the other – 'I think I can run it to earth. They hanged, in those days, you know,' he added as if he had seen something in their faces, 'for almost any trifle!'

'Oh, I hope it wasn't for a trifle!' Miss Susan strangely tittered.

'Yes, of course one would like that, while he was about it – well, it had been, as they say,' Mr Patten laughed, 'rather for a sheep than for a lamb!'

'Did they hang at that time for a sheep?' Miss Amy wonderingly asked.

It made their friend laugh again. 'The question's whether *he* did! But we'll find out. Upon my word, you know, I quite want to myself. I'm awfully busy, but I think I can promise you that you shall hear. You *don't* mind?' he insisted.

'I think we could bear *anything*,' said Miss Amy.

Miss Susan gazed at her, on this, as for reference and appeal. 'And what is he, after all, at this time of day, *to* us?'

Her kinswoman, meeting the eyeglass fixedly, spoke with gravity. 'Oh, an ancestor's always an ancestor.'

'Well said and well felt, dear lady!' the vicar declared. 'Whatever they may have done – '

'It isn't every one,' Miss Amy replied, 'that has them to be ashamed of.'

'And we're not ashamed *yet*!' Miss Frush jerked out.

'Let me promise you then that you shan't be. Only, for I am busy,' said Mr Patten, 'give me time.'

'Ah, but we want the truth!' they cried with high emphasis as he quitted them. They were much excited now.

He answered by pulling up and turning round as short as if his professional character had been challenged. 'Isn't it just in the truth – and the truth only – that I deal?'

This they recognized as much as his love of a joke, and so they were left there together in the pleasant, if slightly overdone, void of the square, which wore at moments the air of a conscious demonstration, intended as an appeal, of the shrinkage of the population of Marr to a solitary cat. They walked on after a little, but they waited till the vicar was ever so far away before they spoke again; all the more that their doing so must bring them once more to a pause. Then they had a long look. 'Hanged!' said Miss Amy – yet almost exultantly.

This was, however, because it was not she who had seen. 'That's why his head – ' but Miss Susan faltered.

Her companion took it in. 'Oh, has such a dreadful twist?'

'It *is* dreadful!' Miss Susan at last dropped, speaking as if she had been present at twenty executions.

There would have been no saying, at any rate, what it didn't evoke from Miss Amy. 'It breaks their neck,' she contributed after a moment.

Miss Susan looked away. 'That's why, I suppose, the head turns so fearfully awry. It's a most peculiar effect.'

So peculiar, it might have seemed, that it made them silent afresh. 'Well then, I hope he killed some one!' Miss Amy broke out at last.

Her companion thought. 'Wouldn't it depend on whom – ?'

'No!' she returned with her characteristic briskness – a briskness that set them again into motion.

That Mr Patten was tremendously busy was evident indeed, as even by the end of the week he had nothing more to impart. The whole thing meanwhile came up again – on the Sunday afternoon; as the younger Miss Frush had been quite confident that, from one day to the other, it must. They went inveterately to evening church, to the close of which supper was postponed; and Miss Susan, on this occasion, ready the first, patiently awaited her mate at the foot of the stairs. Miss Amy at last came down, buttoning a glove, rustling the tail of a frock and looking, as her kinswoman always thought, conspicuously young and smart. There was no one at Marr, she held, who dressed like her; and Miss Amy, it must be owned, had also settled to this view of Miss Susan, though taking it in a different spirit. Dusk had gathered, but our frugal pair were always tardy lighters, and the grey close of day, in which the elder lady, on a high-backed hall chair, sat with hands patiently folded, had for all cheer the subdued glow – always subdued – of the small fire in the drawing-room, visible through a door that stood open. Into the drawing-room Miss Amy passed in search of the prayer-book she had laid down there after morning church, and from it, after a minute, without this volume, she returned to her companion. There was something in her movement that spoke – spoke for a moment so largely that nothing more was said till, with a quick unanimity, they had got themselves straight out of the house. There, before the door, in the cold, still twilight of the winter's end, while the church bells rang and the windows of the great choir showed across the empty square faintly red, they had it out again. But it was Miss Susan herself, this time, who had to bring it.

'He's there?'

'Before the fire – with his back to it.'

'Well, now you see!' Miss Susan exclaimed with elation and as if her friend had hitherto doubted her.

'Yes, I see – and what you mean.' Miss Amy was deeply thoughtful.

'About his head?'

'It *is* on one side,' Miss Amy went on. 'It makes him –' she considered. But she faltered as if still in his presence.

'It makes him awful!' Miss Susan murmured. 'The way,' she softly moaned, 'he looks at you!'

Miss Amy, with a glance, met this recognition. 'Yes – doesn't he?' Then her eyes attached themselves to the red windows of the church. 'But it means something.'

'The Lord knows what it means!' her associate gloomily sighed.
Then, after an instant, 'Did he move?' Miss Susan asked.

'No – and *I* didn't.'

'Oh, I did!' Miss Susan declared, recalling to her more precipitous retreat.

'I mean I took my time. I waited.'

'To see him fade?'

Miss Amy for a moment said nothing. 'He doesn't fade. That's *it*.'

'Oh, then you did move!' her relative rejoined.

Again for a little she was silent. 'One *has* to. But I don't know what
really happened. Of course I came back to you. What I mean is that I
took him thoroughly in. He's young,' she added.

'But he's *bad*!' said Miss Susan.

'He's handsome!' Miss Amy brought out after a moment. And she
showed herself even prepared to continue: 'Splendidly.'

'"Splendidly!" – with his neck broken and with that terrible look?'

'It's just the look that makes him so. It's the wonderful eyes. They
mean something,' Amy Frush brooded.

She spoke with a decision of which Susan presently betrayed the
effect. 'And what do they mean?'

Her friend had stared again at the glimmering windows of St Thomas
of Canterbury. 'That it's time we should get to church.'

III

The curate that evening did duty alone; but on the morrow the vicar
called and, as soon as he got into the room, let them again have it. 'He
was hanged for smuggling!'

They stood there before him almost cold in their surprise and diffusing
an air in which, somehow, this misdemeanour sounded out as the
coarsest of all. '*Smuggling?*' Miss Susan disappointedly echoed – as if it
presented itself to the first chill of their apprehension that he had then
only been vulgar.

'Ah, but they hanged for it freely, you know, and I was an idiot for
not having taken it, in his case, for granted. If a man swung, hereabouts,
it *was* mostly for that. Don't you know it's on that we stand here today,

such as we are – on the fact of what our bold, bad forefathers were not afraid of? It's in the floors we walk on and under the roofs that cover us. They smuggled so hard that they never had time to do anything else; and if they broke a head not their own it was only in the awkwardness of landing their brandy-kegs. I mean, dear ladies,' good Mr Patten wound up, 'no disrespect to *your* forefathers when I tell you that – as I've rather been supposing that, like all the rest of us, you were aware – they conveniently lived by it.'

Miss Susan wondered – visibly almost doubted. 'Gentlefolks?'

'It was the gentlefolks who were the worst.'

'They must have been the bravest!' Miss Amy interjected. She had listened to their visitor's free explanation with a rapid return of colour. 'And since if they lived by it they also died for it – '

'There's nothing at all to be said against them? I quite agree with you,' the vicar laughed, 'for all my cloth; and I even go so far as to say, shocking as you may think me, that we owe them, in our shabby little shrunken present, the sense of a bustling background, a sort of undertone of romance. They give us' – he humorously kept it up, verging perilously near, for his cloth, upon positive paradox – 'our little handful of legend and our small possibility of ghosts.' He paused an instant, with his lighter pulpit manner, but the ladies exchanged no look. They were in fact already, with an immense revulsion, carried quite as far away. 'Every penny in the place, really, that hasn't been earned by subtler – not nobler – arts in our own virtuous time, and though it's a pity there are not more of 'em: every penny in the place was picked up, somehow, by a clever trick, and at the risk of your neck, when the backs of the king's officers were turned. It's shocking, you know, what I'm saying to you, and I wouldn't say it to every one, but I think of some of the shabby old things about us, that represent such pickings, with a sort of sneaking kindness – as of relics of our heroic age. What are we now? We were at any rate devils of fellows then!'

Susan Frush considered it all solemnly, struggling with the spell of this evocation. 'But must we forget that they were wicked?'

'Never!' Mr Patten laughed. 'Thank you, dear friend, for reminding me. Only I'm worse than they!'

'But would you do it?'

'Murder a coastguard – ?' The vicar scratched his head.

'I hope,' said Miss Amy rather surprisingly, 'you'd defend yourself.' And she gave Miss Susan a superior glance. '*I* would!' she distinctly added.

Her companion anxiously took it up. 'Would you defraud the revenue?'

Miss Amy hesitated but a moment; then with a strange laugh, which she covered, however, by turning instantly away, 'Yes!' she remarkably declared.

Their visitor, at this, amused and amusing, eagerly seized her arm. 'Then may I count on you on the stroke of midnight to help me – ?'

'To help you – ?'

'To land the last new Tauchnitz.'

She met the proposal as one whose fancy had kindled, while her cousin watched them as if they had suddenly improvised a drawing-room charade. 'A service of danger?'

'Under the cliff – when you see the lugger stand in!'

'Armed to the teeth?'

'Yes – but invisibly. Your old waterproof – !'

'Mine is new. I'll take Susan's!'

This good lady, however, had her reserves. 'Mayn't one of them, all the same – here and there – have been sorry?'

Mr Patten wondered, 'For the jobs he muffed?'

'For the wrong – as it *was* wrong – he did.'

'"One" of them?' She had gone too far, for the vicar suddenly looked as if he divined in the question a reference.

They became, however, as promptly unanimous in meeting this danger, as to which Miss Susan in particular showed an inspired presence of mind. 'Two of them!' she sweetly smiled. 'May not Amy and I – ?'

'Vicariously repent?' said Mr Patten. 'That depends – for the true honour of Marr – on how you show it.'

'Oh, we *sha'n't* show it!' Miss Amy cried.

'Ah, then,' Mr Patten returned, 'though atonements, to be efficient, are supposed to be public, you may do penance in secret as much as you please!'

'Well, *I* shall do it,' said Susan Frush.

Again, by something in her tone, the vicar's attention appeared to be caught. 'Have you then in view a particular form — ?'

'Of atonement?' She coloured now, glaring rather helplessly, in spite of herself, at her companion. 'Oh, if you're sincere you'll always find one.'

Amy came to her assistance. 'The way she often treats me has made her — though there's after all no harm in her — familiar with remorse. Mayn't we, at any rate,' the younger lady continued, 'now have our letters back?' And the vicar left them with the assurance that they should receive the bundle on the morrow.

They were indeed so at one as to shrouding their mystery that no explicit agreement, no exchange of vows, needed to pass between them; they only settled down, from this moment, to an unshared possession of their secret, an economy in the use and, as may even be said, the enjoyment of it, that was part of their general instinct and habit of thrift. It had been the disposition, the practice, the necessity of each to keep, fairly indeed to clutch, everything that, as they often phrased it, came their way; and this was not the first time such an influence had determined for them an affirmation of property in objects to which ridicule, suspicion, or some other inconvenience, might attach. It was their simple philosophy that one never knew of what service an odd object might *not* be; and there were days now on which they felt themselves to have made a better bargain with their aunt's executors than was witnessed in those law-papers which they had at first timorously regarded as the record of advantages taken of them in matters of detail. They had got, in short, more than was vulgarly, more than was even shrewdly supposed — such an indescribable unearned increment as might scarce more be divulged as a dread than as a delight. They drew together, old-maidishly, in a suspicious, invidious grasp of the idea that a dread of their very own — and blissfully not, of course, that of a failure of any essential supply — might, on nearer acquaintance, positively turn to a delight.

Upon some such attempted consideration of it, at all events, they found themselves embarking after their last interview with Mr Patten, an understanding conveyed between them in no redundancy of discussion, no flippant repetitions nor profane recurrences, yet resting on a sense of added margin, of appropriated history, of liberties taken with time and space, that would leave them prepared both for the worst and for the best. The best would be that something that would turn out to their advantage might prove to be hidden about the place; the worst would be that they might find themselves growing to depend only too much on excitement. They found themselves amazingly reconciled, on Mr Patten's information, to the particular character thus fixed on their visitor; they knew by tradition and fiction that even the highwaymen of the same picturesque age were often gallant gentlemen; therefore a smuggler, by such a measure, fairly belonged to the aristocracy of crime. When their packet of documents came back from the vicarage Miss Amy, to whom her associate continued to leave them, took them once more in hand; but with an effect, afresh, of discouragement and languor – a headachy sense of faded ink, of strange spelling and crabbed characters, of allusions she couldn't follow and parts she couldn't match. She placed the tattered papers piously together, wrapping them tenderly in a piece of old figured silken stuff; then, as solemnly as if they had been archives or statutes or title-deeds, laid them away in one of the several small cupboards lodged in the thickness of the wainscoted walls. What really most sustained our friends in all ways was their consciousness of having, after all – and so contrariwise to what appeared – a man in the house. It removed them from that category of the manless into which no lady really lapses till every issue is closed. Their visitor was an issue – at least to the imagination, and they arrived finally, under provocation, at intensities of flutter in which they felt themselves so compromised by his hoverings that they could only consider with relief the fact of nobody's knowing.

The real complication indeed at first was that for some weeks after their talks with Mr Patten the hoverings quite ceased; a circumstance that brought home to them in some degree a sense of indiscretion and indelicacy. They hadn't mentioned him, no; but they had come perilously near it, and they had doubtless, at any rate, too recklessly let in the light of old buried and sheltered things, old sorrows and shames. They roamed about the house themselves at times, fitfully and singly, when each supposed the other out or engaged; they paused and lingered, like soundless apparitions, in corners, doorways, passages, and sometimes suddenly met, in these experiments, with a suppressed start and a mute confession. They talked of him practically never; but each knew how the other thought – all the more that it was (oh yes, unmistakably!) in a manner different from her own. They were together, none the less, in feeling, while, week after week, he failed again to show, as if they had been guilty of blowing, with an effect of sacrilege, on old gathered silvery ashes. It frankly came out for them that, possessed as they so strangely, yet so ridiculously were, they should be able to settle to nothing till their consciousness was yet again confirmed. Whatever the subject of it might have for them of fear or favour, profit or loss, he had taken the taste from everything else. He had converted *them* into wandering ghosts. At last, one day, with nothing they could afterwards perceive to have determined it, the change came – came, as the previous splash in their stillness had come, by the pale testimony of Miss Susan.

She waited till after breakfast to speak of it – or Miss Amy, rather, waited to hear her; for she showed during the meal the face of controlled commotion that her comrade already knew and that must, with the game loyally played, serve as preface to a disclosure. The younger of the friends really watched the elder, over their tea and toast, as if seeing her for the first time as possibly tortuous, suspecting in her some intention of keeping back what had happened. What had happened was that the image of the hanged man had reappeared in the night; yet only after they had moved together to the drawing-room did Miss Amy learn the facts.

'I was beside the bed – in that low chair; about' – since Miss Amy must know – 'to take off my right shoe. I had noticed nothing before, and had had time partly to undress – had got into my wrapper. So suddenly – as I happened to look – there he was. And there,' said Susan Frush, 'he stayed.'

'But where do you mean?'

'In the high-backed chair, the old flowered chintz "ear-chair" beside the chimney.'

'All night? – and you in your wrapper?' Then as if this image almost challenged her credulity, 'Why didn't you go to bed?' Miss Amy inquired.

'With a – a person in the room?' her friend wonderfully asked; adding after an instant as with positive pride: 'I never broke the spell!'

'And didn't freeze to death?'

'Yes, almost. To say nothing of not having slept, I can assure you, one wink. I shut my eyes for long stretches, but whenever I opened them he was still there, and I never for a moment lost consciousness.'

Miss Amy gave a groan of conscientious sympathy. 'So that you're feeling now of course half dead.'

Her companion turned to the chimney-glass a wan, glazed eye. 'I dare say I *am* looking impossible.'

Miss Amy, after an instant, found herself still conscientious. 'You are.' Her own eyes strayed to the glass, lingering there while she lost herself in thought. 'Really,' she reflected with a certain dryness, 'if that's the kind of thing it's to be − !' there would seem, in a word, to be no withstanding it for either. Why, she afterwards asked herself in secret, should the restless spirit of a dead adventurer have addressed itself, in its trouble, to such a person as her queer, quaint, inefficient housemate? It was in *her*, she dumbly and somewhat sorely argued, that an unappeased soul of the old race should show a confidence. To this conviction she was the more directed by the sense that Susan had, in relation to the preference shown, vain and foolish complacencies. She had her idea of what, in their prodigious predicament, should be, as she called it, 'done', and that was a question that Amy from this time began to nurse the small aggression of not so much as discussing with her. She had certainly, poor Miss Frush, a new, an obscure reticence, and since she wouldn't speak first she should have silence to her fill. Miss Amy, however, peopled the silence with conjectural visions of her kinswoman's secret communion. Miss Susan, it was true, showed nothing, on any particular occasion, more than usual; but this was just a part of the very felicity that had begun to harden and uplift her. Days and nights hereupon elapsed without bringing felicity of any order to Amy Frush. If she had no emotions it was, she suspected, because Susan had them all; and − it would have been preposterous had it not been pathetic − she proceeded rapidly to hug the opinion that Susan was selfish and even something of a sneak. Politeness, between them, still reigned, but confidence had flown, and its place was taken by open ceremonies and confessed precautions. Miss Susan looked blank but resigned; which maintained again, unfortunately, her superior air and the presumption of her duplicity. Her manner was of not knowing where her friend's shoe pinched; but it might have been taken by a jaundiced eye for surprise at the challenge of her monopoly. The unexpected resistance of her nerves was indeed a wonder: was that then the result, even for a shaky old woman, of shocks sufficiently repeated? Miss Amy brooded on the rich inference that, if the first of them didn't prostrate and the rest didn't undermine, one might keep them up as easily as – well, say an unavowed acquaintance or a private commerce of letters. She was startled at the comparison into which she fell – but what was this but an intrigue like another? And fancy Susan carrying one on! That history of the long night hours of the pair in the two chairs kept before her – for it was always present – the extraordinary measure. Was the situation it involved only grotesque – or was it quite grimly grand? It struck her as both; but that was the case with all their situations. Would it be in herself, at any rate, to show such a front? She put herself such questions till she was tired of them. A few good moments of her own would have cleared the air. Luckily they were to come.

IV

It was on a Sunday morning in April, a day brimming over with the turn of the season. She had gone into the garden before church; they cherished alike, with pottering intimacies and opposed theories and a wonderful apparatus of old gloves and trowels and spuds and little botanical cards on sticks, this feature of their establishment, where they could still differ without fear and agree without diplomacy, and which now, with its vernal promise, threw beauty and gloom and light and space, a great good-natured ease, into their wavering scales. She was dressed for church; but when Susan, who had, from a window, seen her wandering, stooping, examining, touching, appeared in the doorway to signify a like readiness, she suddenly felt her intention checked. 'Thank you,' she said, drawing near; 'I think that, though I've dressed, I won't, after all, go. Please therefore, proceed without me.'

Miss Susan fixed her. 'You're not well?'

'Not particularly. I shall be better – the morning's so perfect – here.'

'Are you really ill?'

'Indisposed; but not enough so, thank you, for you to stay with me.'

'Then it has come on but just now?'

'No – I felt not quite fit when I dressed. But it won't do.'

'Yet you'll stay out here?'

Miss Amy looked about. 'It will depend!'

Her friend paused long enough to have asked what it would depend on, but abruptly, after this contemplation, turned instead and, merely throwing over her shoulder an 'At least take care of yourself!' went rustling, in her stiffest Sunday fashion, about her business. Miss Amy, left alone, as she clearly desired to be, lingered a while in the garden, where the sense of things was somehow made still more delicious by the sweet, vain sounds from the church tower; but by the end of ten minutes she had returned to the house. The sense of things was not delicious there, for what it had at last come to was that, as they thought of each other what they couldn't say, all their contacts were hard and false. The real wrong was in what Susan thought – as to which she was much too proud and too sore to undeceive her. Miss Amy went vaguely to the drawing-room.

They sat as usual, after church, at their early Sunday dinner, face to face; but little passed between them save that Miss Amy felt better, that the curate had preached, that nobody else had stayed away, and that everybody had asked why Amy had. Amy, hereupon, satisfied everybody by feeling well enough to go in the afternoon; on which occasion, on the other hand – and for reasons even less luminous than those that had operated with her mate in the morning – Miss Susan remained within. Her comrade came back late, having, after church, paid visits; and found her, as daylight faded, seated in the drawing-room, placid and dressed, but without so much as a Sunday book – the place contained whole shelves of such reading – in her hand. She looked so as if a visitor had just left her that Amy put the question: 'Has any one called?'

'Dear, no; I've been quite alone.'

This again was indirect, and it instantly determined for Miss Amy a conviction – a conviction that, on her also sitting down just as she was and in a silence that prolonged itself, promoted in its turn another determination. The April dusk gathered, and still, without further speech, the companions sat there. But at last Miss Amy said in a tone not quite her commonest: 'This morning he came – while you were at church. I suppose it must have been really – though of course I couldn't know it – what I was moved to stay at home for.' She spoke now – out of her contentment – as if to oblige with explanations.

But it was strange how Miss Susan met her. 'You stay at home for him? *I* don't!' She fairly laughed at the triviality of the idea.

Miss Amy was naturally struck by it and after an instant even nettled. 'Then why did you do so this afternoon?'

'Oh, it wasn't for *that*!' Miss Susan lightly quavered. She made her distinction. 'I *really* wasn't well.'

At this her cousin brought it out. 'But he has been with you?'

'My dear child,' said Susan, launched unexpectedly even to herself, 'he's with me so often that if I put myself out for him – !' But as if at sight of something that showed, through the twilight, in her friend's face, she pulled herself up.

Amy, however, spoke with studied stillness. 'You've ceased then to put yourself out? You gave me, you remember, an instance of how you once did!' And she tried, on her side, a laugh.

'Oh yes – that was at first. But I've seen such a lot of him since. Do you mean *you* hadn't?' Susan asked. Then as her companion only sat looking at her: 'Has this been really the first time for you – since we last talked?'

Miss Amy for a minute said nothing. 'You've actually believed me –'

'To be enjoying on your own account what *I* enjoy? How couldn't I, at the very least,' Miss Susan cried – 'so grand and strange as you must allow me to say you've struck me?'

Amy hesitated. 'I hope I've sometimes struck you as decent!'

But it was a touch that, in her friend's almost amused preoccupation with the simple fact, happily fell short. 'You've only been waiting for what didn't come?'

Miss Amy coloured in the dusk. 'It came, as I tell you, today.'

'Better late than never!' And Miss Susan got up.

Amy Frush sat looking. 'It's because you thought you had ground for jealousy that *you've* been extraordinary?'

Poor Susan, at this, quite bounced about. 'Jealousy?'

It was a tone – never heard from her before – that brought Amy Frush to her feet; so that for a minute, in the unlighted room where, in honour of the spring, there had been no fire and the evening chill had gathered, they stood as enemies. It lasted, fortunately, even long enough to give one of them time suddenly to find it horrible. 'But why should we quarrel *now*?' Amy broke out in a different voice.

Susan was not too alienated quickly enough to meet it. 'It *is* rather wretched.'

'Now when we're equal,' Amy went on.

'Yes – I suppose we are.' Then, however, as if just to attenuate the admission, Susan had her last lapse from grace. 'They say, you know, that when women do quarrel it's usually about a man.'

Amy recognized it, but also with a reserve. 'Well then, let there first *be* one!'

'And don't you call *him* – ?'

'No!' Amy declared and turned away, while her companion showed her a vain wonder for what she could in that case have expected. Their identity of privilege was thus established, but it is not certain that the air with which she indicated that the subject had better drop didn't press down for an instant her side of the balance. She knew that she knew most about men.

The subject did drop for the time, it being agreed between them that neither should from that hour expect from the other any confession or report. They would treat all occurrences now as not worth mentioning – a course easy to pursue from the moment the suspicion of jealousy had, on each side, been so completely laid to rest. They led their life a month or two on the smooth ground of taking everything for granted; by the end of which time, however, try as they would, they had set up no question that – while they met as a pair of gentlewomen living together only must meet – could successfully pretend to take the place of that of Cuthbert Frush. The spring softened and deepened, reached out its tender arms and scattered its shy graces; the earth broke, the air stirred, with emanations that were as touches and voices of the past; our friends bent their backs in their garden and their noses over its symptoms; they opened their windows to the mildness and tracked it in the lanes and by the hedges; yet the plant of conversation between them markedly failed to renew itself with the rest. It was not indeed that the mildness was not within them as well as without; all asperity, at least, had melted away; they were more than ever pleased with their general acquisition, which, at the winter's end, seemed to give out more of its old secrets, to hum, however faintly, with more of its old echoes, to creak, here and there, with the expiring throb of old aches. The deepest sweetness of the spring at Marr was just in its being in this way an attestation of age and rest. The place never seemed to have lived and lingered so long as when kind nature, like a maiden blessing a crone, laid rosy hands on its grizzled head. Then the new season was a light held up to show all the dignity of the years, but also all the wrinkles and scars. The good ladies in whom we are interested changed, at any rate, with the happy days, and it finally came out not only that the invidious note had dropped, but that it had positively turned to music. The whole tone of the time made so for tenderness that it really seemed as if at moments they were sad for each other. They had their grounds at last: each found them in her own consciousness; but it was as if each waited, on the other hand, to be sure she could speak without offence. Fortunately, at last, the tense cord snapped.

The old churchyard at Marr is still liberal; it does its immemorial utmost to people, with names and dates and memories and eulogies, with generations fore-shortened and confounded, the high empty table at which the grand old cripple of the church looks down over the low wall. It serves as an easy thoroughfare, and the stranger finds himself pausing in it with a sense of respect and compassion for the great maimed, ivied shoulders – as the image strikes him – of stone. Miss Susan and Miss Amy were strangers enough still to have sunk down one May morning on the sun-warmed tablet of an ancient tomb and to have remained looking about them in a sort of anxious peace. Their walks were all pointless now, as if they always stopped and turned, for an unconfessed want of interest, before reaching their object. That object presented itself at every start as the same to each, but they had come back too often without having got near it. This morning, strangely, on the return and almost in sight of their door, they were more in presence of it than they had ever been, and they seemed fairly to touch it when Susan said at last, quite in the air and with no traceable reference: 'I hope you don't mind, dearest, if I'm awfully sorry for you.'

'Oh, I know it,' Amy returned – 'I've felt it. But what does it do for us?' she asked.

Then Susan saw, with wonder and pity, how little resentment for penetration or patronage she had had to fear and out of what a depth of sentiment similar to her own her companion helplessly spoke. 'You're sorry for *me*?'

Amy at first only looked at her with tired eyes, putting out a hand that remained a while on her arm. 'Dear old girl! You might have told me before,' she went on as she took everything in; 'though, after all, haven't we each really known it?'

'Well,' said Susan, 'we've waited. We could only wait.'

'Then if we've waited together,' her friend returned, 'that *has* helped us.'

'Yes – to keep him in his place. Who would ever believe in him?' Miss Susan wearily wondered. 'If it wasn't for you and for me –'

'Not doubting of each other?' – her companion took her up: 'yes, there wouldn't be a creature. It's lucky for us,' said Miss Amy, 'that we *don't* doubt.'

'Oh, if we did we shouldn't be sorry.'

'No – except, selfishly, for ourselves. I am, I assure you, for *my* self – it has made me older. But, luckily, at any rate, we trust each other.'

'We do,' said Miss Susan.

'We do,' Miss Amy repeated – they lingered a little on that. 'But except making one feel older, what has it done for one?'

'There it is!'

'And though we've kept him in his place,' Miss Amy continued, 'he has also kept us in ours. We've lived with it,' she declared in melancholy justice. 'And we wondered at first if we could!' she ironically added. 'Well, isn't just what we feel now that we can't any longer?'

'No – it must stop. And I've my idea,' said Susan Frush.

'Oh, I assure you I've mine!' her cousin responded.

'Then if you want to act, don't mind me.'

'Because you certainly won't *me*? No, I suppose not. Well!' Amy sighed, as if, merely from this, relief had at last come. Her comrade echoed it; they remained side by side; and nothing could have had more oddity than what was assumed alike in what they had said and in what they still kept back. There would have been this at least in their favour for a questioner of their case, that each, charged dejectedly with her own experience, took, on the part of the other, the extraordinary – the ineffable, in fact – all for granted. They never named it again – as indeed it was not easy to name; the whole matter shrouded itself in personal discriminations and privacies; the comparison of notes had become a thing impossible. What was definite was that they had lived into their queer story, passed through it as through an observed, a studied, eclipse of the usual, a period of reclusion, a financial, social or moral crisis, and only desired now to live out of it again. The questioner we have been supposing might even have fancied that each, on her side, had hoped for something from it that she finally perceived it was never to give, which would have been exactly, moreover, the core of her secret and the explanation of her reserve. They at least, as the business stood, put each other to no test, and, if they were in fact disillusioned and disappointed, came together, after their long blight, solidly on that. It fully appeared between them that they felt a great deal older. When they got up from their sun-warmed slab, however, reminding each other of luncheon, it was with a visible increase of ease and with Miss Susan's hand drawn, for the walk home, into Miss Amy's arm. Thus the 'idea' of each had continued unspoken and ungrudged. It was as if each wished the other to try her own first; from which it might have been gathered that they alike presented difficulty and even entailed expense. The great questions remained. What then did he mean? What then did he want? Absolution, peace, rest, his final reprieve – merely to say *that* saw them no further on the way than they had already come. What were they at last to do for him? What could they give him that he would take? The ideas they respectively nursed still bore no fruit, and at the end of another month Miss Susan was frankly anxious about Miss Amy. Miss Amy as freely admitted that people *must* have begun to notice strange marks in them and to look for reasons. They were changed – they must change back.

v

Yet it was not till one morning at midsummer, on their meeting for breakfast, that the elder lady fairly attacked the younger's last entrenchment. 'Poor, poor Susan!' Miss Amy had said to herself as her cousin came into the room; and a moment later she brought out, for very pity, her appeal. 'When then *is* yours?'

'My idea?' It was clearly, at last, a vague comfort to Miss Susan to be asked. Yet her answer was desolate. 'Oh, it's no use!'

'But how do you know?'

'Why, I tried it – ten days ago, and I thought at first it had answered. But it hasn't.'

'He's back again?'

Wan, tired, Miss Susan gave it up. 'Back again.'

Miss Amy, after one of the long, odd looks that had now become their most frequent form of intercourse, thought it over. 'And just the same?'

'Worse.'

'Dear!' said Miss Amy, clearly knowing what that meant. 'Then what did you do?'

Her friend brought it roundly out. 'I made my sacrifice.'

Miss Amy, though still more deeply interrogative, hesitated. 'But of what?'

'Why, of my little all – or almost.'

The 'almost' seemed to puzzle Miss Amy, who, moreover, had plainly no clue to the property or attribute so described. 'Your "little all?"'

'Twenty pounds.'

'Money?' Miss Amy gasped.

Her tone produced on her companion's part a wonder as great as her own. 'What then is it yours to give?'

'My idea? It's not to *give*!' cried Amy Frush.

At the finer pride that broke out in this poor Susan's blankness flushed. 'What then is it to do?'

But Miss Amy's bewilderment outlasted her reproach. 'Do you mean he takes money?'

'The Chancellor of the Exchequer does – for "conscience."'

Her friend's exploit shone larger. 'Conscience-money? You sent it to Government?' Then while, as the effect of her surprise, her mate looked too much a fool, Amy melted to kindness. 'Why, you secretive old thing!'

Miss Susan presently pulled herself more together. 'When your ancestor has robbed the revenue and his spirit walks for remorse – '

'You pay to get rid of him? I see – and it becomes what the vicar called his atonement by deputy. But what if it isn't remorse?' Miss Amy shrewdly asked.

'But it *is* – or it seemed to me so.'

'Never to me,' said Miss Amy.

Again they searched each other. 'Then, evidently, with you he's different.'

Miss Amy looked away. 'I dare say!'

'So what *is* your idea?'

Miss Amy thought. 'I'll tell you only if it works.'

'Then, for God's sake, try it!'

Miss Amy, still with averted eyes and now looking easily wise, continued to think. 'To try it I shall have to leave you. That's why I've waited so long.' Then she fully turned, and with expression: 'Can you face three days alone?'

'Oh – "alone!" I wish I ever were!'

At this her friend, as for very compassion, kissed her; for it seemed really to have come out at last – and welcome! – that poor Susan was the worse beset. 'I'll do it! But I must go up to town. Ask me no questions. All I can tell you now is – '

'Well!' Susan appealed while Amy impressively fixed her.

'It's no more remorse than *I'm* a smuggler.'

'What is it then?'

'It's bravado.'

An 'Oh!' more shocked and scared than any that, in the whole business, had yet dropped from her, wound up poor Susan's share in this agreement, appearing as it did to represent for her a somewhat lurid inference. Amy, clearly, had lights of her own. It was by their aid, accordingly, that she immediately prepared for the first separation they had had yet to suffer; of which the consequence, two days later, was that Miss Susan, bowed and anxious, crept singly, on the return from their parting, up the steep hill that leads from the station of Marr and passed ruefully under the ruined town-gate, one of the old defences, that arches over it.

But the full sequel was not for a month – one hot August night when, under the dim stars, they sat together in their little walled garden. Though they had by this time, in general, found again – as women only can find – the secret of easy speech, nothing, for the half-hour, had passed between them: Susan had only sat waiting for her comrade to wake up. Miss Amy had taken of late to interminable dozing – as if with forfeits and arrears to recover; she might have been a convalescent from fever repairing tissue and getting through time. Susan Frush watched her in the warm dimness, and the question between them was fortunately at last so simple that she had freedom to think her pretty in slumber and to fear that she herself, so unguarded, presented an appearance less graceful. She was impatient, for her need had at last come, but she waited, and while she waited she thought. She had already often done so, but the mystery deepened tonight in the story told, as it seemed to her, by her companion's frequent relapses. What had been, three weeks before, the effort intense enough to leave behind such a trail of fatigue? The marks, sure enough, had shown in the poor girl that morning of the termination of the arranged absence for which not three days, but ten, without word or sign, were to prove no more than sufficient. It was at an unnatural hour that Amy had turned up, dusty, dishevelled, inscrutable, confessing for the time to nothing more than a long night-journey. Miss Susan prided herself on having played the game and respected, however tormenting, the conditions. She had her conviction that her friend had been out of the country, and she marvelled, thinking of her own old wanderings and her present settled fears, at the spirit with which a person who, whatever she had previously done, had not travelled, could carry off such a flight. The hour had come at last for this person to name her remedy. What determined it was that, as Susan Frush sat there, she took home the fact that the remedy was by this time not to be questioned. It had acted as her own had not, and Amy, to all appearance, had only waited for her to admit it. Well, she was ready when Amy woke – woke immediately to meet her eyes and to show, after a moment, in doing so, a vision of what was in her mind. 'What *was* it now?' Susan finally said.

'My idea? Is it possible you've not guessed?'

'Oh, you're deeper, much deeper,' Susan sighed, 'than I.'

Amy didn't contradict that – seemed indeed, placidly enough, to take it for truth; but she presently spoke as if the difference, after all, didn't matter now. 'Happily for us today – isn't it so? – our case is the same. I can speak, at any rate, for myself. He has left me.'

'Thank God then!' Miss Susan devoutly murmured. 'For he has left *me*.'

'Are you sure?'

'Oh, I think so.'

'But how?'

'Well,' said Miss Susan after an hesitation, 'how are *you*?'

Amy, for a little, matched her pause. 'Ah, that's what I can't tell you. I can only answer for it that he's gone.'

'Then allow me also to prefer not to explain. The sense of relief has for some reason grown strong in me during the last half-hour. That's such a comfort that it's enough, isn't it?'

'Oh, plenty!' The garden-side of their old house, a window or two dimly lighted, massed itself darkly in the summer night, and, with a common impulse, they gave it, across the little lawn, a long, fond look. Yes, they could be sure. 'Plenty!' Amy repeated. 'He's gone.'

Susan's elder eyes hovered, in the same way, through her elegant glass, at his purified haunt. 'He's gone. And how,' she insisted, '*did* you do it?'

'Why, you dear goose' – Miss Amy spoke a little strangely – 'I went to Paris.'

'To Paris?'

'To see what I could bring back – that I mightn't, that I shouldn't. To do a stroke with!' Miss Amy brought out.

But it left her friend still vague. 'A stroke – ?'

'To get through the Customs – under their nose.'

It was only with this that, for Miss Susan, a pale light dawned. 'You wanted to smuggle? *That* was your idea?'

'It was *his*,' said Miss Amy. 'He wanted no "conscience money" spent for him,' she now more bravely laughed: 'it was quite the other way about – he wanted some bold deed done, of the old wild kind; he wanted some big risk taken. And I took it.' She sprang up, rebounding, in her triumph.

Her companion, gasping, gazed at her. 'Might they have hanged you too?'

Miss Amy looked up at the dim stars. 'If I had defended myself. But luckily it didn't come to that. What I brought in I brought' – she rang out, more and more lucid, now, as she talked – 'triumphantly. To appease him – I braved them. I chanced it, at Dover, and they never knew.'

'Then you hid it – ?'

'About my person.'

With the shiver of this Miss Susan got up, and they stood there duskily together. 'It was so small?' the elder lady wonderingly murmured.

'It was big enough to have satisfied him,' her mate replied with just a shade of sharpness. 'I chose it, with much thought, from the forbidden list.'

The forbidden list hung a moment in Miss Susan's eyes, suggesting to her, however, but a pale conjecture. 'A Tauchnitz?'

Miss Amy communed again with the August stars. 'It was the *spirit* of the deed that told.'

'A Tauchnitz?' her friend insisted.

Then at last her eyes again dropped, and the Misses Frush moved together to the house. 'Well, he's satisfied.'

'Yes, and' – Miss Susan mused a little ruefully as they went – 'you got at last your week in Paris!'

BROKEN WINGS

I

CONSCIOUS as he was of what was between them, though perhaps less conscious than ever of why there should at that time of day be anything, he would yet scarce have supposed they could be so long in a house together without some word or some look. It had been since the Saturday afternoon, and that made twenty-four hours. The party — five-and-thirty people, and some of them great — was one in which words and looks might more or less have gone astray. The effect, none the less, he judged, would have been, for her quite as for himself, that no sound and no sign from the other had been picked up by either. They had happened, both at dinner and at luncheon, to be so placed as not to have to glare — or to grin — across; and for the rest they could each, in such a crowd, as freely help the general ease to keep them apart as assist it to bring them together. One chance there was, of course, that might be beyond their control. He had been the night before half surprised at not finding her his 'fate' when the long procession to the dining-room solemnly hooked itself together. He would have said in advance — recognizing it as one of the sharp 'notes' of Mundham — that, should the gathering contain a literary lady, the literary lady would, for congruity, be apportioned to the arm, when there was a question of arms, of the gentleman present who represented the nearest thing to literature. Poor Straith represented 'art,' and that, no doubt, would have been near enough had not the party offered for choice a slight excess of men. The representative of art had been of the two or three who went in alone, whereas Mrs Harvey had gone in with one of the representatives of banking.

It was certain, however, that she would not again be consigned to Lord Belgrove, and it was just possible that he himself should not be again alone. She would be, on the whole, the most probable remedy to that state, on his part, of disgrace; and this precisely was the great interest of their situation – they were the only persons present without some advantage over somebody else. They hadn't a single advantage; they could be named for nothing but their cleverness; they were at the bottom of the social ladder. The social ladder, even at Mundham, had – as they might properly have been told, as indeed practically they *were* told – to end somewhere; which is no more than to say that, as he strolled about and thought of many things, Stuart Straith had, after all, a good deal the sense of helping to hold it up. Another of the things he thought of was the special oddity – for it was nothing else – of his being there at all, and being there in particular so out of his order and his turn. He couldn't answer for Mrs Harvey's turn. It might well be that she was *in* hers; but these Saturday-to-Monday occasions had hitherto mostly struck him as great gilded cages as to which care was taken that the birds should be birds of a feather.

There had been a wonderful walk in the afternoon, within the limits of the place, to a far-away tea-house; and, in spite of the combinations and changes of this episode, he had still escaped the necessity of putting either his old friend or himself to the test. Also it had been all, he flattered himself, without the pusillanimity of his avoiding her. Life was, indeed, well understood in these great conditions; the conditions constituted in their greatness a kind of fundamental facility, provided a general exemption, bathed the hour, whatever it was, in a universal blandness, that were all a happy solvent for awkward relations. It was beautiful, for instance, that if their failure to meet amid so much meeting had been of Mrs Harvey's own contrivance he couldn't be in the least vulgarly sure of it. There were places in which he would have had no doubt, places different enough from Mundham. He felt all the same and without anguish that these were much more *his* places – even if she didn't feel that they were much more hers. The day had been warm and splendid, and this moment of its wane – with dinner in sight, but as across a field of polished pink marble which seemed to say that wherever in such a house there was space there was also, benignantly, time – formed, of the whole procession of the hours, the one dearest to our friend, who on such occasions interposed it, whenever he could, between the set of impressions that ended and the set that began with 'dressing.' The great terraces and gardens were almost void; people had scattered, though not altogether even yet to dress. The air of the place, with the immense house all seated aloft in strength, robed with summer and crowned with success, was such as to contribute something of its own to the poetry of early evening. This visitor, at any rate, saw and felt it all through one of those fine hazes of August that remind you – at least, they reminded *him* – of the artful gauze stretched across the stage of a theatre when an effect of mystery or some particular pantomimic ravishment is desired.

Should he, in fact, have to pair with Mrs Harvey for dinner it would be a shame to him not to have addressed her sooner; and should she, on the contrary, be put with someone else the loss of so much of the time would have but the greater ugliness. Didn't he meanwhile make out that there were ladies in the lower garden, from which the sound of voices, faint, but as always in the upper air of Mundham, exceedingly sweet, was just now borne to him? She might be among them, and if he should find her he would let her know he had sought her. He would treat it frankly as an occasion for declaring that what had happened between them – or rather what had *not* happened – was too absurd. What at present occurred, however, was that in his quest of her he suddenly, at the turn of an alley, perceived her, not far off, seated in a sort of bower with the Ambassador. With this he pulled up, going another way and pretending not to see them. Three times already that afternoon he had observed her in different situations with the Ambassador. He was the more struck accordingly when, upward of an hour later, again alone and with his state unremedied, he saw her placed for dinner next his Excellency. It was not at all what would have been at Mundham her right seat, so that it could only be explained by his Excellency's direct request. She *was* a success! This time Straith was well in her view and could see that in the candlelight of the wonderful room, where the lustres were, like the table, all crystal and silver, she was as handsome as anyone, taking the women of her age, and also as 'smart' as the evening before, and as true as any of the others to the law of a marked difference in her smartness. If the beautiful way she held herself

– for decidedly it *was* beautiful – came in a great measure from the good thing she professionally made of it all, our observer could reflect that the poor thing *he* professionally made of it probably affected his attitude in just the opposite way; but they communicated neither in the glare nor in the grin that he had dreaded. Still, their eyes did now meet, and then it seemed to him that her own were strange.

II

She, on her side, had her private consciousness, and quite as full a one, doubtless, as he, but with the advantage that, when the company separated for the night, she was not, like her friend, reduced to a vigil unalloyed. Lady Claude, at the top of the stairs, had said, 'May I look in – in five minutes – if you don't mind?' and then had arrived in due course and in a wonderful new beribboned gown, the thing just launched for such occasions. Lady Claude was young and earnest and delightfully bewildered and bewildering, and however interesting she might, through certain elements in her situation, have seemed to a literary lady, her own admirations and curiosities were such as from the first promised to rule the hour. She had already expressed to Mrs Harvey a really informed enthusiasm. She not only delighted in her numerous books, which was a tribute the author had not infrequently met, but she even appeared to have read them – an appearance with which her inter-locutress was much less acquainted. The great thing was that she also yearned to write, and that she had turned up in her fresh furbelows not only to reveal this secret and to ask for direction and comfort, but literally to make a stranger confidence, for which the mystery of midnight seemed propitious. Midnight was, indeed, as the situation developed, well over before her confidence was spent, for it had ended by gathering such a current as floated forth, with everything in Lady Claude's own life, many things more in that of her adviser. Mrs Harvey was, at all events, amused, touched, and effectually kept awake; and at the end of half an hour they had quite got what might have been called their second wind of frankness and were using it for a discussion of the people in the house. Their primary communion had been simply on the question of the pecuniary profits of literature as the producer of so many admired volumes was prepared to present them to an aspirant. Lady Claude was in financial difficulties and desired the literary issue. This was the breathless revelation she had rustled over a mile of crimson velvet corridor to make.

'Nothing?' she had three minutes later incredulously gasped. 'I can make nothing at all?' But the gasp was slight compared with the stupefaction produced in her by a brief further parley, in the course of which Mrs Harvey had, after a hesitation, taken her own plunge. '*You* make so little – wonderful *you*!' And then, as the producer of the admired volumes simply sat there in her dressing-gown, with the saddest of slow head-shakes, looking suddenly too wan even to care that it was at last all out: 'What, in that case, is the use of success and celebrity and genius? You *have* no success?' She had looked almost awestruck at this further confession of her friend. They were face to face in a poor human crudity, which transformed itself quickly into an effusive embrace. 'You've had it and lost it? Then when it has been as great as yours one *can* lose it?'

'More easily than one can get it.'

Lady Claude continued to marvel. 'But you do so much – and it's so beautiful!' On which Mrs Harvey simply smiled again in her handsome despair, and after a moment found herself again in the arms of her visitor. The younger woman had remained for a little a good deal arrested and hushed, and had, at any rate, sensitive and charming, immediately dropped, in the presence of this almost august unveiling, the question of her own thin troubles. But there are short cuts at that hour of night that morning scarce knows, and it took but little more of the breath of the real to suggest to Lady Claude more questions in such a connection than she could answer for herself. 'How, then, if you haven't private means, do you get on?'

'Ah! I don't get on.'

Lady Claude looked about. There were objects scattered in the fine old French room. 'You have lovely things.'

'Two.'

'Two?'

'Two frocks. I couldn't stay another day.'

'Ah, what is *that*? I couldn't either,' said Lady Claude soothingly. 'And you have,' she continued, in the same spirit, 'your nice maid – '

'Who's indeed a charming woman, but my cook in disguise!' Mrs Harvey dropped.

'Ah, you *are* clever!' her friend cried, with a laugh that was as a climax of reassurance.

'Extraordinarily. But don't think,' Mrs Harvey hastened to add, 'that I mean that that's why I'm here.'

Her companion candidly thought. 'Then why are you?'

'I haven't the least idea. I've been wondering all the while, as I've wondered so often before on such occasions, and without arriving at any other reason than that London is so wild.'

Lady Claude wondered. 'Wild?'

'Wild!' said her friend, with some impatience. 'That's the way London strikes.'

'But do you call such an invitation a blow?'

'Yes – crushing. No one else, at all events, either,' Mrs Harvey added, 'could tell you why I'm here.'

Lady Claude's power to receive – and it was perhaps her most attaching quality – was greater still, when she felt strongly, than her power to protest. 'Why, how can you say that when you've only to see how everyone likes and admires you? Just look at the Ambassador,' she had earnestly insisted. And this was what had precisely, as I have mentioned, carried the stream of their talk a good deal away from its source. It had therefore not much further to go before setting in motion the name of Stuart Straith, as to whom Lady Claude confessed to an interest – good-looking, distinguished, 'sympathetic', as he was – that she could really almost hate him for having done nothing whatever to encourage. He had not spoken to her once.

'But, my dear, if he hasn't spoken to *me!*'

Lady Claude appeared to regret this not too much for a hint that, after all, there might be a difference. 'Oh, but *could* he?'

'Without my having spoken to him first?' Mrs Harvey turned it over. 'Perhaps not; but I couldn't have done that.' Then, to explain, and not only because Lady Claude was naturally vague, but because what was still visibly most vivid to her was her independent right to have been 'made up' to: 'And yet not because we're not acquainted.'

'You know him, then?'

'But too well.'

'You mean you don't like him?'

'On the contrary, I like him – to distraction.'

'Then what's the matter?' Lady Claude asked with some impatience. Her friend hesitated but a moment. 'Well, he wouldn't have me.'

'"Have" you?'

'Ten years ago, after Mr Harvey's death, when, if he had lifted a finger, I would have married him.'

'But he didn't lift it?'

'He was too grand. I was too small – by *his* measure. He wanted to keep himself; he saw his future.'

Lady Claude earnestly followed. 'His present position?'

'Yes – everything that was to come to him; his steady rise in value.'

'Has it been so great?'

'Surely – his situation and name. Don't you know his lovely work and what's thought of it?'

'Oh yes, I know. That's why – ' But Lady Claude stopped. After which: 'But if he's still keeping himself?'

'Oh, it's not for me,' said Mrs Harvey.

'And evidently not for *me*. Whom then,' her visitor asked, 'does he think good enough?'

'Oh, these great people!' Mrs Harvey smiled.

'But *we're* great people – you and I!' And Lady Claude kissed her good night.

'You mustn't, all the same,' the elder woman said, 'betray the secret of *my* greatness, which I've told you, please remember, only in the deepest confidence.'

Her tone had a quiet purity of bitterness that for a moment longer held her friend, after which Lady Claude had the happy inspiration of meeting it with graceful gaiety. 'It's quite for the best, I'm sure, that Mr Straith wouldn't have you. You've kept yourself too; you'll marry yet – an ambassador!' And with another good night she reached the door. 'You say you don't get on, but you do.'

'Ah!' said Mrs Harvey with vague attenuation.

'Oh yes, you do,' Lady Claude insisted, while the door emphasized it with a little clap that sounded through the still house.

The first night of *The New Girl* occurred, as everyone remembers, three years ago, and the play is running yet, a fact that may render strange the failure to be widely conscious of which two persons in the audience were guilty. It was not till afterward present either to Mrs Harvey or to Stuart Straith that *The New Girl*[1] was one of the greatest successes of modern times. Indeed if the question had been put to them on the spot they might have appeared much at sea. But this, I may as well immediately say, was the result of their having found themselves side by side in the stalls and thereby given most of their attention to their own predicament. Straith showed that he felt the importance of meeting it promptly, for he turned to his neighbour, who was already in her place, as soon as her identity had come distinct through his own arrival and subsidence. 'I don't quite see how you can help speaking to me now.'

Her face could only show him how long she had been aware of his approach. 'The sound of your voice, coming to me straight, makes it indeed as easy for me as I could possibly desire.'

He looked about at the serried rows, the loaded galleries and the stuffed boxes, with recognitions and nods; and this made between them another pause, during which, while the music seemed perfunctory and the bustle that, in a London audience, represents concentration increased, they felt how effectually, in the thick, preoccupied medium, how extraordinarily, they were together.

'Well, that second afternoon at Mundham, just before dinner, I was very near forcing your hand. But something put me off. You're really too grand.'

'Oh!' she murmured.

'Ambassadors,' said Stuart Straith.

'Oh!' she again sounded. And before anything more could pass the curtain was up. It came down in due course and achieved, after various intervals, the rest of its movements without interrupting, for our friends, the sense of an evening of talk. They said when it was down almost nothing about the play, and when one of them toward the end put to the other, vaguely, 'Is – a – this thing going?' the question had scarce the effect of being even relevant. What was clearest to them was that the people about were somehow enough taken up to leave them at their ease – but what taken up with they but half made out. Mrs Harvey had, none the less, mentioned early that her presence had a reason and that she ought to attend, and her companion had asked her what she thought of a certain picture made at a given moment by the stage, in the reception of which he was so interested that it was really what had brought him. These were glances, however, that quickly strayed – strayed, for instance (as this could carry them far), in its coming to one of them to say that, whatever the piece might be, the real thing, as they had seen it at Mundham, was more than a match for any piece. For it was Mundham that *was*, theatrically, the real thing; better for scenery, dresses, music, pretty women, bare shoulders, everything – even incoherent dialogue; a much bigger and braver show, and got up, as it were, infinitely more 'regardless'. By Mundham they were held long enough to find themselves, though with an equal surprise, quite at one as to the special oddity of their having caught each other in such a plight. Straith said that he supposed what his friend meant was that it was odd *he* should have been there; to which she returned that she had been imputing to him exactly that judgement of her own presence.

'But why shouldn't *you* be?' he asked. 'Isn't that just what you *are*? Aren't you, in your way – like those people – a child of fortune and fashion?'

He got no more answer to this for some time than if he had fairly wounded her; he indeed that evening got no answer at all that was direct. But in the next interval she brought out with abruptness, taking no account of some other matter he had just touched, 'Don't you really know – ?'

She had paused.

'Know what?'

Again she went on without heeding. 'A place like Mundham is, for me, a survival, though poor Mundham in particular won't, for me, have survived that visit – for which it's to be pitied, isn't it? It was a glittering ghost – since laid! – of my old time.'

Straith at this almost gave a start. 'Have *you* got a new time?'

'Do you mean that you have?'

'Well,' said Straith, 'mine may now be called middle-aged. It seems so long, I mean, since I set my watch to it.'

'Oh, I haven't even a watch!' she returned with a laugh. 'I'm beyond watches.' After which she added: 'We *might* have met more – or, I should say perhaps, have got more out of it when we *have* met.'

'Yes, it has been too little. But I've always explained it by our living in such different worlds.'

Mrs Harvey had an occasional incoherence. 'Are you unhappy?'

He gave her a singular smile. 'You said just now that you're beyond watches. I'm beyond unhappiness.'

She turned from him and presently brought out: 'I ought absolutely to take away *something* of the play.'

'By all means. There's certainly something *I* shall take.'

'Ah, then you must help me – give it me.'

'With all my heart,' said Straith, 'if it *can* help you. It's my feeling of our renewal.'

She had one of the sad, slow head-shakes that at Mundham had been impressive to Lady Claude. 'That won't help me.'

'Then you must let me put to you now what I should have tried to get near enough to you there to put if I hadn't been so afraid of the Ambassador. What has it been so long – our impossibility?'

'Well, I can only answer for my own vision of it, which is – which always was – that you were sorry for me, but felt a sort of scruple of showing me that you had nothing better than pity to give.'

'May I come to see you?' Straith asked some minutes after this.

Her words, for which he had also awhile to wait, had, in truth, as little as his own the appearance of a reply. '*Are* you unhappy – really? Haven't you everything?'

'You're beautiful!' he said for all answer. 'Mayn't I come?'

She hesitated.

'Where is your studio?'

'Oh, not too far to reach from it. Don't be anxious; I can walk, or even take the bus.'

Mrs Harvey once more delayed. Then she answered: 'Mayn't I rather come there?'

'I shall be but too delighted.'

It was said with promptness, even precipitation; yet the understanding, shortly after, appeared to have left between them a certain awkwardness, and it was almost as if to change the subject and relieve them equally that she suddenly reminded him of something he had spoken earlier. 'You were to tell me why in particular you had to be here.'

'Oh yes. To see my dresses.'

'Yours!' She wondered.

'The second act. I made them out for them – drew them.'

Before she could check it her tone escaped. 'You?'

'I.' He looked straight before him. 'For the fee.[2] And we didn't even notice them.'

'*I* didn't,' she confessed. But it offered the fact as a sign of her kindness for him, and this kindness was traceably what inspired something she said in the draughty porch, after the performance, while the footman of the friend, a fat, rich, immensely pleased lady, who had given her a lift and then rejoined her from a seat in the balcony, went off to make sure of the brougham. 'May I do something about your things?'

' "Do something?" '

'When I've paid you my visit. Write something – about your pictures. I do a correspondence,' said Mrs Harvey.

He wondered as she had done in the stalls. 'For a paper?'

'The *Blackport Banner*. A "London Letter." The new books, the new plays, the new twaddle of any sort – a little music, a little gossip, a little "art." You'll help me – I need it awfully – with the art. I do three a month.'

'*You* – wonderful you?' He spoke as Lady Claude had done, and could no more help it again than Mrs Harvey had been able to help it in the stalls.

'Oh, as you say, for the fee!' On which, as the footman signalled, her old lady began to plunge through the crowd.

IV

At the studio, where she came to him within the week, her first movement had been to exclaim on the splendid abundance of his work.

She had looked round charmed — so struck as to be, as she called it, crushed. 'You've such a wonderful lot to show.'

'Indeed I have!' said Stuart Straith.

'That's where you beat *us*.'

'I think it may very well be,' he went on, 'where I beat almost everyone.'

'And is much of it new?'

He looked about with her. 'Some of it is pretty old. But my things have a way, I admit, of growing old extraordinarily fast. They seem to me in fact, nowadays, quite "born old."'

She had the manner, after a little, of coming back to something. 'You *are* unhappy. You're *not* beyond it. You're just nicely, just fairly and squarely, in the middle of it.'

'Well,' said Straith, 'if it surrounds me like a desert, so that I'm lost in it, that comes to the same thing. But I want you to tell me about yourself.'

She had continued at first to move about, and had taken out a pocket-book, which she held up at him. 'This time I shall insist on notes. You made my mind a blank about that play, which is the sort of thing we can't afford. If it hadn't been for my fat old lady and the next day's papers!' She kept looking, going up to things, saying, 'How wonderful!' and 'Oh, your *way*!' and then stopping for a general impression, something in the whole charm. The place, high, handsome, neat, with two or three pale tapestries and several rare old pieces of furniture, showed a perfection of order, an absence of loose objects, as if it had been swept and squared for the occasion and made almost too immaculate. It was polished and cold — rather cold for the season and the weather; and Stuart Straith himself, buttoned and brushed, as fine and as clean as his room, might at her arrival have reminded her of the master of a neat, bare ship on his deck awaiting a cargo. 'May I see everything? May I "use" everything?'

'Oh no; you mayn't by any means use everything. You mayn't use half. *Did* I spoil your "London Letter?"' he continued after a moment.

'No one can spoil them as I spoil them myself. I can't do them — I don't know how, and don't want to. I do them wrong, and the people want such trash. Of course they'll sack me.'

She was in the centre, and he had the effect of going round her, restless and vague, in large, slow circles. "Have you done them long?'

'Two or three months – this lot. But I've done others, and I know what happens. Oh, my dear, I've done strange things!'

'And is it a good job?'

She hesitated, then puffed, prettily enough, an indifferent sigh. 'Three-and-ninepence. Is that good?' He had stopped before her, looking at her up and down. 'What do you get,' she went on, 'for what you do for a play?'

'A little more, it would seem, than you. Four-and-six-pence. But I've only done, as yet, that one. Nothing else has offered.'

'I see. But something *will*, eh?'

Poor Straith took a turn again. 'Did you like them – for colour?' But again he pulled up. 'Oh, I forgot; we didn't notice them!'

For a moment they could laugh about it. 'I noticed them, I assure you, in the *Banner*. "The costumes in the second act are of the most marvellous beauty." That's what I said.'

'Oh, that will fetch the managers!' But before her again he seemed to take her in from head to foot. 'You speak of "using" things. If you'd only use yourself – for my enlightenment. Tell me all.'

'You look at me,' said Mrs Harvey, 'as with the wonder of who designs *my* costumes. How I dress on it, how I do even what I still do on it, is *that* what you want to know?'

'What has happened to you?' Straith asked.

'How do I keep it up?' she continued, as if she had not heard him. 'But I *don't* keep it up. *You* do,' she declared as she again looked round her.

Once more it set him off, but for a pause once more almost as quick. 'How long have you been – ?'

'Been what?' she asked as he faltered.

'Unhappy.'

She smiled at him from a depth of indulgence. 'As long as you've been ignorant – that what I've been *wanting* is your pity. Ah, to have to know, as I believed I did, that you supposed it would wound me, and not to have been able to make you see that it was the one thing left to me that would help me! Give me your pity now. It's all I want. I don't care for anything else. But give me that.'

He had, as it happened at the moment, to do a smaller and a usual thing before he could do one so great and so strange. The youth whom he kept for service arrived with a tea-tray, in arranging a place for which, with the sequel of serving Mrs Harvey, seating her and seeing the youth again out of the room, some minutes passed.

'What pity could I dream of for you,' he demanded as he at last dropped near her, 'when I was myself so miserably sore?'

'Sore?' she wondered. 'But you were happy – then.'

'Happy not to have struck you as good enough? For I didn't, you know,' he insisted. 'You had your success, which was so immense. You had your high value, your future, your big possibilities; and I perfectly understood that, given those things, and given also my very much smaller situation, you should wish to keep yourself.'

'Oh, oh!' She gasped as if hurt.

'I understand it; but how could it really make me "happy?"' he asked.

She turned at him as with her hand on the old scar she could now carry. 'You mean that all these years you've really not known – ?'

'But not known what?'

His voice was so blank that at the sound of it, and at something that looked out from him, she only found another 'Oh, oh!' which became the next instant a burst of tears.

V

She had appeared at first unwilling to receive him at home; but he understood it after she had left him, turning over more and more everything their meeting had shaken to the surface, and piecing together memories that at last, however darkly, made a sense. He was to call on her, it was finally agreed, but not till the end of the week, when she should have finished 'moving' – she had but just changed quarters; and meanwhile, as he came and went, mainly in the cold chamber of his own past endeavour, which looked even to himself as studios look when artists are dead and the public, in the arranged place, are admitted to stare, he had plenty to think about. What had come out – he could see it now – was that each, ten years before, had miserably misunderstood and then had turned for relief from pain to a perversity of pride. But it was himself above all that he now sharply judged, since women, he felt, have to get on as they can, and for the mistake of this woman there were reasons he had, with a sore heart, to acknowledge. She had really found in the pomp of his early success, at the time they used to meet, and to care to, exactly the ground for her sense of failure with him that he had found in the vision of her gross popularity for his conviction that she judged him as comparatively small. Each had blundered, as sensitive souls of the 'artistic temperament' blunder, into a conception not only of the other's attitude, but of the other's material situation at the moment, that had thrown them back on stupid secrecy, where their estrangement had grown like an evil plant in the shade. He had positively believed her to have gone on all the while making the five thousand a year that the first eight or ten of her so supremely happy novels had brought her in, just as she, on her side, had read into the felicity of his first new hits, his pictures 'of the year' at three or four Academies, the absurdest theory of the sort of career that, thanks to big dealers and intelligent buyers, his gains would have built up for him. It looked vulgar enough now, but it had been grave enough then. His long, detached delusion about her 'prices,' at any rate, appeared to have been more than matched by the strange stories occasionally floated to her — and all to make her but draw more closely in — on the subject of his own.

It was with each equally that everything had changed — everything but the stiff consciousness in either of the need to conceal changes from the other. If she had cherished for long years the soreness of her not being 'good' enough, so this was what had counted most in her sustained effort to appear at least as good as he. London, meanwhile, was big; London was blind and benighted; and nothing had ever occurred to undermine for him the fiction of her prosperity. Before his eyes there, while she sat with him, she had pulled off one by one those vain coverings of her state that she confessed she had hitherto done her best — and so always with an eye on himself — deceptively to draw about it. He had felt frozen, as he listened, at such likenesses to things he knew. He recognized as she talked, and he groaned as he understood. He understood — oh, at last, whatever he had not done before! And yet he could well have smiled, out of their common abyss, at such odd identities and recurrences. Truly the arts were sisters, as was so often said; for what apparently could be more like the experience of one than the experience of another? And she spared him things with it all. He felt that too, just as, even while showing her how he followed, he had bethought himself of closing his lips for the hour, none too soon, on his own stale story. There had been a beautiful intelligence, for that matter, in her having asked him nothing more. She had overflowed because shaken by not finding him happy, and her surrender had somehow offered itself to him as her way — the first that sprang up — of considering his trouble. She had left him, at all events, in full possession of all the phases through which in 'literary circles' acclaimed states may pass on their regular march to eclipse and extinction. One had but one's hour, and if one had it soon — it was really almost a case of choice — one didn't have it late. It might, moreover, never even remotely have approached, at its best, things ridiculously rumoured. Straith felt, on the whole, how little he had known of literary circles or of any mystery but his own, indeed; on which, up to actual impending collapse, he had mounted such anxious guard.

It was when he went on the Friday to see her that he took in the latest of the phases in question, which might very well be almost the final one; there was at least that comfort in it. She had just settled in a small flat, where he recognized in the steady disposal, for the best, of various objects she had not yet parted with, her reason for having made him wait. Here they had together — those two worn and baffled workers — a wonderful hour of gladness in their lost battle and of freshness in their lost youth; for it was not till Stuart Straith had also raised the heavy mask and laid it beside her own on the table, that they began really to feel themselves recover something of that possibility of each other they had so wearily wasted. Only she couldn't get over it that he was like herself, and that what she had shrunken to in her three or four simplified rooms had its perfect image in the hollow show of his ordered studio and his accumulated work. He told her everything now, kept as little back as she had kept at their previous meeting, while she repeated over and over, 'You — wonderful you?' as if the knowledge made a deeper darkness of fate, as if the pain of his having come down at all almost quenched the joy of his having come so much nearer. When she learned that he had not for three years sold a picture – 'You, beautiful you?' – it seemed a new cold breath out of the dusk of her own outlook. Disappointment and despair were in such relations contagious, and there was clearly as much less again left to her as the little that was left to him. He showed her, laughing at the long queerness of it, how awfully little, as they called it, this was. He let it all come, but with more mirth than misery, and with a final abandonment of pride that was like changing at the end of a dreadful day from tight boots to slippers. There were moments when they might have resembled a couple united by some misdeed and meeting to decide on some desperate course; they gave themselves so to the great irony – the vision of the comic in contrasts – that precedes surrenders and extinctions.

They went over the whole thing, remounted the dwindling stream, reconstructed, explained, understood – recognized, in short, the particular example they gave, and how, without mutual suspicion, they had been giving it side by side. 'We're simply the case,' Straith familiarly put it, 'of having been had enough of. No case is perhaps more common, save that, for you and for me, each in our line, it did look in the good time – didn't it? – as if nobody *could* have enough.' With which they counted backward, gruesome as it was, the symptoms of satiety up to the first dawn, and lived again together the unforgettable hours – distant now – out of which it had begun to glimmer that the truth had to be faced and the right names given to the wrong facts. They laughed at their original explanations and the minor scale, even, of their early fears; compared notes on the fallibility of remedies and hopes, and, more and more united in the identity of their lesson, made out perfectly that, though there appeared to be many kinds of success, there was only one kind of failure. And yet what had been hardest had not been to have to shrink, but – the long game of bluff, as Straith called it – to have to keep up. It fairly swept them away at present, however, the hugeness of the relief of no longer keeping up as against each other. This gave them all the measure of the motive their courage, on either side, in silence and gloom, had forced into its service.

'Only what shall we do now for a motive?' Straith went on.

She thought. 'A motive for courage?'

'Yes – to keep up.'

'And go again, for instance, do you mean, to Mundham? We shall, thank heaven, never go again to Mundham. The Mundhams are over.'

> *'Nous n'irons plus au bois;*
> *Les lauriers sont coupés,'*[3]

sang Straith. 'It does cost.'

'As everything costs that one does for the rich. It's not our poor relations who make us pay.'

'No; one must have means to acknowledge the others. We can't afford the opulent. But it isn't only the money they take.'

'It's the imagination,' said Mrs Harvey. 'As they have none themselves – '

'It's an article we have to supply? We have certainly to use a lot to protect ourselves,' Straith agreed. 'And the strange thing is that they like us.'

She thought again. 'That's what makes it easy to cut them. They forgive.'

'Yes,' her companion laughed; 'once they really don't know you enough – !'

'They treat you as old friends. But what do we want now of courage?' she went on.

He wondered. 'Yes, after all, what?'

'To keep up, I mean. Why *should* we keep up?'

It seemed to strike him. 'I see. After all, why? The courage *not* to keep up – '

'We have *that*, at least,' she declared, 'haven't we?' Standing there at her little high-perched window, which overhung grey housetops, they let the consideration of this pass between them in a deep look, as well as in a hush of which the intensity had something commensurate. 'If we're beaten!' she then continued.

'Let us at least be beaten together!' He took her in his arms; she let herself go, and he held her long and close for the compact. But when they had recovered themselves enough to handle their agreement more responsibly, the words in which they confirmed it broke in sweetness as well as sadness from both together· 'And now to work!'

THE BEAST IN THE JUNGLE

I

WHAT determined the speech that startled him in the course of their encounter scarcely matters, being probably but some words spoken by himself quite without intention – spoken as they lingered and slowly moved together after their renewal of acquaintance. He had been conveyed by friends, an hour or two before, to the house at which she was staying; the party of visitors at the other house, of whom he was one, and thanks to whom it was his theory, as always, that he was lost in the crowd, had been invited over to luncheon. There had been after luncheon much dispersal, all in the interest of the original motive, a view of Weatherend itself and the fine things, intrinsic features, pictures, heirlooms, treasures of all the arts, that made the place almost famous; and the great rooms were so numerous that guests could wander at their will, hang back from the principal group, and, in cases where they took such matters with the last seriousness, give themselves up to mysterious appreciations and measurements. There were persons to be observed, singly or in couples, bending towards objects in out-of-the-way corners with their hands on their knees and their heads nodding quite as with the emphasis of an excited sense of smell. When they were two they either mingled their sounds of ecstasy or melted into silences of even deeper import, so that there were aspects of the occasion that gave it for Marcher much the air of the 'look round,' previous to a sale highly advertised, that excites or quenches, as may be, the dream of acquisition. The dream of acquisition at Weatherend would have had to be wild indeed, and John Marcher found himself, among such sugges-tions, disconcerted almost equally by the presence of those who knew too much and by that of those who knew nothing. The great rooms caused so much poetry and history to press upon him that he needed to wander apart to feel in a proper relation with them, though his doing so was not, as happened, like the gloating of some of his companions, to be compared to the movements of a dog sniffing a cupboard. It had an issue promptly enough in a direction that was not to have been calculated.

It led, in short, in the course of the October afternoon, to his closer meeting with May Bartram, whose face, a reminder, yet not quite a remembrance, as they sat, much separated, at a very long table, had begun merely by troubling him rather pleasantly. It affected him as the sequel of something of which he had lost the beginning. He knew it, and for the time quite welcomed it, as a continuation, but didn't know what it continued, which was an interest, or an amusement, the greater as he was also somehow aware — yet without a direct sign from her — that the young woman herself had not lost the thread. She had not lost it, but she wouldn't give it back to him, he saw, without some putting forth of his hand for it; and he not only saw that, but saw several things more, things odd enough in the light of the fact that at the moment some accident of grouping brought them face to face he was still merely fumbling with the idea that any contact between them in the past would have had no importance. If it had had no importance he scarcely knew why his actual impression of her should so seem to have so much; the answer to which, however, was that in such a life as they all appeared to be leading for the moment one could but take things as they came. He was satisfied, without in the least being able to say why, that this young lady might roughly have ranked in the house as a poor relation; satisfied also that she was not there on a brief visit, but was more or less a part of the establishment — almost a working, a remunerated part. Didn't she enjoy at periods a protection that she paid for by helping, among other services, to show the place and explain it, deal with the tiresome people, answer questions about the dates of the buildings, the styles of the furniture, the authorship of the pictures, the favourite haunts of the ghost? It wasn't that she looked as if you could have given her shillings — it was impossible to look less so. Yet when she finally drifted toward him, distinctly handsome, though ever so much older – older than when he had seen her before – it might have been as an effect of her guessing that he had, within the couple of hours, devoted more imagination to her than to all the others put together, and had thereby penetrated to a kind of truth that the others were too stupid for. She *was* there on harder terms than anyone; she was there as a consequence of things suffered, in one way and another, in the interval of years; and she remembered him very much as she was remembered – only a good deal better.

By the time they at last thus came to speech they were alone in one of the rooms – remarkable for a fine portrait over the chimney-place – out of which their friends had passed, and the charm of it was that even before they had spoken they had practically arranged with each other to stay behind for talk. The charm, happily, was in other things too; it was partly in there being scarce a spot at Weatherend without something to stay behind for. It was in the way the autumn day looked into the high windows as it waned; in the way the red light, breaking at the close from under a low, sombre sky, reached out in a long shaft and played over old wainscots, old tapestry, old gold, old colour. It was most of all perhaps in the way she came to him as if, since she had been turned on to deal with the simpler sort, he might, should he choose to keep the whole thing down, just take her mild attention for a part of her general business. As soon as he heard her voice, however, the gap was filled up and the missing link supplied; the slight irony he divined in her attitude lost its advantage. He almost jumped at it to get there before her. 'I met you years and years ago in Rome. I remember all about it.' She confessed to disappointment – she had been so sure he didn't; and to prove how well he did he began to pour forth the particular recollections that popped up as he called for them. Her face and her voice, all at his service now, worked the miracle – the impression operating like the torch of a lamplighter who touches into flame, one by one, a long row of gas jets. Marcher flattered himself that the illumination was brilliant, yet he was really still more pleased on her showing him, with amusement, that in his haste to make everything right he had got most things rather wrong. It hadn't been at Rome – it had been at Naples; and it hadn't been seven years before – it had been more nearly ten. She hadn't been either with her uncle and aunt, but with her mother and her brother; in addition to which it was not with the Pembles that *he* had been, but with the Boyers, coming down in the company from Rome – a point on which she insisted, a little to his confusion, and as to which she had her evidence in hand. The Boyers she had known, but she didn't know the Pembles, though she had heard of them, and it was the people he was with who had made them acquainted. The incident of the thunderstorm that had raged round them with such violence as to drive them for refuge into an excavation – this incident had not occurred at the Palace of the Caesars, but at Pompeii, on an occasion when they had been present there at an important find.

He accepted her amendments, he enjoyed her corrections, though the moral of them was, she pointed out, that he *really* didn't remember the least thing about her; and he only felt it as a drawback that when all was made comfortable to the truth there didn't appear much of anything left. They lingered together still, she neglecting her office – for from the moment he was so clever she had no proper right to him – and both neglecting the house, just waiting as to see if a memory or two more wouldn't again breathe upon them. It had not taken them many minutes, after all, to put down on the table, like the cards of a pack, those that constituted their respective hands; only what came out was that the pack was unfortunately not perfect – that the past, invoked, invited, encouraged, could give them, naturally, no more than it had. It had made them meet – her at twenty, him at twenty-five; but nothing was so strange, they seemed to say to each other, as that, while so occupied, it hadn't done a little more for them. They looked at each other as with the feeling of an occasion missed; the present one would have been so much better if the other, in the far distance, in the foreign land, hadn't been so stupidly meagre. There weren't, apparently, all counted, more than a dozen little old things that had succeeded in coming to pass between them; trivialities of youth, simplicities of freshness, stupidities of ignorance, small possible germs, but too deeply buried – too deeply (didn't it seem?) to sprout after so many years. Marcher said to himself that he ought to have rendered her some service – saved her from a capsized boat in the bay, or at least recovered her dressing-bag, filched from her cab, in the streets of Naples, by a lazzarone with a stiletto. Or it would have been nice if he could have been taken with fever, alone, at his hotel, and she could have come to look after him, to write to his people, to drive him out in convalescence. *Then* they would be in possession of the something or other that their actual show seemed to lack. It yet somehow presented itself, this show, as too good to be spoiled; so that they were reduced for a few minutes more to wondering a little helplessly why – since they seemed to know a certain number of the same people – their reunion had been so long averted. They didn't use that name for it, but their delay from minute to minute to join the others was a kind of confession that they didn't quite want it to be a failure. Their attempted supposition of reasons for their not having met but showed how little they knew of each other. There came in fact a moment when Marcher felt a positive pang. It was vain to pretend she was an old friend, for all the communities were wanting, in spite of which it was as an old friend that he saw she would have suited him. He had new ones enough – was surrounded with them, for instance, at that hour at the other house; as a new one he probably wouldn't have so much as noticed her. He would have liked to invent something, get her to make-believe with him that some passage of a romantic or critical kind *had* originally occurred. He was really almost reaching out in imagination – as against time – for something that would do, and saying to himself that if it didn't come this new incident would simply and rather awkwardly close. They would separate, and now for no second or for no third chance. They would have tried and not succeeded. Then it was, just at the turn, as he afterwards made it out to himself, that, everything else failing, she herself decided to take up the case and, as it were, save the situation. He felt as soon as she spoke that she had been consciously keeping back what she said and hoping to get on without it; a scruple in her that immensely touched him when, by the end of three or four minutes more, he was able to measure it. What she brought out, at any rate, quite cleared the air and supplied the link – the link it was such a mystery he should frivolously have managed to lose.

'You know you told me something that I've never forgotten and that again and again has made me think of you since; it was that tremendously hot day when we went to Sorrento, across the bay, for the breeze. What I allude to was what you said to me, on the way back, as we sat, under the awning of the boat, enjoying the cool. Have you forgotten?'

He had forgotten, and he was even more surprised than ashamed. But the great thing was that he saw it was no vulgar reminder of any 'sweet' speech. The vanity of women had long memories, but she was making no claim on him of a compliment or a mistake. With another woman, a totally different one, he might have feared the recall possibly even some imbecile 'offer'. So, in having to say that he had indeed forgotten, he was conscious rather of a loss than of a gain; he already saw an interest in the matter of her reference. 'I try to think – but I give it up. Yet I remember the Sorrento day.'

'I'm not very sure you do,' May Bartram after a moment said; 'and I'm not very sure I ought to want you to. It's dreadful to bring a person back, at any time, to what he was ten years before. If you've lived away from it,' she smiled, 'so much the better.'

'Ah, if *you* haven't why should I?' he asked.

'Lived away, you mean, from what I myself was?'

'From what *I* was. I was of course an ass,' Marcher went on; 'but I would rather know from you just the sort of ass I was than – from the moment you have something in your mind – not know anything.'

Still, however, she hesitated. 'But if you've completely ceased to be that sort – ?'

'Why, I can then just so all the more bear to know. Besides, perhaps I haven't.'

'Perhaps. Yet if you haven't,' she added, 'I should suppose you would remember. Not indeed that *I* in the least connect with my impression the invidious name you use. If I had only thought you foolish,' she explained, 'the thing I speak of wouldn't so have remained with me. It was about yourself.' She waited, as if it might come to him; but as, only meeting her eyes in wonder, he gave no sign, she burnt her ships. 'Has it ever happened?'

Then it was that, while he continued to stare, a light broke for him and the blood slowly came to his face, which began to burn with recognition. 'Do you mean I told you – ?' But he faltered, lest what came to him shouldn't be right, lest he should only give himself away.

'It was something about yourself that it was natural one shouldn't forget – that is if one remembered you at all. That's why I ask you,' she smiled, 'if the thing you then spoke of has ever come to pass?'

Oh, then he saw, but he was lost in wonder and found himself embarrassed. This, he also saw, made her sorry for him, as if her allusion had been a mistake. It took him but a moment, however, to feel that it had not been, much as it had been a surprise. After the first little shock of it her knowledge on the contrary began, even if rather strangely, to taste sweet to him. She was the only other person in the world then who would have it, and she had had it all these years, while the fact of his having so breathed his secret had unaccountably faded from him. No wonder they couldn't have met as if nothing had happened. 'I judge,' he finally said, 'that I know what you mean. Only I had strangely enough lost the consciousness of having taken you so far into my confidence.'

'Is it because you've taken so many others as well?'

'I've taken nobody. Not a creature since then.'

'So that I'm the only person who knows?'

'The only person in the world.'

'Well,' she quickly replied, 'I myself have never spoken. I've never, never repeated of you what you told me.' She looked at him so that he perfectly believed her. Their eyes met over it in such a way that he was without a doubt. 'And I never will.'

She spoke with an earnestness that, as if almost excessive, put him at ease about her possible derision. Somehow the whole question was a new luxury to him – that is, from the moment she was in possession. If she didn't take the ironic view she clearly took the sympathetic, and that was what he had had, in all the long time, from no one whomsoever. What he felt was that he couldn't at present have begun to tell her and yet could profit perhaps exquisitely by the accident of having done so of old. 'Please don't then. We're just right as it is.'

'Oh, I am,' she laughed, 'if you are!' To which she added: 'Then you do still feel in the same way?'

It was impossible to him not to take to himself that she was really interested, and it all kept coming as a sort of revelation. He had thought of himself so long as abominably alone, and, lo, he wasn't alone a bit. He hadn't been, it appeared, for an hour – since those moments on the Sorrento boat. It was *she* who had been, he seemed to see as he looked at her – she who had been made so by the graceless fact of his lapse of fidelity. To tell her what he had told her — what had it been but to ask something of her? something that she had given, in her charity, without his having, by a remembrance, by a return of the spirit, failing another encounter, so much as thanked her. What he had asked of her had been simply at first not to laugh at him. She had beautifully not done so for ten years, and she was not doing so now. So he had endless gratitude to make up. Only for that he must see just how he had figured to her. 'What, exactly, was the account I gave — ?'

'Of the way you did feel? Well, it was very simple. You said you had had from your earliest time, as the deepest thing within you, the sense of being kept for something rare and strange, possibly prodigious and terrible, that was sooner or later to happen to you, that you had in your bones the foreboding and the conviction of, and that would perhaps overwhelm you.'

'Do you call that very simple?' John Marcher asked.

She thought a moment. 'It was perhaps because I seemed, as you spoke, to understand it.'

'You do understand it?' he eagerly asked.

Again she kept her kind eyes on him. 'You still have the belief?'

'Oh!' he exclaimed helplessly. There was too much to say.

'Whatever it is to be,' she clearly made out, 'it hasn't yet come.'

He shook his head in complete surrender now. 'It hasn't yet come. Only, you know, it isn't anything I'm to *do*, to achieve in the world, to be distinguished or admired for. I'm not such an ass as *that*. It would be much better, no doubt, if I were.'

'It's to be something you're merely to suffer?'

'Well, say to wait for — to have to meet, to face, to see suddenly break out in my life; possibly destroying all further consciousness, possibly annihilating me; possibly, on the other hand, only altering everything, striking at the root of all my world and leaving me to the consequences, however they shape themselves.'

She took this in, but the light in her eyes continued for him not to be that of mockery. 'Isn't what you describe perhaps but the expectation — or, at any rate, the sense of danger, familiar to so many people — of falling in love?'

John Marcher thought. 'Did you ask me that before?'

'No – I wasn't so free-and-easy then. But it's what strikes me now.'

'Of course,' he said after a moment, 'it strikes you. Of course it strikes *me*. Of course what's in store for me may be no more than that. The only thing is,' he went on, 'that I think that if it had been that, I should by this time know.'

'Do you mean because you've *been* in love?' And then as he but looked at her in silence: 'You've been in love, and it hasn't meant such a cataclysm, hasn't proved the great affair?'

'Here I am, you see. It hasn't been overwhelming.'

'Then it hasn't been love,' said May Bartram.

'Well, I at least thought it was. I took it for that – I've taken it till now. It was agreeable, it was delightful, it was miserable,' he explained. 'But it wasn't strange. It wasn't what *my* affair's to be.'

'You want something all to yourself – something that nobody else knows or *has* known?'

'It isn't a question of what I "want" – God knows I don't want anything. It's only a question of the apprehension that haunts me – that I live with day by day.'

He said this so lucidly and consistently that, visibly, it further imposed itself. If she had not been interested before she would have been interested now. 'Is it a sense of coming violence?'

Evidently now too, again, he liked to talk of it. 'I don't think of it as – when it does come – necessarily violent. I only think of it as natural and as of course, above all, unmistakable. I think of it simply as *the* thing. *The* thing will of itself appear natural.'

'Then how will it appear strange?'

Marcher bethought himself. 'It won't – to *me*.'

'To whom then?'

'Well,' he replied, smiling at last, 'say to you.'

'Oh then, I'm to be present?'

'Why, you *are* present – since you know.'

'I see.' She turned it over. 'But I mean at the catastrophe.'

At this, for a minute, their lightness gave way to their gravity; it was as if the long look they exchanged held them together. 'It will only depend on yourself – if you'll watch with me.'

'Are you afraid?' she asked.

'Don't leave me *now*,' he went on.

'Are you afraid?' she repeated.

'Do you think me simply out of my mind?' he pursued instead of answering. 'Do I merely strike you as a harmless lunatic?'

'No,' said May Bartram. 'I understand you. I believe you.'

'You mean you feel how my obsession – poor old thing! – may correspond to some possible reality?'

'To some possible reality.'

'Then you *will* watch with me?'

She hesitated, then for the third time put her question. 'Are you afraid?'

'Did I tell you I was – at Naples?'

'No, you said nothing about it.'

'Then I don't know. And I should *like* to know,' said John Marcher. 'You'll tell me yourself whether you think so. If you'll watch with me you'll see.'

'Very good then.' They had been moving by this time across the room, and at the door, before passing out, they paused as if for the full wind-up of their understanding. 'I'll watch with you,' said May Bartram.

II

The fact that she 'knew' – knew and yet neither chaffed him nor betrayed him – had in a short time begun to constitute between them a sensible bond, which became more marked when, within the year that followed their afternoon at Weatherend, the opportunities for meeting multiplied. The event that thus promoted these occasions was the death of the ancient lady, her great-aunt, under whose wing, since losing her mother, she had to such an extent found shelter, and who, though but the widowed mother of the new successor to the property, had succeeded – thanks to a high tone and a high temper – in not forfeiting the supreme position at the great house. The deposition of this personage arrived but with her death, which, followed by many changes, made in particular a difference for the young woman in whom Marcher's expert attention had recognized from the first a dependent with a pride that might ache though it didn't bristle. Nothing for a long time had made him easier than the thought that the aching must have been much soothed by Miss Bartram's now finding herself able to set up a small home in London. She had acquired property, to an amount that made that luxury just possible, under her aunt's extremely complicated will, and when the whole matter began to be straightened out, which indeed took time, she let him know that the happy issue was at last in view. He had seen her again before that day, both because she had more than once accompanied the ancient lady to town and because he had paid another visit to the friends who so conveniently made of Weatherend one of the charms of their own hospitality. These friends had taken him back there; he had achieved there again with Miss Bartram some quiet detachment; and he had in London succeeded in persuading her to more than one brief absence from her aunt. They went together, on these latter occasions, to the National Gallery and the South Kensington Museum, where, among vivid reminders, they talked of Italy at large – not now attempting to recover, as at first, the taste of their youth and their ignorance. That recovery, the first day at Weatherend, had served its purpose well, had given them quite enough; so that they were, to Marcher's sense, no longer hovering about the head-waters of their stream, but had felt their boat pushed sharply off and down the current.

They were literally afloat together; for our gentleman this was marked, quite as marked as that the fortunate cause of it was just the buried treasure of her knowledge. He had with his own hands dug up this little hoard, brought to light – that is to within reach of the dim day constituted by their discretions and privacies – the object of value the hiding-place of which he had, after putting it into the ground himself, so strangely, so long forgotten. The exquisite luck of having again just stumbled on the spot made him indifferent to any other question; he would doubtless have devoted more time to the odd accident of his lapse of memory if he had not been moved to devote so much to the sweetness, the comfort, as he felt, for the future, that this accident itself had helped to keep fresh. It had never entered into his plan that anyone should 'know,' and mainly for the reason that it was not in him to tell anyone. That would have been impossible, since nothing but the amusement of a cold world would have waited on it. Since, however, a mysterious fate had opened his mouth in youth, in spite of him, he would count that a compensation and profit by it to the utmost. That the right person *should* know tempered the asperity of his secret more even than his shyness had permitted him to imagine; and May Bartram was clearly right, because – well, because there she was. Her knowledge simply settled it; he would have been sure enough by this time had she been wrong. There was that in his situation, no doubt, that disposed him too much to see her as a mere confidant, taking all her light for him from the fact – the fact only – of her interest in his predicament, from her mercy, sympathy, seriousness, her consent not to regard him as the funniest of the funny. Aware, in fine, that her price for him was just in her giving him this constant sense of his being admirably spared, he was careful to remember that she had, after all, also a life of her own, with things that might happen to *her*, things that in friendship one should likewise take account of. Something fairly remarkable came to pass with him, for that matter, in this connection – something represented by a certain passage of his consciousness, in the suddenest way, from one extreme to the other.

He had thought himself, so long as nobody knew, the most disinterested person in the world, carrying his concentrated burden, his perpetual suspense, ever so quietly, holding his tongue about it, giving others no glimpse of it nor of its effect upon his life, asking of them no allowance and only making on his side all those that were asked. He had disturbed nobody with the queerness of having to know a haunted man, though he had had moments of rather special temptation on hearing people say that they were 'unsettled'. If they were as unsettled as he was – he who had never been settled for an hour in his life – they would know what it meant. Yet it wasn't, all the same, for him to make them, and he listened to them civilly enough. This was why he had such good – though possibly such rather colourless – manners; this was why, above all, he could regard himself, in a greedy world, as decently – as, in fact, perhaps even a little sublimely – unselfish. Our point is accordingly that he valued this character quite sufficiently to measure his present danger of letting it lapse, against which he promised himself to be much on his guard. He was quite ready, none the less, to be selfish just a little, since, surely, no more charming occasion for it had come to him. 'Just a little,' in a word, was just as much as Miss Bartram, taking one day with another, would let him. He never would be in the least coercive, and he would keep well before him the lines on which consideration for her – the very highest – ought to proceed. He would thoroughly establish the heads under which her affairs, her requirements, her peculiarities – he went so far as to give them the latitude of that name – would come into their intercourse. All this naturally was a sign of how much he took the intercourse itself for granted. There was nothing more to be done about *that*. It simply existed; had sprung into being with her first penetrating question to him in the autumn light there at Weatherend. The real form it should have taken on the basis that stood out large was the form of their marrying. But the devil in this was that the very basis itself put marrying out of the question. His conviction, his apprehension, his obsession, in short, was not a condition he could invite a woman to share; and that consequence of it was precisely what was the matter with him. Something or other lay in wait for him, amid the twists and turns of the months and the years, like a crouching beast in the jungle. It signified little whether the crouching beast were destined to slay him or to be slain. The definite point was the inevitable spring of the creature; and the definite lesson from that was that a man of feeling didn't cause himself to be accompanied by a lady on a tiger-hunt. Such was the image under which he had ended by figuring his life.

They had at first, none the less, in the scattered hours spent together, made no allusion to that view of it; which was a sign he was handsomely ready to give that he didn't expect, that he in fact didn't care always to be talking about it. Such a feature in one's outlook was really like a hump on one's back. The difference it made every minute of the day existed quite independently of discussion. One discussed, of course, *like* a hunchback, for there was always, if nothing else, the hunchback face. That remained, and she was watching him; but people watched best, as a general thing, in silence, so that such would be predominantly the manner of their vigil. Yet he didn't want, at the same time, to be solemn; solemn was what he imagined he too much tended to be with other people. The thing to be, with the one person who knew, was easy and natural – to make the reference rather than be seeming to avoid it, to avoid it rather than be seeming to make it, and to keep it, in any case, familiar, facetious even, rather than pedantic and portentous. Some such consideration as the latter was doubtless in his mind, for instance, when he wrote pleasantly to Miss Bartram that perhaps the great thing he had so long felt as in the lap of the gods was no more than this circumstance, which touched him so nearly, of her acquiring a house in London. It was the first allusion they had yet again made, needing any other hitherto so little; but when she replied, after having given him the news, that she was by no means satisfied with such a trifle, as the climax to so special a suspense, she almost set him wondering if she hadn't even a larger conception of singularity for him than he had for himself. He was at all events destined to become aware little by little, as time went by, that she was all the while looking at his life, judging it, measuring it, in the light of the thing she knew, which grew to be at last, with the consecration of the years, never mentioned between them save as 'the real truth' about him. That had always been his own form of reference to it, but she adopted the form so quietly that, looking back at the end of a period, he knew there was no moment at which it was traceable that she had, as he might say, got inside his condition, or exchanged the attitude of beautifully indulging for that of still more beautifully believing him.

It was always open to him to accuse her of seeing him but as the most harmless of maniacs, and this, in the long run – since it covered so much ground – was his easiest description of their friendship. He had a screw loose for her, but she liked him in spite of it, and was practically, against the rest of the world, his kind, wise keeper, unremunerated, but fairly amused and, in the absence of other near ties, not disreputably occupied. The rest of the world of course thought him queer, but she, she only, knew how, and above all why, queer; which was precisely what enabled her to dispose the concealing veil in the right folds. She took his gaiety from him – since it had to pass with them for gaiety – as she took everything else; but she certainly so far justified by her unerring touch his finer sense of the degree to which he had ended by convincing her. *She* at least never spoke of the secret of his life except as 'the real truth about you,' and she had in fact a wonderful way of making it seem, as such, the secret of her own life too. That was in fine how he so constantly felt her as allowing for him; he couldn't on the whole call it anything else. He allowed for himself, but she, exactly, allowed still more; partly because, better placed for a sight of the matter, she traced his unhappy perversion through portions of its course into which he could scarce follow it. He knew how he felt, but, besides knowing that, she knew how he *looked* as well; he knew each of the things of importance he was insidiously kept from doing, but she could add up the amount they made, understand how much, with a lighter weight on his spirit, he might have done, and thereby establish how, clever as he was, he fell short. Above all she was in the secret of the difference between the forms he went through — those of his little office under Government, those of caring for his modest patrimony, for his library, for his garden in the country, for the people in London whose invitations he accepted and repaid — and the detachment that reigned beneath them and that made of all behaviour, all that could in the least be called behaviour, a long act of dissimulation. What it had come to was that he wore a mask painted with the social simper, out of the eye-holes of which there looked eyes of an expression not in the least matching the other features. This the stupid world, even after years, had never more than half discovered. It was only May Bartram who had, and she achieved, by an art indescribable, the feat of at once — or perhaps it was only alternately — meeting the eyes from in front and mingling her own vision, as from over his shoulder, with their peep through the apertures.

So, while they grew older together, she did watch with him, and so she let this association give shape and colour to her own existence. Beneath *her* forms as well detachment had learned to sit, and behaviour had become for her, in the social sense, a false account of herself. There was but one account of her that would have been true all the while, and that she could give, directly, to nobody, least of all to John Marcher. Her whole attitude was a virtual statement, but the perception of that only seemed destined to take its place for him as one of the many things necessarily crowded out of his consciousness. If she had, moreover, like himself, to make sacrifices to their real truth, it was to be granted that her compensation might have affected her as more prompt and more natural. They had long periods, in this London time, during which, when they were together, a stranger might have listened to them without in the least pricking up his ears; on the other hand, the real truth was equally liable at any moment to rise to the surface, and the auditor would then have wondered indeed what they were talking about. They had from an early time made up their mind that society was, luckily, unintelligent, and the margin that this gave them had fairly become one of their commonplaces. Yet there were still moments when the situation turned almost fresh – usually under the effect of some expression drawn from herself. Her expressions doubtless repeated themselves, but her intervals were generous. 'What saves us, you know, is that we answer so completely to so usual an appearance: that of the man and woman whose friendship has become such a daily habit, or almost, as to be at last indispensable.' That, for instance, was a remark she had frequently enough had occasion to make, though she had given it at different times different developments. What we are especially concerned with is the turn it happened to take from her one afternoon when he had come to see her in honour of her birthday. This anniversary had fallen on a Sunday, at a season of thick fog and general outward gloom; but he had brought her his customary offering, having known her now long enough to have established a hundred little customs. It was one of his proofs to himself, the present he made her on her birthday, that he had not sunk into real selfishness. It was mostly nothing more than a small trinket, but it was always fine of its kind, and he was regularly careful to pay for it more than he thought he could afford. 'Our habit saves you, at least, don't you see? because it makes you, after all, for the vulgar, indistinguishable from other men. What's the most inveterate mark of men in general? Why, the capacity to spend endless time with dull women – to spend it, I won't say without being bored, but without minding that they are, without being driven off at a tangent by it; which comes to the same thing. I'm your dull woman, a part of the daily bread for which you pray at church. That covers your tracks more than anything.'

'And what covers yours?' asked Marcher, whom his dull woman could mostly to this extent amuse. 'I see of course what you mean by your saving me, in one way and another, so far as other people are concerned – I've seen it all along. Only, what is it that saves you? I often think, you know, of that.'

She looked as if she sometimes thought of that too, but in rather a different way. 'Where other people, you mean, are concerned?'

'Well, you're really so in with me, you know – as a sort of result of my being so in with yourself. I mean of my having such an immense regard for you, being so tremendously grateful for all you've done for me. I sometimes ask myself if it's quite fair. Fair I mean to have so involved and – since one may say it – interested you. I almost feel as if you hadn't really had time to do anything else.'

'Anything else but be interested?' she asked. 'Ah, what else does one ever want to be? If I've been "watching" with you, as we long ago agreed that I was to do, watching is always in itself an absorption.'

'Oh certainly,' John Marcher said, 'if you hadn't had your curiosity – ! Only, doesn't it sometimes come to you, as time goes on, that your curiosity is not being particularly repaid?'

May Bartram had a pause. 'Do you ask that, by any chance, because you feel at all that yours isn't? I mean because you have to wait so long.'

Oh, he understood what she meant. 'For the thing to happen that never does happen? For the beast to jump out? No, I'm just where I was about it. It isn't a matter as to which I can *choose*, I can decide for a change. It isn't one as to which there *can* be a change. It's in the lap of the gods. One's in the hands of one's law – there one is. As to the form the law will take, the way it will operate, that's its own affair.'

'Yes,' Miss Bartram replied; 'of course one's fate is coming, of course it *has* come, in its own form and its own way, all the while. Only, you know, the form and the way in your case were to have been – well, something so exceptional and, as one may say, so particularly *your* own.'

Something in this made him look at her with suspicion. 'You say "were to *have* been," as if in your heart you had begun to doubt.'

'Oh!' she vaguely protested.

'As if you believed,' he went on, 'that nothing will now take place.'

She shook her head slowly, but rather inscrutably. 'You're far from my thought.'

He continued to look at her. 'What then is the matter with you?'

'Well,' she said after another wait, 'the matter with me is simply that I'm more sure than ever my curiosity, as you call it, will be but too well repaid.'

They were frankly grave now; he had got up from his seat, had turned once more about the little drawing-room to which, year after year, he brought his inevitable topic; in which he had, as he might have said, tasted their intimate community with every sauce, where every object was as familiar to him as the things of his own house and the very carpets were worn with his fitful walk very much as the desks in old counting-houses are worn by the elbows of generations of clerks. The generations of his nervous moods had been at work there, and the place was the written history of his whole middle life. Under the impression of what his friend had just said he knew himself, for some reason, more aware of these things, which made him, after a moment, stop again before her. 'Is it, possibly, that you've grown afraid?'

'Afraid?' He thought, as she repeated the word, that his question had made her, a little, change colour; so that, lest he should have touched on a truth, he explained very kindly, 'You remember that that was what you asked *me* long ago – that first day at Weatherend.'

'Oh yes, and you told me you didn't know – that I was to see for myself. We've said little about it since, even in so long a time.'

'Precisely,' Marcher interposed – 'quite as if it were too delicate a matter for us to make free with. Quite as if we might find, on pressure, that I *am* afraid. For then,' he said, 'we shouldn't, should we? quite know what to do.'

She had for the time no answer to this question. 'There have been days when I thought you were. Only, of course,' she added, 'there have been days when we have thought almost anything.'

'Everything. Oh!' Marcher softly groaned as with a gasp, half spent, at the face, more uncovered just then than it had been for a long while, of the imagination always with them. It had always had its incalculable moments of glaring out, quite as with the very eyes of the very Beast, and, used as he was to them, they could still draw from him the tribute of a sigh that rose from the depths of his being. All that they had thought, first and last, rolled over him; the past seemed to have been reduced to mere barren speculation. This in fact was what the place had just struck him as so full of – the simplification of everything but the state of suspense. That remained only by seeming to hang in the void surrounding it. Even his original fear, if fear it had been, had lost itself in the desert. 'I judge, however,' he continued, 'that you see I'm not afraid now.'

'What I see is, as I make it out, that you've achieved something almost unprecedented in the way of getting used to danger. Living with it so long and so closely, you've lost your sense of it; you know it's there, but you're indifferent, and you cease even, as of old, to have to whistle in the dark. Considering what the danger is,' May Bartram wound up, 'I'm bound to say that I don't think your attitude could well be surpassed.'

John Marcher faintly smiled. 'It's heroic?'

'Certainly – call it that.'

He considered. 'I *am*, then, a man of courage?'

'That's what you were to show me.'

He still, however, wondered. 'But doesn't the man of courage know what he's afraid of – or *not* afraid of? I don't know *that*, you see. I don't focus it. I can't name it. I only know I'm exposed.'

'Yes, but exposed – how shall I say? – so directly. So intimately. That's surely enough.'

'Enough to make you feel, then – as what we may call the end of our watch – that I'm not afraid?'

'You're not afraid. But it isn't,' she said, 'the end of our watch. That is it isn't the end of yours. You've everything still to see.'

'Then why haven't you?' he asked. He had had, all along, today, the sense of her keeping something back, and he still had it. As this was his first impression of that, it made a kind of date. The case was the more marked as she didn't at first answer; which in turn made him go on. 'You know something I don't.' Then his voice, for that of a man of courage, trembled a little. 'You know what's to happen.' Her silence, with the face she showed, was almost a confession – it made him sure. 'You know, and you're afraid to tell me. It's so bad that you're afraid I'll find out.'

All this might be true, for she did look as if, unexpectedly to her, he had crossed some mystic line that she had secretly drawn round her. Yet she might, after all, not have worried; and the real upshot was that he himself, at all events, needn't. 'You'll never find out.'

III

It was all to have made, none the less, as I have said, a date; as came out in the fact that again and again, even after long intervals, other things that passed between them wore, in relation to this hour, but the character of recalls and results. Its immediate effect had been indeed rather to lighten insistence – almost to provoke a reaction; as if their topic had dropped by its own weight and as if moreover, for that matter, Marcher had been visited by one of his occasional warnings against egotism. He had kept up, he felt, and very decently on the whole, his consciousness of the importance of not being selfish, and it was true that he had never sinned in that direction without promptly enough trying to press the scales the other way. He often repaired his fault, the season permitting, by inviting his friend to accompany him to the opera; and it not infrequently thus happened that, to show he didn't wish her to have but one sort of food for her mind, he was the cause of her appearing there with him a dozen nights in the month. It even happened that, seeing her home at such times, he occasionally went in with her to finish, as he called it, the evening, and, the better to make his point, sat down to the frugal but always careful little supper that awaited his pleasure. His point was made, he thought, by his not eternally insisting with her on himself; made for instance, at such hours, when it befell that, her piano at hand and each of them familiar with it, they went over passages of the opera together. It chanced to be on one of these occasions, however, that he reminded her of her not having answered a certain question he had put to her during the talk that had taken place between them on her last birthday. 'What is it that saves *you*?' – saved her, he meant, from that appearance of variation from the usual human type. If he had practically escaped remark, as she pretended, by doing, in the most important particular, what most men do – find the answer to life in patching up an alliance of a sort with a woman no better than himself – how had she escaped it, and how could the alliance, such as it was, since they must suppose it had been more or less noticed, have failed to make her rather positively talked about?

'I never said,' May Bartram replied, 'that it hadn't made me talked about.'

'Ah well then, you're not "saved."'

'It has not been a question for me. If you've had your woman, I've had,' she said, 'my man.'

'And you mean that makes you all right?'

She hesitated. 'I don't know why it shouldn't make me – humanly, which is what we're speaking of – as right as it makes you.'

'I see,' Marcher returned. '"Humanly," no doubt, as showing that you're living for something. Not, that is, just for me and my secret.'

May Bartram smiled. 'I don't pretend it exactly shows that I'm not living for you. It's my intimacy with you that's in question.'

He laughed as he saw what she meant. 'Yes, but since, as you say, I'm only, so far as people make out, ordinary, you're – aren't you? – no more than ordinary either. You help me to pass for a man like another. So if I *am*, as I understand you, you're not compromised. Is that it?'

She had another hesitation, but she spoke clearly enough. 'That's it. It's all that concerns me – to help you to pass for a man like another.'

He was careful to acknowledge the remark handsomely. 'How kind, how beautiful, you are to me! How shall I ever repay you?'

She had her last grave pause, as if there might be a choice of ways. But she chose. 'By going on as you are.'

It was into this going on as he was that they relapsed, and really for so long a time that the day inevitably came for a further sounding of their depths. It was as if these depths, constantly bridged over by a structure that was firm enough in spite of its lightness and of its occasional oscillation in the somewhat vertiginous air, invited on occasion, in the interest of their nerves, a dropping of the plummet and a measurement of the abyss. A difference had been made moreover, once for all, by the fact that she had, all the while, not appeared to feel the need of rebutting his charge of an idea within her that she didn't dare to express, uttered just before one of the fullest of their later discussions ended. It had come up for him then that she 'knew' something and that what she knew was bad – too bad to tell him. When he had spoken of it as visibly so bad that she was afraid he might find it out, her reply had left the matter too equivocal to be let alone and yet, for Marcher's special sensibility, almost too formidable again to touch. He circled about it at a distance that alternately narrowed and widened and that yet was not much affected by the consciousness in him that there was nothing she could 'know,' after all, any better than he did. She had no source of knowledge that he hadn't equally – except of course that she might have finer nerves. That was what women had where they were interested; they made out things, where people were concerned, that the people often couldn't have made out for themselves. Their nerves, their sensibility, their imagination, were conductors and revealers, and the beauty of May Bartram was in particular that she had given herself so to his case. He felt in these days what, oddly enough, he had never felt before, the growth of a dread of losing her by some catastrophe – some catastrophe that yet wouldn't at all be *the* catastrophe: partly because she had, almost of a sudden, begun to strike him as useful to him as never yet, and partly by reason of an appearance of uncertainty in her health, coincident and equally new. It was characteristic of the inner detachment he had hitherto so successfully cultivated and to which our whole account of him is a reference, it was characteristic that his complications, such as they were, had never yet seemed so as at this crisis to thicken about him, even to the point of making him ask himself if he were, by any chance, of a truth, within sight or sound, within touch or reach, within the immediate jurisdiction of the thing that waited.

When the day came, as come it had to, that his friend confessed to him her fear of a deep disorder in her blood, he felt somehow the shadow of a change and the chill of a shock. He immediately began to imagine aggravations and disasters, and above all to think of her peril as the direct menace for himself of personal privation. This indeed gave him one of those partial recoveries of equanimity that were agreeable to him – it showed him that what was still first in his mind was the loss she herself might suffer. 'What if she should have to die before knowing, before seeing – ?' It would have been brutal, in the early stages of her trouble, to put that question to her; but it had immediately sounded for him to his own concern, and the possibility was what most made him sorry for her. If she did 'know,' moreover, in the sense of her having had some – what should he think? – mystical, irresistible light, this would make the matter not better, but worse, inasmuch as her original adoption of his own curiosity had quite become the basis of her life. She had been living to see what would *be* to be seen, and it would be cruel to her to have to give up before the accomplishment of the vision. These reflections, as I say, refreshed his generosity; yet, make them as he might, he saw himself, with the lapse of the period, more and more disconcerted. It lapsed for him with a strange, steady sweep, and the oddest oddity was that it gave him, independently of the threat of much inconvenience, almost the only positive surprise his career, if career it could be called, had yet offered him. She kept the house as she had never done; he had to go to her to see her – she could meet him nowhere now, though there was scarce a corner of their loved old London in which she had not in the past, at one time or another, done so; and he found her always seated by her fire in the deep, old-fashioned chair she was less and less able to leave. He had been struck one day, after an absence exceeding his usual measure, with her suddenly looking much older to him than he had ever thought of her being; then he recognized that the suddenness was all on his side – he had just been suddenly struck. She looked older because inevitably, after so many years, she *was* old, or almost; which was of course true in still greater measure of her companion. If she was old, or almost, John Marcher assuredly was, and yet it was her showing of the lesson, not his own, that brought the truth home to him. His surprises began here; when once they had begun they multiplied; they came rather with a rush: it was as if, in the oddest way in the world, they had all been kept back, sown in a thick cluster, for the late afternoon of life, the time at which, for people in general, the unexpected has died out.

One of them was that he should have caught himself – for he *had* so done – *really* wondering if the great accident would take form now as nothing more than his being condemned to see this charming woman, this admirable friend, pass away from him. He had never so unreservedly qualified her as while confronted in thought with such a possibility; in spite of which there was small doubt for him that as an answer to his long riddle the mere effacement of even so fine a feature of his situation would be an abject anticlimax. It would represent, as connected with his past attitude, a drop of dignity under the shadow of which his existence could only become the most grotesque of failures. He had been far from holding it a failure – long as he had waited for the appearance that was to make it a success. He had waited for a quite other thing, not for such a one as that. The breath of his good faith came short, however, as he recognized how long he had waited, or how long, at least, his companion had. That she, at all events, might be recorded as having waited in vain – this affected him sharply, and all the more because of his at first having done little more than amuse himself with the idea. It grew more grave as the gravity of her condition grew, and the state of mind it produced in him, which he ended by watching, himself, as if it had been some definite disfigurement of his outer person, may pass for another of his surprises. This conjoined itself still with another, the really stupefying consciousness of a question that he would have allowed to shape itself had he dared. What did everything mean – what, that is, did *she* mean, she and her vain waiting and her probable death and the soundless admonition of it all – unless that, at this time of day, it was simply, it was overwhelmingly too late? He had never, at any stage of his queer consciousness, admitted the whisper of such a correction; he had never, till within these last few months, been so false to his conviction as not to hold that what was to come to him had time, whether *he* struck himself as having it or not. That at last, at last, he certainly hadn't it, to speak of, or had it but in the scantiest measure – such, soon enough, as things went with him, became the inference with which his old obsession had to reckon: and this it was not helped to do by the more and more confirmed appearance that the great vagueness casting the long shadow in which he had lived had, to attest itself, almost no margin left. Since it was in Time that he was to have met his fate, so it was in Time that his fate was to have acted; and as he waked up to the sense of no longer being young, which was exactly the sense of being stale, just as that, in turn, was the sense of being weak, he waked up to another matter beside. It all hung together; they were subject, he and the great vagueness, to an equal and indivisible law. When the possibilities themselves had, accordingly, turned stale, when the secret of the gods had grown faint, had perhaps even quite evaporated, that, and that only, was failure. It wouldn't have been failure to be bankrupt, dishonoured, pilloried, hanged; it was failure not to be anything. And so, in the dark valley into which his path had taken its unlooked-for twist, he wondered not a little as he groped. He didn't care what awful crash might overtake him, with what ignominy or what monstrosity he might yet be associated – since he wasn't, after all, too utterly old to suffer – if it would only be decently proportionate to the posture he had kept, all his life, in the promised presence of it. He had but one desire left – that he shouldn't have been 'sold'.

IV

Then it was that one afternoon, while the spring of the year was young and new, she met, all in her own way, his frankest betrayal of these alarms. He had gone in late to see her, but evening had not settled, and she was presented to him in that long, fresh light of waning April days which affects us often with a sadness sharper than the greyest hours of autumn. The week had been warm, the spring was supposed to have begun early, and May Bartram sat, for the first time in the year, without a fire, a fact that, to Marcher's sense, gave the scene of which she formed part a smooth and ultimate look, an air of knowing, in its immaculate order and its cold, meaningless cheer, that it would never see a fire again. Her own aspect – he could scarce have said why – intensified this note. Almost as white as wax, with the marks and signs in her face as numerous and as fine as if they had been etched by a needle, with soft white draperies relieved by a faded green scarf, the delicate tone of which had been consecrated by the years, she was the picture of a serene, exquisite, but impenetrable sphinx, whose head, or indeed all whose person, might have been powdered with silver. She was a sphinx, yet with her white petals and green fronds she might have been a lily too – only an artificial lily, wonderfully imitated and constantly kept, without dust or stain, though not exempt from a slight droop and a complexity of faint creases, under some clear glass bell. The perfection of household care, of high polish and finish, always reigned in her rooms, but they especially looked to Marcher at present as if everything had been wound up, tucked in, put away, so that she might sit with folded hands and with nothing more to do. She was 'out of it,' to his vision; her work was over; she communicated with him as across some gulf, or from some island of rest that she had already reached, and it made him feel strangely abandoned. Was it – or, rather, wasn't it – that if for so long she had been watching with him the answer to their question had swum into her ken and taken on its name, so that her occupation was verily gone? He had as much as charged her with this in saying to her, many months before, that she even then knew something she was keeping from him. It was a point he had never since ventured to press, vaguely fearing, as he did, that it might become a difference, perhaps a disagreement, between them. He had in short, in this later time, turned nervous, which was what, in all the other years, he had never been; and the oddity was that his nervousness should have waited till he had begun to doubt, should have held off so long as he was sure. There was something, it seemed to him, that the wrong word would bring down on his head, something that would so at least put an end to his suspense. But he wanted not to speak the wrong word; that would make everything ugly. He wanted the knowledge he lacked to drop on him, if drop it could, by its own august weight. If she was to forsake him it was surely for her to take leave. This was why he didn't ask her again, directly, what she knew; but it was also why, approaching the matter from another side, he said to her in the course of his visit: 'What do you regard as the very worst that, at this time of day, *can* happen to me?'

He had asked her that in the past often enough; they had, with the odd, irregular rhythm of their intensities and avoidances, exchanged ideas about it and then had seen the ideas washed away by cool intervals, washed like figures traced in sea-sand. It had ever been the mark of their talk that the oldest allusions in it required but a little dismissal and reaction to come out again, sounding for the hour as new. She could thus at present meet his inquiry quite freshly and patiently. 'Oh yes, I've repeatedly thought, only it always seemed to me of old that I couldn't quite make up my mind. I thought of dreadful things, between which it was difficult to choose; and so must you have done.'

'Rather! I feel now as if I had scarce done anything else. I appear to myself to have spent my life in thinking of nothing *but* dreadful things. A great many of them I've at different times named to you, but there were others I couldn't name.'

'They were too, too dreadful?'

'Too, too dreadful – some of them.'

She looked at him a minute, and there came to him as he met it an inconsequent sense that her eyes, when one got their full clearness, were still as beautiful as they had been in youth, only beautiful with a strange, cold light – a light that somehow was a part of the effect, if it wasn't rather a part of the cause, of the pale, hard sweetness of the season and the hour. 'And yet,' she said at last, 'there are horrors we have mentioned.'

It deepened the strangeness to see her, as such a figure in such a picture, talk of 'horrors,' but she was to do, in a few minutes, something stranger yet – though even of this he was to take the full measure but afterwards – and the note of it was already in the air. It was, for the matter of that, one of the signs that her eyes were having again such a high flicker of their prime. He had to admit, however, what she said. 'Oh yes, there were times when we did go far.' He caught himself in the act of speaking as if it all were over. Well, he wished it were; and the consummation depended, for him, clearly, more and more on his companion.

But she had now a soft smile. 'Oh, far – !'

It was oddly ironic. 'Do you mean you're prepared to go further?'

She was frail and ancient and charming as she continued to look at him, yet it was rather as if she had lost the thread. 'Do you consider that we went so far?'

'Why, I thought it the point you were just making – that we *had* looked most things in the face.'

'Including each other?' She still smiled. 'But you're quite right. We've had together great imaginations, often great fears; but some of them have been unspoken.'

'Then the worst – we haven't faced that. I *could* face it, I believe, if I knew what you think it. I feel,' he explained, 'as if I had lost my power to conceive such things.' And he wondered if he looked as blank as he sounded. 'It's spent.'

'Then why do you assume,' she asked, 'that mine isn't?'

'Because you've given me signs to the contrary. It isn't a question for you of conceiving, imagining, comparing. It isn't a question now of choosing.' At last he came out with it. 'You know something that I don't. You've shown me that before.'

These last words affected her, he could see in a moment, remarkably, and she spoke with firmness. 'I've shown you, my dear, nothing.'

He shook his head. 'You can't hide it.'

'Oh, oh!' May Bartram murmured over what she couldn't hide. It was almost a smothered groan.

'You admitted it months ago, when I spoke of it to you as of something you were afraid I would find out. Your answer was that I couldn't, that I wouldn't, and I don't pretend I have. But you had something therefore in mind, and I see now that it must have been, that it still is, the possibility that, of all possibilities, has settled itself for you as the worst. This,' he went on, 'is why I appeal to you. I'm only afraid of ignorance now – I'm not afraid of knowledge.' And then as for a while she said nothing: 'What makes me sure is that I see in your face and feel here, in this air and amid these appearances, that you're out of it. You've done. You've had your experience. You leave me to my fate.'

Well, she listened, motionless and white in her chair, as if she had in fact a decision to make, so that her whole manner was a virtual confession, though still with a small, fine, inner stiffness, an imperfect surrender. 'It *would* be the worst,' she finally let herself say. 'I mean the thing that I've never said.'

It hushed him a moment. 'More monstrous than all the monstrosities we've named?'

'More monstrous. Isn't that what you sufficiently express,' she asked, 'in calling it the worst?'

Marcher thought. 'Assuredly – if you mean, as I do, something that includes all the loss and all the shame that are thinkable.'

'It would if it *should* happen,' said May Bartram. 'What we're speaking of, remember, is only my idea.'

'It's your belief,' Marcher returned. 'That's enough for me. I feel your beliefs are right. Therefore if, having this one, you give me no more light on it, you abandon me.'

'No, no!' she repeated. 'I'm with you – don't you see? – still.' And as if to make it more vivid to him she rose from her chair – a movement she seldom made in these days – and showed herself, all draped and all soft, in her fairness and slimness. 'I haven't forsaken you.'

It was really, in its effort against weakness, a generous assurance, and had the success of the impulse not, happily, been great, it would have touched him to pain more than to pleasure. But the cold charm in her eyes had spread, as she hovered before him, to all the rest of her person, so that it was, for the minute, almost like a recovery of youth. He couldn't pity her for that; he could only take her as she showed – as capable still of helping him. It was as if, at the same time, her light might at any instant go out; wherefore he must make the most of it. There passed before him with intensity the three or four things he wanted most to know; but the question that came of itself to his lips really covered the others. 'Then tell me if I shall consciously suffer.'

She promptly shook her head. 'Never!'

It confirmed the authority he imputed to her, and it produced on him an extraordinary effect. 'Well, what's better than that? Do you call that the worst?'

'You think nothing is better?' she asked.

She seemed to mean something so special that he again sharply wondered, though still with the dawn of a prospect of relief. 'Why not, if one doesn't *know*?' After which, as their eyes, over his question, met in a silence, the dawn deepened and something to his purpose came, prodigiously, out of her very face. His own, as he took it in, suddenly flushed to the forehead, and he gasped with the force of a perception to which, on the instant, everything fitted. The sound of his gasp filled the air; then he became articulate. 'I see – if I don't suffer!'

In her own look, however, was doubt. 'You see what?'

'Why, what you mean – what you've always meant.'

She again shook her head. 'What I mean isn't what I've always meant. It's different.'

'It's something new?'

She hesitated. 'Something new. It's not what you think. I see what you think.'

His divination drew breath then; only her correction might be wrong. 'It isn't that I *am* a donkey?' he asked between faintness and grimness. 'It isn't that it's all a mistake?'

'A mistake?' she pityingly echoed. *That* possibility, for her, he saw, would be monstrous; and if she guaranteed him the immunity from pain it would accordingly not be what she had in mind. 'Oh, no,' she declared; 'it's nothing of that sort. You've been right.'

Yet he couldn't help asking himself if she weren't, thus pressed, speaking but to save him. It seemed to him he should be most lost if his history should prove all a platitude. 'Are you telling me the truth, so that I sha'n't have been a bigger idiot than I can bear to know? I *haven't* lived with a vain imagination, in the most besotted illusion? I haven't waited but to see the door shut in my face?'

She shook her head again. 'However the case stands *that* isn't the truth. Whatever the reality, it *is* a reality. The door isn't shut. The door's open,' said May Bartram.

'Then something's to come?'

She waited once again, always with her cold, sweet eyes on him. 'It's never too late.' She had, with her gliding step, diminished the distance between them, and she stood nearer to him, close to him, a minute, as if still full of the unspoken. Her movement might have been for some finer emphasis of what she was at once hesitating and deciding to say. He had been standing by the chimney-piece, fireless and sparely adorned, a small, perfect old French clock and two morsels of rosy Dresden constituting all its furniture; and her hand grasped the shelf while she kept him waiting, grasped it a little as for support and encouragement. She only kept him waiting, however; that is he only waited. It had become suddenly, from her movement and attitude, beautiful and vivid to him that she had something more to give him; her wasted face delicately shone with it, and it glittered, almost as with the white lustre of silver, in her expression. She was right, incontestably, for what he saw in her face was the truth, and strangely, without consequence, while their talk of it as dreadful was still in the air, she appeared to present it as inordinately soft. This, prompting bewilderment, made him but gape the more gratefully for her revelation, so that they continued for some minutes silent, her face shining at him, her contact imponderably pressing, and his stare all kind, but all expectant. The end, none the less, was that what he had expected failed to sound. Something else took place instead, which seemed to consist at first in the mere closing of her eyes. She gave way at the same instant to a slow, fine shudder, and though he remained staring – though he stared, in fact, but the harder – she turned off and regained her chair. It was the end of what she had been intending, but it left him thinking only of that.

'Well, you don't say – ?'

She had touched in her passage a bell near the chimney and had sunk back, strangely pale. 'I'm afraid I'm too ill.'

'Too ill to tell me?' It sprang up sharp to him, and almost to his lips, the fear that she would die without giving him light. He checked himself in time from so expressing his question but she answered as if she had heard the words.

'Don't you know – now?'

' "Now" – ?' She had spoken as if something that had made a difference had come up within the moment. But her maid, quickly obedient to her bell, was already with them. 'I know nothing.' And he was afterwards to say to himself that he must have spoken with odious impatience, such an impatience as to show that, supremely disconcerted, he washed his hands of the whole question.

'Oh!' said May Bartram.

'Are you in pain?' he asked, as the woman went to her.

'No,' said May Bartram.

Her maid, who had put an arm round her as if to take her to her room, fixed on him eyes that appealingly contradicted her; in spite of which, however, he showed once more his mystification. 'What then has happened?'

She was once more, with her companion's help, on her feet, and, feeling withdrawal imposed on him, he had found, blankly, his hat and gloves and had reached the door. Yet he waited for her answer. 'What *was* to,' she said.

V

He came back the next day, but she was then unable to see him, and as it was literally the first time this had occurred in the long stretch of their acquaintance he turned away, defeated and sore, almost angry – or feeling at least that such a break in their custom was really the beginning of the end – and wandered alone with his thoughts, especially with one of them that he was unable to keep down. She was dying, and he would lose her; she was dying, and his life would end. He stopped in the park, into which he had passed, and stared before him at his recurrent doubt.

Away from her the doubt pressed again; in her presence he had believed her, but as he felt his forlornness he threw himself into the explanation that, nearest at hand, had most of a miserable warmth for him and least of a cold torment. She had deceived him to save him – to put him off with something in which he should be able to rest. What could the thing that was to happen to him be, after all, but just this thing that had begun to happen? Her dying, her death, his consequent solitude – *that* was what he had figured as the beast in the jungle, that was what had been in the lap of the gods. He had had her word for it as he left her; for what else, on earth, could she have meant? It wasn't a thing of a monstrous order, not a fate rare and distinguished; not a stroke of fortune that overwhelmed and immortalized; it had only the stamp of the common doom. But poor Marcher, at this hour, judged the common doom sufficient. It would serve his turn, and even as the consummation of infinite waiting he would bend his pride to accept it. He sat down on a bench in the twilight. He hadn't been a fool. Something had *been*, as she had said, to come. Before he rose indeed it had quite struck him that the final fact really matched with the long avenue through which he had had to reach it. As sharing his suspense, and as giving herself all, giving her life, to bring it to an end, she had come with him every step of the way. He had lived by her aid, and to leave her behind would be cruelly, damnably to miss her. What could be more overwhelming than that?

Well, he was to know within the week, for though she kept him a while at bay, left him restless and wretched during a series of days on each of which he asked about her only again to have to turn away, she ended his trial by receiving him where she had always received him. Yet she had been brought out at some hazard into the presence of so many of the things that were, consciously, vainly, half their past, and there was scant service left in the gentleness of her mere desire, all too visible, to check his obsession and wind up his long trouble. That was clearly what she wanted; the one thing more, for her own peace, while she could still put out her hand. He was so affected by her state that, once seated by her chair, he was moved to let everything go; it was she herself therefore who brought him back, took up again, before she dismissed him, her last word of the other time. She showed how she wished to leave their affair in order. 'I'm not sure you understood. You've nothing to wait for more. It *has* come.'

Oh, how he looked at her! 'Really?'

'Really.'

'The thing that, as you said, *was* to?'

'The thing that we began in our youth to watch for.'

Face to face with her once more he believed her; it was a claim to which he had so abjectly little to oppose. 'You mean that it has come as a positive, definitive occurrence, with a name and a date?'

'Positive. Definite. I don't know about the "name," but, oh, with a date!'

He found himself again too helplessly at sea. 'But come in the night — come and passed me by?'

May Bartram had her strange, faint smile. 'Oh no, it hasn't passed you by!'

'But if I haven't been aware of it, and it hasn't touched me — ?'

'Ah, your not being aware of it,' and she seemed to hesitate an instant to deal with this — 'your not being aware of it is the strangeness *in* the strangeness. It's the wonder *of* the wonder.' She spoke as with the softness almost of a sick child, yet now at last, at the end of all, with the perfect straightness of a sibyl. She visibly knew that she knew, and the effect on him was of something co-ordinate, in its high character, with the law that had ruled him. It was the true voice of the law; so on her lips would the law itself have sounded. 'It *has* touched you,' she went on. 'It has done its office. It has made you all its own.'

'So utterly without my knowing it?'

'So utterly without your knowing it.' His hand, as he leaned to her, was on the arm of her chair, and, dimly smiling always now, she placed her own on it. 'It's enough if *I* know it.'

'Oh!' he confusedly sounded, as she herself of late so often had done.

'What I long ago said is true. You'll never know now, and I think you ought to be content. You've *had* it,' said May Bartram.

'But had what?'

'Why, what was to have marked you out. The proof of your law. It has acted. I'm too glad,' she said then bravely added, 'to have been able to see what it's *not*.'

He continued to attach his eyes to her, and with the sense that it was all beyond him, and that *she* was too, he would still have sharply

THE BEAST IN THE JUNGLE

challenged her, had he not felt it an abuse of her weakness to do more than take devoutly what she gave him, take it as hushed as to a revelation. If he did speak, it was out of the foreknowledge of his loneliness to come. 'If you're glad of what it's "not," it might then have been worse?'

She turned her eyes away, she looked straight before her with which, after a moment: 'Well, you know our fears.'

He wondered. 'It's something then we never feared?'

On this, slowly, she turned to him. 'Did we ever dream, with all our dreams, that we should sit and talk of it thus?'

He tried for a little to make out if they had; but it was as if their dreams, numberless enough, were in solution in some thick, cold mist, in which thought lost itself. 'It might have been that we couldn't talk?'

'Well' – she did her best for him – 'not from this side. This, you see,' she said, 'is the *other* side.'

'I think,' poor Marcher returned, 'that all sides are the same to me.' Then, however, as she softly shook her head in correction: 'We mightn't, as it were, have got across – ?'

'To where we are – no. We're *here*' – she made her weak emphasis.

'And much good does it do us!' was her friend's frank comment.

'It does us the good it can. It does us the good that *it* isn't here. It's past. It's behind,' said May Bartram. 'Before – ' but her voice dropped.

He had got up, not to tire her, but it was hard to combat his yearning. She after all told him nothing but that his light had failed – which he knew well enough without her. 'Before – ?' he blankly echoed.

'Before, you see, it was always to *come*. That kept it present.'

'Oh, I don't care what comes now! Besides,' Marcher added, 'it seems to me I liked it better present, as you say, than I can like it absent with *your* absence.'

'Oh, mine!' – and her pale hands made light of it.

'With the absence of everything.' He had a dreadful sense of standing there before her for – so far as anything but this proved, this bottomless drop was concerned – the last time of their life. It rested on him with a weight he felt he could scarce bear, and this weight it apparently was that still pressed out what remained in him of speakable protest. 'I

97

believe you; but I can't begin to pretend I understand. *Nothing*, for me, is past; nothing *will* pass until I pass myself, which I pray my stars may be as soon as possible. Say, however,' he added, 'that I've eaten my cake, as you contend, to the last crumb – how can the thing I've never felt at all be the thing I was marked out to feel?'

She met him, perhaps, less directly, but she met him unperturbed. 'You take your "feelings" for granted. You were to suffer your fate. That was not necessarily to know it.'

'How in the world – when what is such knowledge but suffering?'

She looked up at him a while, in silence. 'No – you don't understand.'

'I suffer,' said John Marcher.

'Don't, don't!'

'How can I help at least *that*?'

'*Don't!*' May Bartram repeated.

She spoke it in a tone so special, in spite of her weakness, that he stared an instant – stared as if some light, hitherto hidden, had shimmered across his vision. Darkness again closed over it, but the gleam had already become for him an idea. 'Because I haven't the right – ?'

'Don't *know* – when you needn't,' she mercifully urged. 'You needn't – for we shouldn't.'

'Shouldn't?' If he could but know what she meant!

'No – it's too much.'

'Too much?' he still asked – but with a mystification that was the next moment, of a sudden, to give way. Her words, if they meant something, affected him in this light – the light also of her wasted face – as meaning *all*, and the sense of what knowledge had been for herself came over him with a rush which broke through into a question. 'Is it of that, then, you're dying?'

She but watched him, gravely at first, as if to see, with this, where he was, and she might have seen something, or feared something, that moved her sympathy. 'I would live for you still – if I could.' Her eyes closed for a little, as if, withdrawn into herself, she were, for a last time, trying. 'But I can't!' she said as she raised them again to take leave of him.

She couldn't indeed, as but too promptly and sharply appeared, and he had no vision of her after this that was anything but darkness and doom. They had parted for ever in that strange talk; access to her chamber of pain, rigidly guarded, was almost wholly forbidden him; he was feeling now moreover, in the face of doctors, nurses, the two or three relatives attracted doubtless by the presumption of what she had to 'leave,' how few were the rights, as they were called in such cases, that he had to put forward, and how odd it might even seem that their intimacy shouldn't have given him more of them. The stupidest fourth cousin had more, even though she had been nothing in such a person's life. She had been a feature of features in *his*, for what else was it to have been so indispensable? Strange beyond saying were the ways of existence, baffling for him the anomaly of his lack, as he felt it to be, of producible claim. A woman might have been, as it were, everything to him, and it might yet present him in no connection that anyone appeared obliged to recognize. If this was the case in these closing weeks it was the case more sharply on the occasion of the last offices rendered, in the great grey London cemetery, to what had been mortal, to what had been precious, in his friend. The concourse at her grave was not numerous, but he saw himself treated as scarce more nearly concerned with it than if there had been a thousand others. He was in short from this moment face to face with the fact that he was to profit extraordinarily little by the interest May Bartram had taken in him. He couldn't quite have said what he expected, but he had somehow not expected this approach to a double privation. Not only had her interest failed him, but he seemed to feel himself unattended – and for a reason he couldn't sound – by the distinction, the dignity, the propriety, if nothing else, of the man markedly bereaved. It was as if, in the view of society, he had not *been* markedly bereaved, as if there still failed some sign or proof of it, and as if, none the less, his character could never be affirmed, nor the deficiency ever made up. There were moments, as the weeks went by, when he would have liked, by some almost aggressive act, to take his stand on the intimacy of his loss, in order that it *might* be questioned and his retort, to the relief of his spirit, so recorded; but the moments of an irritation more helpless followed fast on these, the moments during which, turning things over with a good conscience but with a bare horizon, he found himself wondering if he oughtn't to have begun, so to speak, further back.

He found himself wondering indeed at many things, and this last speculation had others to keep it company. What could he have done, after all, in her lifetime, without giving them both, as it were, away? He couldn't have made it known she was watching him, for that would have published the superstition of the Beast. This was what closed his mouth now — now that the Jungle had been threshed to vacancy and that the Beast had stolen away. It sounded too foolish and too flat; the difference for him in this particular, the extinction in his life of the element of suspense, was such in fact as to surprise him. He could scarce have said what the effect resembled; the abrupt cessation, the positive prohibition, of music perhaps, more than anything else, in some place all adjusted and all accustomed to sonority and to attention. If he could at any rate have conceived lifting the veil from his image at some moment of the past (what had he done, after all, if not lift it to *her*?), so to do this today, to talk to people at large of the jungle cleared and confide to them that he now felt it as safe, would have been not only to see them listen as to a goodwife's tale, but really to hear himself tell one. What it presently came to in truth was that poor Marcher waded through his beaten grass, where no life stirred, where no breath sounded, where no evil eye seemed to gleam from a possible lair, very much as if vaguely looking for the Beast, and still more as if missing it. He walked about in an existence that had grown strangely more spacious, and, stopping fitfully in places where the undergrowth of life struck him as closer, asked himself yearningly, wondered secretly, and sorely, if it would have lurked here or there. It would have at all events *sprung*; what was at least complete was his belief in the truth itself of the assurance given him. The change from his old sense to his new was absolute and final: what was to happen *had* so absolutely and finally happened that he was as little able to know a fear for his future as to know a hope; so absent in short was any question of anything still to come. He was to live entirely with the other question, that of his unidentified past, that of his having to see his fortune impenetrably muffled and masked.

The torment of this vision became then his occupation; he couldn't perhaps have consented to live but for the possibility of guessing. She had told him, his friend, not to guess; she had forbidden him, so far as

he might, to know, and she had even in a sort denied the power in him
to learn: which were so many things, precisely, to deprive him of rest. It
wasn't that he wanted, he argued for fairness, that anything that had
happened to him should happen over again; it was only that he shouldn't,
as an anticlimax, have been taken sleeping so sound as not to be able to
win back by an effort of thought the lost stuff of consciousness. He
declared to himself at moments that he would either win it back or have
done with consciousness for ever; he made this idea his one motive, in
fine, made it so much his passion that none other, to compare with it,
seemed ever to have touched him. The lost stuff of consciousness
became thus for him as a strayed or stolen child to an unappeasable
father; he hunted it up and down very much as if he were knocking at
doors and inquiring of the police. This was the spirit in which, inevitably, he set himself to travel; he started on a journey that was to be as
long as he could make it; it danced before him that, as the other side of
the globe couldn't possibly have less to say to him, it might, by a
possibility of suggestion, have more. Before he quitted London, however, he made a pilgrimage to May Bartram's grave, took his way to it
through the endless avenues of the grim suburban necropolis, sought it
out in the wilderness of tombs, and, though he had come but for the
renewal of the act of farewell, found himself, when he had at last stood
by it, beguiled into long intensities. He stood for an hour, powerless to
turn away and yet powerless to penetrate the darkness of death; fixing
with his eyes her inscribed name and date, beating his forehead against
the fact of the secret they kept, drawing his breath, while he waited as if,
in pity of him, some sense would rise from the stones. He kneeled on
the stones, however, in vain; they kept what they concealed; and if the
face of the tomb did become a face for him it was because her two
names were like a pair of eyes that didn't know him. He gave them a
last long look, but no palest light broke.

VI

He stayed away, after this, for a year; he visited the depths of Asia,
spending himself on scenes of romantic interest, of superlative sanctity;
but what was present to him everywhere was that for a man who had

THE BEAST IN THE JUNGLE

known what *he* had known the world was vulgar and vain. The state of mind in which he had lived for so many years shone out to him, in reflection, as a light that coloured and refined, a light beside which the glow of the East was garish, cheap and thin. The terrible truth was that he had lost – with everything else – a distinction as well; the things he saw couldn't help being common when he had become common to look at them. He was simply now one of them himself – he was in the dust, without a peg for the sense of difference; and there were hours when, before the temples of gods and the sepulchres of kings, his spirit turned, for nobleness of association, to the barely discriminated slab in the London suburb. That had become for him, and more intensely with time and distance, his one witness of a past glory. It was all that was left to him for proof or pride, yet the past glories of Pharaohs were nothing to him as he thought of it. Small wonder then that he came back to it on the morrow of his return. He was drawn there this time as irresistibly as the other, yet with a confidence, almost, that was doubtless the effect of the many months that had elapsed. He had lived, in spite of himself, into his change of feeling, and in wandering over the earth had wandered, as might be said, from the circumference to the centre of his desert. He had settled to his safety and accepted perforce his extinction; figuring to himself, with some colour, in the likeness of certain little old men he remembered to have seen, of whom, all meagre and wizened as they might look, it was related that they had in their time fought twenty duels or been loved by ten princesses. They indeed had been wondrous for others, while he was but wondrous for himself; which, however, was exactly the cause of his haste to renew the wonder by getting back, as he might put it, into his own presence. That had quickened his steps and checked his delay. If his visit was prompt it was because he had been separated so long from the part of himself that alone he now valued.

It is accordingly not false to say that he reached his goal with a certain elation and stood there again with a certain assurance. The creature beneath the sod *knew* of his rare experience, so that, strangely now, the place had lost for him its mere blankness of expression. It met him in mildness – not, as before, in mockery; it wore for him the air of conscious greeting that we find, after absence, in things that have closely belonged to us which seem to confess of themselves to the connection. The plot of ground, the graven tablet, the tended flowers affected him so as belonging to him that he quite felt for the hour like a contented landlord reviewing a piece of property. Whatever had happened – well, had happened. He had not come back this time with the vanity of that question, his former worrying, 'What, *what*?' now practically so spent. Yet he would, none the less, never again so cut himself off from the spot; he would come back to it every month, for if he did nothing else by its aid he at least held up his head. It thus grew for him, in the oddest way, a positive resource; he carried out his idea of periodical returns, which took their place at last among the most inveterate of his habits. What it all amounted to, oddly enough, was that, in his now so simplified world, this garden of death gave him the few square feet of earth on which he could still most live. It was as if, being nothing anywhere else for anyone, nothing even for himself, he were just everything here, and if not for a crowd of witnesses, or indeed for any witness but John Marcher, then by clear right of the register that he could scan like an open page. The open page was the tomb of his friend, and *there* were the facts of the past, there the truth of his life, there the backward reaches in which he could lose himself. He did this, from time to time, with such effect that he seemed to wander through the old years with his hand in the arm of a companion who was, in the most extraordinary manner, his other, his younger self; and to wander, which was more extraordinary yet, round and round a third presence – not wandering she, but stationary, still, whose eyes, turning with his revolution, never ceased to follow him, and whose seat was his point, so to speak, of orientation. Thus in short he settled to live – feeding only on the sense that he once *had* lived, and dependent on it not only for a support but for an identity.

It sufficed him, in its way, for months, and the year elapsed; it would doubtless even have carried him further but for an accident, superficially slight, which moved him, in a quite other direction, with a force beyond any of his impressions of Egypt or of India. It was a thing of the merest chance – the turn, as he afterwards felt, of a hair, though he was indeed to live to believe that if light hadn't come to him in this particular fashion it would still have come in another. He was to live to believe this, I say, though he was not to live, I may not less definitely mention, to do much else. We allow him at any rate the benefit of the conviction, struggling up for him at the end, that, whatever might have happened or not happened, he would have come round of himself to the light. The incident of an autumn day had put the match to the train laid from of old by his misery. With the light before him he knew that even of late his ache had only been smothered. It was strangely drugged, but it throbbed; at the touch it began to bleed. And the touch, in the event, was the face of a fellow-mortal. This face, one grey afternoon when the leaves were thick in the alleys, looked into Marcher's own, at the cemetery, with an expression like the cut of a blade. He felt it, that is, so deep down that he winced at the steady thrust. The person who so mutely assaulted him was a figure he had noticed, on reaching his own goal, absorbed by a grave a short distance away, a grave apparently fresh, so that the emotion of the visitor would probably match it for frankness. This fact alone forbade further attention, though during the time he stayed he remained vaguely conscious of his neighbour, a middle-aged man apparently, in mourning, whose bowed back, among the clustered monuments and mortuary yews, was constantly presented. Marcher's theory that these were elements in contact with which he himself revived, had suffered, on this occasion, it may be granted, a sensible though inscrutable check. The autumn day was dire for him as none had recently been, and he rested with a heaviness he had not yet known on the low stone table that bore May Bartram's name. He rested without power to move, as if some spring in him, some spell vouchsafed, had suddenly been broken forever. If he could have done that moment as he wanted he would simply have stretched himself on the slab that was ready to take him, treating it as a place prepared to receive his last sleep. What in all the wide world had he now to keep awake for? He stared before him with the question, and it was then that, as one of the cemetery walks passed near him, he caught the shock of the face.

His neighbour at the other grave had withdrawn, as he himself, with force in him to move, would have done by now, and was advancing along the path on his way to one of the gates. This brought him near, and his pace was slow, so that – and all the more as there was a kind of hunger in his look – the two men were for a minute directly confronted.

Marcher felt him on the spot as one of the deeply stricken – a perception so sharp that nothing else in the picture lived for it, neither his dress, his age, nor his presumable character and class; nothing lived but the deep ravage of the features that he showed. He *showed* them – that was the point; he was moved, as he passed, by some impulse that was either a signal for sympathy or, more possibly, a challenge to another sorrow. He might already have been aware of our friend, might, at some previous hour, have noticed in him the smooth habit of the scene, with which the state of his own senses so scantly consorted, and might thereby have been stirred as by a kind of overt discord. What Marcher was at all events conscious of was, in the first place, that the image of scarred passion presented to him was conscious too – of something that profaned the air; and, in the second, that, roused, startled, shocked, he was yet the next moment looking after it, as it went, with envy. The most extraordinary thing that had happened to him – though he had given that name to other matters as well – took place, after his immediate vague stare, as a consequence of this impression. The stranger passed, but the raw glare of his grief remained, making our friend wonder in pity what wrong, what wound it expressed, what injury not to be healed. What had the man *had* to make him, by the loss of it, so bleed and yet live?

Something – and this reached him with a pang – that *he*, John Marcher, hadn't; the proof of which was precisely John Marcher's arid end. No passion had ever touched him, for this was what passion meant; he had survived and maundered and pined, but where had been *his* deep ravage? The extraordinary thing we speak of was the sudden rush of the result of this question. The sight that had just met his eyes named to him, as in letters of quick flame, something he had utterly, insanely missed, and what he had missed made these things a train of fire, made them mark themselves in an anguish of inward throbs. He had seen *outside* of his life, not learned it within, the way a woman was mourned when she had been loved for herself; such was the force of his conviction of the meaning of the stranger's face, which still flared for him like a smoky torch. It had not come to him, the knowledge, on the wings of experience; it had brushed him, jostled him, upset him, with the disrespect of chance, the insolence of an accident. Now that the illumination had begun, however, it blazed to the zenith, and what he presently stood there gazing at was the sounded void of his life. He gazed, he drew breath, in pain; he turned in his dismay, and, turning, he had before him in sharper incision than ever the open page of his story. The name on the table smote him as the passage of his neighbour had done, and what it said to him, full in the face, was that *she* was what he had missed. This was the awful thought, the answer to all the past, the vision at the dread clearness of which he turned as cold as the stone beneath him. Everything fell together, confessed, explained, over-whelmed; leaving him most of all stupefied at the blindness he had cherished. The fate he had been marked for he had met with a vengeance – he had emptied the cup to the lees; he had been the man of his time, *the* man, to whom nothing on earth was to have happened. That was the rare stroke – that was his visitation. So he saw it, as we say, in pale horror, while the pieces fitted and fitted. So *she* had seen it, while he didn't, and so she served at this hour to drive the truth home. It was the truth, vivid and monstrous, that all the while he had waited the wait was itself his portion. This the companion of his vigil had at a given moment perceived, and she had then offered him the chance to baffle his doom. One's doom, however, was never baffled, and on the day she had told him that his own had come down she had seen him but stupidly stare at the escape she offered him.

The escape would have been to love her; then, *then* he would have lived. *She* had lived – who could say now with what passion? – since she had loved him for himself; whereas he had never thought of her (ah, how it hugely glared at him!) but in the chill of his egotism and the light of her use. Her spoken words came back to him, and the chain stretched and stretched. The beast had lurked indeed, and the beast, at its hour, had sprung; it had sprung in that twilight of the cold April when, pale, ill, wasted, but all beautiful, and perhaps even then recoverable, she had risen from her chair to stand before him and let him imaginably guess. It had sprung as he didn't guess; it had sprung as she hopelessly turned from him, and the mark, by the time he left her, had fallen where it *was* to fall. He had justified his fear and achieved his fate; he had failed, with the last exactitude, of all he was to fail of; and a moan now rose to his lips as he remembered she had prayed he mightn't know. This horror of waking — *this* was knowledge, knowledge under the breath of which the very tears in his eyes seemed to freeze. Through them, none the less, he tried to fix it and hold it; he kept it there before him so that he might feel the pain. That at least, belated and bitter, had something of the taste of life. But the bitterness suddenly sickened him, and it was as if, horribly, he saw, in the truth, in the cruelty of his image, what had been appointed and done. He saw the Jungle of his life and saw the lurking Beast; then, while he looked, perceived it, as by a stir of the air, rise, huge and hideous, for the leap that was to settle him. His eyes darkened — it was close; and, instinctively turning, in his hallucination, to avoid it, he flung himself, on his face, on the tomb.

THE BIRTHPLACE

I

IT seemed to them at first, the offer, too good to be true, and their friend's letter, addressed to them to feel, as he said, the ground, to sound them as to inclinations and possibilities, had almost the effect of a brave joke at their expense. Their friend, Mr Grant-Jackson, a highly preponderant, pushing person, great in discussion and arrangement, abrupt in overture, unexpected, if not perverse, in attitude, and almost equally acclaimed and objected to in the wide midland region to which he had taught, as the phrase was, the size of his foot — their friend had launched his bolt quite out of the blue and had thereby so shaken them as to make them fear almost more than hope. The place had fallen vacant by the death of one of the two ladies, mother and daughter, who had discharged its duties for fifteen years; the daughter was staying on alone, to accommodate, but had found, though extremely mature, an opportunity of marriage that involved retirement, and the question of the new incumbents was not a little pressing. The want thus determined was of a united couple of some sort, of the right sort, a pair of educated and competent sisters possibly preferred, but a married pair having its advantage if other qualifications were marked. Applicants, candidates, besiegers of the door of everyone supposed to have a voice in the matter, were already beyond counting, and Mr Grant-Jackson, who was in his way diplomatic and whose voice, though not perhaps of the loudest, possessed notes of insistence, had found his preference fixing itself on some person or brace of persons who had been decent and dumb. The Gedges appeared to have struck him as waiting in silence — though absolutely, as happened, no busybody had brought them, far

away in the north, a hint either of bliss or of danger; and the happy
spell, for the rest, had obviously been wrought in him by a remembrance
which, though now scarcely fresh, had never before borne any such
fruit.

Morris Gedge had for a few years, as a young man, carried on a small
private school of the order known as preparatory, and had happened
then to receive under his roof the small son of the great man, who was
not at that time so great. The little boy, during an absence of his parents
from England, had been dangerously ill, so dangerously that they had
been recalled in haste, though with inevitable delays, from a far country
– they had gone to America, with the whole continent and the great sea
to cross again – and had got back to find the child saved, but saved, as
couldn't help coming to light, by the extreme devotion and perfect
judgement of Mrs Gedge. Without children of her own, she had
particularly attached herself to this tiniest and tenderest of her husband's
pupils, and they had both dreaded as a dire disaster the injury to their
little enterprise that would be caused by their losing him. Nervous,
anxious, sensitive persons, with a pride – as they were for that matter
well aware – above their position, never, at the best, to be anything but
dingy, they had nursed him in terror and had brought him through in
exhaustion. Exhaustion, as befell, had thus overtaken them early and
had for one reason and another managed to assert itself as their permanent portion. The little boy's death would, as they said, have done for
them, yet his recovery hadn't saved them; with which it was doubtless
also part of a shy but stiff candour in them that they didn't regard
themselves as having in a more indirect manner laid up treasure.
Treasure was not to be, in any form whatever, of their dreams or of
their waking sense; and the years that followed had limped under their
weight, had now and then rather grievously stumbled, had even barely
escaped laying them in the dust. The school had not prospered, had but
dwindled to a close. Gedge's health had failed, and, still more, every
sign in him of a capacity to publish himself as practical. He had tried
several things, he had tried many, but the final appearance was of their
having tried him not less. They mostly, at the time I speak of, were
trying his successors, while he found himself, with an effect of dull
felicity that had come in this case from the mere postponement of

change, in charge of the grey town-library of Blackport-on-Dwindle, all granite, fog and female fiction. This was a situation in which his general intelligence – acknowledged as his strong point – was doubtless conceived, around him, as feeling less of a strain than that mastery of particulars in which he was recognized as weak.

It was at Blackport-on-Dwindle that the silver shaft reached and pierced him; it was as an alternative to dispensing dog's-eared volumes the very titles of which, on the lips of innumerable glib girls, were a challenge to his temper, that the wardenship of so different a temple presented itself. The stipend named differed little from the slim wage at present paid him, but even had it been less the interest and the honour would have struck him as determinant. The shrine at which he was to preside – though he had always lacked occasion to approach it – figured to him as the most sacred known to the steps of men, the early home of the supreme poet, the Mecca of the English-speaking race. The tears came into his eyes sooner still than into his wife's while he looked about with her at their actual narrow prison, so grim with enlightenment, so ugly with industry, so turned away from any dream, so intolerable to any taste. He felt as if a window had opened into a great green woodland, a woodland that had a name, glorious, immortal, that was peopled with vivid figures, each of them renowned, and that gave out a murmur, deep as the sound of the sea, which was the rustle in forest shade of all the poetry, the beauty, the colour of life. It would be prodigious that of this transfigured world *he* should keep the key. No – he couldn't believe it, not even when Isabel, at sight of his face, came and helpfully kissed him. He shook his head with a strange smile. 'We shan't get it. Why should we? It's perfect.'

'If we don't he'll simply have been cruel; which is impossible when he has waited all this time to be kind.' Mrs Gedge did believe – she *would*; since the wide doors of the world of poetry had suddenly pushed back for them it was in the form of poetic justice that they were first to know it. She had her faith in their patron; it was sudden, but it was now complete. 'He remembers – that's all; and that's our strength.'

'And what's *his*?' Gedge asked. 'He may *want* to put us through, but that's a different thing from being able. What are our special advantages?'

'Well, that we're just the thing.' Her knowledge of the needs of the case was, as yet, thanks to scant information, of the vaguest, and she had never, more than her husband, stood on the sacred spot; but she saw herself waving a nicely-gloved hand over a collection of remarkable objects and saying to a compact crowd of gaping, awe-struck persons: 'And now, please, *this* way.' She even heard herself meeting with promptness and decision an occasional inquiry from a visitor in whom audacity had prevailed over awe. She had been once, with a cousin, years before, to a great northern castle, and that was the way the housekeeper had taken them round. And it was not moreover, either, that she thought of herself as a housekeeper: she was well above that, and the wave of her hand wouldn't fail to be such as to show it. This, and much else, she summed up as she answered her mate. 'Our special advantages are that you're a gentleman.'

'Oh!' said Gedge, as if he had never thought of it, and yet as if too it were scarce worth thinking of.

'I see it all,' she went on; 'they've *had* the vulgar – they find they don't do. We're poor and we're modest, but anyone can see what we are.'

Gedge wondered. 'Do you mean – ?' More modest than she, he didn't know quite what she meant.

'We're refined. We know how to speak.'

'Do we?' – he still, suddenly, wondered.

But she was, from the first, surer of everything than he; so that when a few weeks more had elapsed and the shade of uncertainty – though it was only a shade – had grown almost to sicken him, her triumph was to come with the news that they were fairly named. 'We're on poor pay, though we manage' – she had on the present occasion insisted on her point. 'But we're highly cultivated, and for them to get *that*, don't you see? without getting too much with it in the way of pretensions and demands, must be precisely their dream. We've no social position, but we don't *mind* that we haven't, do we? a bit; which is because we know the difference between realities and shams. We hold to reality, and that gives us common sense, which the vulgar have less than anything, and which yet must be wanted there, after all, as well as anywhere else.'

Her companion followed her, but musingly, as if his horizon had within a few moments grown so great that he was almost lost in it and required a new orientation. The shining spaces surrounded him; the association alone gave a nobler arch to the sky. 'Allow that we hold also a little to the romance. It seems to me that that's the beauty. We've missed it all our life, and now it's come. We shall be at head-quarters for it. We shall have our fill of it.'

She looked at his face, at the effect in it of these prospects, and her own lighted as if he had suddenly grown handsome. 'Certainly – we shall live as in a fairy-tale. But what I mean is that we shall give, in a way – and so gladly – quite as much as we get. With all the rest of it we're, for instance, neat.' Their letter had come to them at breakfast, and she picked a fly out of the butter-dish. 'It's the way we'll *keep* the place' – with which she removed from the sofa to the top of the cottage-piano a tin of biscuits that had refused to squeeze into the cupboard. At Blackport they were in lodgings – of the lowest description, she had been known, with a freedom felt by Blackport to be slightly invidious, to declare. The Birthplace – and that itself, after such a life, was exaltation – wouldn't be lodgings, since a house close beside it was set apart for the warden, a house joining on to it as a sweet old parsonage is often annexed to a quaint old church. It would all together be their home, and such a home as would make a little world that they would never want to leave. She dwelt on the gain, for that matter, to their income; as, obviously, though the salary was not a change for the better, the house, given them, would make all the difference. He assented to this, but absently, and she was almost impatient at the range of his thoughts. It was as if something, for him – the very swarm of them – veiled the view; and he presently, of himself, showed what it was.

'What I can't get over is its being such a man – !' He almost, from inward emotion, broke down.

'Such a man – ?'

'Him, *him*, HIM – !' It was too much.

'Grant-Jackson? Yes, it's a surprise, but one sees how he has been meaning, all the while, the right thing by us.'

'I mean *Him*,' Gedge returned more coldly; 'our becoming familiar and intimate – for that's what it will come to. We shall just live with Him.'

'Of course – it *is* the beauty.' And she added quite gaily: 'The more we do the more we shall love Him.'

'No doubt – but it's rather awful. The more we *know* Him,' Gedge reflected, 'the more we shall love Him. We don't as yet, you see, know Him so very tremendously.'

'We do so quite as well, I imagine, as the sort of people they've had. And that probably isn't – unless you care, as we do – so awfully necessary. For there are the facts.'

'Yes – there are the facts.'

'I mean the principal ones. They're all that the people – the people who come – want.'

'Yes – they must be all *they* want.'

'So that they're all that those who've been in charge have needed to know.'

'Ah,' he said as if it were a question of honour, '*we* must know everything.'

She cheerfully acceded: she had the merit, he felt, of keeping the case within bounds. 'Everything. But about him personally,' she added, 'there isn't, is there? so very, very much.'

'More, I believe, than there used to be. They've made discoveries.'

It was a grand thought. 'Perhaps *we* shall make some!'

'Oh, I shall be content to be a little better up in what has been done.' And his eyes rested on a shelf of books, half of which, little worn but much faded, were of the florid 'gift' order and belonged to the house. Of those among them that were his own most were common specimens of the reference sort, not excluding an old Bradshaw and a catalogue of the town-library. 'We've not even a Set of our own. Of the Works,' he explained in quick repudiation of the sense, perhaps more obvious, in which she might have taken it.

As a proof of their scant range of possessions this sounded almost abject, till the painful flush with which they met on the admission melted presently into a different glow. It was just for that kind of poorness that their new situation was, by its intrinsic charm, to console them. And Mrs Gedge had a happy thought. 'Wouldn't the Library more or less have them?'

'Oh no, we've nothing of that sort: for what do you take us?' This, however, was but the play of Gedge's high spirits: the form both depression and exhilaration most frequently took with him being a bitterness on the subject of the literary taste of Blackport. No one was so deeply acquainted with it. It acted with him in fact as so lurid a sign of the future that the charm of the thought of removal was sharply enhanced by the prospect of escape from it. The institution he served didn't of course deserve the particular reproach into which his irony had flowered; and indeed if the several Sets in which the Works were present were a trifle dusty, the dust was a little his own fault. To make up for that now he had the vision of immediately giving his time to the study of them; he saw himself indeed, inflamed with a new passion, earnestly commenting and collating. Mrs Gedge, who had suggested that they ought, till their move should come, to read Him regularly of an evening – certain as they were to do it still more when in closer quarters with Him – Mrs Gedge felt also, in her degree, the spell; so that the very happiest time of their anxious life was perhaps to have been the series of lamp-light hours, after supper, in which, alternately taking the book, they declaimed, they almost performed, their beneficent author. He became speedily more than their author – their personal friend, their universal light, their final authority and divinity. Where in the world, they were already asking themselves, would they have been without him? By the time their appointment arrived in form their relation to him had immensely developed. It was amusing to Morris Gedge that he had so lately blushed for his ignorance, and he made this remark to his wife during the last hour they were able to give to their study, before proceeding, across half the country, to the scene of their romantic future. It was as if, in deep, close throbs, in cool after-waves that broke of a sudden and bathed his mind, all possession and comprehension and sympathy, all the truth and the life and the story, had come to him, and come, as the newspapers said, to stay. 'It's absurd,' he didn't hesitate to say, 'to talk of our not "knowing." So far as we don't it's because we're donkeys. He's *in* the thing, over His ears, and the more we get into it the more we're with Him. I seem to myself at any rate,' he declared, 'to *see* Him in it as if He were painted on the wall.'

'Oh, *doesn't* one rather, the dear thing? And don't you feel where it is?' Mrs Gedge finely asked. 'We see Him because we love Him – that's what we do. How can we not, the old darling – with what He's doing for us? There's no light' – she had a sententious turn – 'like true affection.'

'Yes, I suppose that's it. And yet,' her husband mused, 'I see, confound me, the faults.'

'That's because you're so critical. You see them, but you don't mind them. You see them, but you forgive them. You mustn't mention them *there*. We shan't, you know, be there for *that*.'

'Dear no!' he laughed: 'we'll chuck out anyone who hints at them.'

II

If the sweetness of the preliminary months had been great, great too, though almost excessive as agitation, was the wonder of fairly being housed with Him, of treading day and night in the footsteps He had worn, of touching the objects, or at all events the surfaces, the substances, over which His hands had played, which his arms, his shoulders had rubbed, of breathing the air – or something not too unlike it – in which His voice had sounded. They had had a little at first their bewilderments, their disconcertedness; the place was both humbler and grander than they had exactly prefigured, more at once of a cottage and of a museum, a little more archaically bare and yet a little more richly official. But the sense was strong with them that the point of view, for the inevitable ease of the connection, patiently, indulgently awaited them; in addition to which, from the first evening, after closing-hour, when the last blank pilgrim had gone, the mere spell, the mystic presence – as if they had had it quite to themselves – were all they could have desired. They had received, by Grant-Jackson's care and in addition to a table of instructions and admonitions by the number, and in some particulars by the nature, of which they found themselves slightly depressed, various little guides, handbooks, travellers' tributes, literary memorials and other catch-penny publications, which, however, were to be for the moment swallowed up in the interesting episode of the induction or initiation appointed for them in advance at the hands of several persons whose connection with the establishment was, as superior to their own, still more official, and at those in especial of one of the ladies who had for so many years borne the brunt. About the instructions from above, about the shilling books and the well-known facts and the full-blown legend, the supervision, the subjection, the submission, the view as of a cage in which he should circulate and a groove in which he should slide, Gedge had preserved a certain play of mind; but all power of reaction appeared suddenly to desert him in the presence of his so visibly competent predecessor and as an effect of her good offices. He had not the resource, enjoyed by his wife, of seeing himself, with impatience, attired in black silk of a make characterised by just the right shade of austerity; so that this firm, smooth, expert and consummately respectable middle-aged person had him somehow, on the whole ground, completely at her mercy.

It was evidently something of a rueful moment when, as a lesson – she being for the day or two still in the field – he accepted Miss Putchin's suggestion of 'going round' with her and with the successive squads of visitors she was there to deal with. He appreciated her method – he saw there had to *be* one; he admired her as succinct and definite; for there were the facts, as his wife had said at Blackport, and they were to be disposed of in the time; yet he felt like a very little boy as he dangled, more than once, with Mrs Gedge, at the tail of the human comet. The idea had been that they should, by this attendance, more fully embrace the possible accidents and incidents, as it were, of the relation to the great public in which they were to find themselves; and the poor man's excited perception of the great public rapidly became such as to resist any diversion meaner than that of the admirable manner of their guide. It wandered from his gaping companions to that of the priestess in black silk, whom he kept asking himself if either he or Isabel could hope by any possibility ever remotely to resemble; then it bounded restlessly back to the numerous persons who revealed to him, as it had never yet been revealed, the happy power of the simple to hang upon the lips of the wise. The great thing seemed to be – and quite surprisingly – that the business was easy and the strain, which as a strain they had feared, moderate; so that he might have been puzzled, had he fairly caught himself in the act, by his recognizing as the last effect of the impression an odd absence of the ability to rest in it, an agitation deep within him that vaguely threatened to grow. 'It isn't, you see, so very complicated,' the black silk lady seemed to throw off, with everything else, in her neat, crisp, cheerful way; in spite of which he already, the very first time – that is after several parties had been in and out and up and down – went so far as to wonder if there weren't more in it than she imagined. She was, so to speak, kindness itself – was all encouragement and reassurance; but it was just her slightly coarse redolence of these very things that, on repetition, before they parted, dimmed a little, as he felt, the light of his acknowledging smile. That, again, she took for a symptom of some pleading weakness in him – he could never be as brave as she; so that she wound up with a few pleasant words from the very depth of her experience. 'You'll get into it, never fear – it will *come*; and then you'll feel as if you had never done anything else.' He was afterwards to know that, on the spot, at this moment, he must have begun to wince a little at such a menace; that he might come to feel as if he had never done anything but what Miss Putchin did loomed for him, in germ, as a penalty to pay. The support she offered, none the less, continued to strike him; she put the whole thing on so sound a basis when she said: 'You see they're so nice about it – they take such an interest. And they never do a thing they shouldn't. That was always everything to mother and me.' 'They,' Gedge had already noticed, referred constantly and hugely, in the good woman's talk, to the millions who shuffled through the house; the pronoun in question was forever on her lips, the hordes it represented filled her consciousness, the addition of their numbers ministered to her glory. Mrs Gedge promptly met her. 'It must be indeed delightful to see the effect on so many, and to feel that one may perhaps do something to make it – well, permanent.' But he was kept silent by his becoming more sharply aware that this was a new view, for him, of the reference made, that he had never thought of the quality of the place as derived from Them, but from Somebody Else, and that They, in short, seemed to have got into the way of crowding out Him. He found himself even a little resenting this for Him, which perhaps had something to do with the slightly invidious cast of his next inquiry.

'And are They always, as one might say – a – stupid?'

'Stupid!' She stared, looking as if no one *could* be such a thing in such a connection. No one had ever been anything but neat and cheerful and fluent, except to be attentive and unobjectionable and, so far as was possible, American.

'What I mean is,' he explained, 'is there any perceptible proportion that take an interest in Him?'

His wife stepped on his toe; she deprecated irony. But his mistake fortunately was lost on their friend. 'That's just why they come, that they take such an interest. I sometimes think they take more than about anything else in the world.' With which Miss Putchin looked about at the place. 'It *is* pretty, don't you think, the way they've got it now?' This, Gedge saw, was a different 'They'; it applied to the powers that were – the people who had appointed him, the governing, visiting Body, in respect to which he was afterwards to remark to Mrs Gedge that a fellow – it was the difficulty – didn't know 'where to have her.' His wife, at a loss, questioned at that moment the necessity of having her anywhere, and he said, good-humouredly, 'Of course; it's all right.' He was in fact content enough with the last touches their friend had given the picture. 'There are many who know all about it when they come, and the Americans often are tremendously up. Mother and me really enjoyed' – it was her only slip – 'the interest of the Americans. We've sometimes had ninety a day, and all wanting to see and hear everything. But you'll work them off; you'll see the way – it's all experience.' She came back, for his comfort, to that. She came back also to other things: she did justice to the considerable class who arrived positive and primed. 'There are those who know more about it than you do. But *that* only comes from their interest.'

'Who know more about what?' Gedge inquired.

'Why, about the place. I mean they have their ideas – of what everything is, and *where* it is, and what it isn't, and where it *should* be. They do ask questions,' she said, yet not so much in warning as in the complacency of being seasoned and sound; 'and they're down on you when they think you go wrong. As if you ever could! You know too much,' she sagaciously smiled; 'or you *will*.'

'Oh, you mustn't know *too* much, must you?' And Gedge now smiled as well. He knew, he thought, what he meant.

'Well, you must know as much as anybody else. I claim, at any rate, that I do,' Miss Putchin declared. 'They never really caught me.'

'I'm very sure of *that*,' Mrs Gedge said with an elation almost personal.

'Certainly,' he added, 'I don't want to be caught.' She rejoined that, in such a case, he would have *Them* down on him, and he saw that this time she meant the powers above. It quickened his sense of all the elements that were to reckon with, yet he felt at the same time that the powers above were not what he should most fear. 'I'm glad,' he observed, 'that they ever ask questions; but I happened to notice, you know, that no one did today.'

'Then you missed several – and no loss. There were three or four put to me too silly to remember. But of course they mostly *are* silly.'

'You mean the questions?'

She laughed with all her cheer. 'Yes, sir; I don't mean the answers.'

Whereupon, for a moment snubbed and silent, he felt like one of the crowd. Then it made him slightly vicious. 'I didn't know but you meant the people in general – till I remembered that I'm to understand from you that *they're* wise, only occasionally breaking down.'

It was not really till then, he thought, that she lost patience; and he had had, much more than he meant no doubt, a cross-questioning air. 'You'll see for yourself.' Of which he was sure enough. He was in fact so ready to take this that she came round to full accommodation, put it frankly that every now and then they broke out – not the silly, oh no, the intensely inquiring. 'We've had quite lively discussions, don't you know, about well-known points. They want it all *their* way, and I know the sort that are going to as soon as I see them. That's one of the things you do – you get to know the sorts. And if it's what you're afraid of – their taking you up,' she was further gracious enough to say, 'you needn't mind a bit. What *do* they know, after all, when for us it's our life? I've never moved an inch, because, you see, I shouldn't have been here if I didn't know where I was. No more will *you* be a year hence – you know what I mean, putting it impossibly – if *you* don't. I expect you do, in spite of your fancies.' And she dropped once more to bed-rock. 'There are the facts. Otherwise where would any of us be? That's all you've got to go upon. A person, however cheeky, can't have them *his* way just because he takes it into his head. There can only be *one* way, and,' she gaily added as she took leave of them, 'I'm sure it's quite enough!'

III

Gedge not only assented eagerly — one way *was* quite enough if it were the right one — but repeated it, after this conversation, at odd moments, several times over to his wife. 'There can only be one way, one way,' he continued to remark — though indeed much as if it were a joke; till she asked him how many more he supposed she wanted. He failed to answer this question, but resorted to another repetition, 'There are the facts, the facts,' which, perhaps, however, he kept a little more to himself, sounding it at intervals in different parts of the house. Mrs Gedge was full of comment on their clever introductress, though not restrictively save in the matter of her speech, 'Me and mother,' and a general tone — which certainly was not their sort of thing. 'I don't know,' he said, 'perhaps it comes with the place, since speaking in immortal verse doesn't seem to come. It must be, one seems to see, one thing or the other. I dare say that in a few months I shall also be at it — "me and the wife."'

'Why not me and the missus at once?' Mrs Gedge resentfully inquired. 'I don't think,' she observed at another time, 'that I quite know what's the matter with you.'

'It's only that I'm excited, awfully excited — as I don't see how one can not be. You wouldn't have a fellow drop into this berth as into an appointment at the Post Office. Here on the spot it goes to my head; how can that be helped? But we shall live into it, and perhaps,' he said with an implication of the other possibility that was doubtless but part of his fine ecstasy, 'we shall live through it.' The place acted on his imagination — how, surely, shouldn't it? And his imagination acted on his nerves, and these things together, with the general vividness and the new and complete immersion, made rest for him almost impossible, so that he could scarce go to bed at night and even during the first week more than once rose in the small hours to move about, up and down, with his lamp, standing, sitting, listening, wondering, in the stillness, as if positively to recover some echo, to surprise some secret, of the *genius loci*. He couldn't have explained it — and didn't in fact need to explain it, at least to himself, since the impulse simply held him and shook him; but the time after closing, the time above all after the people — Them, as he felt himself on the way to think of them, predominant, insistent, all in the foreground – brought him, or ought to have brought him, he seemed to see, nearer to the enshrined Presence, enlarged the opportunity for communion and intensified the sense of it. These nightly prowls, as he called them, were disquieting to his wife, who had no disposition to share in them, speaking with decision of the whole place as just the place to be forbidding after dark. She rejoiced in the distinctness, contiguous though it was, of their own little residence, where she trimmed the lamp and stirred the fire and heard the kettle sing, repairing the while the omissions of the small domestic who slept out; she foresaw herself with some promptness, drawing rather sharply the line between her own precinct and that in which the great spirit might walk. It would be with them, the great spirit, all day – even if indeed on her making that remark, and in just that form, to her husband, he replied with a queer 'But will he though?' And she vaguely imaged the development of a domestic antidote after a while, precisely, in the shape of curtains more markedly drawn and everything most modern and lively, tea, 'patterns,' the newspapers, the female fiction itself that they had reacted against at Blackport, quite defiantly cultivated.

These possibilities, however, were all right, as her companion said it was, all the first autumn – they had arrived at summer's end; as if he were more than content with a special set of his own that he had access to from behind, passing out of their low door for the few steps between it and the Birthplace. With his lamp ever so carefully guarded, and his nursed keys that made him free of treasures, he crossed the dusky interval so often that she began to qualify it as a habit that 'grew.' She spoke of it almost as if he had taken to drink, and he humoured that view of it by confessing that the cup was strong. This had been in truth, altogether, his immediate sense of it; strange and deep for him the spell of silent sessions before familiarity and, to some small extent, disappointment had set in. The exhibitional side of the establishment had struck him, even on arrival, as qualifying too much its character; he scarce knew what he might best have looked for, but the three or four rooms bristled overmuch, in the garish light of day, with busts and relics, not even ostensibly always *His*, old prints and old editions, old objects fashioned in His likeness, furniture 'of the time' and autographs of celebrated worshippers. In the quiet hours and the deep dusk, none the less, under the play of the shifted lamp and that of his own emotion, these things too recovered their advantage, ministered to the mystery, or at all events to the impression, seemed consciously to offer themselves as personal to the poet. Not one of them was really or unchallengeably so, but they had somehow, through long association, got, as Gedge always phrased it, into the secret, and it was about the secret he asked them while he restlessly wandered. It was not till months had elapsed that he found how little they had to tell him, and he was quite at his ease with them when he knew they were by no means where his sensibility had first placed them. They were as out of it as he; only, to do them justice, they had made him immensely feel. And still, too, it was not they who had done that most, since his sentiment had gradually cleared itself to deep, to deeper refinements.

The Holy of Holies of the Birthplace was the low, the sublime Chamber of Birth, sublime because, as the Americans usually said – unlike the natives they mostly found words – it was so pathetic; and pathetic because it was – well, really nothing else in the world that one could name, number or measure. It was as empty as a shell of which the kernel has withered, and contained neither busts nor prints nor early copies; it contained only the Fact – *the* Fact itself – which, as he stood sentient there at midnight, our friend, holding his breath, allowed to sink into him. He *had* to take it as the place where the spirit would most walk and where he would therefore be most to be met, with possibilities of recognition and reciprocity. He hadn't, most probably – *He* hadn't – much inhabited the room, as men weren't apt, as a rule, to convert to their later use and involve in their wider fortune the scene itself of their nativity. But as there were moments when, in the conflict of theories, the sole certainty surviving for the critic threatened to be that He had not – unlike other successful men – *not* been born, so Gedge, though little of a critic, clung to the square feet of space that connected themselves, however feebly, with the positive appearance. He was little of a critic – he was nothing of one; he hadn't pretended to the character before coming, nor come to pretend to it; also, luckily for him, he was seeing day by day how little use he could possibly have for it. It would be to him, the attitude of a high expert, distinctly a stumbling-block, and that he rejoiced, as the winter waned, in his ignorance, was one of the propositions he betook himself, in his odd manner, to enunciating to his wife. She denied it, for hadn't she, in the first place, been present, wasn't she still present, at his pious, his tireless study of everything connected with the subject? – so present that she had herself learned more about it than had ever seemed likely. Then, in the second place, he was not to proclaim on the housetops any point at which he might be weak, for who knew, if it should get abroad that they were ignorant, what effect might be produced – ?

'On the attraction' – he took her up – 'of the Show?'

He had fallen into the harmless habit of speaking of the place as the 'Show'; but she didn't mind this so much as to be diverted by it. 'No; on the attitude of the Body. You know they're pleased with us, and I don't see why you should want to spoil it. We got in by a tight squeeze – you know we've had evidence of that, and that it was about as much as our backers could manage. But we're proving a comfort to them, and it's absurd of you to question your suitability to people who were content with the Putchins.'

'I don't, my dear,' he returned, 'question anything; but if I should do so it would be precisely because of the greater advantage constituted for the Putchins by the simplicity of their spirit. They were kept straight by the quality of their ignorance – which was denser even than mine. It was a mistake in us, from the first, to have attempted to correct or to disguise ours. We should have waited simply to become good parrots, to learn our lesson – all on the spot here, so little of it is wanted – and squawk it off.'

'Ah, "squawk," love – what a word to use about Him!'

'It isn't about Him – nothing's about Him. None of Them care tuppence about Him. The only thing They care about is this empty shell – or rather, for it isn't empty, the extraneous, preposterous stuffing of it.'

'Preposterous?' – he made her stare with this as he had not yet done.

At sight of her look, however – the gleam, as it might have been, of a queer suspicion – he bent to her kindly and tapped her cheek. 'Oh, it's all right. We *must* fall back on the Putchins. Do you remember what she said? – "They've made it so pretty now." They *have* made it pretty, and it's a first-rate show. It's a first-rate show and a first-rate billet, and He was a first-rate poet, and you're a first-rate woman – to put up so sweetly, I mean, with my nonsense.'

She appreciated his domestic charm and she justified that part of his tribute which concerned herself. 'I don't care how much of your nonsense you talk to me, so long as you *keep* it all for me and don't treat *Them* to it.'

'The pilgrims? No,' he conceded – 'it isn't fair to Them. They mean well.'

'What complaint have we, after all, to make of Them so long as They don't break off bits – as They used, Miss Putchin told us, so awfully – to conceal about Their Persons? She broke them at least of that.'

'Yes,' Gedge mused again; 'I wish awfully she hadn't!'

'You would like the relics destroyed, removed? That's all that's wanted!'

'There *are* no relics.'

'There won't be any soon, unless you take care.' But he was already laughing, and the talk was not dropped without his having patted her once more. An impression or two, however, remained with her from it, as he saw from a question she asked him on the morrow. 'What did you mean yesterday about Miss Putchin's simplicity – its keeping her "straight?" Do you mean mentally?'

Her 'mentally' was rather portentous, but he practically confessed. 'Well, it kept her up. I mean,' he amended, laughing, 'it kept her down.'

It was really as if she had been a little uneasy. 'You consider there's a danger of your being affected? You know what I mean. Of its going to your head. You do know,' she insisted as he said nothing. 'Through your caring for Him so. You'd certainly be right in that case about its having been a mistake for you to plunge so deep.' And then as his listening without reply, though with his look a little sad for her, might have denoted that, allowing for extravagance of statement, he saw there was something in it: 'Give up your prowls. Keep it for daylight. Keep it for *Them*.'

'Ah,' he smiled, 'if one could! My prowls,' he added, 'are what I most enjoy. They're the only time, as I've told you before, that I'm really with *Him*. Then I don't see the place. He isn't the place.'

'I don't care for what you "don't" see,' she replied with vivacity; 'the question is of what you do see.'

Well, if it was, he waited before meeting it. 'Do you know what I sometimes do?' And then as she waited too: 'In the Birthroom there, when I look in late, I often put out my light. That makes it better.'

'Makes what – ?'

'Everything.'

'What is it then you see in the dark?'

'Nothing!' said Morris Gedge.

'And what's the pleasure of that?'

'Well, what the American ladies say. It's so fascinating.'

IV

The autumn was brisk, as Miss Putchin had told them it would be, but business naturally fell off with the winter months and the short days. There was rarely an hour indeed without a call of some sort, and they were never allowed to forget that they kept the shop in all the world, as they might say, where custom was least fluctuating. The seasons told on it, as they tell upon travel, but no other influence, consideration or convulsion to which the population of the globe is exposed. This population, never exactly in simultaneous hordes, but in a full, swift and steady stream, passed through the smoothly working mill and went, in its variety of degrees duly impressed and edified, on its artless way. Gedge gave himself up, with much ingenuity of spirit, to trying to keep in relation with it; having even at moments, in the early time, glimpses of the chance that the impressions gathered from so rare an opportunity for contact with the general mind might prove as interesting as anything else in the connection. Types, classes, nationalities, manners, diversities of behaviour, modes of seeing, feeling, of expression, would pass before him and become for him, after a fashion, the experience of an untravelled man. His journeys had been short and saving, but poetic justice again seemed inclined to work for him in placing him just at the point in all Europe perhaps where the confluence of races was thickest. The theory, at any rate, carried him on, operating helpfully for the term of his anxious beginnings and gilding in a manner – it was the way he characterized the case to his wife – the somewhat stodgy gingerbread of their daily routine. They had not known many people, and their visiting-list was small – which made it again poetic justice that they should be visited on such a scale. They dressed and were at home, they were under arms and received, and except for the offer of refreshment – and Gedge had his view that there would eventually be a *buffet* farmed out to a great firm – their hospitality would have made them princely if mere hospitality ever did. Thus they were launched, and it was interesting, and from having been ready to drop, originally, with fatigue, they emerged even-winded and strong in the legs, as if they had had an Alpine holiday. This experience, Gedge opined, also represented, as a gain, a like seasoning of the spirit – by which he meant a certain command of impenetrable patience.

The patience was needed for the particular feature of the ordeal that, by the time the lively season was with them again, had disengaged itself as the sharpest – the immense assumption of veracities and sanctities, of the general soundness of the legend with which everyone arrived. He was well provided, certainly, for meeting it, and he gave all he had, yet he had sometimes the sense of a vague resentment on the part of his pilgrims at his not ladling out their fare with a bigger spoon. An irritation had begun to grumble in him during the comparatively idle months of winter when a pilgrim would turn up singly. The pious individual, entertained for the half-hour, had occasionally seemed to offer him the promise of beguilement or the semblance of a personal relation; it came back again to the few pleasant calls he had received in the course of a life almost void of social amenity. Sometimes he liked the person, the face, the speech: an educated man, a gentleman, not one of the herd; a graceful woman, vague, accidental, unconscious of him, but making him wonder, while he hovered, who she was. These chances represented for him light yearnings and faint flutters; they acted indeed, within him, in a special, an extraordinary way. He would have liked to talk with such stray companions, to talk with them *really*, to talk with them as he might have talked if he had met them where he couldn't meet them – at dinner, in the 'world,' on a visit at a country-house. Then he could have said – and about the shrine and the idol always – things he couldn't say now. The form in which his irritation first came to him was that of his feeling obliged to say to them – to the single visitor, even when sympathetic, quite as to the gaping group – the particular things, a dreadful dozen or so, that they expected. If he had thus arrived at characterizing these things as dreadful the reason touches the very point that, for a while turning everything over, he kept dodging, not facing, trying to ignore. The point was that he was on his way to become two quite different persons, the public and the private, and yet that it would somehow have to be managed that these persons should live together. He was splitting into halves, unmistakably – he who, whatever else he had been, had at least always been so entire and in his way, so solid. One of the halves, or perhaps even, since the split promised to be rather unequal, one of the quarters, was the keeper, the showman, the priest of the idol; the other piece was the poor unsuccessful honest man he had always been.

There were[1] moments when he recognized this primary character as he had never done before; when he in fact quite shook in his shoes at the idea that it perhaps had in reserve some supreme assertion of its identity. It was honest, verily, just by reason of the possibility. It was poor and unsuccessful because here it was just on the verge of quarrelling with its bread and butter. Salvation would be of course – the salvation of the showman – rigidly to *keep* it on the verge; not to let it, in other words, overpass by an inch. He might count on this, he said to himself, if there weren't any public – if there weren't thousands of people demanding of him what he was paid for. He saw the approach of the stage at which they would affect him, the thousands of people – and perhaps even more the earnest individual – as coming really to see if he were earning his wage. Wouldn't he soon begin to fancy them in league with the Body, practically deputed by it – given, no doubt, a kindled suspicion – to look in and report observations? It was the way he broke down with the lonely pilgrim that led to his first heart-searchings – broke down as to the courage required for damping an uncritical faith. What they all most wanted was to feel that everything was 'just as it was'; only the shock of having to part with that vision was greater than any individual could bear unsupported. The bad moments were upstairs in the Birth-room, for here the forces pressing on the very edge assumed a dire intensity. The mere expression of eye, all-credulous, omnivorous and fairly moistening in the act, with which many persons gazed about, might eventually make it difficult for him to remain fairly civil. Often they came in pairs – sometimes one had come before – and then they explained to each other. He never in that case corrected; he listened, for the lesson of listening: after which he would remark to his wife that there was no end to what he was learning. He saw that if he should really ever break down it would be with her he would begin. He had given her hints and digs enough, but she was so inflamed with appreciation that she either didn't feel them or pretended not to understand.

This was the greater complication that, with the return of the spring and the increase of the public, her services were more required. She took the field with him, from an early hour; she was present with the party above while he kept an eye, and still more an ear, on the party below; and how could he know, he asked himself, what she might say to them and what she might suffer *Them* to say – or in other words, poor wretches, to believe – while removed from his control? Some day or other, and before too long, he couldn't but think, he must have the matter out with her – the matter, namely, of the *morality* of their position. The morality of women was special – he was getting lights on that. Isabel's conception of her office was to cherish and enrich the legend. It was already, the legend, very taking, but what was she there for but to make it more so? She certainly wasn't there to chill any natural piety. If it was all in the air – all in their 'eye,' as the vulgar might say – that He *had* been born in the Birthroom, where was the value of the sixpences they took? Where the equivalent they had engaged to supply? 'Oh dear, yes – just about *here*'; and she must tap the place with her foot. 'Altered? Oh dear, no – save in a few trifling particulars; you see the place – and isn't that just the charm of it? – quite as *He* saw it. Very poor and homely, no doubt; but that's just what's so wonderful.' He didn't want to hear her, and yet he didn't want to give her her head; he didn't want to make difficulties or to snatch the bread from her mouth. But he must none the less give her a warning before they had gone *too* far. That was the way, one evening in June, he put it to her; the affluence, with the finest weather, having lately been of the largest, and the crowd, all day, fairly gorged with the story. 'We mustn't, you know, go *too* far.'

The odd thing was that she had now ceased to be even conscious of what troubled him – she was so launched in her own career. 'Too far for what?'

'To save our immortal souls. We mustn't, love, tell too many lies.'

She looked at him with dire reproach. 'Ah now, are you going to begin again?'

'I never *have* begun; I haven't wanted to worry you. But, you know, we don't know anything about it.' And then as she stared, flushing: 'About His having been born up there. About anything, really. Not the least little scrap that would weigh, in any other connection, as evidence. So don't rub it in so.'

'Rub it in how?'

'That He *was* born – ' But at sight of her face he only sighed. 'Oh dear, oh dear!'

'Don't you think,' she replied cuttingly, 'that He was born anywhere?'

He hesitated – it was such an edifice to shake. 'Well, we don't know. There's very little *to* know. He covered His tracks as no other human being has ever done.'

She was still in her public costume and had not taken off the gloves that she made a point of wearing as a part of that uniform; she remembered how the rustling housekeeper in the Border castle, on whom she had begun by modelling herself, had worn them. She seemed official and slightly distant. 'To cover His tracks He must have had to exist. Have we got to give *that* up?'

'No, I don't ask you to give it up *yet*. But there's very little to go upon.'

'And is that what I'm to tell Them in return for everything?'

Gedge waited – he walked about. The place was doubly still after the bustle of the day, and the summer evening rested on it as a blessing, making it, in its small state and ancientry, mellow and sweet. It was good to be there, and it would be good to stay. At the same time there was something incalculable in the effect on one's nerves of the great gregarious density. That was an attitude that had nothing to do with degrees and shades, the attitude of wanting all or nothing. And you couldn't talk things over with it. You could only do this with friends, and then but in cases where you were sure the friends wouldn't betray you. 'Couldn't you adopt,' he replied at last, 'a slightly more discreet method? What we can say is that things have been *said*; that's all *we* have to do with. "And is this really" – when they jam their umbrellas into the floor – "the very *spot* where He was born?" "So it has, from a long time back, been described as being." Couldn't one meet Them, to be decent a little, in some such way as that?'

She looked at him very hard. 'Is that the way *you* meet them?'

'No; I've kept on lying – without scruple, without shame.'

'Then why do you haul me up?'

'Because it has seemed to me that we might, like true companions, work it out a little together.'

This was not strong, he felt, as, pausing with his hands in his pockets, he stood before her; and he knew it as weaker still after she had looked at him a minute. 'Morris Gedge, I propose to be *your* true companion, and I've come here to stay. That's all I've got to say.' It was not, however, for 'You had better try yourself and see,' she presently added. 'Give the place, give the story away, by so much as a look, and – well, I'd allow you about nine days. Then you'd see.'

He feigned, to gain time, an innocence. 'They'd take it so ill?' And then, as she said nothing; 'They'd turn and rend me? They'd tear me to pieces?'

But she wouldn't make a joke of it. 'They wouldn't *have* it, simply.'

'No – they wouldn't. That's what I saw. They won't.'

'You had better,' she went on, 'begin with Grant-Jackson. But even that isn't necessary. It would get to him, it would get to the Body, like wildfire.'

'I see,' said poor Gedge. And indeed for the moment he did see, while his companion followed up what she believed her advantage.

'Do you consider it's *all* a fraud?'

'Well, I grant you there was somebody. But the details are naught. The links are missing. The evidence – in particular about that room upstairs, in itself our Casa Santa – is *nil*. It was so awfully long ago.' Which he knew again sounded weak.

'Of course it was awfully long ago – that's just the beauty and the interest. Tell Them, *tell* Them,' she continued, 'that the evidence is *nil*, and I'll tell them something else.' She spoke it with such meaning that his face seemed to show a question, to which she was on the spot of replying 'I'll tell them that you're a – ' She stopped, however, changing it. 'I'll tell them exactly the opposite. And I'll find out what you say – it won't take long – to do it. If we tell different stories, *that* possibly may save us.'

'I see what you mean. It would perhaps, as an oddity, have a success of curiosity. It might become a draw. Still, they but want broad masses.' And he looked at her sadly. 'You're no more than one of Them.'

'If it's being no more than one of them to love it,' she answered, 'then I certainly am. And I am not ashamed of my company.'

'To love *what*?' said Morris Gedge.

'To love to think He was born there.'

'You think too much. It's bad for you.' He turned away with his chronic moan. But it was without losing what she called after him.

'I decline to let the place down.' And what was there indeed to say? They *were* there to keep it up.

V

He kept it up through the summer, but with the queerest consciousness, at times, of the want of proportion between his secret rage and the spirit of those from whom the friction came. He said to himself – so sore as his sensibility had grown – that They were gregariously ferocious at the very time he was seeing Them as individually mild. He said to himself that They were mild only because *he* was – he flattered himself that he was divinely so, considering what he might be; and that he should, as his wife had warned him, soon enough have news of it were he to deflect by a hair's breadth from the line traced for him. *That* was the collective fatuity – that it was capable of turning, on the instant, both to a general and to a particular resentment. Since the least breath of discrimination would get him the sack without mercy, it was absurd, he reflected, to speak of his discomfort as light. He was gagged, he was goaded, as in omnivorous companies he doubtless sometimes showed by a strange silent glare. They would get him the sack for that as well, if he didn't look out; therefore wasn't it in effect ferocity when you mightn't even hold your tongue? They wouldn't let you off with silence – They insisted on your committing yourself. It was the pound of flesh – They would have it; so under his coat he bled. But a wondrous peace, by exception, dropped on him one afternoon at the end of August. The pressure had, as usual, been high, but it had diminished with the fall of day, and the place was empty before the hour for closing. Then it was that, within a few minutes of this hour, there presented themselves a pair of pilgrims to whom in the ordinary course he would have remarked that they were, to his regret, too late. He was to wonder afterwards why the course had, at sight of the visitors – a gentleman and a lady, appealing and fairly young – shown for him as other than ordinary; the consequence sprang doubtless from something rather fine and unnameable, something, for instance, in the tone of the young man, or in the light of his eye, after hearing the statement on the subject of the hour. 'Yes, we know it's late; but it's just, I'm afraid, *because* of that. We've had rather a notion of escaping the crowd – as, I suppose, you mostly have one now; and it was really on the chance of finding you alone – !'

These things the young man said before being quite admitted, and they were words that any one might have spoken who had not taken the trouble to be punctual or who desired, a little ingratiatingly, to force the door. Gedge even guessed at the sense that might lurk in them, the hint of a special tip if the point were stretched. There were no tips, he had often thanked his stars, at the Birthplace; there was the charged fee and nothing more; everything else was out of order, to the relief of a palm not formed by nature for a scoop. Yet in spite of everything, in spite especially of the almost audible chink of the gentleman's sovereigns, which might in another case exactly have put him out, he presently found himself, in the Birthroom, access to which he had gracefully enough granted, almost treating the visit as personal and private. The reason – well, the reason would have been, if anywhere, in something naturally persuasive on the part of the couple, unless it had been, rather, again, in the way the young man, once he was in place, met the caretaker's expression of face, held it a moment and seemed to wish to sound it. That they were Americans was promptly clear, and Gedge could very nearly have told what kind; he had arrived at the point of distinguishing kinds, though the difficulty might have been with him now that the case before him was rare. He saw it, in fact, suddenly, in the light of the golden midland evening, which reached them through low old windows, saw it with a rush of feeling, unexpected and smothered, that made him wish for a moment to keep it before him as a case of inordinate happiness. It made him feel old, shabby, poor, but he watched it no less intensely for its doing so. They were children of fortune, of the greatest, as it might seem to Morris Gedge, and they were of course lately married; the husband, smooth-faced and soft, but resolute and fine, several years older than the wife, and the wife vaguely, delicately, irregularly, but mercilessly pretty. Somehow, the world was theirs; they gave the person who took the sixpences at the Birthplace such a sense of the high luxury of freedom as he had never had. The thing was that the world was theirs not simply because they had money — he had seen rich people enough — but because they could in a supreme degree think and feel and say what they liked. They had a nature and a culture, a tradition, a facility of some sort — and all producing in them an effect of positive beauty — that gave a light to their liberty and an ease to their tone. These things moreover suffered nothing from the fact that they happened to be in mourning; this was probably worn for some lately-deceased opulent father, or some delicate mother who would be sure to have been a part of the source of the beauty, and it affected Gedge, in the gathered twilight and at his odd crisis, as the very uniform of their distinction.

He couldn't quite have said afterwards by what steps the point had been reached, but it had become at the end of five minutes a part of their presence in the Birthroom, a part of the young man's look, a part of the charm of the moment, and a part, above all, of a strange sense within him of 'Now or never!' that Gedge had suddenly, thrillingly, let himself go. He had not been definitely conscious of drifting to it; he had been, for that, too conscious merely of thinking how different, in all their range, were such a united couple from another united couple that he knew. They were everything he and his wife were not; this was more than anything else the lesson at first of their talk. Thousands of couples of whom the same was true certainly had passed before him, but none of whom it was true with just that engaging intensity. This was *because* of their transcendent freedom; that was what, at the end of five minutes, he saw it all come back to. The husband had been there at some earlier time, and he had his impression, which he wished now to make his wife share. But he already, Gedge could see, had not concealed it from her. A pleasant irony, in fine, our friend seemed to taste in the air – he who had not yet felt free to taste his own.

'I think you weren't here four years ago' – that was what the young man had almost begun by remarking. Gedge liked his remembering it, liked his frankly speaking to him; all the more that he had given him, as it were, no opening. He had let them look about below, and then had taken them up, but without words, without the usual showman's song, of which he would have been afraid. The visitors didn't ask for it; the young man had taken the matter out of his hands by himself dropping for the benefit of the young woman a few detached remarks. What Gedge felt, oddly, was that these remarks were not inconsiderate of him; he had heard others, both of the priggish order and the crude, that might have been called so. And as the young man had not been aided to this cognition of him as new, it already began to make for them a certain common ground. The ground became immense when the visitor presently added with a smile: 'There was a good lady, I recollect, who had a great deal to say.'

It was the gentleman's smile that had done it; the irony *was* there. 'Ah, there has been a great deal said.' And Gedge's look at his interlocutor doubtless showed his sense of being sounded. It was extraordinary of course that a perfect stranger should have guessed the travail of his spirit, should have caught the gleam of his inner commentary. That probably, in spite of him, leaked out of his poor old eyes. 'Much of it, in such places as this,' he heard himself adding, 'is of course said very irresponsibly.' *Such places as this!* – he winced at the words as soon as he had uttered them.

There was no wincing, however, on the part of his pleasant companions. 'Exactly so; the whole thing becomes a sort of stiff, smug convention, like a dressed-up sacred doll in a Spanish church – which you're a monster if you touch.'

'A monster,' said Gedge, meeting his eyes.

The young man smiled, but he thought he looked at him a little harder. 'A blasphemer.'

'A blasphemer.'

It seemed to do his visitor good – he certainly *was* looking at him harder. Detached as he was he was interested – he was at least amused. 'Then you don't claim, or at any rate you don't insist – ? I mean you personally.'

He had an identity for him, Gedge felt, that he couldn't have had for a Briton, and the impulse was quick in our friend to testify to this perception. 'I don't insist to *you*.'

The young man laughed. 'It really – I assure you if I may – wouldn't do any good. I'm too awfully interested.'

'Do you mean,' his wife lightly inquired, 'in – a – pulling it down? That is in what you've said to me.'

'Has he said to you,' Gedge intervened, though quaking a little, 'that he would like to pull it down?'

She met, in her free sweetness, this directness with such a charm! 'Oh, perhaps not quite the *house* – !'

'Good. You see we live on it – I mean *we* people.'

The husband had laughed, but had now so completely ceased to look about him that there seemed nothing left for him but to talk avowedly with the caretaker. 'I'm interested,' he explained, 'in what, I think, is *the* interesting thing – or at all events the eternally tormenting one. The fact of the abysmally little that, in proportion, we know.'

'In proportion to what?' his companion asked.

'Well, to what there must have been – to what in fact there *is* – to wonder about. That's the interest; it's immense. He escapes us like a thief at night,[2] carrying off – well, carrying off everything. And people pretend to catch Him like a flown canary, over whom you can close your hand and put Him back. He won't *go* back; he won't *come* back. He's not' – the young man laughed – 'such a fool! It makes Him the happiest of all great men.'

He had begun by speaking to his wife, but had ended, with his friendly, his easy, his indescribable competence, for Gedge – poor Gedge who quite held his breath and who felt, in the most unexpected way, that he had somehow never been in such good society. The young wife, who for herself meanwhile had continued to look about, sighed out, smiled out – Gedge couldn't have told which – her little answer to these remarks. 'It's rather a pity, you know, that He *isn't* here. I mean as Goethe's at Weimar. For Goethe *is* at Weimar.'

'Yes, my dear; that's Goethe's bad luck. There he sticks. *This* man isn't anywhere. I defy you to catch Him.'

'Why not say, beautifully,' the young woman laughed, 'that, like the wind, He's everywhere?'

It wasn't of course the tone of discussion, it was the tone of joking, though of better joking, Gedge seemed to feel, and more within his own appreciation, than he had ever listened to; and this was precisely why the young man could go on without the effect of irritation, answering his wife but still with eyes for their companion. 'I'll be hanged if He's *here*!'

It was almost as if he were taken — that is, struck and rather held — by their companion's unruffled state, which they hadn't meant to ruffle, but which suddenly presented its interest, perhaps even projected its light. The gentleman didn't know, Gedge was afterwards to say to himself, how that hypocrite was inwardly all of a tremble, how it seemed to him that his fate was being literally pulled down on his head. He was trembling for the moment certainly too much to speak; abject he might be, but he didn't want his voice to have the absurdity of a quaver. And the young woman — charming creature! — still had another word. It was for the guardian of the spot, and she made it, in her way, delightful. They had remained in the Holy of Holies, and she had been looking for a minute, with a ruefulness just marked enough to be pretty, at the queer old floor. 'Then if you say it *wasn't* in this room He was born — well, what's the use?'

'What's the use of what?' her husband asked. 'The use, you mean, of our coming here? Why, the place is charming in itself. And it's also interesting,' he added to Gedge, 'to know how you get on.'

Gedge looked at him a moment in silence, but he answered the young woman first. If poor Isabel, he was thinking, could only have been like that! — not as to youth, beauty, arrangement of hair or picturesque grace of hat — these things he didn't mind; but as to sympathy, facility, light perceptive, and yet not cheap, detachment! 'I don't say it wasn't — but I don't say it *was*.'

'Ah, but doesn't that,' she returned, 'come very much to the same thing? And don't They want also to see where He had His dinner and where He had His tea?'

'They want everything,' said Morris Gedge. 'They want to see where He hung up His hat and where He kept His boots and where His mother boiled her pot.'

'But if you don't show them — ?'

'They show *me*. It's in all their little books.'

'You mean,' the husband asked, 'that you've only to hold your tongue?'

'I try to,' said Gedge.

'Well,' his visitor smiled, 'I see you *can*.'

Gedge hesitated. 'I can't.'

'Oh, well,' said his friend, 'what does it matter?'

'I do speak,' he continued. 'I can't sometimes not.'

'Then how do you get on?'

Gedge looked at him more abjectly, to his own sense, than he had ever looked at anyone — even at Isabel when she frightened him. 'I don't get on. I speak,' he said, 'since I've spoken to *you*.'

'Oh, *we* shan't hurt you!' the young man reassuringly laughed.

The twilight meanwhile had sensibly thickened; the end of the visit was indicated. They turned together out of the upper room, and came down the narrow stair. The words just exchanged might have been felt as producing an awkwardness which the young woman gracefully felt the impulse to dissipate. 'You must rather wonder why we've come.' And it was the first note, for Gedge, of a further awkwardness — as if he had definitely heard it make the husband's hand, in a full pocket, begin to fumble.

It was even a little awkwardly that the husband still held off. 'Oh, we like it as it is. There's always *something*.' With which they had approached the door of egress.

'What is there, please?' asked Morris Gedge, not yet opening the door, as he would fain have kept the pair on, and conscious only for a moment after he had spoken that his question was just having, for the young man, too dreadfully wrong a sound. This personage wondered, yet feared, had evidently for some minutes been asking himself; so that, with his preoccupation, the caretaker's words had represented to him, inevitably, 'What is there, please, for *me*?' Gedge already knew, with it, moreover, that he wasn't stopping him in time. He had put his question, to show he himself wasn't afraid, and he must have had in consequence, he was subsequently to reflect, a lamentable air of waiting.

The visitor's hand came out. 'I hope I may take the liberty – ?' What afterwards happened our friend scarcely knew, for it fell into a slight confusion, the confusion of a queer gleam of gold – a sovereign fairly thrust at him; of a quick, almost violent motion on his own part, which, to make the matter worse, might well have sent the money rolling on the floor; and then of marked blushes all round, and a sensible embarrassment; producing indeed, in turn, rather oddly, and ever so quickly, an increase of communion. It was as if the young man had offered him money to make up to him for having, as it were, led him on, and then, perceiving the mistake, but liking him the better for his refusal, had wanted to obliterate this aggravation of his original wrong. He had done so, presently, while Gedge got the door open, by saying the best thing he could, and by saying it frankly and gaily. 'Luckily it doesn't at all affect the *work*!'

The small town-street, quiet and empty in the summer eventide, stretched to right and left, with a gabled and timbered house or two, and fairly seemed to have cleared itself to congruity with the historic void over which our friends, lingering an instant to converse, looked at each other. The young wife, rather, looked about a moment at all there wasn't to be seen, and then, before Gedge had found a reply to her husband's remark, uttered, evidently in the interest of conciliation, a little question of her own that she tried to make earnest. 'It's our unfortunate ignorance, you mean, that doesn't?'

'Unfortunate or fortunate. I like it so,' said the husband. ' "The play's the thing." Let the author alone.'

Gedge, with his key on his forefinger, leaned against the doorpost, took in the stupid little street, and was sorry to see them go – they seemed so to abandon him. 'That's just what They won't do – not let *me* do. It's all I want – to let the author alone. Practically' – he felt himself getting the last of his chance – 'there *is* no author; that is for us to deal with. There are all the immortal people – *in* the work; but there's nobody else.'

'Yes,' said the young man — 'that's what it comes to. There should really, to clear the matter up, be no such Person.'

'As you say,' Gedge returned, 'it's what it comes to. There *is* no such Person.'

The evening air listened, in the warm, thick midland stillness, while the wife's little cry rang out. 'But *wasn't* there — ?'

'There was somebody,' said Gedge, against the doorpost. 'But They've killed Him. And, dead as He is, They keep it up, They do it over again, They kill Him every day.'

He was aware of saying this so grimly — more grimly than he wished — that his companions exchanged a glance and even perhaps looked as if they felt him extravagant. That was the way, really, Isabel had warned him all the others would be looking if he should talk to Them as he talked to *her*. He liked, however, for that matter, to hear how he should sound when pronounced incapable through deterioration of the brain. 'Then if there's no author, if there's nothing to be said but that there isn't anybody,' the young woman smilingly asked, 'why in the world should there be a house?'

'There shouldn't,' said Morris Gedge.

Decidedly, yes, he affected the young man. 'Oh, I don't say, mind you, that you should pull it down!'

'Then where would you *go*?' their companion sweetly inquired.

'That's what my wife asks,' Gedge replied.

'Then keep it up, keep it up!' And the husband held out his hand.

'That's what my wife says,' Gedge went on as he shook it.

The young woman, charming creature, emulated the other visitor; she offered their remarkable friend her handshake. 'Then mind your wife.'

The poor man faced her gravely. 'I would if she were such a wife as you!'

VI

It had made for him, all the same, an immense difference; it had given him an extraordinary lift, so that a certain sweet aftertaste of his freedom might, a couple of months later, have been suspected of aiding to produce for him another, and really a more considerable, adventure. It was an odd way to think of it, but he had been, to his imagination, for twenty minutes in good society – that being the term that best described for him the company of people to whom he hadn't to talk, as he further phrased it, rot. It was his title to society that he had, in his doubtless awkward way, affirmed; and the difficulty was just that, having affirmed it, he couldn't take back the affirmation. Few things had happened to him in life, that is few that were agreeable, but at least *this* had, and he wasn't so constructed that he could go on as if it hadn't. It was going on as if it had, however, that landed him, alas! in the situation unmistakeably marked by a visit from Grant-Jackson, late one afternoon towards the end of October. This had been the hour of the call of the young Americans. Every day that hour had come round something of the deep throb of it, the successful secret, woke up; but the two occasions were, of a truth, related only by being so intensely opposed. The secret had been successful in that he had said nothing of it to Isabel, who, occupied in their own quarter while the incident lasted, had neither heard the visitors arrive nor seen them depart. It was on the other hand scarcely successful in guarding itself from indirect betrayals. There were two persons in the world, at least, who felt as he did; they were persons also, who had treated him, benignly, as feeling as *they* did, who had been ready in fact to overflow in gifts as a sign of it, and though they were now off in space they were still with him sufficiently in spirit to make him play, as it were, with the sense of their sympathy. This in turn made him, as he was perfectly aware, more than a shade or two reckless, so that, in his reaction from that gluttony of the public for false facts which had from the first tormented him, he fell into the habit of sailing, as he would have said, too near the wind, or in other words – all in presence of the people – of washing his hands of the legend. He had crossed the line – he knew it; he had struck wild – They drove him to it; he had substituted, by a succession of uncontrollable profanities, an attitude that couldn't be understood for an attitude that but too evidently *had* been.

This was of course the franker line, only he hadn't taken it, alas! for frankness – hadn't in the least, really, *taken* it, but had been simply himself caught up and disposed of by it, hurled by his fate against the bedizened walls of the temple, quite in the way of a priest possessed to excess of the god, or, more vulgarly, that of a blind bull in a china-shop – an animal to which he often compared himself. He had let himself fatally go, in fine, just for irritation, for rage, having, in his predicament, nothing at all to do with frankness – a luxury reserved for quite other situations. It had always been his sentiment that one lived to learn; he had learned something every hour of his life, though people mostly never knew what, in spite of its having generally been – hadn't it? – at somebody's expense. What he was at present continually learning was the sense of a form of words heretofore so vain – the famous 'false position' that had so often helped out a phrase. One used names in that way without knowing what they were worth; then of a sudden, one fine day, their meaning was bitter in the mouth. This was a truth with the relish of which his fireside hours were occupied, and he was quite conscious that a man was exposed who looked so perpetually as if something had disagreed with him. The look to be worn at the Birth-place was properly the beatific, and when once it had fairly been missed by those who took it for granted, who, indeed, paid sixpence for it – like the table-wine in provincial France, it was *compris* – one would be sure to have news of the remark.

News accordingly was what Gedge had been expecting – and what he knew, above all, had been expected by his wife, who had a way of sitting at present as with an ear for a certain knock. She didn't watch him, didn't follow him about the house, at the public hours, to spy upon his treachery; and that could touch him even though her averted eyes went through him more than her fixed. Her mistrust was so perfectly expressed by her manner of showing she trusted that he never felt so nervous, never so tried to keep straight, as when she most let him alone. When the crowd thickened and they had of necessity to receive together he tried himself to get off by allowing her as much as possible the word. When people appealed to him he turned to her – and with more of ceremony than their relation warranted: he couldn't help *this* either, if it seemed ironic – as to the person most concerned or most competent. He flattered himself at these moments that no one would have guessed her being his wife; especially as, to do her justice, she met his manner with a wonderful grim bravado – grim, so to say, for himself, grim by its outrageous cheerfulness for the simple-minded. The lore she *did* produce for them, the associations of the sacred spot that she developed, multiplied, embroidered; the things in short she said and the stupendous way she said them! She wasn't a bit ashamed; for why need virtue be ever ashamed? It *was* virtue, for it put bread into his mouth – he meanwhile, on his side, taking it out of hers. He had seen Grant-Jackson, on the October day, in the Birthplace itself – the right setting of course for such an interview; and what occurred was that, precisely, when the scene had ended and he had come back to their own sitting-room, the question she put to him for information was: 'Have you settled it that I'm to starve?'

She had for a long time said nothing to him so straight – which was but a proof of her real anxiety; the straightness of Grant-Jackson's visit, following on the very slight sinuosity of a note shortly before received from him, made tension show for what it was. By this time, really, however, his decision had been taken; the minutes elapsing between his reappearance at the domestic fireside and his having, from the other threshold, seen Grant-Jackson's broad, well-fitted back, the back of a banker and a patriot, move away, had, though few, presented themselves to him as supremely critical. They formed, as it were, the hinge of his door, that door actually ajar so as to show him a possible fate beyond it, but which, with his hand, in a spasm, thus tightening on the knob, he might either open wide or close partly and altogether. He stood, in the autumn dusk, in the little museum that constituted the vestibule of the temple, and there, as with a concentrated push at the crank of a windlass, he brought himself round. The portraits on the walls seemed vaguely to watch for it; it was in their august presence – kept dimly august, for the moment, by Grant-Jackson's impressive check of his application of a match to the vulgar gas – that the great man had uttered, as if it said all, his 'You know, my dear fellow, really –!' He had managed it with the special tact of a fat man, always, when there *was* any, very fine; he had got the most out of the time, the place, the setting, all the little massed admonitions and symbols; confronted there with his victim on the spot that he took occasion to name to him afresh as, to *his* piety and patriotism, the most sacred on earth, he had given it to be understood that in the first place he was lost in amazement and

142

that in the second he expected a single warning now to suffice. Not to insist too much moreover on the question of gratitude, he would let his remonstrance rest, if need be, solely on the question of taste. *As* a matter of taste alone — ! But he was surely not to be obliged to follow that up. Poor Gedge indeed would have been sorry to oblige him, for he saw it was precisely to the atrocious taste of unthankfulness that the allusion was made. When he said he wouldn't dwell on what the fortunate occupant of the post owed him for the stout battle originally fought on his behalf, he simply meant he *would*. That was his tact — which, with everything else that had been mentioned, in the scene, to help, really had the ground to itself. The day *had* been when Gedge couldn't have thanked him enough — though he had thanked him, he considered, almost fulsomely — and nothing, nothing that he could coherently or reputably name, had happened since then. From the moment he was pulled up, in short, he had no case, and if he exhibited, instead of one, only hot tears in his eyes, the mystic gloom of the temple either prevented his friend from seeing them or rendered it possible that they stood for remorse. He had dried them, with the pads formed by the base of his bony thumbs, before he went in to Isabel. This was the more fortunate as, in spite of her inquiry, prompt and pointed, he but moved about the room looking at her hard. Then he stood before the fire a little with his hands behind him and his coat-tails divided, quite as the person in permanent possession. It was an indication his wife appeared to take in; but she put nevertheless presently another question. 'You object to telling me what he said?'

'He said "You know, my dear fellow, really — !"'

'And is that all?'

'Practically. Except that I'm a thankless beast.'

'Welll!' she responded, not with dissent.

'You mean that I *am*?'

'Are those the words he used?' she asked with a scruple.

Gedge continued to think. 'The words he used were that I give away the Show and that, from several sources, it has come round to Them.'

'As of course a baby would have known!' And then as her husband said nothing: 'Were *those* the words he used?'

'Absolutely. He couldn't have used better ones.'

'Did he call it,' Mrs Gedge inquired, 'the "Show?"'

'Of course he did. The Biggest on Earth.'

She winced, looking at him hard – she wondered, but only for a moment. 'Well, it *is*.'

'Then it's something,' Gedge went on, 'to have given *that* away. But,' he added, 'I've taken it back.'

'You mean you've been convinced?'

'I mean I've been scared.'

'At last, at last!' she gratefully breathed.

'Oh, it was easily done. It was only two words. But here I am.'

Her face was now less hard for him. 'And what two words?'

'"You know, Mr Gedge, that it simply won't do." That was all. But it was the way such a man says them.'

'I'm glad, then,' Mrs Gedge frankly averred, 'that he *is* such a man. How did you ever think it *could* do?'

'Well, it was my critical sense. I didn't ever know I had one – till They came and (by putting me here) waked it up in me. Then I had, somehow, don't you see? to live with it; and I seemed to feel that, somehow or other, giving it time and in the long run, it might, it *ought* to, come out on top of the heap. Now that's where, he says, it simply won't do. So I must put it – I *have* put it – at the bottom.'

'A very good place, then, for a critical sense!' And Isabel, more placidly now, folded her work. '*If*, that is, you can only keep it there. If it doesn't struggle up again.'

'It can't struggle.' He was still before the fire, looking round at the warm, low room, peaceful in the lamplight, with the hum of the kettle for the ear, with the curtain drawn over the leaded casement, a short moreen curtain artfully chosen by Isabel for the effect of the olden time, its virtue of letting the light within show ruddy to the street. 'It's dead,' he went on; 'I killed it just now.'

He spoke, really, so that she wondered. 'Just now?'

'There in the other place – I strangled it, poor thing, in the dark. If you'll go out and see, there must be blood. Which, indeed,' he added, 'on an altar of sacrifice, is all right. But the place is for ever spattered.'

'I don't want to go out and see.' She rested her locked hands on the needlework folded on her knee, and he knew, with her eyes on him, that a look he had seen before was in her face. 'You're off your head you know, my dear, in a way.' Then, however, more cheeringly: 'It's a good job it hasn't been too late.'

'Too late to get it under?'

'Too late for Them to give you the second chance that I thank God you accept.'

'Yes, if it *had* been – !' And he looked away as through the ruddy curtain and into the chill street. Then he faced her again. 'I've scarcely got over my fright yet. I mean,' he went on, 'for you.'

'And I mean for *you*. Suppose what you had come to announce to me now were that we had *got* the sack. How should I enjoy, do you think, seeing you turn out? Yes, out *there*?' she added as his eyes again moved from their little warm circle to the night of early winter on the other side of the pane, to the rare, quick footsteps, to the closed doors, to the curtains drawn like their own, behind which the small flat town, intrinsically dull, was sitting down to supper.

He stiffened himself as he warmed his back; he held up his head, shaking himself a little as if to shake the stoop out of his shoulders, but he had to allow she was right. 'What would have become of us?'

'What indeed? We should have begged our bread – or I should be taking in washing.'

He was silent a little. 'I'm too old. I should have begun sooner.'

'Oh, God forbid!' she cried.

'The pinch,' he pursued, 'is that I can do nothing else.'

'Nothing whatever!' she agreed with elation.

'Whereas here – if I cultivate it – I perhaps *can* still lie. But I must cultivate it.'

'Oh, you old dear!' And she got up to kiss him.

'I'll do my best,' he said.

VII

'Do you remember us?' the gentleman asked and smiled – with the lady beside him smiling too; speaking so much less as an earnest pilgrim or as a tiresome tourist than as an old acquaintance. It was history repeating itself as Gedge had somehow never expected, with almost everything the same except that the evening was now a mild April-end, except that the visitors had put off mourning and showed all their bravery — besides showing, as he doubtless did himself, though so differently, for a little older; except, above all, that — oh, seeing them again suddenly affected him as not a bit the thing he would have thought it. 'We're in England again, and we were near; I've a brother at Oxford with whom we've been spending a day, and we thought we'd come over.' So the young man pleasantly said while our friend took in the queer fact that he must himself seem to them rather coldly to gape. They had come in the same way, at the quiet close; another August had passed, and this was the second spring; the Birthplace, given the hour, was about to suspend operations till the morrow; the last lingerer had gone, and the fancy of the visitors was, once more, for a look round by themselves. This represented surely no greater presumption than the terms on which they had last parted with him seemed to warrant; so that if he did inconsequently stare it was just in fact because he was so supremely far from having forgotten them. But the sight of the pair luckily had a double effect, and the first precipitated the second — the second being really his sudden vision that everything perhaps depended for him on his recognizing no complication. He must go straight on, since it was what had for more than a year now so handsomely answered; he must brazen it out consistently, since that only was what his dignity was at last reduced to. He mustn't be afraid in one way any more than he had been in another; besides which it came over him with a force that made him flush that their visit, in its essence, must have been for himself. It was good society again, and *they* were the same. It wasn't for him therefore to behave as if he couldn't meet them.

These deep vibrations, on Gedge's part, were as quick as they were deep; they came in fact all at once, so that his response, his declaration that it was all right — 'Oh, *rather*; the hour doesn't matter for *you*!' — had hung fire but an instant; and when they were within and the door closed behind them, within the twilight of the temple, where, as before, the votive offerings glimmered on the walls, he drew the long breath of one who might, by a self-betrayal, have done something too dreadful. For what had brought them back was not, indubitably, the sentiment of the shrine itself — since he knew their sentiment; but their intelligent interest in the queer case of the priest. Their call was the tribute of curiosity, of sympathy, of a compassion really, as such things went, exquisite – a tribute *to* that queerness which entitled them to the frankest welcome. They had wanted, for the generous wonder of it, to see how he was getting on, how such a man in such a place *could*; and they had doubtless more than half expected to see the door opened by somebody who had succeeded him. Well, somebody *had* – only with a strange equivocation; as they would have, poor things, to make out for themselves, an embarrassment as to which he pitied them. Nothing could have been more odd, but verily it was this troubled vision of their possible bewilderment, and this compunctious view of such a return for their amenity, that practically determined for him his tone. The lapse of the months had but made their name familiar to him; they had on the other occasion inscribed it, among the thousand names, in the current public register, and he had since then, for reasons of his own, reasons of feeling, again and again turned back to it. It was nothing in itself; it told him nothing – 'Mr and Mrs B. D. Hayes, New York' – one of those American labels that were just like every other American label and that were, precisely, the most remarkable thing about people reduced to achieving an identity in such other ways. They could be Mr and Mrs B. D. Hayes and yet they could be, with all presumptions missing – well, what these callers were. It had quickly enough indeed cleared the situation a little further that his friends had absolutely, the other time, as it came back to him, warned him of his original danger, their anxiety about which had been the last note sounded between them. What he was afraid of, with this reminiscence, was that, finding him still safe, they would, the next thing, definitely congratulate him and perhaps even, no less candidly, ask him how he had managed. It was with the sense of nipping some such inquiry in the bud that, losing no time and holding himself with a firm grip, he began, on the spot, downstairs, to make plain to them how he had managed. He averted the question in short by the assurance of his answer. 'Yes, yes, I'm still here; I suppose it *is* in a manner to one's profit that one does, such as it is, one's best.' He did his best on the present occasion, did it with the gravest face he had ever worn and a soft serenity that was like a large damp sponge passed over their previous meeting – over everything in it, that is, but the fact of its pleasantness.

'We stand here, you see, in the old living-room, happily still to be reconstructed in the mind's eye, in spite of the havoc of time, which we have fortunately, of late years, been able to arrest. It was of course rude and humble, but it must have been snug and quaint, and we have at least the pleasure of knowing that the tradition in respect to the features that do remain is delightfully uninterrupted. Across that threshold He habitually passed; through those low windows, in childhood, He peered out into the world that He was to make so much happier by the gift to it of His genius; over the boards of this floor – that is over *some* of them, for we mustn't be carried away! – his little feet often pattered; and the beams of this ceiling (we must really in some places take care of *our* heads!) he endeavoured, in boyish strife, to jump up and touch. It's not often that in the early home of genius and renown the whole tenor of existence is laid so bare, not often that we are able to retrace, from point to point and from step to step, its connection with objects, with influences – to build it round again with the little solid facts out of which it sprang. This, therefore, I need scarcely remind you, is what makes the small space between these walls – so modest to measurement, so insignificant of aspect – unique on all the earth. *There is nothing like it*,' Morris Gedge went on, insisting as solemnly and softly, for his bewildered hearers, as over a pulpit-edge; 'there is nothing at all like it anywhere in the world. There is nothing, only reflect, for the combination of greatness, and, as we venture to say, of intimacy. You may find elsewhere perhaps absolutely fewer changes, but where shall you find a *presence* equally diffused, uncontested and undisturbed? Where in particular shall you find, on the part of the abiding spirit, an equally towering eminence? You may find elsewhere eminence of a considerable order, but where shall you find *with* it, don't you see, changes, after all, so few, and the contemporary element caught so, as it were, in the very fact?' His visitors, at first confounded, but gradually spellbound, were still gaping with the universal gape – wondering, he judged, into what strange pleasantry he had been suddenly moved to break out, and yet beginning to see in him an intention beyond a joke, so that they started, at this point, almost jumped, when, by as rapid a transition, he made, toward the old fireplace, a dash that seemed to illustrate, precisely, the act of eager catching. 'It is in this old chimney corner, the quaint inglenook of our ancestors – just there in the far angle, where His little stool was placed, and where, I dare say, if we could look close enough, we should find the hearthstone scraped with His little feet – that we see the inconceivable child gazing into the blaze of the old oaken logs and making out there pictures and stories, see Him conning, with curly bent head, His well-worn hornbook, or poring over some scrap of an ancient ballad, some page of some such rudely bound volume of chronicles as lay, we may be sure, in His father's window-seat.'

It was, he even himself felt at this moment, wonderfully done; no auditors, for all his thousands, had ever yet so inspired him. The odd, slightly alarmed shyness in the two faces, as if in a drawing-room, in their 'good society', exactly, some act incongruous, something grazing the indecent, had abruptly been perpetrated, the painful reality of which faltered before coming home – the visible effect on his friends, in fine, wound him up as to the sense that *they* were worth the trick. It came of itself now – he had got it so by heart; but perhaps really it had never come so well, with the staleness so disguised, the interest so renewed and the clerical unction, demanded by the priestly character, so successfully distilled. Mr Hayes of New York had more than once looked at his wife, and Mrs Hayes of New York had more than once looked at her husband – only, up to now, with a stolen glance, with eyes it had not been easy to detach from the remarkable countenance by the aid of which their entertainer held them. At present, however, after an exchange less furtive, they ventured on a sign that they had not been appealed to in vain. 'Charming, charming, Mr Gedge!' Mr Hayes broke out; 'we feel that we've caught you in the mood.'

His wife hastened to assent – it eased the tension. 'It *would* be quite the way; except,' she smiled, 'that you'd be too dangerous. You've really a genius!'

Gedge looked at her hard, but yielding no inch, even though she touched him there at a point of consciousness that quivered. This was the prodigy for him, and had been, the year through – that he did it all, he found, easily, did it better than he had done anything else in his life; with so high and broad an effect, in truth, an inspiration so rich and free, that his poor wife now, literally, had been moved more than once to fresh fear. She had had her bad moments, he knew, after taking the measure of his new direction – moments of readjusted suspicion in which she wondered if he had not simply embraced another, a different perversity. There would be more than one fashion of giving away the show, and wasn't *this* perhaps a question of giving it away by excess? He could dish them by too much romance as well as by too little; she had not hitherto fairly apprehended that there might *be* too much. It was a way like another, at any rate, of reducing the place to the absurd; which reduction, if he didn't look out, would reduce *them* again to the prospect of the streets, and this time surely without an appeal. It all depended, indeed – he knew she knew that – on how much Grant-Jackson and the others, how much the Body, in a word, would take. He knew she knew what he himself held it would take – that he considered no limit could be drawn to the quantity. They simply wanted it piled up, and so did everybody else; wherefore, if no one reported him, as before, why were They to be uneasy? It was in consequence of idiots brought to reason that he had been dealt with before; but as there was now no form of idiocy that he didn't systematically flatter, goading it on really to its *own* private doom, who was ever to pull the string of the guillotine? The axe was in the air – yes; but in a world gorged to satiety there were no revolutions. And it had been vain for Isabel to ask if the other thunder-growl also hadn't come out of the blue. There was actually proof positive that the winds were now at rest. How could they be more so? – he appealed to the receipts. These were golden days – the show had never so flourished. So he had argued, so he was arguing still – and, it had to be owned, with every appearance in his favour. Yet if he inwardly winced at the tribute to his plausibility rendered by his flushed friends, this was because he felt in it the real ground of his optimism. The charming woman before him acknowledged his 'genius' as he himself had had to do. He had been surprised at his facility until he had grown used to it. Whether or no he had, as a fresh menace to his future, found a new perversity, he had found a vocation much older, evidently, than he had at first been prepared to recognize. He had done himself injustice. He liked to be brave because it came so easy; he could measure it off by the yard. It was in the Birthroom, above all, that he continued to do this, having ushered up his companions without, as he was still more elated to feel, the turn of a hair. She might take it as she liked, but he had had the lucidity – all, that is, for his own safety – to meet without the grace of an answer the homage of her beautiful smile. She took it apparently, and her husband took it, but as a part of his odd humour, and they followed him aloft with faces now a little more responsive to the manner in which, on *that* spot, he would naturally come out. He came out, according to the word of his assured private receipt, 'strong'. He missed a little, in truth, the usual round-eyed question from them – the inveterate artless cue with which, from moment to moment, clustered troops had, for a year, obliged him. Mr and Mrs Hayes were from New York, but it was a little like singing, as he had heard one of his Americans once say about something, to a Boston audience. He did none the less what he could, and it was ever his practice to stop still at a certain spot in the room and, after having secured attention by look and gesture, suddenly shoot off: 'Here!'

They always understood, the good people – he could fairly love them now for it; they always said, breathlessly and unanimously, 'There?' and stared down at the designated point quite as if some trace of the grand event were still to be made out. This movement produced, he again looked round. 'Consider it well: *the* spot of earth – !' 'Oh, but it isn't *earth*!' the boldest spirit – there was always a boldest – would generally pipe out. Then the guardian of the Birthplace would be truly superior – as if the unfortunate had figured the Immortal coming up, like a potato, through the soil. 'I'm not suggesting that He was born on the bare ground. He was born *here*!' – with an uncompromising dig of his heel. 'There ought to be a brass, with an inscription, let in.' 'Into the floor?' – it always came. 'Birth and burial: seedtime, summer, autumn!' – that always, with its special, right cadence, thanks to his unfailing spring, came too. 'Why not as well as into the pavement of the church? – you've *seen* our grand old church?' The former of which questions nobody ever answered – abounding, on the other hand, to make up, in relation to the latter. Mr and Mrs Hayes even were at first left dumb by it – not indeed, to do them justice, having uttered the word that produced it. They had uttered no word while he kept the game up, and (though that made it a little more difficult) he could yet stand triumphant before them after he had finished with his flourish. Then it was only that Mr Hayes of New York broke silence.

'Well, if we wanted to see, I think I may say we're quite satisfied. As my wife says, it *would* seem to be your line.' He spoke now, visibly, with more ease, as if a light had come: though he made no joke of it, for a reason that presently appeared. They were coming down the little stair, and it was on the descent that his companion added her word.

'Do you know what we half *did* think – ?' And then to her husband: 'Is it dreadful to tell him?' They were in the room below, and the young woman, also relieved, expressed the feeling with gaiety. She smiled, as before, at Morris Gedge, treating him as a person with whom relations were possible, yet remaining just uncertain enough to invoke Mr Hayes's opinion. 'We *have* awfully wanted – from what we had heard.' But she met her husband's graver face; he was not quite out of the wood. At this she was slightly flurried – but she cut it short. 'You must know – don't you? – that, with the crowds who listen to you, we'd have heard.'

He looked from one to the other, and once more again, with force, something came over him. They had kept him in mind, they were neither ashamed nor afraid to show it, and it was positively an interest, on the part of this charming creature and this keen, cautious gentleman, an interest resisting oblivion and surviving separation, that had governed their return. Their other visit had been the brightest thing that had ever happened to him, but this was the gravest; so that at the end of a minute something broke in him and his mask, of itself, fell off. He chucked, as he would have said, consistency; which, in its extinction, left the tears in his eyes. His smile was therefore queer. 'Heard how I'm going it?'

The young man, though still looking at him hard, felt sure, with this, of his own ground. 'Of course, you're tremendously talked about. You've gone round the world.'

'You've heard of me in America?'

'Why, almost of nothing else!'

'That was what made us feel – !' Mrs Hayes contributed.

'That you must see for yourselves?' Again he compared, poor Gedge, their faces. 'Do you mean I excite – a – scandal?'

'Dear no! Admiration. You renew so,' the young man observed, 'the interest.'

'Ah, there it is!' said Gedge with eyes of adventure that seemed to rest beyond the Atlantic.

'They listen, month after month, when they're out here, as you must have seen; and they go home and talk. But they sing your praise.'

Our friend could scarce take it in. 'Over *there*?'

'Over there. I think you must be even in the papers.'

'Without abuse?'

'Oh, we don't abuse everyone.'

Mrs Hayes, in her beauty, it was clear, stretched the point. 'They rave about you.'

'Then they *don't* know?'

'Nobody knows,' the young man declared; 'it wasn't anyone's knowledge, at any rate, that made us uneasy.'

'It was your own? I mean your own sense?'

'Well, call it that. We remembered, and we wondered what had happened. So,' Mr Hayes now frankly laughed, 'we came to see.'

Gedge stared through his film of tears. 'Came from America to see *me*?'

'Oh, a part of the way. But we wouldn't, in England, not have seen you.'

'And now we *have*!' the young woman soothingly added.

Gedge still could only gape at the candour of the tribute. But he tried to meet them — it was what was least poor for him — in their own key. 'Well, how do you like it?'

Mrs Hayes, he thought — if their answer were important — laughed a little nervously. 'Oh, you see.'

Once more he looked from one to the other. 'It's too beastly easy, you know.'

Her husband raised his eyebrows. 'You conceal your art. The emotion — yes; that must be easy; the general tone must flow. But about your facts — you've so many: how do you get *them* through?'

Gedge wondered. 'You think I get too many — ?'

At this they were amused together. 'That's just what we came to see!'

'Well, you know, I've felt my way; I've gone step by step; you wouldn't believe how I've tried it on. *This* — where you see me — is where I've come out.' After which, as they said nothing: 'You hadn't thought I *could* come out?'

Again they just waited, but the husband spoke: 'Are you so awfully sure you *are* out?'

Gedge drew himself up in the manner of his moments of emotion, almost conscious even that, with his sloping shoulders, his long lean neck and his nose so prominent in proportion to other matters, he looked the more like a giraffe. It was now at last that he really caught on. 'I *may* be in danger again – and the danger is what has moved you? Oh!' the poor man fairly moaned. His appreciation of it quite weakened him, yet he pulled himself together. 'You've your view of my danger?'

It was wondrous how, with that note definitely sounded, the air was cleared. Lucid Mr Hayes, at the end of a minute, had put the thing in a nutshell. 'I don't know what you'll think of us – for being so beastly curious.'

'I think,' poor Gedge grimaced, 'you're only too beastly kind.'

'It's all your own fault,' his friend returned, 'for presenting us (who are not idiots, say) with so striking a picture of a crisis. At our other visit, you remember,' he smiled, 'you created an anxiety for the opposite reason. Therefore if *this* should again be a crisis for you, you'd really give us the case with an ideal completeness.'

'You make me wish,' said Morris Gedge, 'that it might be one.'

'Well, don't try – for our amusement – to bring one on. I don't see, you know, how you can have much margin. Take care – take care.'

Gedge took it pensively in. 'Yes, that was what you said a year ago. You did me the honour to be uneasy as my wife was.'

Which determined on the young woman's part an immediate question. 'May I ask, then, if Mrs Gedge is now at rest?'

'No; since you do ask. *She* fears, at least, that I go too far; *she* doesn't believe in my margin. You see, we *had* our scare after your visit. They came down.'

His friends were all interest. 'Ah! They came down?'

'Heavy. They brought *me* down. That's *why* – '

'Why you are down?' Mrs Hayes sweetly demanded.

'Ah, but my dear man,' her husband interposed, 'you're not down; you're *up*! You're only up a different tree, but you're up at the tip-top.'

'You mean I take it too high?'

'That's exactly the question,' the young man answered; 'and the possibility, as matching your first danger, is just what we felt we couldn't, if you didn't mind, miss the measure of.'

Gedge looked at him. 'I feel that I know what you at bottom *hoped*.'

'We at bottom "hope," surely, that you're all right.'

'In spite of the fool it makes of everyone?'

Mr Hayes of New York smiled. 'Say *because* of that. We only ask to believe that everyone *is* a fool!'

'Only you haven't been, without reassurance, able to imagine fools of the size that my case demands?' And Gedge had a pause, while, as if on the chance of some proof, his companion waited. 'Well, I won't pretend to you that your anxiety hasn't made me, doesn't threaten to make me, a bit nervous; though I don't quite understand it if, as you say, people but rave about me.'

'Oh, *that* report was from the other side; people in our country so very easily rave. You've seen small children laugh to shrieks when tickled in a new place. So there are amiable millions with us who are but small children. They perpetually present new places for the tickler. What we've seen in further lights,' Mr Hayes good-humouredly pursued, 'is your people *here* – the Committee, the Board, or whatever the powers to whom you're responsible.'

'Call them my friend Grant-Jackson then – my original backer, though I admit, for that reason, perhaps my most formidable critic. It's with him, practically, I deal; or rather it's by him I'm dealt with – *was* dealt with before. I stand or fall by him. But he has given me my head.'

'Mayn't he then want you,' Mrs Hayes inquired, 'just to show as flagrantly running away.'

'Of course – I see what you mean. I'm riding, blindly, for a fall, and They're watching (to be tender of me!) for the smash that may come of itself. It's Machiavellic – but everything's possible. And what did you just now mean,' Gedge asked – 'especially if you've only heard of my prosperity – by your "further lights?"'

His friends for an instant looked embarrassed, but Mr Hayes came to the point. 'We've heard of your prosperity, but we've also, remember, within a few minutes, heard *you*.'

'I was determined you *should*,' said Gedge. 'I'm good then – but I overdo?' His strained grin was still sceptical.

Thus challenged, at any rate, his visitor pronounced. 'Well, if you don't; if at the end of six months more it's clear that you haven't overdone; then, *then* – '

'Then what?'

'Then it's great.'

'But it *is* great – greater than anything of the sort ever was. I overdo, thank goodness, yes; or I would if it were a thing you *could*.'

'Oh, well, if there's *proof* that you can't – !' With which, and an expressive gesture, Mr Hayes threw up his fears.

His wife, however, for a moment, seemed unable to let them go. 'Don't They want then *any* truth? – none even for the mere look of it?'

'The look of it,' said Morris Gedge, 'is what I give!'

It made them, the others, exchange a look of their own. Then she smiled. 'Oh, well, if they think so – !'

'You at least don't? You're like my wife – which indeed, I remember,' Gedge added, 'is a similarity I expressed a year ago the wish for! At any rate I frighten *her*.'

The young husband, with an 'Ah, wives are terrible!' smoothed it over, and their visit would have failed of further excuse had not, at this instant, a movement at the other end of the room suddenly engaged them. The evening had so nearly closed in, though Gedge, in the course of their talk, had lighted the lamp nearest them, that they had not distinguished, in connection with the opening of the door of communication to the warden's lodge, the appearance of another person, an eager woman, who, in her impatience, had barely paused before advancing. Mrs Gedge – her identity took but a few seconds to become vivid – was upon them, and she had not been too late for Mr Hayes's last remark. Gedge saw at once that she had come with news; no need even, for that certitude, of her quick retort to the words in the air – 'You may say as well, sir, that they're often, poor wives, terrified!' She knew nothing of the friends whom, at so unnatural an hour, he was showing about; but there was no livelier sign for him that this didn't matter than the possibility with which she intensely charged her 'Grant-Jackson, to see you at once!' – letting it, so to speak, fly in his face.

'He has been with you?'

'Only a minute – he's there. But it's you he wants to see.'

He looked at the others. 'And what does he want, dear?'

'God knows! There it is. It's his horrid hour – it *was* that other time.'

She had nervously turned to the others, overflowing to them, in her dismay, for all their strangeness – quite, as he said to himself, like a woman of the people. She was the bare-headed goodwife talking in the street about the row in the house, and it was in this character that he instantly introduced her: 'My dear doubting wife, who will do her best to entertain you while I wait upon our friend.' And he explained to her as he could his now protesting companions – 'Mr and Mrs Hayes of New York, who have been here before.' He knew, without knowing why, that her announcement chilled him; he failed at least to see why it should chill him so much. His good friends had themselves been visibly affected by it, and heaven knew that the depths of brooding fancy in him were easily stirred by contact. If they had wanted a crisis they accordingly had found one, albeit they had already asked leave to retire before it. This he wouldn't have. 'Ah no, you must really see!'

'But we shan't be able to bear it, you know,' said the young woman, 'if it *is* to turn you out.'

Her crudity attested her sincerity, and it was the latter, doubtless, that instantly held Mrs Gedge. 'It *is* to turn us out.'

'Has he told you that, madam?' Mr Hayes inquired of her – it being wondrous how the breath of doom had drawn them together.

'No, not told me; but there's something in him there – I mean in his awful manner – that matches too well with other things. We've seen,' said the poor pale lady, 'other things enough.'

The young woman almost clutched her. 'Is his manner very awful?'

'It's simply the manner,' Gedge interposed, 'of a very great man.'

'Well, very great men,' said his wife, 'are very awful things.'

'It's exactly,' he laughed, 'what we're finding out! But I mustn't keep him waiting. Our friends here,' he went on, 'are directly interested. You mustn't, mind you, let them go until we know.'

Mr Hayes, however, held him; he found himself stayed. 'We're so directly interested that I want you to understand this. If anything happens – '

'Yes?' said Gedge, all gentle as he faltered.

'Well, *we* must set you up.'

Mrs Hayes quickly abounded. 'Oh, *do* come to us!'

Again he could but look at them. They were really wonderful folk. And but Mr and Mrs Hayes! It affected even Isabel, through her alarm;

though the balm, in a manner, seemed to foretell the wound. He had reached the threshold of his own quarters; he stood there as at the door of the chamber of judgement. But he laughed; at least he could be gallant in going up for sentence. 'Very good then – I'll come to you!'

This was very well, but it didn't prevent his heart, a minute later, at the end of the passage, from thumping with beats he could count. He had paused again before going in; on the other side of this second door his poor future was to be let loose at him. It was broken, at best, and spiritless, but wasn't Grant-Jackson there, like a beast-tamer in a cage, all tights and spangles and circus attitudes, to give it a cut with the smart official whip and make it spring at him? It was during this moment that he fully measured the effect for his nerves of the impression made on his so oddly earnest friends – whose earnestness he in fact, in the spasm of this last effort, came within an ace of resenting. They had upset him by contact; he was afraid, literally, of meeting his doom on his knees; it wouldn't have taken much more, he absolutely felt, to make him approach with his forehead in the dust the great man whose wrath was to be averted. Mr and Mrs Hayes of New York had brought tears to his eyes; but was it to be reserved for Grant-Jackson to make him cry like a baby? He wished, yes, while he palpitated, that Mr and Mrs Hayes of New York hadn't had such an eccentricity of interest, for it seemed somehow to come from *them* that he was going so fast to pieces. Before he turned the knob of the door, however, he had another queer instant; making out that it had been, strictly, his case that was interesting, his funny power, however accidental, to show as in a picture the attitude of others – not his poor, dingy personality. It was this latter quantity, none the less, that was marching to execution. It is to our friend's credit that he *believed*, as he prepared to turn the knob, that he was going to be hanged; and it is certainly not less to his credit that his wife, on the chance, had his supreme thought. Here it was that – possibly with his last articulate breath – he thanked his stars, such as they were, for Mr and Mrs Hayes of New York. At least they would take care of her.

They were doing that certainly with some success when, ten minutes later, he returned to them. She sat between them in the beautiful Birthplace, and he couldn't have been sure afterwards that each wasn't holding her hand. The three together, at any rate, had the effect of recalling to him – it was too whimsical – some picture, a sentimental print, seen and admired in his youth, a 'Waiting for the Verdict,' a 'Counting the Hours,' or something of that sort; humble respectability in suspense about humble innocence. He didn't know how he himself looked, and he didn't care; the great thing was that he wasn't crying – though he might have been; the glitter in his eyes was assuredly dry, though that there *was* a glitter, or something slightly to bewilder, the faces of the others, as they rose to meet him, sufficiently proved. His wife's eyes pierced his own, but it was Mrs Hayes of New York who spoke. '*Was* it then for that – ?'

He only looked at them at first – he felt he might now enjoy it. 'Yes, it was for "that". I mean it was about the way I've been going on. He came to speak of it.'

'And he's gone?' Mr Hayes permitted himself to inquire.

'He's gone.'

'It's over?' Isabel hoarsely asked.

'It's over.'

'Then we go?'

This it was that he enjoyed. 'No, my dear; we stay.'

There was fairly a triple gasp; relief took time to operate. 'Then why did he come?'

'In the fulness of his kind heart and of *Their* discussed and decreed satisfaction. To express Their sense – !'

Mr Hayes broke into a laugh, but his wife wanted to know. 'Of the grand work you're doing?'

'Of the way I polish it off. They're most handsome about it. The receipts, it appears, speak – '

He was nursing his effect; Isabel intently watched him, and the others hung on his lips. 'Yes, speak – ?'

'Well, volumes. They tell the truth.'

At this Mr Hayes laughed again. 'Oh, *they* at least do?'

Near him thus, once more, Gedge knew their intelligence as one – which was so good a consciousness to get back that his tension now relaxed as by the snap of a spring and he felt his old face at ease. 'So you can't say,' he continued, 'that we don't want it.'

'I bow to it,' the young man smiled. 'It's what I said then. It's *great*.'

'It's great,' said Morris Gedge. 'It couldn't be greater.'

His wife still watched him; her irony hung behind. 'Then we're just as we were?'

'No, not as we were.'

She jumped at it. 'Better?'

'Better. They give us a rise.'

'Of income?'

'Of our sweet little stipend — by a vote of the Committee. That's what, as Chairman, he came to announce.'

The very echoes of the Birthplace were themselves, for the instant, hushed; the warden's three companions showed, in the conscious air, a struggle for their own breath. But Isabel, with almost a shriek, was the first to recover hers. 'They double us?'

'Well — call it that. "In recognition." There you are.'

Isabel uttered another sound — but this time inarticulate; partly because Mrs Hayes of New York had already jumped at her to kiss her. Mr Hayes meanwhile, as with too much to say, but put out his hand, which our friend took in silence. So Gedge had the last word. 'And there *you* are!'

THE JOLLY CORNER

I

'Every one asks me what I "think" of everything,' said Spencer Brydon; 'and I make answer as I can — begging or dodging the question, putting them off with any nonsense. It wouldn't matter to any of them really,' he went on, 'for, even were it possible to meet in that stand-and-deliver way so silly a demand on so big a subject, my "thoughts" would still be almost altogether about something that concerns only myself.' He was talking to Miss Staverton, with whom for a couple of months now he had availed himself of every possible occasion to talk; this disposition and this resource, this comfort and support, as the situation in fact presented itself, having promptly enough taken the first place in the considerable array of rather unattenuated surprises attending his so strangely belated return to America. Everything was somehow a surprise; and that might be natural when one had so long and so consistently neglected everything, taken pains to give surprises so much margin for play. He had given them more than thirty years — thirty-three, to be exact; and they now seemed to him to have organized their performance quite on the scale of that licence. He had been twenty-three on leaving New York — he was fifty-six today: unless indeed he were to reckon as he had sometimes, since his repatriation found himself feeling; in which case he would have lived longer than is often allotted to man. It would have taken a century, he repeatedly said to himself, and said also to Alice Staverton, it would have taken a longer absence and a more averted mind than those even of which he had been guilty, to pile up the differences, the newnesses, the queernesses, above all the bignesses, for the better or the worse, that at present assaulted his vision wherever he looked.

The great fact all the while however had been the incalculability; since he *had* supposed himself, from decade to decade, to be allowing, and in the most liberal and intelligent manner, for brilliancy of change. He actually saw that he had allowed for nothing; he missed what he would have been sure of finding, he found what he would never have imagined. Proportions and values were upside-down; the ugly things he had expected, the ugly things of his far-away youth, when he had too promptly waked up to a sense of the ugly – these uncanny phenomena placed him rather, as it happened, under the charm; whereas the 'swagger' things, the modern, the monstrous, the famous things, those he had more particularly, like thousands of ingenuous inquirers every year, come over to see, were exactly his sources of dismay. They were as so many set traps for displeasure, above all for reaction, of which his restless tread was constantly pressing the spring. It was interesting, doubtless, the whole show, but it would have been too disconcerting hadn't a certain finer truth saved the situation. He had distinctly not, in this steadier light, come over *all* for the monstrosities; he had come, not only in the last analysis but quite on the face of the act, under an impulse with which they had nothing to do. He had come – putting the thing pompously – to look at his 'property,' which he had thus for a third of a century not been within four thousand miles of; or, expressing it less sordidly, he had yielded to the humour of seeing again his house on the jolly corner, as he usually, and quite fondly, described it – the one in which he had first seen the light, in which various members of his family had lived and had died, in which the holidays of his overschooled boyhood had been passed and the few social flowers of his chilled adolescence gathered, and which, alienated then for so long a period, had, through the successive deaths of his two brothers and the termination of old arrangements, come wholly into his hands. He was the owner of another, not quite so 'good' – the jolly corner having been, from far back, superlatively extended and consecrated; and the value of the pair represented his main capital, with an income consisting, in their later years, of their respective rents which (thanks precisely to their original excellent type) had never been depressingly low. He could live in 'Europe,' as he had been in the habit of living, on the product of these flourishing New York leases, and all the better since, that of the second structure, the mere number in its long row, having within a twelve-month fallen in, renovation at a high advance had proved beautifully possible.

These were items of property indeed, but he had found himself since his arrival distinguishing more than ever between them. The house within the street, two bristling blocks westward, was already in course of reconstruction as a tall mass of flats; he had acceded, some time before, to overtures for this conversion – in which, now that it was going forward, it had been not the least of his astonishments to find himself able, on the spot, and though without a previous ounce of such experience, to participate with a certain intelligence, almost with a certain authority. He had lived his life with his back so turned to such concerns and his face addressed to those of so different an order that he scarce knew what to make of this lively stir, in a compartment of his mind never yet penetrated, of a capacity for business and a sense for construction. These virtues, so common all round him now, had been dormant in his own organism – where it might be said of them perhaps that they had slept the sleep of the just. At present, in the splendid autumn weather – the autumn at least was a pure boon in the terrible place – he loafed about his 'work' undeterred, secretly agitated; not in the least 'minding' that the whole proposition, as they said, was vulgar and sordid, and ready to climb ladders, to walk the plank, to handle materials and look wise about them, to ask questions, in fine, and challenge explanations and really 'go into' figures.

It amused, it verily quite charmed him; and, by the same stroke, it amused, and even more, Alice Staverton, though perhaps charming her perceptibly less. She wasn't however going to be better-off for it, as *he* was – and so astonishingly much: nothing was now likely, he knew, ever to make her better-off than she found herself, in the afternoon of life, as the delicately frugal possessor and tenant of the small house in Irving Place to which she had subtly managed to cling through her almost unbroken New York career. If he knew the way to it now better than to any other address among the dreadful multiplied numberings which seemed to him to reduce the whole place to some vast ledger-page, overgrown, fantastic, of ruled and criss-crossed lines and figures – if he had formed, for his consolation, that habit, it was really not a little because of the charm of his having encountered and recognized, in the vast wilderness of the wholesale, breaking through the mere gross generalization of wealth and force and success, a small still scene where items and shades, all delicate things, kept the sharpness of the notes of a high voice perfectly trained, and where economy hung about like the scent of a garden. His old friend lived with one maid and herself dusted her relics and trimmed her lamps and polished her silver; she stood off, in the awful modern crush, when the could, but she sallied forth and did battle when the challenge was really to 'spirit', the spirit she after all confessed to, proudly and a little shyly, as to that of the better time, that of *their* common, their quite far-away and antediluvian social period and order. She made use of the street-cars when need be, the terrible things that people scrambled for as the panic-stricken at sea scramble for the boats; she affronted, inscrutably, under stress, all the public concussions and ordeals; and yet, with that slim mystifying grace of her appearance, which defied you to say if she were a fair young woman who looked older through trouble, or a fine smooth older one who looked young through successful indifference; with her precious reference, above all, to memories and histories into which he could enter, she was as exquisite for him as some pale pressed flower (a rarity to begin with), and, failing other sweetnesses, she was a sufficient reward of his effort. They had communities of knowledge, 'their' knowledge (this discriminating possessive was always on her lips) of presences of the other age, presences all overlaid, in his case, by the experience of a man and the freedom of a wanderer, overlaid by pleasure, by infidelity, by passages of life that were strange and dim to her, just by 'Europe' in short, but still unobscured, still exposed and cherished, under that pious visitation of the spirit from which she had never been diverted.

She had come with him one day to see how his 'apartment-house' was rising; he had helped her over gaps and explained to her plans, and while they were there had happened to have, before her, a brief but lively discussion with the man in charge, the representative of the building-firm that had undertaken his work. He had found himself quite 'standing-up' to this personage over a failure on the latter's part to observe some detail of one of their noted conditions, and had so lucidly argued his case that, besides ever so prettily flushing, at the time, for sympathy in his triumph, she had afterwards said to him (though to a slightly greater effect of irony) that he had clearly for too many years neglected a real gift. If he had but stayed at home he would have anticipated the inventor of the sky-scraper. If he had but stayed at home he would have discovered his genius in time really to start some new variety of awful architectural hare and run it till it burrowed in a goldmine. He was to remember these words, while the weeks elapsed, for the small silver ring they had sounded over the queerest and deepest of his own lately most disguised and most muffled vibrations.

It had begun to be present to him after the first fortnight, it had broken out with the oddest abruptness, this particular wanton wonderment: it met him there – and this was the image under which he himself judged the matter, or at least, not a little, thrilled and flushed with it – very much as he might have been met by some strange figure, some unexpected occupant, at a turn of one of the dim passages of an empty house. The quaint analogy quite hauntingly remained with him, when he didn't indeed rather improve it by a still intenser form: that of his opening a door behind which he would have made sure of finding nothing, a door into a room shuttered and void, and yet so coming, with a great suppressed start, on some quite erect confronting presence, something planted in the middle of the place and facing him through the dusk. After that visit to the house in construction he walked with his companion to see the other and always so much the better one, which in the eastward direction formed one of the corners, the 'jolly' one precisely, of the street now so generally dishonoured and disfigured in its westward reaches and of the comparatively conservative Avenue. The Avenue still had pretensions, as Miss Staverton said, to decency; the old people had mostly gone, the old names were unknown, and here and there an old association seemed to stray, all vaguely, like some very aged person, out too late, whom you might meet and feel the impulse to watch or follow, in kindness, for safe restoration to shelter.

They went in together, our friends; he admitted himself with his key, as he kept no one there, he explained, preferring, for his reasons, to leave the place empty, under a simple arrangement with a good woman living in the neighbourhood and who came for a daily hour to open windows and dust and sweep. Spencer Brydon had his reasons and was growingly aware of them; they seemed to him better each time he was there, though he didn't name them all to his companion, any more than he told her as yet how often, how quite absurdly often, he himself came. He only let her see for the present, while they walked through the great blank rooms, that absolute vacancy reigned and that, from top to bottom, there was nothing but Mrs Muldoon's broomstick, in a corner, to tempt the burglar. Mrs Muldoon was then on the premises, and she loquaciously attended the visitors, preceding them from room to room and pushing back shutters and throwing up sashes – all to show them, as she remarked, how little there was to see. There was little indeed to see in the great gaunt shell where the main dispositions and the general apportionment of space, the style of an age of ampler allowances, had nevertheless for its master their honest pleading message, affecting him as some good old servant's, some lifelong retainer's appeal for a character, or even for a retiring-pension; yet it was also a remark of Mrs Muldoon's that, glad as she was to oblige him by her noonday round, there was a request she greatly hoped he would never make of her. If he should wish her for any reason to come in after dark she would just tell him, if he 'plased,' that he must ask it of somebody else.

The fact that there was nothing to see didn't militate for the worthy woman against what one *might* see, and she put it frankly to Miss Staverton that no lady could be expected to like, could she? 'craping up to thim top storeys in the ayvil hours.' The gas and the electric light were off the house, and she fairly evoked a gruesome vision of her march through the great grey rooms – so many of them as there were too! – with her glimmering taper. Miss Staverton met her honest glare with a smile and the profession that she herself certainly would recoil from such an adventure. Spencer Brydon meanwhile held his peace – for the moment; the question of the 'evil' hours in his old home had already become too grave for him. He had begun some time since to 'crape,' and he knew just why a packet of candles addressed to that pursuit had been stowed by his own hand, three weeks before, at the back of a drawer of the fine old sideboard that occupied, as a 'fixture,' the deep recess in the dining-room. Just now he laughed at his companions – quickly however changing the subject; for the reason that, in the first place, his laugh struck him even at that moment as starting the odd echo, the conscious human resonance (he scarce knew how to qualify it) that sounds made while he was there alone sent back to his ear or his fancy; and that, in the second, he imagined Alice Staverton for the instant on the point of asking him, with a divination, if he ever so prowled. There were divinations he was unprepared for, and he had at all events averted inquiry by the time Mrs Muldoon had left them, passing on to other parts.

There was happily enough to say, on so consecrated a spot, that could be said freely and fairly; so that a whole train of declarations was precipitated by his friend's having herself broken out, after a yearning look round: 'But I hope you don't mean they want you to pull *this* to pieces!' His answer came, promptly, with his re-awakened wrath: it was of course exactly what they wanted, and what they were 'at' him for, daily, with the iteration of people who couldn't for their life understand a man's liability to decent feelings. He had found the place, just as it stood and beyond what he could express, an interest and a joy. There were values other than the beastly rent-values, and in short, in short – ! But it was thus Miss Staverton took him up. 'In short you're to make so good a thing of your sky-scraper that, living in luxury on *those* ill-gotten gains, you can afford for a while to be sentimental here!' Her smile had for him, with the words, the particular mild irony with which he found half her talk suffused; an irony without bitterness and that came, exactly, from her having so much imagination – not, like the cheap sarcasms with which one heard most people, about the world of 'society,' bid for the reputation of cleverness, from nobody's really having any. It was agreeable to him at this very moment to be sure that when he had answered, after a brief demur, 'Well yes: so, precisely, you may put it!' her imagination would still do him justice. He explained that even if never a dollar were to come to him from the other house he would nevertheless cherish this one; and he dwelt, further, while they lingered and wandered, on the fact of the stupefaction he was already exciting, the positive mystification he felt himself create.

He spoke of the value of all he read into it, into the mere sight of the walls, mere shapes of the rooms, mere sound of the floors, mere feel, in his hand, of the old silver-plated knobs of the several mahogany doors, which suggested the pressure of the palms of the dead; the seventy years of the past in fine that these things represented, the annals of nearly three generations, counting his grandfather's, the one that had ended there, and the impalpable ashes of his long-extinct youth, afloat in the very air like microscopic motes. She listened to everything; she was a woman who answered intimately but who utterly didn't chatter. She scattered abroad therefore no cloud of words; she could assent, she could agree, above all she could encourage, without doing that. Only at the last she went a little further than he had done himself. 'And then how do you know? You may still, after all, want to live here.' It rather indeed pulled him up, for it wasn't what he had been thinking, at least in her sense of the words. 'You mean I may decide to stay on for the sake of it?'

'Well, *with* such a home – !' But, quite beautifully, she had too much tact to dot so monstrous an *i*, and it was precisely an illustration of the way she didn't rattle. How could any one – of any wit – insist on any one else's 'wanting' to live in New York?

'Oh,' he said, 'I *might* have lived here (since I had my opportunity early in life); I might have put in here all these years. Then everything would have been different enough – and, I dare say, "funny" enough. But that's another matter. And then the beauty of it – I mean of my perversity, of my refusal to agree to a "deal" – is just in the total absence of a reason. Don't you see that if I had a reason about the matter at all it would *have* to be the other way, and would then be inevitably a reason of dollars? There are no reasons here *but* of dollars. Let us therefore have none whatever – not the ghost of one.'

They were back in the hall then for departure, but from where they stood the vista was large, through an open door, into the great square main saloon, with its almost antique felicity of brave spaces between windows. Her eyes came back from that reach and met his own a moment. 'Are you very sure the "ghost" of one doesn't, much rather, serve – ?'

He had a positive sense of turning pale. But it was as near as they were then to come. For he made answer, he believed, between a glare and a grin: 'Oh ghosts – of course the place must swarm with them! I should be ashamed of it if it didn't. Poor Mrs Muldoon's right, and it's why I haven't asked her to do more than look in.'

Miss Staverton's gaze again lost itself, and things she didn't utter, it was clear, came and went in her mind. She might even for the minute, off there in the fine room, have imagined some element dimly gathering. Simplified like the death-mask of a handsome face, it perhaps produced for her just then an effect akin to the stir of an expression in the 'set' commemorative plaster. Yet whatever her impression may have been she produced instead a vague platitude. 'Well, if it were only furnished and lived in – '

She appeared to imply that in case of its being still furnished he might have been a little less opposed to the idea of a return. But she passed straight into the vestibule as if to leave her words behind her, and the next moment he had opened the house-door and was standing with her on the steps. He closed the door and, while he re-pocketed his key, looking up and down, they took in the comparatively harsh actuality of the Avenue, which reminded him of the assault of the outer light of the Desert on the traveller emerging from an Egyptian tomb. But he risked before they stepped into the street his gathered answer to her speech. 'For me it *is* lived in. For me it *is* furnished.' At which it was easy for her to sigh. 'Ah yes – !' all vaguely and discreetly; since his parents and his favourite sister, to say nothing of other kin, in numbers, had run their course and met their end there. That represented, within the walls, ineffaceable life.

It was a few days after this that, during an hour passed with her again, he had expressed his impatience of the too flattering curiosity – among the people he met – about his appreciation of New York. He had arrived at none at all that was socially producible, and as for that matter of his 'thinking' (thinking the better or the worse of anything there) he was wholly taken up with one subject of thought. It was mere vain egoism, and it was moreover, if she liked, a morbid obsession. He found all things come back to the question of what he personally might have been, how he might have led his life and 'turned out,' if he had not so, at the outset, given it up. And confessing for the first time to the intensity within him of this absurd speculation – which but proved also, no doubt, the habit of too selfishly thinking – he affirmed the impotence there of any other source of interest, any other native appeal. 'What would it have made of me, what would it have made of me? I keep for ever wondering, all idiotically; as if I could possibly know! I see what it has made of dozens of others, those I meet, and it positively aches within me, to the point of exasperation, that it would have made something of me as well. Only I can't make out *what*, and the worry of it, the small rage of curiosity never to be satisfied, brings back what I remember to have felt, once or twice, after judging best, for reasons, to burn some important letter unopened. I've been sorry, I've hated it – I've never known what was in the letter. You may of course say it's a trifle – !'

'I don't say it's a trifle,' Miss Staverton gravely interrupted.

She was seated by her fire, and before her, on his feet and restless, he turned to and fro between this intensity of his idea and a fitful and unseeing inspection, through his single eye-glass, of the dear little old objects on her chimney-piece. Her interruption made him for an instant look at her harder. 'I shouldn't care if you did!' he laughed, however; 'and it's only a figure, at any rate, for the way I now feel. *Not* to have followed my perverse young course – and almost in the teeth of my father's curse, as I may say; not to have kept it up, so, "over there," from that day to this, without a doubt or a pang; not, above all, to have liked it, to have loved it, so much, loved it, no doubt, with such an abysmal conceit of my own preference: some variation from *that*, I say, must have produced some different effect for my life and for my "form." I should have stuck here – if it had been possible; and I was too young, at twenty-three, to judge, *pour deux sous*, whether it *were* possible. If I had waited I might have seen it was, and then I might have been, by staying here, something nearer to one of these types who have been hammered so hard and made so keen by their conditions. It isn't that I admire them so much – the question of any charm in them, or of any charm, beyond that of the rank money-passion, exerted by their conditions *for* them, has nothing to do with the matter: it's only a question of what fantastic, yet perfectly possible, development of my own nature I mayn't have missed. It comes over me that I had then a strange *alter ego* deep down somewhere within me, as the full-blown flower is in the small tight bud, and that I just took the course, I just transferred him to the climate, that blighted him for once and for ever.'

'And you wonder about the flower,' Miss Staverton said. 'So do I, if you want to know; and so I've been wondering these several weeks. I believe in the flower,' she continued, 'I feel it would have been quite splendid, quite huge and monstrous.'

'Monstrous above all!' her visitor echoed; 'and I imagine, by the same stroke quite hideous and offensive.'

'You don't believe that,' she returned; 'if you did you wouldn't wonder. You'd know, and that would be enough for you. What you feel – and what I feel *for* you – is that you'd have had power.'

'You'd have liked me that way?' he asked.

She barely hung fire. 'How should I not have liked you?'

'I see. You'd have liked me, have preferred me, a billionaire!'

'How should I not have liked you?' she simply again asked.

He stood before her still – her question kept him motionless. He took it in, so much there was of it; and indeed his not otherwise meeting it testified to that. 'I know at least what I am,' he simply went on; 'the other side of the medal's clear enough. I've not been edifying – I believe I'm thought in a hundred quarters to have been barely decent. I've followed strange paths and worshipped strange gods; it must have come to you again and again – in fact you've admitted to me as much – that I was leading at any time these thirty years, a selfish frivolous scandalous life. And you see what it has made of me.'

She just waited, smiling at him. 'You see what it has made of *me*.'

'Oh, you're a person whom nothing can have altered. You were born to be what you are, anywhere, anyway: you've the perfection nothing else could have blighted. And don't you see how, without my exile, I shouldn't have been waiting till now – ?' But he pulled up for the strange pang.

'The great thing to see,' she presently said, 'seems to me to be that it has spoiled nothing. It hasn't spoiled your being here at last. It hasn't spoiled this. It hasn't spoiled your speaking –' She also however faltered.

He wondered at everything her controlled emotion might mean. 'Do you believe then – too dreadfully! – that I *am* as good as I might ever have been?'

'Oh no! Far from it!' With which she got up from her chair and was nearer to him. 'But I don't care,' she smiled.

'You mean I'm good enough?'

She considered a little. 'Will you believe it if I say so? I mean will you let that settle your question for you?' And then as if making out in his face that he drew back from this, that he had some idea which, however absurd, he couldn't yet bargain away: 'Oh you don't care either – but very differently: you don't care for anything but yourself.'

Spencer Brydon recognized it – it was in fact what he had absolutely professed. Yet he importantly qualified. '*He* isn't myself. He's the just so totally other person. But I do want to see him,' he added. 'And I can. And I shall.'

Their eyes met for a minute while he guessed from something in hers that she divined his strange sense. But neither of them otherwise expressed it, and her apparent understanding, with no protesting shock, no easy derision, touched him more deeply than anything yet, constituting for his stifled perversity, on the spot, an element that was like breatheable air. What she said however was unexpected. 'Well, *I've* seen him.'

'You – ?'

'I've seen him in a dream.'

'Oh a "dream" – !' It let him down.

'But twice over,' she continued. 'I saw him as I see you now.'

'You've dreamed the same dream – ?'

'Twice over,' she repeated. 'The very same.'

This did somehow a little speak to him, as it also gratified him. 'You dream about me at that rate?'

'Ah about *him*!' she smiled.

His eyes again sounded her. 'Then you know all about him.' And as she said nothing more: 'What's the wretch like?'

She hesitated, and it was as if he were pressing her so hard that, resisting for reasons of her own, she had to turn away. 'I'll tell you some other time!'

II

It was after this that there was most of a virtue for him, most of a cultivated charm, most of a preposterous secret thrill, in the particular form of surrender to his obsession and of address to what he more and more believed to be his privilege. It was what in these weeks he was living for – since he really felt life to begin but after Mrs Muldoon had retired from the scene and, visiting the ample house from attic to cellar, making sure he was alone, he knew himself in safe possession and, as he tacitly expressed it, let himself go. He sometimes came twice in the twenty-four hours; the moments he liked best were those of gathering dusk, of the short autumn twilight; this was the time of which, again and again, he found himself hoping most. Then he could, as seemed to him, most intimately wander and wait, linger and listen, feel his fine attention, never in his life before so fine, on the pulse of the great vague place: he preferred the lampless hour and only wished he might have prolonged each day the deep crepuscular spell. Later – rarely much before midnight, but then for a considerable vigil – he watched with his glimmering light; moving slowly, holding it high, playing it far, rejoicing above all, as much as he might, in open vistas, reaches of communication between rooms and by passages; the long straight chance or show as he would have called it, for the revelation he pretended to invite. It was a practice he found he could perfectly 'work' without exciting remark; no one was in the least the wiser for it; even Alice Staverton, who was moreover a well of discretion, didn't quite fully imagine.

He let himself in and let himself out with the assurance of calm proprietorship; and accident so far favoured him that, if a fat Avenue 'officer' had happened on occasion to see him entering at eleven-thirty, he had never yet, to the best of his belief, been noticed as emerging at two. He walked there on the crisp November nights, arrived regularly at the evening's end; it was as easy to do this after dining out as to take his way to a club or to his hotel. When he left his club, if he hadn't been dining out, it was ostensibly to go to his hotel; and when he left his hotel, if he had spent a part of the evening there, it was ostensibly to go to his club. Everything was easy in fine; everything conspired and promoted: there was truly even in the strain of his experience something that glossed over, something that salved and simplified, all the rest of consciousness. He circulated, talked, renewed, loosely and pleasantly, old relations – met indeed, so far as he could, new expectations and seemed to make out on the whole that in spite of the career, of such different contacts, which he had spoken of to Miss Staverton as ministering so little, for those who might have watched it, to edification, he was positively rather liked than not. He was a dim secondary social success – and all with people who had truly not an idea of him. It was all mere surface sound, this murmur of their welcome, this popping of their corks – just as his gestures of response were the extravagant shadows, emphatic in proportion as they meant little, of some game of *ombres chinoises*. He projected himself all day, in thought, straight over the bristling line of hard unconscious heads and into the other, the real, the waiting life; the life that, as soon as he had heard behind him the click of his great house-door, began for him, on the jolly corner, as beguilingly as the slow opening bars of some rich music follows the tap of the conductor's wand.

He had always caught the first effect of the steel point of his stick on the old marble of the hall pavement, large black-and-white squares that he remembered as the admiration of his childhood and that had then made in him, as he now saw, for the growth of an early conception of style. This effect was the dim reverberating tinkle as of some far-off bell hung who should say where? – in the depths of the house, of the past, of that mystical other world that might have flourished for him had he not, for weal or woe, abandoned it. On this impression he did ever the same thing; he put his stick noiselessly away in a corner – feeling the place once more in the likeness of some great glass bowl, all precious concave crystal, set delicately humming by the play of a moist finger round its edge. The concave crystal held, as it were, this mystical other world, and the indescribably fine murmur of its rim was the sigh there, the scarce audible pathetic wail to his strained ear, of all the old baffled forsworn possibilities. What he did therefore by this appeal of his hushed presence was to wake them into such measure of ghostly life as they might still enjoy. They were shy, all but unappeasably shy, but they weren't really sinister; at least they weren't as he had hitherto felt them – before they had taken the Form he so yearned to make them take, the Form he at moments saw himself in the light of fairly hunting on tiptoe, the points of his evening-shoes, from room to room and from storey to storey.

That was the essence of his vision – which was all rank folly, if one would, while he was out of the house and otherwise occupied, but which took on the last verisimilitude as soon as he was placed and posted. He knew what he meant and what he wanted: it was as clear as the figure on a cheque presented in demand for cash. His *alter ego* 'walked' – that was the note of his image of him, while his image of his motive for his own odd pastime was the desire to waylay him and meet him. He roamed, slowly, warily, but all restlessly, he himself did – Mrs Muldoon had been right, absolutely, with her figure of their 'craping'; and the presence he watched for would roam restlessly too. But it would be as cautious and as shifty; the conviction of its probable, in fact its already quite sensible, quite audible evasion of pursuit grew for him from night to night, laying on him finally a rigour to which nothing in his life had been comparable. It had been the theory of many superficially judging persons, he knew, that he was wasting that life in a surrender to sensations, but he had tasted of no pleasure so fine as his actual tension, had been introduced to no sport that demanded at once the patience and the nerve of this stalking of a creature more subtle, yet at bay perhaps more formidable, than any beast of the forest. The terms, the comparisons, the very practices of the chase positively came again into play: there were even moments when passages of his occasional experience as a sportsman, stirred memories, from his younger time, of moor and mountain and desert, revived for him – and to the increase of his keenness – by the tremendous force of analogy. He found himself at moments – once he had placed his single light on some mantelshelf or in some recess – stepping back into shelter or shade, effacing himself behind a door or in an embrasure, as he had sought of old the vantage of rock and tree; he found himself holding his breath and living in the joy of the instant, the supreme suspense created by big game alone.

He wasn't afraid (though putting himself the question as he believed gentlemen on Bengal tiger-shoots or in close quarters with the great bear of the Rockies had been known to confess to having put it); and this indeed – since here at least he might be frank! – because of the impression, so intimate and so strange, that he himself produced as yet a dread, produced certainly a strain, beyond the liveliest he was likely to feel. They fell for him into categories, they fairly became familiar, the signs, for his own perception, of the alarm his presence and his vigilance created; though leaving him always to remark, portentously, on his probably having formed a relation, his probably enjoying a consciousness, unique in the experience of man. People enough, first and last, had been in terror of apparitions, but who had ever before so turned the tables and become himself, in the apparitional world, an incalculable terror? He might have found this sublime had he quite dared to think of it; but he didn't too much insist, truly, on that side of his privilege. With habit and repetition he gained to an extraordinary degree the power to penetrate the dusk of distances and the darkness of corners, to resolve back into their innocence the treacheries of uncertain light, the evil-looking forms taken in the gloom by mere shadows, by accidents of the air, by shifting effects of perspective; putting down his dim luminary he could still wander on without it, pass into other rooms and, only knowing it was there behind him in case of need, see his way about, visually project for his purpose a comparative clearness. It made him feel, this acquired faculty, like some monstrous stealthy cat; he wondered if he would have glanced at these moments with large shining yellow eyes, and what it mightn't verily be, for the poor hard-pressed *alter ego*, to be confronted with such a type.

He liked however the open shutters; he opened everywhere those Mrs Muldoon had closed, closing them as carefully afterwards, so that she shouldn't notice: he liked — oh this he did like, and above all in the upper rooms! — the sense of the hard silver of the autumn stars through the window-panes, and scarcely less the flare of the street-lamps below, the white electric lustre which it would have taken curtains to keep out. This was human actual social; this was of the world he had lived in, and he was more at his ease certainly for the countenance, coldly general and impersonal, that all the while and in spite of his detachment it seemed to give him. He had support of course mostly in the rooms at the wide front and the prolonged side; it failed him considerably in the central shades and the parts at the back. But if he sometimes, on his rounds, was glad of his optical reach, so none the less often the rear of the house affected him as the very jungle of his prey. The place was there more subdivided; a large 'extension' in particular, where small rooms for servants had been multiplied, abounded in nooks and corners, in closets and passages, in the ramifications especially of an ample back staircase over which he leaned, many a time, to look far down – not deterred from his gravity even while aware that he might, for a spectator, have figured some solemn simpleton playing at hide-and-seek. Outside in fact he might himself make that ironic *rapprochement*; but within the walls, and in spite of the clear windows, his consistency was proof against the cynical light of New York.

It had belonged to that idea of the exasperated consciousness of his victim to become a real test for him; since he had quite put it to himself from the first that, oh distinctly! he could 'cultivate' his whole perception. He had felt it as above all open to cultivation – which indeed was but another name for his manner of spending his time. He was bringing it on, bringing it to perfection, by practice; in consequence of which it had grown so fine that he was now aware of impressions, attestations of his general postulate, that couldn't have broken upon him at once. This was the case more specifically with a phenomenon at last quite frequent for him in the upper rooms, the recognition – absolutely unmistakable, and by a turn dating from a particular hour, his resumption of his campaign after a diplomatic drop, a calculated absence of three nights – of his being definitely followed, tracked at a distance carefully taken and to the express end that he should the less confidently, less arrogantly, appear to himself merely to pursue. It worried, it finally quite broke him up, for it proved, of all the conceivable impressions, the one least suited to his book. He was kept in sight while remaining himself – as regards the essence of his position – sightless, and his only recourse then was in abrupt turns, rapid recoveries of ground. He wheeled about, retracing his steps, as if he might so catch in his face at least the stirred air of some other quick revolution. It was indeed true that his fully dislocalized thought of these manoeuvres recalled to him Pantaloon, at the Christmas farce, buffeted and tricked from behind by ubiquitous Harlequin; but it left intact the influence of the conditions themselves each time he was re-exposed to them, so that in fact this association, had he suffered it to become constant, would on a certain side have but ministered to his intenser gravity. He had made, as I have said, to create on the premises the baseless sense of a reprieve, his three absences; and the result of the third was to confirm the after-effect of the second.

On his return, that night – the night succeeding his last intermission –

he stood in the hall and looked up the staircase with a certainty more intimate than any he had yet known. 'He's *there*, at the top, and waiting – not, as in general, falling back for disappearance. He's holding his ground, and it's the first time – which is a proof, isn't it? that something has happened for him.' So Brydon argued with his hand on the banister and his foot on the lowest stair; in which position he felt as never before the air chilled by his logic. He himself turned cold in it, for he seemed of a sudden to know what now was involved. 'Harder pressed? – yes, he takes it in, with its thus making clear to him that I've come, as they say, "to stay." He finally doesn't like and can't bear it, in the sense, I mean, that his wrath, his menaced interest, now balances with his dread. I've hunted him till he has "turned": that, up there, is what has happened – he's the fanged or the antlered animal brought at last to bay.' There came to him, as I say – but determined by an influence beyond my notation! – the acuteness of this certainty; under which however the next moment he had broken into a sweat that he would as little have consented to attribute to fear as he would have dared immediately to act upon it for enterprise. It marked none the less a prodigious thrill, a thrill that represented sudden dismay, no doubt, but also represented, and with the selfsame throb, the strangest, the most joyous, possibly the next minute almost the proudest, duplication of consciousness.

'He has been dodging, retreating, hiding, but now, worked up to anger, he'll fight!' – this intense impression made a single mouthful, as it were, of terror and applause. But what was wondrous was that the applause, for the felt fact, was so eager, since, if it was his other self he was running to earth, this ineffable identity was thus in the last resort not unworthy of him. It bristled there – somewhere near at hand, however unseen still – as the hunted thing, even as the trodden worm of the adage *must* at last bristle; and Brydon at this instant tasted probably of a sensation more complex than had ever before found itself consistent with sanity. It was as if it would have shamed him that a character so associated with his own should triumphantly succeed in just skulking, should to the end not risk the open; so that the drop of this danger was, on the spot, a great lift of the whole situation. Yet with another rare shift of the same subtlety he was already trying to measure by how much more he himself might now be in peril of fear; so rejoicing that he could, in another form, actively inspire that fear, and simultaneously quaking for the form in which he might passively know it.

The apprehension of knowing it must after a little have grown in him, and the strangest moment of his adventure perhaps, the most memorable or really most interesting, afterwards, of his crisis, was the lapse of certain instants of concentrated conscious *combat*, the sense of a need to hold on to something, even after the manner of a man slipping and slipping on some awful incline; the vivid impulse, above all, to move, to act, to charge, somehow and upon something – to show himself, in a word, that he wasn't afraid. The state of 'holding-on' was thus the state to which he was momentarily reduced; if there had been anything, in the great vacancy, to seize, he would presently have been aware of having clutched it as he might under a shock at home have clutched the nearest chair-back. He had been surprised at any rate – of this he *was* aware – into something unprecedented since his original appropriation of the place; he had closed his eyes, held them tight, for a long minute, as with that instinct of dismay and that terror of vision. When he opened them the room, the other contiguous rooms, extraordinarily, seemed lighter – so light, almost, that at first he took the change for day. He stood firm, however that might be, just where he had paused; his resistance had helped him – it was as if there were something he had tided over. He knew after a little what this was – it had been in the imminent danger of flight. He had stiffened his will against going; without this he would have made for the stairs, and it seemed to him that, still with his eyes closed, he would have descended them, would have known how, straight and swiftly, to the bottom.

Well, as he had held out, here he was – still at the top, among the more intricate upper rooms and with the gauntlet of the others, of all the rest of the house, still to run when it should be his time to go. He would go at his time – only at his time: didn't he go every night very much at the same hour? He took out his watch – there was light for that: it was scarcely a quarter past one, and he had never withdrawn so soon. He reached his lodgings for the most part at two – with his walk of a quarter of an hour. He would wait for the last quarter – he wouldn't stir till then; and he kept his watch there with his eyes on it, reflecting while he held it that this deliberate wait, a wait with an effort, which he recognized, would serve perfectly for the attestation he desired to make. It would prove his courage – unless indeed the latter might most be proved by his budging at last from his place. What he mainly felt now was that, since he hadn't originally scuttled, he had his dignities – which had never in his life seemed so many – all to preserve and to carry aloft. This was before him in truth as a physical image, an image almost worthy of an age of greater romance. That remark indeed glimmered for him only to glow the next instant with a finer light; since what age of romance, after all, could have matched either the state of his mind or, 'objectively,' as they said, the wonder of his situation? The only difference would have been that, brandishing his dignities over his head as in a parchment scroll, he might then – that is in the heroic time – have proceeded downstairs with a drawn sword in his other grasp.

At present, really, the light he had set down on the mantel of the next room would have to figure his sword; which utensil, in the course of a minute, he had taken the requisite number of steps to possess himself of. The door between the rooms was open, and from the second another door opened to a third. These rooms, as he remembered, gave all three upon a common corridor as well, but there was a fourth, beyond them, without issue save through the preceding. To have moved, to have heard his step again, was appreciably a help; though even in recognizing this he lingered once more a little by the chimney-piece on which his light had rested. When he next moved, just hesitating where to turn, he found himself considering a circumstance that, after his first and comparatively vague apprehension of it, produced in him the start that often attends some pang of recollection, the violent shock of having ceased happily to forget. He had come into sight of the door in which the brief chain of communication ended and which he now surveyed from the nearer threshold, the one not directly facing it. Placed at some distance to the left of this point, it would have admitted him to the last room of the four, the room without other approach or egress, had it not, to his intimate conviction, been closed *since* his former visitation, the matter probably of a quarter of an hour before. He stared with all his eyes at the wonder of the fact, arrested again where he stood and again holding his breath while he sounded its sense. Surely it had been *subsequently* closed – that is it had been on his previous passage indubitably open!

He took it full in the face that something had happened between –
that he couldn't not have noticed before (by which he meant on his
original tour of all the rooms that evening) that such a barrier had
exceptionally presented itself. He had indeed since that moment under-
gone an agitation so extraordinary that it might have muddled for
him any earlier view; and he tried to convince himself that he might
perhaps then have gone into the room and, inadvertently, automatically,
on coming out, have drawn the door after him. The difficulty was that
this exactly was what he never did; it was against his whole policy, as he
might have said, the essence of which was to keep vistas clear. He had
them from the first, as he was well aware, quite on the brain: the strange
apparition, at the far end of one of them, of his baffled 'prey' (which
had become by so sharp an irony so little the term now to apply!) was
the form of success his imagination had most cherished, projecting into
it always a refinement of beauty. He had known fifty times the start of
perception that had afterwards dropped; had fifty times gasped to
himself 'There!' under some fond brief hallucination. The house, as the
case stood, admirably lent itself; he might wonder at the taste, the native
architecture of the particular time, which could rejoice so in the multiplication of doors – the opposite extreme to the modern, the actual
almost complete proscription of them; but it had fairly contributed to
provoke this obsession of the presence encountered telescopically, as he
might say, focused and studied in diminishing perspective and as by a
rest for the elbow.

It was with these considerations that his present attention was charged
– they perfectly availed to make what he saw portentous. He *couldn't*, by
any lapse, have blocked that aperture; and if he hadn't, if it was
unthinkable, why what else was clear but that there had been another
agent? Another agent? – he had been catching, as he felt, a moment
back, the very breath of him; but when had he been so close as in this
simple, this logical, this completely personal act? It was so logical, that is,
that one might have *taken* it for personal; yet for what did Brydon take
it, he asked himself, while, softly panting, he felt his eyes almost leave
their sockets. Ah this time at last they *were*, the two, the opposed
projections of him, in presence; and this time, as much as one would,
the question of danger loomed. With it rose, as not before, the question

of courage – for what he knew the blank face of the door to say to him was 'Show us how much you have!' It stared, it glared back at him with that challenge; it put to him the two alternatives: should he just push it open or not? Oh to have this consciousness was to *think* – and to think, Brydon knew, as he stood there, was, with the lapsing moments, not to have acted! Not to have acted – that was the misery and the pang – was even still not to act; was in fact *all* to feel the thing in another, in a new and terrible way. How long did he pause and how long did he debate? There was presently nothing to measure it; for his vibration had already changed – as just by the effect of its intensity. Shut up there, at bay, defiant, and with the prodigy of the thing palpably proveably *done*, thus giving notice like some stark signboard – under that accession of accent the situation itself had turned; and Brydon at last remarkably made up his mind on what it had turned to.

It had turned altogether to a different admonition; to a supreme hint, for him, of the value of Discretion! This slowly dawned, no doubt – for it could take its time; so perfectly, on his threshold, had he been stayed, so little as yet had he either advanced or retreated. It was the strangest of all things that now when, by his taking ten steps and applying his hand to a latch, or even his shoulder and his knee, if necessary, to a panel, all the hunger of his prime need might have been met, his high curiosity crowned, his unrest assuaged – it was amazing, but it was also exquisite and rare, that insistence should have, at a touch, quite dropped from him. Discretion – he jumped at that; and yet not, verily, at such a pitch, because it saved his nerves or his skin, but because, much more valuably, it saved the situation. When I say he 'jumped' at it I feel the consonance of this term with the fact that – at the end indeed of I know not how long – he did move again, he crossed straight to the door. He wouldn't touch it – it seemed now that he might *if* he would: he would only just wait there a little, to show, to prove, that he wouldn't. He had thus another station, close to the thin partition by which revelation was denied him; but with his eyes bent and his hands held off in a mere intensity of stillness. He listened as if there had been something to hear, but this attitude, while it lasted, was his own communication. 'If you won't then – good: I spare you and I give up. You affect me as by the appeal positively for pity: you convince me that for reasons rigid and sublime – what do I know? – we both of us should have suffered. I respect them then, and, though moved and privileged as, I believe, it has never been given to man, I retire, I renounce – never, on my honour, to try again. So rest for ever – and let *me*!'

That, for Brydon was the deep sense of this last demonstration – solemn, measured, directed, as he felt it to be. He brought it to a close, he turned away; and now verily he knew how deeply he had been stirred. He retraced his steps, taking up his candle, burnt, he observed, well-nigh to the socket, and marking again, lighten it as he would, the distinctness of his footfall; after which, in a moment, he knew himself at the other side of the house. He did here what he had not yet done at these hours – he opened half a casement, one of those in the front, and let in the air of the night; a thing he would have taken at any time previous for a sharp rupture of his spell. His spell was broken now, and it didn't matter – broken by his concession and his surrender, which made it idle henceforth that he should ever come back. The empty street – its other life so marked even by the great lamplit vacancy – was within call, within touch; he stayed there as to be in it again, high above it though he was still perched; he watched as for some comforting common fact, some vulgar human note, the passage of a scavenger or a thief, some night-bird however base. He would have blessed that sign of life; he would have welcomed positively the slow approach of his friend the policeman, whom he had hitherto only sought to avoid, and was not sure that if the patrol had come into sight he mightn't have felt the impulse to get into relation with it, to hail it, on some pretext, from his fourth floor.

The pretext that wouldn't have been too silly or too compromising, the explanation that would have saved his dignity and kept his name, in such a case, out of the papers, was not definite to him: he was so occupied with the thought of recording his Discretion – as an effect of the vow he had just uttered to his intimate adversary – that the importance of this loomed large and something had overtaken all ironically his sense of proportion. If there had been a ladder applied to the front of the house, even one of the vertiginous perpendiculars employed by painters and roofers and sometimes left standing overnight, he would have managed somehow, astride of the window-sill, to compass by outstretched leg and arm that mode of descent. If there had been some such uncanny thing as he had found in his room at hotels, a workable fire-escape in the form of notched cable or a canvas shoot, he would have availed himself of it as a proof — well, of his present delicacy. He nursed that sentiment, as the question stood, a little in vain, and even — at the end of he scarce knew, once more, how long — found it, as by the action on his mind of the failure of response of the outer world, sinking back to vague anguish. It seemed to him he had waited an age for some stir of the great grim hush; the life of the town was itself under a spell — so unnaturally, up and down the whole prospect of known and rather ugly objects, the bleakness and the silence lasted. Had they ever, he asked himself, the hard-faced houses, which had begun to look livid in the dim dawn, had they ever spoken so little to any need of his spirit? Great built voids, great crowded stillnesses put on, often, in the heart of cities, for the small hours, a sort of sinister mask, and it was of this large collective negation that Brydon presently became conscious — all the more that the break of day was, almost incredibly, now at hand, proving to him what a night he had made of it.

He looked again at his watch, saw what had become of his time-values (he had taken hours for minutes — not, as in other tense situations, minutes for hours) and the strange air of the streets was but the weak, the sullen flush of a dawn in which everything was still locked up. His choked appeal from his own open window had been the sole note of life, and he could but break off at last as for a worse despair. Yet while so deeply demoralised he was capable again of an impulse denoting — at least by his present measure — extraordinary resolution; of retracing his steps to the spot where he had turned cold with the extinction of his last pulse of doubt as to there being in the place another presence than his own. This required an effort strong enough to sicken him; but he had his reason, which overmastered for the moment everything else. There was the whole of the rest of the house to traverse, and how should he screw himself to that if the door he had seen closed were at present open? He could hold to the idea that the closing had practically been for him an act of mercy, a chance offered him to descend, depart, get off the ground and never again profane it. This conception held together, it worked; but what it meant for him depended now clearly on the amount of forbearance his recent action, or rather his recent inaction, had engendered. The image of the 'presence,' whatever it was, waiting there for him to go – this image had not yet been so concrete for his nerves as when he stopped short of the point at which certainty would have come to him. For, with all his resolution, or more exactly with all his dread, he did stop short – he hung back from really seeing. The risk was too great and his fear too definite: it took at this moment an awful specific form.

He knew – yes, as he had never known anything – that, *should* he see the door open, it would all too abjectly be the end of him. It would mean that the agent of his shame – for his shame was the deep abjection – was once more at large and in general possession; and what glared him thus in the face was the act that this would determine for him. It would send him straight about to the window he had left open, and by that window, be long ladder and dangling rope as absent as they would, he saw himself uncontrollably insanely fatally take his way to the street. The hideous chance of this he at least could avert; but he could only avert it by recoiling in time from assurance. He had the whole house to deal with, this fact was still there; only he now knew that uncertainty alone could start him. He stole back from where he had checked himself – merely to do so was suddenly like safety – and, making blindly for the greater staircase, left gaping rooms and sounding passages behind. Here was the top of the stairs, with a fine large dim descent and three spacious landings to mark off. His instinct was all for mildness, but his feet were harsh on the floors, and, strangely, when he had in a couple of minutes become aware of this, it counted somehow for help. He couldn't have spoken, the tone of his voice would have scared him, and the common conceit or resource of 'whistling in the dark' (whether literally or figuratively) have appeared basely vulgar; yet he liked none the less to hear himself go, and when he had reached his first landing – taking it all with no rush, but quite steadily – that stage of success drew from him a gasp of relief.

The house, withal, seemed immense, the scale of space again inordinate; the open rooms, to no one of which his eyes deflected, gloomed in their shuttered state like mouths of caverns; only the high skylight that formed the crown of the deep well created for him a medium in which he could advance, but which might have been, for queerness of colour, some watery under-world. He tried to think of something noble, as that his property was really grand, a splendid possession; but this nobleness took the form too of the clear delight with which he was finally to sacrifice it. They might come in now, the builders, the destroyers – they might come as soon as they would. At the end of two flights he had dropped to another zone, and from the middle of the third, with only one more left, he recognized the influence of the lower windows, of half-drawn blinds, of the occasional gleam of street-lamps, of the glazed spaces of the vestibule. This was the bottom of the sea, which showed an illumination of its own and which he even saw paved – when at a given moment he drew up to sink a long look over the banisters – with the marble squares of his childhood. By that time indubitably he felt, as he might have said in a commoner cause, better; it had allowed him to stop and draw breath, and the ease increased with the sight of the old black-and-white slabs. But what he most felt was that now surely, with the element of impunity pulling him as by hard firm hands, the case was settled for what he might have seen above had he dared that last look. The closed door, blessedly remote now, was still closed – and he had only in short to reach that of the house.

He came down further, he crossed the passage forming the access to the last flight; and if here again he stopped an instant it was almost for the sharpness of the thrill of assured escape. It made him shut his eyes – which opened again to the straight slope of the remainder of the stairs. Here was impunity still, but impunity almost excessive; inasmuch as the side-lights and the high fan-tracery of the entrance were glimmering straight into the hall; an appearance produced, he the next instant saw, by the fact that the vestibule gaped wide, that the hinged halves of the inner door had been thrown far back. Out of that again the *question* sprang at him, making his eyes, as he felt, half-start from his head, as they had done, at the top of the house, before the sign of the other door. If he had left that one open, hadn't he left this one closed, and wasn't he now in *most* immediate presence of some inconceivable occult activity? It was as sharp, the question, as a knife in his side, but the answer hung fire still and seemed to lose itself in the vague darkness to which the thin admitted dawn, glimmering archwise over the whole outer door, made

THE JOLLY CORNER

a semicircular margin, a cold silvery nimbus that seemed to play a little as he looked – to shift and expand and contract.

It was as if there had been something within it, protected by indistinctness and corresponding in extent with the opaque surface behind, the painted panels of the last barrier to his escape, of which the key was in his pocket. The indistinctness mocked him even while he stared, affected him as somehow shrouding or challenging certitude, so that after faltering an instant on his step he let himself go with the sense that here *was* at last something to meet, to touch, to take, to know – something all unnatural and dreadful, but to advance upon which was the condition for him either of liberation or of supreme defeat. The penumbra, dense and dark, was the virtual screen of a figure which stood in it as still as some image erect in a niche or as some black-vizored sentinel guarding a treasure. Brydon was to know afterwards, was to recall and make out, the particular thing he had believed during the rest of his descent. He saw, in its great grey glimmering margin, the central vagueness diminish, and he felt it to be taking the very form toward which, for so many days, the passion of his curiosity had yearned. It gloomed, it loomed, it was something, it was somebody, the prodigy of a personal presence.

Rigid and conscious, spectral yet human, a man of his own substance and stature waited there to measure himself with his power to dismay. This only could it be – this only till he recognized, with his advance, that what made the face dim was the pair of raised hands that covered it and in which, so far from being offered in defiance, it was buried as for dark deprecation. So Brydon, before him, took him in; with every fact of him now, in the higher light, hard and acute – his planted stillness, his vivid truth, his grizzled bent head and white masking hands, his queer actuality of evening-dress, of dangling double eye-glass, of gleaming silk lappet and white linen, of pearl button and gold watch-guard and polished shoe. No portrait by a great modern master could have presented him with more intensity, thrust him out of his frame with more art, as if there had been 'treatment,' of the consummate sort, in his every shade and salience. The revulsion, for our friend, had become, before he knew it, immense – this drop, in the act of apprehension, to the sense of his adversary's inscrutable manoeuvre. That meaning at least, while he gaped, it offered him; for he could but gape at his other self in this other anguish, gape as a proof that *he*, standing there for the achieved, the enjoyed, the triumphant life, couldn't be faced in his triumph. Wasn't the proof in the splendid covering hands, strong and completely spread? – so spread and so intentional that, in spite of a special verity that surpassed every other, the fact that one of these hands had lost two fingers, which were reduced to stumps, as if accidentally shot away, the face was effectually guarded and saved.

'Saved,' though, *would* it be? – Brydon breathed his wonder till the very impunity of his attitude and the very insistence of his eyes produced, as he felt, a sudden stir which showed the next instant as a deeper portent, while the head raised itself, the betrayal of a braver purpose. The hands, as he looked, began to move, to open; then, as if deciding in a flash, dropped from the face and left it uncovered and presented. Horror, with the sight, had leaped into Brydon's throat, gasping there in a sound he couldn't utter; for the bared identity was too hideous as *his*, and his glare was the passion of his protest. The face, *that* face, Spencer Brydon's? – he searched it still, but looking away from it in dismay and denial, falling straight from his height of sublimity. It was unknown, inconceivable, awful, disconnected from any possibility – ! He had been 'sold,' he inwardly moaned, stalking such game as this: the presence before him was a presence, the horror within him a horror, but the waste of his nights had been only grotesque and the success of his adventure an irony. Such an identity fitted his at *no* point, made its alternative monstrous. A thousand times yes, as it came upon him nearer now – the face was the face of a stranger. It came upon him nearer now, quite as one of those expanding fantastic images projected by the magic lantern of childhood; for the stranger, whoever he might be, evil, odious, blatant, vulgar, had advanced as for aggression, and he knew himself give ground. Then harder pressed still, sick with the force of his shock, and falling back as under the hot breath and the roused passion of a life larger than his own, a rage of personality before which his own collapsed, he felt the whole vision turn to darkness and his very feet give way. His head went round; he was going; he had gone.

What had next brought him back, clearly – though after how long? – was Mrs Muldoon's voice, coming to him from quite near, from so near that he seemed presently to see her as kneeling on the ground before him while he lay looking up at her; himself not wholly on the ground, but half-raised and upheld – conscious, yes, of tenderness of support and, more particularly, of a head pillowed in extraordinary softness and fainly refreshing fragrance. He considered, he wondered, his wit but half at his service; then another face intervened, bending more directly over him, and he finally knew that Alice Staverton had made her lap an ample and perfect cushion to him, and that she had to this end seated herself on the lowest degree of the staircase, the rest of his long person remaining stretched on his old black-and-white slabs. They were cold, these marble squares of his youth; but *he* somehow was not, in this rich return of consciousness – the most wonderful hour, little by little, that he had ever known, leaving him, as it did, so gratefully, so abysmally passive, and yet as with a treasure of intelligence waiting all round him for quiet appropriation; dissolved, he might call it, in the air of the place and producing the golden glow of a late autumn afternoon. He had come back, yes – come back from further away than any man but himself had ever travelled; but it was strange how with this sense what he had come back *to* seemed really the great thing, and if this prodigious journey had been all for the sake of it. Slowly but surely his consciousness grew, his vision of his state thus completing itself: he had been miraculousy *carried* back – lifted and carefully borne as from where he had been picked up, the uttermost end of an interminable grey passage. Even with this he was suffered to rest, and what had now brought him to knowledge was the break in the long mild motion.

It had brought him to knowledge, to knowledge – yes, this was the beauty of his state; which came to resemble more and more that of a man who has gone to sleep on some news of a great inheritance, and then, after dreaming it away, after profaning it with matters strange to it, has waked up again to serenity of certitude and has only to lie and watch it grow. This was the drift of his patience – that he had only to let it shine on him. He must moreover, with intermissions, still have been lifted and borne; since why and how else should he have known himself, later on, with the afternoon glow intenser, no longer at the foot of his stairs – situated as these now seemed at that dark other end of his tunnel – but on a deep window-bench of his high saloon, over which had been spread, couch-fashion, a mantle of soft stuff lined with grey fur that was familiar to his eyes and that one of his hands kept fondly feeling as for its pledge of truth. Mrs Muldoon's face had gone, but the other, the second he had recognized, hung over him in a way that showed how he was still propped and pillowed. He took it all in, and the more he took it the more it seemed to suffice: he was as much at peace as if he had had food and drink. It was the two women who had found him, on Mrs Muldoon's having plied, at her usual hour, her latch-key – and on her having above all arrived while Miss Staverton still lingered near the house. She had been turning away, all anxiety, from worrying the vain bell-handle – her calculation having been of the hour of the good woman's visit; but the latter, blessedly, had come up while she was still there, and they had entered together. He had then lain, beyond the vestibule, very much as he was lying now – quite, that is, as he appeared to have fallen, but all so wondrously without bruise or gash; only in a depth of stupor. What he most took in, however, at present, with the steadier clearance, was that Alice Staverton had for a long unspeakable moment not doubted he was dead.

'It must have been that I *was*.' He made it out as she held him. 'Yes – I can only have died. You brought me literally to life. Only,' he wondered, his eyes rising to her, 'only, in the name of all the benedictions, how?'

It took her but an instant to bend her face and kiss him, and something in the manner of it, and in the way her hands clasped and locked his head while he felt the cool charity and virtue of her lips, something in all this beatitude somehow answered everything. 'And now I keep you,' she said.

'Oh keep me, keep me!' he pleaded while her face still hung over him: in response to which it dropped again and stayed close, clingingly close. It was the seal of their situation – of which he tasted the impress for a long blissful moment in silence. But he came back. 'Yet how did you know – ?'

'I was uneasy. You were to have come, you remember – and you had sent no word.'

'Yes, I remember — I was to have gone to you at one to-day.' It caught on to their 'old' life and relation — which were so near and so far. 'I was still out there in my strange darkness — where was it, what was it? I must have stayed there so long.' He could but wonder at the depth and the duration of his swoon.

'Since last night?' she asked with a shade of fear for her possible indiscretion.

'Since this morning — it must have been: the cold dim dawn of to-day. Where have I been,' he vaguely wailed, 'where have I been?' He felt her hold him close, and it was as if this helped him now to make in all security his mild moan. 'What a long dark day!'

All in her tenderness she had waited a moment. 'In the cold dim dawn?' she quavered.

But he had already gone on piecing together the parts of the whole prodigy. 'As I didn't turn up you came straight — ?'

She barely cast about. 'I went first to your hotel — where they told me of your absence. You had dined out last evening and hadn't been back since. But they appeared to know you had been at your club.'

'So you had the idea of *this* — ?'

'Of what?' she asked in a moment.

'Well — of what has happened.'

'I believed at least you'd have been here. I've known, all along,' she said, 'that you've been coming.'

'"Known" it — ?'

'Well, I've believed it. I said nothing to you after that talk we had a month ago — but I felt sure. I knew you *would*,' she declared.

'That I'd persist, you mean?'

'That you'd see him.'

'Ah but I didn't!' cried Brydon with his long wail. 'There's somebody — an awful beast; whom I brought, too horribly, to bay. But it's not me.'

At this she bent over him again, and her eyes were in his eyes. 'No — it's not you.' And it was as if, while her face hovered, he might have made out in it, hadn't it been so near, some particular meaning blurred by a smile. 'No, thank heaven,' she repeated — 'it's not you! Of course it wasn't to have been.'

'Ah but it *was*,' he gently insisted. And he stared before him now as he had been staring for so many weeks. 'I was to have known myself.'

'You couldn't!' she returned consolingly. And then reverting, and as if to account further for what she had herself done, 'But it wasn't only *that*, that you hadn't been at home,' she went on. 'I waited till the hour at which we had found Mrs Muldoon that day of my going with you; and she arrived, as I've told you, while, failing to bring any one to the door, I lingered in my despair on the steps. After a little, if she hadn't come, by such a mercy, I should have found means to hunt her up. But it wasn't,' said Alice Staverton, as if once more with her fine intention – 'it wasn't only that.'

His eyes, as he lay, turned back to her. 'What more then?'

She met it, the wonder she had stirred. 'In the cold dim dawn, you say? Well, in the cold dim dawn of this morning I too saw you.'

'Saw *me* – ?'

'Saw *him*,' said Alice Staverton. 'It must have been at the same moment.'

He lay an instant taking it in – as if he wished to be quite reasonable. 'At the same moment?'

'Yes – in my dream again, the same one I've named to you. He came back to me. Then I knew it for a sign. He had come to you.'

At this Brydon raised himself; he had to see her better. She helped him when she understood his movement, and he sat up, steadying himself beside her there on the window-bench and with his right hand grasping her left. '*He* didn't come to me.'

'You came to yourself,' she beautifully smiled.

'Ah I've come to myself now – thanks to you, dearest. But this brute, with his awful face – this brute's a black stranger. He's none of *me*, even as I *might* have been,' Brydon sturdily declared.

But she kept the clearness that was like the breath of infallibility. 'Isn't the whole point that you'd have been different?'

He almost scowled for it. 'As different as *that* – ?'

Her look again was more beautiful to him than the things of this world. 'Haven't you exactly wanted to know *how* different? So this morning,' she said, 'you appeared to me.'

'Like *him*?'

'A black stranger!'

'Then how did you know it was I?'

'Because, as I told you weeks ago, my mind, my imagination, had worked so over what you might, what you mightn't have been – to show you, you see, how I've thought of you. In the midst of that you came to me – that my wonder might be answered. So I knew,' she went on; 'and believed that, since the question held you too so fast, as you told me that day, you too would see for yourself. And when this morning I again saw I knew it would be because you had – and also then, from the first moment, because you somehow wanted me. *He* seemed to tell me of that. So why,' she strangely smiled, 'shouldn't I like him?'

It brought Spencer Brydon to his feet. 'You "like" that horror – ?'

'I *could* have liked him. And to me,' she said, 'he was no horror. I had accepted him.'

'"Accepted" – ?' Brydon oddly sounded.

'Before, for the interest of his difference – yes. And as *I* didn't disown him, as *I* knew him – which you at last, confronted with him in his difference, so cruelly didn't, my dear – well, he must have been, you see, less dreadful to me. And it may have pleased him that I pitied him.'

She was beside him on her feet, but still holding his hand – still with her arm supporting him. But though it all brought for him thus a dim light, 'You "pitied" him?' he grudgingly, resentfully asked.

'He has been unhappy, he has been ravaged,' she said.

'And haven't I been unhappy? Am not I – you've only to look at me! – ravaged?'

'Ah I don't say I like him *better*,' she granted after a thought. 'But he's grim, he's worn – and things have happened to him. He doesn't make shift, for sight, with your charming monocle.'

'No' – it struck Brydon: 'I couldn't have sported mine "downtown." They'd have guyed me there.'

'His great convex pince-nez – I saw it, I recognized the kind – is for his poor ruined sight. And his poor right hand – !'

'Ah!' Brydon winced – whether for his proved identity or for his lost fingers. Then, 'He has a million a year,' he lucidly added. 'But he hasn't you.'

'And he isn't – no, he isn't – *you*!' she murmured as he drew her to his breast.

THE VELVET GLOVE

H E thought he had already, poor John Berridge, tasted in their fullness the sweets of success; but nothing yet had been more charming to him than when the young Lord, as he irresistibly and, for greater certitude, quite correctly figured him, fairly sought out, in Paris, the new literary star that had begun to hang, with a fresh red light, over the vast, even though rather confused, Anglo-Saxon horizon; positively approaching that celebrity with a shy and artless appeal. The young Lord invoked on this occasion the celebrity's prized judgement of a special literary case; and Berridge could take the whole manner of it for one of the 'quaintest' little acts displayed to his amused eyes, up to now, on the stage of European society – albeit these eyes were quite aware, in general, of missing everywhere no more of the human scene than possible, and of having of late been particularly awake to the large extensions of it spread before him (since so he could but fondly read his fate) under the omen of his prodigious 'hit.' It was because of his hit that he was having rare opportunities – of which he was so honestly and humbly proposing, as he would have said, to make the most: it was because every one in the world (so far had the thing gone) was reading *The Heart of Gold* as just a slightly too fat volume, or sitting out the same as just a fifth-act too long play, that he found himself floated on a tide he would scarce have dared to show his favourite hero sustained by, found a hundred agreeable and interesting things happen to him which were all, one way or another, affluents of the golden stream.

The great renewed resonance – renewed by the incredible luck of the play – was always in his ears without so much as a conscious turn of his head to listen; so that the queer world of his fame was not the mere usual field of the Anglo-Saxon boom, but positively the bottom of the *whole* theatric sea, unplumbed source of the wave that had borne him in the course of a year or two over German, French, Italian, Russian, Scandinavian footlights. Paris itself really appeared for the hour the centre of his cyclone, with reports and 'returns,' to say nothing of agents and emissaries, converging from the minor capitals; though his impatience was scarce the less keen to get back to London, where his work had had no such critical excoriation to survive, no such lesson of anguish to learn, as it had received at the hand of supreme authority, of that French authority which was in such a matter the only one to be artistically reckoned with. If his spirit indeed had had to reckon with it his fourth act practically hadn't: it continued to make him blush every night for the public more even than the inimitable *feuilleton* had made him blush for himself.

This had figured, however, after all, the one bad drop in his cup; so that, for the rest, his high-water mark might well have been, that evening at Gloriani's[1] studio, the approach of his odd and charming applicant, vaguely introduced at the latter's very own request by their hostess, who, with an honest, helpless, genial gesture, washed her fat begemmed hands of the name and identity of either, but left the fresh, fair, ever so habitually assured, yet ever so easily awkward Englishman with his plea to put forth. There was that in this pleasant personage which could still make Berridge wonder what conception of profit from him might have, all incalculably, taken form in such a head – these being truly the last intrenchments of our hero's modesty. He wondered, the splendid young man, he wondered awfully, he wondered (it was unmistakable) quite nervously, he wondered, to John's ardent and acute imagination, quite beautifully, if the author of *The Heart of Gold* would mind just looking at a book by a friend of his, a great friend, which he himself believed rather clever, and had in fact found very charming, but as to which – if it really wouldn't bore Mr Berridge – he should so like the verdict of some one who knew. His friend was awfully ambitious, and he thought there was something in it – with all of which might he send the book to any address?

Berridge thought of many things while the young Lord thus charged upon him, and it was odd that no one of them was any question of the possible worth of the offered achievement – which, for that matter, was certain to be of the quality of *all* the books, to say nothing of the plays, and the projects for plays, with which, for some time past, he had seen his daily postbag distended. He had made out, on looking at these things, no difference at all from one to the other. Here, however, was something more – something that made his fellow-guest's overture *independently* interesting and, as he might imagine, important. He smiled, he was friendly and vague; said 'A work of fiction, I suppose?' and that he didn't pretend ever to pronounce, that he in fact quite hated, always, to have to, not 'knowing,' as he felt, any better than anyone else; but would gladly look at anything, under that demur, if it would give any pleasure. Perhaps the very brightest and most diamond-like twinkle he had yet seen the star of his renown emit was just the light brought into his young Lord's eyes by this so easy consent to oblige. It was easy because the presence before him was from moment to moment referring itself back to some recent observation or memory; something caught somewhere, within a few weeks or months, as he had moved about, and that seemed to flutter forth at this stir of the folded leaves of his recent experience very much as a gathered faded flower, placed there for 'pressing,' might drop from between the pages of a volume opened at hazard.

He had seen him before, this splendid and sympathetic person – whose flattering appeal was by no means *all* that made him sympathetic; he had met him, had noted, had wondered about him, had in fact imaginatively, intellectually, so to speak, quite yearned over him, in some conjunction lately, though ever so fleetingly, apprehended: which circumstance constituted precisely an association as tormenting, for the few minutes, as it was vague, and set him to sounding, intensely and vainly, the face that itself figured everything agreeable except recognition. He couldn't remember, and the young man didn't; distinctly, yes, they had been in presence, during the previous winter, by some chance of travel, through Sicily, through Italy, through the south of France, but his *Seigneurie* – so Berridge liked exotically to phrase it – had then (in ignorance of the present reasons) not noticed *him*. It was positive for the man of established identity, all the while too, and through the perfect lucidity of his sense of achievement in an air 'conducting' nothing but the loudest bang, that this was fundamentally much less remarkable than the fact of his being made up to in such a quarter now. That was the disservice, in a manner, of one's having so much imagination: the mysterious values of other types kept looming larger before you than the doubtless often higher but comparatively familiar ones of your own, and if you had anything of the artist's real feeling for life the attraction and amusement of possibilities so projected were worth more to you, in nineteen moods out of twenty, than the sufficiency, the serenity, the felicity, whatever it might be, of your stale personal certitudes. You were intellectually, you were 'artistically' rather abject, in fine, if your curiosity (in the grand sense of the term) wasn't worth more to you than your dignity. What *was* your dignity, 'anyway,' but just the consistency of your curiosity, and what moments were ever so ignoble for you as, under the blighting breath of the false gods, stupid conventions, traditions, examples, your lapses from that consistency? His *Seigneurie*, at all events, delightfully, hadn't the least real idea of what any John Berridge was talking about, and the latter felt that if he had been less beautifully witless, and thereby less true to his right figure, it might scarce have been forgiven him.

His right figure was that of life in irreflective joy and at the highest thinkable level of prepared security and unconscious insolence. What was the pale page of fiction compared with the intimately personal adventure that, in almost any direction, he would have been all so stupidly, all so gallantly, all so instinctively and, by every presumption, so prevailingly ready for? Berridge would have given six months' 'royalties' for even an hour of his looser dormant consciousness – since one was oneself, after all, no worm, but an heir of all the ages too – and yet without being able to supply chapter and verse for the felt, the huge difference. His *Seigneurie* was tall and straight, but so, thank goodness, was the author of *The Heart of Gold*, who had no such vulgar 'mug' either; and there was no intrinsic inferiority in being a bit inordinately, and so it might have seemed a bit strikingly, black-browed instead of being fair as the morning. Again while his new friend delivered himself our own tried in vain to place him; he indulged in plenty of pleasant, if rather restlessly headlong sound, the confessed incoherence of a happy mortal who had always many things 'on,' and who, while waiting at any moment for connections and consummations, had fallen into the way of talking, as they said, all artlessly, and a trifle more betrayingly, against time. He would always be having appointments, and somehow of a high 'romantic' order, to keep, and the imperfect punctualities of others to wait for – though who would be of a quality to make such a pampered personage wait very much our young analyst could only enjoy asking himself. There were women who might be of a quality – half a dozen of those perhaps, of those alone, about the world; our friend was as sure of this, by the end of four minutes, as if he knew all about it.

After saying he would send him the book the young Lord indeed dropped that subject; he had asked where he might send it, and had had an 'Oh, I shall remember!' on John's mention of an hotel; but he had made no further dash into literature, and it was ten to one that this would be the last the distinguished author might hear of the volume. Such again was a note of these high existences – that made one content to ask of them no whit of other consistency than that of carrying off the particular occasion, whatever it might be, in a dazzle of amiability and felicity and leaving *that* as a sufficient trace of their passage. Sought and achieved consistency was but an angular, a secondary motion; compared with the air of complete freedom it might have an effect of deformity. There was no placing this figure of radiant ease, for Berridge, in any relation that didn't appear not good enough – that is among the relations that hadn't been too good for Berridge himself. He was all right where he was; the great Gloriani somehow made that law; his house, with his supreme artistic position, was good enough for anyone, and tonight in especial there were charming people, more charming than our friend could recall from any other scene, as the natural train or circle, as he might say, of such a presence. For an instant he thought he had got the face as a specimen of imperturbability watched, with wonder, across the hushed rattle of roulette at Monte Carlo; but this quickly became as improbable as any question of a vulgar *table d'hôte*, or a steamboat deck, or a herd of fellow-pilgrims cicerone-led, or even an opera-box serving, during a performance, for frame of a type observed from the stalls. One placed young gods and goddesses only when one placed them on Olympus, and it met the case, always, that they were of Olympian race, and that they glimmered for one, at the best, through their silver cloud, like the visiting apparitions in an epic.

This was brief and beautiful indeed till something happened that gave it, for Berridge, on the spot, a prodigious extension – an extension really as prodigious, after a little, as if he had suddenly seen the silver clouds multiply and then the whole of Olympus presently open. Music, breaking upon the large air, enjoined immediate attention, and in a moment he was listening, with the rest of the company, to an eminent tenor, who stood by the piano; and was aware, with it, that his Englishman had turned away and that in the vast, rich, tapestried room where, in spite of figures and objects so numerous, clear spaces, wide vistas and, as they might be called, becoming situations abounded, there had been from elsewhere, at the signal of unmistakable song, a rapid accession of guests. At first he but took this in, and the way that several young women, for whom seats had been found, looked charming in the rapt attitude; while even the men, mostly standing and grouped, 'composed,' in their stillness, scarce less impressively, under the sway of the divine voice. It ruled the scene, to the last intensity, and yet our young man's fine sense found still a resource in the range of the eyes, without sound or motion, while all the rest of consciousness was held down as by a hand mailed in silver.[2] It was better, in this way, than the opera – John alertly thought of that: the composition sung might be Wagnerian, but no Tristram, no Iseult, no Parsifal and no Kundry of them all could ever show, could ever 'act' to the music, as our friend had thus the power of seeing his dear contemporaries of either sex (armoured *they* so otherwise than in cheap Teutonic tinsel!) just continuously and inscrutably sit to it.

It made, the whole thing together, an enchantment amid which he had in truth, at a given moment, ceased to distinguish parts – so that he was himself certainly at last soaring as high as the singer's voice and forgetting, in a lost gaze at the splendid ceiling, everything of the occasion but what his intelligence poured into it. This, as happened, was a flight so sublime that by the time he had dropped his eyes again a cluster of persons near the main door had just parted to give way to a belated lady who slipped in, through the gap made for her, and stood for some minutes full in his view. It was a proof of the perfect hush that no one stirred to offer her a seat, and her entrance, in her high grace, had yet been so noiseless that she could remain at once immensely exposed and completely unabashed. For Berridge, once more, if the scenic show before him so melted into the music, here precisely might have been the heroine herself advancing to the footlights at her cue. The interest deepened to a thrill, and everything, at the touch of his recognition of this personage, absolutely the most beautiful woman now present, fell exquisitely together and gave him what he had been wanting from the moment of his taking in his young Englishman.

It was there, the missing connection: her arrival had on the instant lighted it by a flash. Olympian herself, supremely, divinely Olympian, she had arrived, could *only* have arrived, for the one person present of really equal race, our young man's late converser, whose flattering demonstration might now stand for one of the odd extravagant forms taken by nervous impatience. This charming, this dazzling woman had been one member of the couple disturbed, to his intimate conviction, the autumn previous, on his being pushed by the officials, at the last moment, into a compartment of the train that was to take him from Cremona to Mantua – where, failing a stop, he had had to keep his place. The other member, by whose felt but unseized identity he had been haunted, was the unconsciously insolent form of guaranteed happiness he had just been engaged with. The sense of the admirable intimacy that, having taken its precautions, had not reckoned with his irruption – this image had remained with him; to say nothing of the interest of aspect of the associated figures, so stamped somehow with rarity, so beautifully distinct from the common occupants of padded corners, and yet on the subject of whom, for the romantic structure he was immediately to raise, he had not had a scrap of evidence.

If he had imputed to them conditions it was all his own doing: it came from his inveterate habit of abysmal imputation, the snatching of the ell wherever the inch peeped out, without which where would have been the tolerability of life? It didn't matter now what he had imputed – and he always held that his expenses of imputation were, at the worst, a compliment to those inspiring them. It only mattered that each of the pair had been then what he really saw each now – full, that is, of the pride of their youth and beauty and fortune and freedom, though at the same time particularly preoccupied: preoccupied, that is, with the affairs, and above all with the passions, of Olympus. Who had they been, and what? Whence had they come, whither were they bound, what tie united them, what adventure engaged, what felicity, tempered by what peril, magnificently, dramatically attended? These had been his questions, all so inevitable and so impertinent, at the time, and to the exclusion of any scruples over his not postulating an inane honeymoon, his not taking the 'tie,' as he should doubtless properly have done, for the mere blest matrimonial; and he now retracted not one of them, flushing as they did before him again with their old momentary life. To feel his two friends renewedly in presence – friends of the fleeting hour though they had but been, and with whom he had exchanged no sign save the vaguest of salutes on finally relieving them of his company – was only to be conscious that he hadn't, on the spot, done them, so to speak, half justice, and that, for his superior entertainment, there would be ever so much more of them to come.

II

It might already have been coming indeed, with an immense stride, when, scarce more than ten minutes later, he was aware that the distinguished stranger had brought the Princess straight across the room to speak to him. He had failed in the interval of any glimpse of their closer meeting; for the great tenor had sung another song and then stopped, immediately on which Madame Gloriani had made his pulse quicken to a different, if not to a finer, throb by hovering before him once more with the man in the world he most admired, as it were, looking at him over her shoulder. The man in the world he most admired, the greatest then of contemporary Dramatists – and bearing, independently, the name inscribed if not in deepest incision at least in thickest gilding on the rich recreative roll – this prodigious personage was actually to suffer 'presentation' to him at the good lady's generous but ineffectual hands, and had in fact the next instant, left alone with him, bowed, in formal salutation, the massive, curly, witty head, so 'romantic' yet so modern, so 'artistic' and ironic yet somehow so civic, so Gallic yet somehow so cosmic, his personal vision of which had not hitherto transcended that of the possessor of a signed and framed photograph in a consecrated quarter of a writing-table.

It was positive, however, that poor John was afterward to remember of this conjunction nothing whatever but the fact of the great man's looking at him very hard, straight in the eyes, and of his not having himself scrupled to do as much, and with a confessed intensity of appetite. It was improbable, he was to recognize, that they had, for the few minutes, only stared and grimaced, like pitted boxers or wrestlers; but what had abode with him later on, none the less, was just the cherished memory of his not having so lost presence of mind as to fail of feeding on his impression. It was precious and precarious, that was perhaps all there would be of it; and his subsequent consciousness was quite to cherish this queer view of the silence, neither awkward nor empty nor harsh, but on the contrary quite charged and brimming, that represented for him his use, his unforgettable enjoyment in fact, of his opportunity. Had nothing passed in words? Well, no misery of murmured 'homage,' thank goodness; though something must have been said, certainly, to lead up, as they put it at the theatre, to John's having asked the head of the profession, before they separated, if he by chance knew who the so radiantly handsome young woman might be, the one who had so lately come in and who wore the pale yellow dress, of the strange tone, and the magnificent pearls. They must have separated soon, it was further to have been noted; since it was before the advance of the pair, their wonderful dazzling charge upon him, that he had distinctly seen the great man, at a distance again, block out from his sight the harmony of the faded gold and the pearls – to speak only of that – and plant himself there (the mere high Atlas-back of renown to Berridge now) as for communion with them. He had blocked everything out, to this tune, effectually; with nothing of the matter left for our friend meanwhile but that, as he had said, the beautiful lady was the Princess. What Princess, or the Princess of what? – our young man had afterward wondered; his companion's reply having lost itself in the prelude of an outburst by another vocalist who had approached the piano.

It was after these things that she so incredibly came to him, attended by her adorer – since he took it for absolute that the young Lord was her adorer, as who indeed mightn't be? – and scarce waiting, in her bright simplicity, for any form of introduction. It may thus be said in a word that this was the manner in which she made our hero's acquaintance, a satisfaction that she on the spot described to him as really wanting of late to her felicity. 'I've read everything, you know, and *The Heart of Gold* three times': she put it all immediately on that ground, while the young Lord now smiled, beside her, as if it were quite the sort of thing he had done too; and while, further, the author of the work yielded to the consciousness that whereas in general he had come at last scarce to be able to bear the iteration of those words, which affected him as mere vain vocal convulsion, so not a breath of this association now attended them, so such a person as the Princess could make of them what she would. Unless it was to be really what *he* would! – this occurred to him in the very thick of the prodigy, no single shade of possibility of which was less prodigious than any other. It was a declaration, simply, the admirable young woman was treating him to, a profession of 'artistic sympathy' – for she was in a moment to use this very term that made for them a large, clear, common ether, an element all uplifted and rare, of which they could equally partake.

If she was Olympian – as in her rich and regular young beauty, that of some divine Greek mask overpainted say by Titian, she more and more appeared to him – this offered air was that of the gods themselves: she might have been, with her long rustle across the room, Artemis decorated, hung with pearls, for her worshippers, yet disconcerting them by having under an impulse just faintly fierce, snatched the cup of gold from Hebe. It was to him, John Berridge, she thus publicly offered it; and it was his over-topping *confrère* of shortly before who was the worshipper most disconcerted. John had happened to catch, even at its distance, after these friends had joined him, the momentary deep, grave estimate, in the great Dramatist's salient watching eyes, of the Princess's so singular performance: the touch perhaps this, in the whole business, that made Berridge's sense of it most sharp. The sense of it as *prodigy* didn't in the least entail his feeling abject – any more, that is, than in the due dazzled degree; for surely there would have been supreme wonder in the eagerness of her exchange of mature glory for thin notoriety, hadn't it still exceeded everything that an Olympian of such race should have found herself bothered, as they said, to 'read' at all – and most of all to read three times!

With the turn the matter took as an effect of this meeting, Berridge was more than once to find himself almost ashamed for her – since it seemed never to occur to her to be so for herself; he was jealous of the type where she might have been taken as insolently careless of it; his advantage (unless indeed it had been his ruin) being that he could inordinately reflect upon it, could wander off thereby into kinds of licence of which she was incapable. He hadn't, for himself, waited till now to be sure of what he would do were *he* an Olympian; he would leave his own stuff snugly unread, to begin with; that would be a beautiful start for an Olympian career. He should have been as unable to write those works in short as to make anything else of them; and he should have had no more arithmetic for computing fingers than any perfect-headed marble Apollo mutilated at the wrists. He should have consented to know but the grand personal adventure on the grand personal basis: nothing short of this, no poor cognizance of confusable, pettifogging things, the sphere of earth-grubbing questions and two-penny issues, would begin to be, on any side, Olympian enough.

Even the great Dramatist, with his tempered and tested steel and his immense 'assured' position, even he was not Olympian: the look, full of the torment of earth, with which he had seen the Princess turn her back, and for such a purpose, on the prized privilege of his notice, testified sufficiently to that. Still, comparatively, it was to be said, the question of a personal relation with an authority so eminent on the subject of the passions – to say nothing of the rest of his charm – might have had for an ardent young woman (and the Princess was unmistakably ardent) the absolute attraction of romance: unless, again, prodigy of prodigies, she were looking for her romance very particularly elsewhere. Yet where could she have been looking for it, Berridge was to ask himself with private intensity, in a manner to leave her so at her ease for appearing to offer *him* everything? – so free to be quite divinely gentle with him, to hover there before him in all her mild, bright, smooth sublimity and to say: 'I should be so very grateful if you'd come to see me.'

There succeeded this a space of time of which he was afterward to lose all account, was never to recover the history; his only coherent view of it being that an interruption, some incident that kept them a while separate, had then taken place, yet that during their separation, of half an hour or whatever, they had still somehow not lost sight of each other, but had found their eyes meeting, in deep communion, all across the great peopled room; meeting and wanting to meet, wanting – it was the most extraordinary thing in the world for the suppression of stages, for confessed precipitate intensity – to use together every instant of the hour that might be left them. Yet to use it for what? – unless, like beautiful fabulous figures in some old-world legend, for the frankest and almost the crudest avowal of the impression they had made on each other. He couldn't have named, later on, any other person she had during this space been engaged with, any more than he was to remember in the least what he had himself ostensibly done, who had spoken to him, whom he had spoken to, or whether he hadn't just stood and publicly gaped or languished.

Ah, Olympians were unconventional indeed – that was a part of their high bravery and privilege; but what it also appeared to attest in this wondrous manner was that they could communicate to their chosen in three minutes, by the mere light of their eyes, the same shining cynicism. He was to wonder of course, tinglingly enough, whether he had really made an ass of himself, and there was this amount of evidence for it that there certainly *had* been a series of moments each one of which glowed with the lucid sense that, as she couldn't like him as much as *that* either for his acted clap-trap or for his printed verbiage, what it must come to was that she liked him, and to such a tune, just for himself and quite after no other fashion than that in which every goddess in the calendar had, when you came to look, sooner or later liked some prepossessing young shepherd. The question would thus have been, for him, with a still sharper eventual ache, of whether he positively *had*, as an effect of the miracle, been petrified, before fifty pair of eyes, to the posture of a prepossessing shepherd – and would perhaps have left him under the shadow of some such imputable fatuity if his consciousness hadn't, at a given moment, cleared up to still stranger things.

The agent of the change was, as quite congruously happened, none other than the shining youth whom he now seemed to himself to have been thinking of for ever so long, for a much longer time than he had ever in his life spent at an evening party, as the young Lord: which personage suddenly stood before him again, holding him up an odd object and smiling, as if in reference to it, with a gladness that at once struck our friend as almost too absurd for belief. The object was incongruous by reason of its being, to a second and less preoccupied glance, a book; and what had befallen Berridge within twenty minutes was that they – the Princess and he, that is – had got such millions of miles, or at least such thousands of years, away from *those* platitudes. The book, he found himself assuming, could only be *his* book (it seemed also to have a tawdry red cover); and there came to him memories, dreadfully false notes sounded so straight again by his new acquaintance, of certain altogether different persons who at certain altogether different parties had flourished volumes before him very much with that insinuating gesture, that arch expression and that fell intention. The meaning of these things – of all possible breaks of the charm at such an hour! – was that he should 'signature' the ugly thing, and with a characteristic quotation or sentiment: that was the way people simpered and squirmed, the way they mouthed and beckoned, when animated by such purposes; and it already, on the spot, almost broke his heart to see such a type as that of the young Lord brought, by the vulgarest of fashions, so low. This state of quick displeasure in Berridge, however, was founded on a deeper question – the question of how in the world he was to remain for himself a prepossessing shepherd if he should consent to come back to these base actualities. It was true that even while this wonderment held him, his aggressor's perfect good conscience had placed the matter in a slightly different light.

'By an extraordinary chance I've found a copy of my friend's novel on one of the tables here – I see by the inscription that she has presented it to Gloriani. So if you'd like to glance at it – !' And the young Lord, in the pride of his association with the eminent thing, held it out to Berridge as artlessly as if it had been a striking natural specimen of some sort, a rosy round apple grown in his own orchard, or an exceptional precious stone, to be admired for its weight and lustre. Berridge accepted the offer mechanically – relieved at the prompt fading of his worst fear, yet feeling in himself a tell-tale facial blankness for the still absolutely anomalous character of his friend's appeal. He was even tempted for a moment to lay the volume down without looking at it — only with some extemporized promise to borrow it of their host and take it home, to give himself to it at an easier moment. Then the very expression of his fellow-guest's own countenance determined in him a different and a still more dreadful view; in fact an immediate collapse of the dream in which he had for the splendid previous space of time been living. The young Lord himself, in his radiant costly barbarism, figured far better than John Berridge could do the prepossessing shepherd, the beautiful mythological mortal 'distinguished' by a goddess; for our hero now saw that his whole manner of dealing with his ridiculous tribute was marked exactly by the grand simplicity, the prehistoric good faith, as one might call it, of far-off romantic and 'plastic' creatures, figures of exquisite Arcadian stamp, glorified rustics like those of the train of peasants in *A Winter's Tale*, who thought nothing of such treasure-trove, on a Claude Lorrain sea-strand, as a royal infant wrapped in purple: something in that fabulous style of exhibition appearing exactly what his present demonstration might have been prompted by.[3]

The Top of the Tree, by Amy Evans — scarce credible words floating before Berridge after he had with an anguish of effort dropped his eyes on the importunate title-page — represented an object as alien to the careless grace of goddess-haunted Arcady as a washed-up 'kodak' from a wrecked ship might have been to the appreciation of some islander of wholly unvisited seas. Nothing could have been more in the tone of an islander deplorably diverted from his native interests and dignities than the glibness with which John's own child of nature went on. 'It's her pen-name, Amy Evans' — he couldn't have said it otherwise had he been a blue-chinned penny-a-liner — yet marking it with a disconnectedness of intelligence that kept up all the poetry of his own situation and only crashed into that of other persons. The reference put the author of *The Heart of Gold* quite into *his* place, but left the speaker absolutely free of Arcady. 'Thanks awfully' — Berridge somehow clutched at that, to keep everything from swimming. 'Yes, I should like to look at it,' he managed, horribly grimacing now, he believed, to say; and there was in fact a strange short interlude after this in which he scarce knew what had become of anyone or of anything; in which he only seemed to himself to stand alone in a desolate place where even its desolation didn't save him from having to stare at the greyest of printed pages. Nothing here helped anything else, since the stamped greyness didn't even in itself make it impossible his eyes should follow such sentences as: 'The loveliness of the face, which was that of the glorious period in which Pheidias reigned supreme, and which owed its most exquisite note to that shell-like curl of the upper lip which always somehow recalls for us the smile with which wind-blown Astarte[4] must have risen from the salt sea to which she owed her birth and her terrible moods'; or 'It was too much for all the passionate woman in her, and she let herself go, over the flowering land that had been, but was no longer, their love, with an effect of blighting desolation that might have proceeded from one of the more physical, though not more awful, convulsions of nature.'

He seemed to know later on that other and much more natural things had occurred; as that, for instance, with now at last a definite intermission of the rare music that for a long time past, save at the briefest intervals, had kept all participants ostensibly attentive and motionless, and that in spite of its high quality and the supposed privilege of listening to it he had allowed himself not to catch a note of, there was a great rustling and shifting and vociferous drop to a lower plane, more marked still with the quick clearance of a way to supper and a lively dispersal of most of the guests. Hadn't he made out, through the queer glare of appearances, though they yet somehow all came to him as confused and unreal, that the Princess was no longer there, wasn't even only crowded out of his range by the immediate multiplication of her court, the obsequious court that the change of pitch had at once permitted to close round her; that Gloriani had offered her his arm, in a gallant official way, as to the greatest lady present, and that he was left with half a dozen persons more knowing than the others, who had promptly taken, singly or in couples, to a closer inspection of the fine small scattered treasures of the studio?

He himself stood there, rueful and stricken, nursing a silly red-bound book under his arm very much as if he might have been holding on tight to an upright stake, or to the nearest piece of furniture, during some impression of a sharp earthquake-shock or of an attack of dyspeptic dizziness; albeit indeed that he wasn't conscious of this absurd, this instinctive nervous clutch till the thing that was to be more wonderful than any yet suddenly flared up for him – the sight of the Princess again on the threshold of the room, poised there an instant, in her exquisite grace, for recovery of some one or of something, and then, at recognition of him, coming straight to him across the empty place as if he alone, and nobody and nothing else, were what she incredibly wanted. She was there, she was radiantly *at* him, as if she had known and loved him for ten years – ten years during which, however, she had never quite been able, in spite of undiscouraged attempts, to cure him, as goddesses *had* to cure shepherds, of his mere mortal shyness.

'Ah no, not *that* one!' she said at once, with her divine familiarity; for she had in the flash of an eye 'spotted' the particular literary production he seemed so very fondly to have possessed himself of and against which all the Amy Evans in her, as she would doubtless have put it, clearly wished on the spot to discriminate. She pulled it away from him; he let it go; he scarce knew what was happening – only made out that she distinguished the right one, the one that should have been shown him, as blue or green or purple, and intimated that her other friend, her fellow-Olympian, as Berridge had thought of him from the first, really did too clumsily bungle matters, poor dear, with his officiousness over the red one! She went on really as if she had come for that, some such rectification, some such eagerness of reunion with dear Mr Berridge, some talk, after all the tiresome music, of questions really urgent; while, thanks to the supreme strangeness of it, the high tide of golden fable floated him afresh, and her pretext and her plea, the queerness of her offered motive, melted away after the fashion of the enveloping clouds that do their office in epics and idylls.

'You didn't perhaps know I'm Amy Evans,' she smiled, 'or even perhaps that I write in English – which I love, I assure you, as much as you can yourself do, and which gives one (doesn't it? for who should know if not you?) the biggest of publics. I "just love" – don't they say? – your American millions; and all the more that they really *take* me for Amy Evans, as I've just wanted to be taken, to be loved too for myself, don't you know? – that they haven't seemed to try at all to "go behind" (don't you say?)[5] my poor dear little *nom de guerre*. But it's the new one, my last, *The Velvet Glove*, that I should like you to judge me by – if such a *corvée* isn't too horrible for you to think of; though I admit it's a move straight in the romantic direction – since after all (for I might as well make a clean breast of it) it's dear old discredited romance that I'm most in sympathy with. I'll send you *The Velvet Glove* tomorrow, if you *can* find half an hour for it; and then – and *then* – !' She paused as for the positive bright glory of her meaning.

It could only be so extraordinary, her meaning, whatever it was, that the need in him that would – whatever it was again! – meet it most absolutely formed the syllables on his lips as: 'Will you be very, *very* kind to me?'

'Ah, "kind," dear Mr Berridge? "Kind,"' she splendidly laughed, 'is nothing to what – !' But she pulled herself up again an instant. 'Well, to what I want to be! Just *see*,' she said, 'how I want to be!' It was exactly, he felt, what he couldn't *but* see – in spite of books and publics and pen-names, in spite of the really 'decadent' perversity, recalling that of the most irresponsibly insolent of the old Romans and Byzantines, that could lead a creature so formed for living and breathing her Romance, and so committed, up to the eyes, to the constant fact of her personal immersion in it and genius for it, the dreadful amateurish dance of ungrammatically scribbling it, with editions and advertisements and reviews and royalties and every other futile item: since what was more of the deep essence of throbbing intercourse itself than this very act of her having broken away from people, in the other room, to whom he was as nought, of her having, with her *crânerie*[6] of audacity and indifference, just turned her back on them all as soon as she had begun to miss him? What was more of it than her having forbidden them, by a sufficient curt ring of her own supremely silver tone, to attempt to check or criticize her freedom, than her having looked him up, at his distance, under all the noses he had put out of joint, so as to let them think whatever they might – not of herself (much she troubled to care!) but of the new champion to be reckoned with, the invincible young lion of the day? What was more of it in short than her having perhaps even positively snubbed for him the great mystified Sculptor and the great bewildered Dramatist, treated to this queer experience for the first time of their lives?

It all came back again to the really great ease of really great ladies, and to the perfect facility of everything when once they were great enough. *That* might become the delicious thing to him, he more and more felt, as soon as it should be supremely attested; it was ground he had ventured on, scenically, representationally, in the artistic sphere, but without ever dreaming he should 'realize' it thus in the social. Handsomely, gallantly just now, moreover, he didn't so much as let it occur to him that the social experience would perhaps on some future occasion richly profit further scenic efforts; he only lost himself in the consciousness of all she invited him to believe. It took licence, this consciousness, the next moment, for a tremendous further throb, from what she had gone on to say to him in so many words – though indeed the words were nothing and it was all a matter but of the implication that glimmered through them: 'Do you *want* very much your supper here?' And then while he felt himself glare, for charmed response, almost to the point of his tears rising with it: 'Because if you don't – !'

'Because if I don't – ?' She had paused, not from the faintest shade of timidity, but clearly for the pleasure of making him press.

'Why shouldn't we go together, letting me drive you home?'

'You'll come home with me?' gasped John Berridge, while the perspiration on his brow might have been the morning dew on a high lawn of Mount Ida.[7]

'No – you had better come with *me*. That's what I mean; but I certainly will come to you with pleasure some time if you'll let me.'

She made no more than that of the most fatuous of freedoms, as he felt directly he had spoken that it might have seemed to her; and before he had even time to welcome the relief of not having then himself, for beastly contrition, to make more of it, she had simply mentioned, with her affectionate ease, that she wanted to get away, that of the bores there she might easily, after a little, have too much, and that if he'd but say the word they'd nip straight out together by an independent door and be sure to find her motor in the court. What word he had found to say, he was afterward to reflect, must have little enough mattered; for he was to have kept, of what then occurred, but a single other impression, that of her great fragrant rustle beside him over the rest of the ample room and toward their nearest and friendliest resource, the door by which he had come in and which gave directly upon a staircase. This independent image was just that of the only other of his fellow-guests with whom he had been closely concerned; he had thought of him rather indeed, up to that moment, as the Princess's fellow-Olympian – but a new momentary vision of him seemed now to qualify it.

The young Lord had reappeared within a minute on the threshold, that of the passage from the supper-room, lately crossed by the Princess herself, and Berridge felt him there, saw him there, wondered about him there, all, for the first minute, without so much as a straight look at him. He would have come to learn the reason of his friend's extraordinary public demonstration – having more right to his curiosity, or his anxiety or whatever, than anyone else; he would be taking in the remarkable appearances that thus completed it, and would perhaps be showing quite a different face for them, at the point they had reached, than any that would have hitherto consorted with the beautiful security of his own position. So much, on our own young man's part, for this first flush of a presumption that he might have stirred the germs of ire in a celestial breast; so much for the moment during which nothing would have induced him to betray, to a possibly rueful member of an old aristocracy, a vulgar elation or a tickled, unaccustomed glee. His inevitable second thought was, however, it has to be confessed, another matter, which took a different turn – for, frankly, all the conscious conqueror in him, as Amy Evans would again have said, couldn't forego a probably supreme consecration. He treated himself to no prolonged reach of vision, but there was something he nevertheless fully measured for five seconds – the sharp truth of the fact, namely, of how the interested observer in the doorway must really have felt about him. Rather disconcertingly, hereupon, the sharp truth proved to be that the most amused, quite the most encouraging and the least invidious of smiles graced the young Lord's handsome countenance – forming, in short, his final contribution to a display of high social candour unprecedented in our hero's experience. No, he wasn't jealous, didn't do John Berridge the honour to be, to the extent of the least glimmer of a spark of it, but was so happy to see his immortal mistress do what she liked that he could positively beam at the odd circumstance of her almost lavishing public caresses on a gentleman not, after all, of negligible importance.

III

Well, it was all confounding enough, but this indication in particular
would have jostled our friend's grasp of the presented cup had he had,
during the next ten minutes, more independence of thought. That,
however, was out of the question when one positively felt, as with a
pang somewhere deep within, as even with a smothered cry for alarm,
one's whole sense of proportion shattered at a blow and ceasing to serve.
'Not *straight*, and not too fast, shall we?' was the ineffable young
woman's appeal to him, a few minutes later, beneath the wide glass
porch-cover that sheltered their brief wait for their chariot of fire. It was
there even as she spoke; the capped charioteer, with a great clean curve,
drew up at the steps of the porch, and the Princess's footman, before
rejoining him in front, held open the door of the car. She got in, and
Berridge was the next instant beside her; he could only say: 'As you
like, Princess – where you will; certainly let us prolong it; let us prolong
everything; don't let us have it over – strange and beautiful as it can
only be! – a moment sooner than we must.' So he spoke, in the security
of their intimate English, while the perpendicular imperturbable *valet-
de-pied*, white-faced in the electric light, closed them in and then took his
place on the box where the rigid liveried backs of the two men,
presented through the glass, were like a protecting wall; such a guarantee
of privacy as might come – it occurred to Berridge's inexpugnable
fancy – from a vision of tall guards erect round Eastern seraglios.

His companion had said something, by the time they started, about
their taking a turn, their looking out for a few of the night-views of
Paris that were so wonderful; and after that, in spite of his constantly
prized sense of knowing his enchanted city and his way about, he ceased
to follow or measure their course, content as he was with the particular
exquisite assurance it gave him. *That* was knowing Paris, of a wondrous
bland April night; that was hanging over it from vague consecrated
lamp-studded heights and taking in, spread below and afar, the great
scroll of all its irresistible story, pricked out, across river and bridge and
radiant *place*, and along quays and boulevards and avenues, and around
monumental circles and squares, in syllables of fire, and sketched and
summarized, further and further, in the dim fire-dust of endless avenues;

that was all of the essence of fond and thrilled and throbbing recognition, with a thousand things understood and a flood of response conveyed, a whole familiar possessive feeling appealed to and attested.

'From you, you know, it *would* be such a pleasure, and I think – in fact I'm sure – it would do so much for the thing in America.' Had she gone on as they went, or had there been pauses of easy and of charmed and of natural silence, breaks and drops from talk, but only into greater confidence and sweetness? – such as her very gesture now seemed a part of; her laying her gloved hand, for emphasis, on the back of his own, which rested on his knee and which took in from the act he scarce knew what melting assurance. The emphasis, it was true – this came to him even while for a minute he held his breath – seemed rather that of Amy Evans; and if her talk, while they rolled, had been in the sense of these words (he had really but felt that they were shut intimately in together, all his consciousness, all his discrimination of meanings and indications being so deeply and so exquisitely merged in that) the case wasn't as surely and sublimely, as extravagantly, as fabulously romantic for him as his excited pulses had been seeming to certify. Her hand was there on his own, in precious living proof, and splendid Paris hung over them, as a consecrating canopy, her purple night embroidered with gold; yet he waited, something stranger still having glimmered for him, waited though she left her hand, which expressed emphasis and homage and tenderness, and anything else he liked indeed – since it was all then a matter of what he next heard and what he slowly grew cold as he took from her.

'You know they do it here so charmingly – it's a compliment a clever man is always so glad to pay a literary friend, and sometimes, in the case of a great name like yours, it renders such a service to a poor little book like mine!' She spoke ever so humbly and yet ever so gaily – and still more than before with this confidence of the sincere admirer and the comrade. That, yes, through his sudden sharpening chill, was what first became distinct for him; she was mentioning somehow her explanation and her conditions – her motive, in fine, disconcerting, deplorable, dreadful, in respect to the experience, otherwise so boundless, that he had taken her as having opened to him; and she was doing it, above all, with the clearest coolness of her general privilege. What in particular she was talking about he as yet, still holding his breath, wondered; it was something she wanted him to do for her – which was exactly what he had hoped, but something of what trivial and, heaven forgive them both, of what dismal order? Most of all, meanwhile, he felt the dire penetration of two or three of the words she had used; so that after a painful minute the quaver with which he repeated them resembled his drawing, slowly, carefully, timidly, some barbed dart out of his flesh.

'A "literary friend?"' he echoed as he turned his face more to her; so that, as they sat, the whites of her eyes, near to his own, gleamed in the dusk like some silver setting of deep sapphires.

It made her smile – which in their relation now was like the breaking of a cool air-wave over the conscious sore flush that maintained itself through his general chill. 'Ah, of course you don't allow that I *am* literary – and of course if you're awfully cruel and critical and incorruptible you won't let it say for me what I so want it should!'

'Where are we, where, in the name of all that's damnably, of all that's grotesquely delusive, are we?' he said, without a sign, to himself; which was the form of his really being quite at sea as to what she was talking about. That uncertainty indeed he could but frankly betray by taking her up, as he cast about him, on the particular ambiguity that his voice perhaps already showed him to find most irritating. 'Let *it* show? "It," dear Princess – ?'

'Why, my dear man, let your Preface show, the lovely, friendly, irresistible log-rolling Preface that I've been asking you if you wouldn't be an angel and write for me.'

He took it in with a deep long gulp – he had never, it seemed to him, had to swallow anything so bitter. 'You've been asking me if I wouldn't write you a Preface?'

'To *The Velvet Glove* – after I've sent it to you and you've judged if you really can. Of course I don't want you to perjure yourself; but' – and she fairly brushed him again, at their close quarters, with her fresh fragrant smile – 'I do want you so to like me, and to say it all out beautifully and publicly.'

'You want me to like you, Princess?'

'But, heaven help us, haven't you understood?'

Nothing stranger could conceivably have been, it struck him – if he was right now – than this exquisite intimacy of her manner of setting him down on the other side of an abyss. It was as if she had lifted him first in her beautiful arms, had raised him up high, high, high, to do it, pressing him to her immortal young breast while he let himself go, and then, by some extraordinary effort of her native force and her alien quality, setting him down exactly where she wanted him to be – which was a thousand miles away from her. Once more, so preposterously face to face with her for these base issues, he took it all in; after which he felt his eyes close, for amazement, despair and shame, and his head, which he had some time before, baring his brow to the mild night, eased of its crush-hat, sink to confounded rest on the upholstered back of the seat. The act, the ceasing to see, and if possible to hear, was for the moment a retreat, an escape from a state that he felt himself fairly flattered by thinking of it as 'awkward'; the state of really wishing that his humiliation might end, and of wondering in fact if the most decent course open to him mightn't be to ask her to stop the motor and let him down.

He spoke no word for a long minute, or for considerably more than that; during which time the motor went and went, now even somewhat faster, and he knew, through his closed eyes, that the outer lights had begun to multiply and that they were getting back somewhere into the spacious and decorative quarters. He knew this, and also that his retreat, for all his attitude as of accommodating thought, his air – *that* presently and quickly came to him – of having perhaps gathered himself in, for an instant, at her behest, to turn over, in his high ingenuity, some humbugging 'rotten' phrase or formula that he might place at her service and make the note of such an effort; he became aware, I say, that his lapse was but a half-retreat, with her strenuous presence and her earnest pressure and the close, cool respiration of her good faith absolutely timing the moments of his stillness and the progress of the car. Yes, it was wondrous well, he had all but made the biggest of all fools of himself, almost as big a one as *she* was still, to every appearance, in her perfect serenity, trying to make of him, and the one straight answer to it *would* be that he should reach forward and touch the footman's shoulder and demand that the vehicle itself should make an end.

That would be an answer, however, he continued intensely to see, only to inanely importunate, to utterly superfluous Amy Evans – not a bit to his at last exquisitely patient companion, who was clearly now quite taking it from him that what kept him in his attitude was the spring of the quick desire to oblige her, the charming loyal impulse to consider a little what he could do for her, say 'handsomely yet conscientiously' (oh, the loveliness!) before he should commit himself. She was enchanted – *that* seemed to breathe upon him; she waited, she hung there, she quite bent over him, as Diana over the sleeping Endymion, while all the conscientious man of letters in him, as she might so supremely have phrased it, struggled with the more peccable, the more muddled and 'squared,' though, for her own ideal, the so much more *banal* comrade. Yes, he could keep it up now – that is he could hold out for his real reply, could meet the rather marked tension of the rest of their passage as well as she; he should be able somehow or other to make his wordless detachment, the tribute of his ostensibly deep consideration of her request, a retreat in good order. She *was*, for herself, to the last point of her guileless fatuity, Amy Evans and an asker for 'lifts,' a conceiver of twaddle both in herself and in him; or at least, so far as she fell short of all this platitude, it was no fault of the really affecting folly of her attempt to become a mere magazine mortal after the only fashion she had made out, to the intensification of her self-complacency, that she might.

Nothing might thus have touched him more – if to be touched, beyond a certain point, hadn't been to be squared – than the way she failed to divine the bearing of his thoughts; so that she had probably at no one small crisis of her life felt so much a promise in the flutter of her own as on the occasion of the beautiful act she indulged in at the very moment, he was afterward to recognize, of their sweeping into her great smooth empty, costly street – a desert, at that hour, of lavish lamplight and sculptured stone. She raised to her lips the hand she had never yet released and kept it there a moment pressed close against them; he himself closing his eyes to the deepest detachment he was capable of while he took in with a smothered sound of pain that this was the conferred bounty by which Amy Evans sought most expressively to encourage, to sustain and to reward. The motor had slackened and in a moment would stop; and meanwhile even after lowering his hand again she hadn't let it go. This enabled it, while he after a further moment roused himself to a more confessed consciousness, to form with his friend's a more active relation, to possess him of hers, in turn, and with an intention the straighter that her glove had by this time somehow come off. Bending over it without hindrance, he returned as firmly and fully as the application of all his recovered wholeness of feeling, under his moustache, might express, the consecration the bareness of his own knuckles had received; only after which it was that, still thus drawing out his grasp of her, and having let down their front glass by his free hand, he signified to the footman his view of their stopping short.

They had arrived; the high, closed *porte-cochère*, in its crested stretch of wall, awaited their approach; but his gesture took effect, the car pulled up at the edge of the pavement, the man, in an instant, was at the door and had opened it; quickly moving across the walk, the next moment, to press the bell at the gate. Berridge, as his hand now broke away, felt he had cut his cable; with which, after he had stepped out, he raised again the glass he had lowered and closed, its own being already down, the door that had released him. During these motions he had the sense of his companion, still radiant and splendid, but somehow momentarily suppressed, suspended, silvered over and celestially blurred, even as a summer moon by the loose veil of a cloud. So it was he saw her while he leaned for farewell on the open window-ledge; he took her in as her visible intensity of bright vagueness filled the circle that the interior of the car made for her. It was such a state as she would have been reduced to – he felt this, was certain of it – for the first time in her life; and it was he, poor John Berridge, after all, who would have created the condition.

'Good-night, Princess. I shan't see you again.'

Vague was indeed no word for it – shine though she might, in her screened narrow niche, as with the liquefaction of her pearls, the glimmer of her tears, the freshness of her surprise. 'You won't come in – when you've had no supper?'

He smiled at her with a purpose of kindness that could never in his life have been greater; and at first but smiled without a word. He presently shook his head, however – doubtless also with as great a sadness. 'I seem to have supped to my fill,[8] Princess. Thank you, I won't come in.'

It drew from her, while she looked at him, a long, low, anxious wail. 'And you won't do my Preface?'

'No, Princess, I won't do your Preface. Nothing would induce me to say a word in print about you. I'm in fact not sure I shall ever mention you in any manner at all as long as ever I live.'

He had felt for an instant as if he were speaking to some miraculously humanized idol, all sacred, all jewelled, all votively hung about, but made mysterious, in the recess of its shrine, by the very thickness of the accumulated lustre. And 'Then you don't like me – ?' was the marvellous sound from the image.

'Princess,' was in response the sound of the worshipper, 'Princess, I adore you. But I'm ashamed for you.'

'Ashamed – ?'

'You *are* Romance – as everything, and by what I make out every one, about you is; so what more do you want? Your Preface – the only one worth speaking of – was written long ages ago by the most beautiful imagination of man.'

Humanized at least for these moments, she could understand enough to declare that she didn't. 'I don't, I don't!'

'You don't need to understand. Don't attempt such base things. Leave those to us. Only live. Only be. *We'll* do the rest.'

She moved over – she had come close to the window. 'Ah, but, Mr Berridge – !'

He raised both hands; he shook them at her gently, in deep and soft deprecation. 'Don't sound my dreadful name. Fortunately, however, you can't help yourself.'

'Ah, *voyons!* I so want – !'

He repeated his gesture, and when he brought down his hands they closed together on both of hers, which now quite convulsively grasped the window-ledge. 'Don't speak, because when you speak you really say things –! You *are* Romance,' he pronounced afresh and with the last intensity of conviction and persuasion. 'That's all you have to do with it,' he continued while his hands, for emphasis, pressed hard on her own.

Their faces, in this way, were nearer together than ever, but with the effect of only adding to the vividness of that dire non-intelligence from which, all perversely and incalculably, her very beauty now appeared to gain relief. This made for him a pang and almost an anguish; the fear of her saying something yet again that would wretchedly prove how little he moved her perception. So his eyes, of remonstrant, of suppliant intention, met hers close, at the same time that these, so far from shrinking, but with their quite other swimming plea all bedimmed now, seemed almost to wash him with the tears of her failure. He soothed, he stroked, he reassured her hands, for tender conveyance of his meaning, quite as she had just before dealt with his own for brave demonstration of hers. It was during these instants as if the question had been which of them *could* most candidly and fraternally plead. Full but of that she kept it up. 'Ah, if you'd only think, if you'd only try – !'

He couldn't stand it – she was capable of believing he had edged away, excusing himself and trumping up a factitious theory, because he hadn't the wit, hadn't the hand, to knock off the few pleasant pages she asked him for and that any proper Frenchman, master of the *métier*, would so easily and gallantly have promised. Should she so begin to commit herself he'd, by the immortal gods, anticipate it in the manner most admirably effective – in fact he'd even thus make her further derogation impossible. Their faces were so close that he could practise any rich freedom – even though for an instant, while the back of the chauffeur guarded them on that side and his own presented breadth, amplified by his loose mantle, filled the whole window-space, leaving him no observation from any quarter to heed, he uttered, in a deep-drawn final groan, an irrepressible echo of his pang for what might have been, the muffled cry of his insistence. 'You *are* Romance!' – he drove it intimately, inordinately home, his lips, for a long moment, sealing it, with the fullest force of authority, on her own; after which, as he broke away and the car, starting again, turned powerfully across the pavement, he had no further sound from her than if, all divinely indulgent but all humanly defeated, she had given the question up, falling back to infinite wonder. He too fell back, but could still wave his hat for her as she passed to disappearance in the great floridly framed aperture whose wings at once came together behind her.[9]

CRAPY CORNELIA

I

THREE times within a quarter of an hour — shifting the while his posture on his chair of contemplation — had he looked at his watch as for its final sharp hint that he should decide, that he should get up. His seat was one of a group fairly sequestered, unoccupied save for his own presence, and from where he lingered he looked off at a stretch of lawn freshened by recent April showers and on which sundry small children were at play. The trees, the shrubs, the plants, every stem and twig just ruffled as by the first touch of the light finger of the relenting year, struck him as standing still in the blest hope of more of the same caress; the quarter about him held its breath after the fashion of the child who waits with the rigour of an open mouth and shut eyes for the promised sensible effect of his having been good. So, in the windless, sun-warmed air of the beautiful afternoon, the Park of the winter's end had struck White-Mason as waiting; even New York, under such an impression, was 'good,' good enough — for *him*: its very sounds were faint, were almost sweet, as they reached him from so seemingly far beyond the wooded horizon that formed the remoter limit of his large shallow glade. The tones of the frolic infants ceased to be nondescript and harsh, were in fact almost as fresh and decent as the frilled and puckered and ribboned garb of the little girls, which had always a way, in those parts, of so portentously flaunting the daughters of the strange native — that is of the overwhelmingly alien — populace at him.

Not that these things in particular were his matter of meditation now; he had wanted, at the end of his walk, to sit apart a little and think

– and had been doing that for twenty minutes, even though as yet to no break in the charm of procrastination. But he had looked without seeing and listened without hearing: all that had been positive for him was that he hadn't failed vaguely to feel. He had felt in the first place, and he continued to feel – yes, at forty-eight quite as much as at any point of the supposed reign of younger intensities – the great spirit of the air, the fine sense of the season, the supreme appeal of Nature, he might have said, to his time of life; quite as if she, easy, indulgent, indifferent, cynical Power, were offering him the last chance it would rest with his wit or his blood to embrace. Then with that he had been entertaining, to the point and with the prolonged consequence of accepted immobilization, the certitude that if he did call on Mrs Worthingham and find her at home he couldn't in justice to himself not put to her the question that had lapsed the other time, the last time, through the irritating and persistent, even if accidental, presence of others. What friends she had – the people who so stupidly, so wantonly stuck! If they *should*, he and she, come to an understanding, that would presumably have to include certain members of her singularly ill-composed circle, in whom it was incredible to him that he should ever take an interest. This defeat, to do himself justice – he had bent rather predominantly on *that*, you see; ideal justice to *her*, with her possible conception of what it should consist of being another and quite a different matter – he had had the fact of the Sunday afternoon to thank for; she didn't 'keep' that day for him, since they hadn't, up to now, quite begun to cultivate the appointment or assignation founded on explicit sacrifices. He might at any rate look to find this pleasant practical Wednesday – should he indeed, at his actual rate, stay it before it ebbed – more liberally and intendingly given him.

The sound he at last most wittingly distinguished in his nook was the single deep note of half-past five borne to him from some high-perched public clock. He finally got up with the sense that the time from then on *ought* at least to be felt as sacred to him. At this juncture it was – while he stood there shaking his garments, settling his hat, his necktie, his shirt-cuffs, fixing the high polish of his fine shoes as if for some reflection in it of his straight and spare and grizzled, his refined and trimmed and dressed, his altogether distinguished person, that of a gentleman abundantly settled, but of a bachelor markedly nervous – at this crisis it was, doubtless, that he at once most measured and least resented his predicament. If he should go he would almost to a certainty find her, and if he should find her he would almost to a certainty come to the point. He wouldn't put it off again – there was that high consideration for him of justice at least to himself. He had never yet denied himself anything so apparently fraught with possibilities as the idea of proposing to Mrs Worthingham – never yet, in other words, denied himself anything he had so distinctly wanted to do; and the results of that wisdom had remained for him precisely the precious parts of experience. Counting only the offers of his honourable hand, these had been on three remembered occasions at least the consequence of an impulse as sharp and a self-respect that hadn't in the least suffered, moreover, from the failure of each appeal. He had been met in the three cases – the only ones he at all compared with his present case – by the frank confession that he didn't somehow, charming as he was, cause himself to be superstitiously believed in; and the lapse of life, afterward, had cleared up many doubts.

It *wouldn't* have done, he eventually, he lucidly saw, each time he had been refused; and the candour of his nature was such that he could live to think of these very passages as a proof of how right he had been – right, that is, to have put himself forward always, by the happiest instinct, only in impossible conditions. He had the happy consciousness of having exposed the important question to the crucial test, and of having escaped, by that persistent logic, a grave mistake. What better proof of his escape than the fact that he was now free to renew the all-interesting inquiry, and should be exactly about to do so in different and better conditions? The conditions were better by as much more – as much more of his career and character, of his situation, his reputation he could even have called it, of his knowledge of life, of his somewhat extended means, of his possibly augmented charm, of his certainly improved mind and temper – as was involved in the actual impending settlement. Once he had got into motion, once he had crossed the Park and passed out of it, entering, with very little space to traverse, one of the short new streets that abutted on its east side, his step became that of a man young enough to find confidence, quite to find felicity, in the sense, in almost any sense, of action. He could still enjoy almost anything, absolutely an unpleasant thing, in default of a better, that might still remind him he wasn't so old. The standing newness of everything about him would, it was true, have weakened this cheer by too much presuming on it; Mrs Worthingham's house, before which he stopped, had that gloss of new money, that glare of a piece fresh from the mint and ringing for the first time on any counter, which seems to claim for it, in any transaction, something more than the 'face' value.

This could but be yet more the case for the impression of the observer introduced and committed. On our friend's part I mean, after his admission and while still in the hall, the sense of the general shining immediacy, of the still unhushed clamour of the shock, was perhaps stronger than he had ever known it. That broke out from every corner as the high pitch of interest, and with a candour that – no, certainly – he had never seen equalled; every particular expensive object shrieking at him in its artless pride that it had just 'come home.' He met the whole vision with something of the grimace produced on persons without goggles by the passage from a shelter to a blinding light; and if he had – by a perfectly possible chance – been 'snap-shotted' on the spot, would have struck you as showing for his first tribute to the temple of Mrs Worthingham's charming presence a scowl almost of anguish. He wasn't constitutionally, it may at once be explained for him, a goggled person; and he was condemned in New York to this frequent violence of transition – having to reckon with it whenever he went out, as who should say, from himself. The high pitch of interest, to his taste, was the pitch of history, the pitch of acquired and earned suggestion, the pitch of association, in a word; so that he lived by preference, incontestably, if not in a rich gloom, which would have been beyond his means and spirits, at least amid objects and images that confessed to the tone of time.

He had ever felt that an indispensable presence – with a need of it moreover that interfered at no point with his gentle habit, not to say his subtle art, of drawing out what was left him of his youth, of thinly and thriftily spreading the rest of that choicest jam-pot of the cupboard of consciousness over the remainder of a slice of life still possibly thick enough to bear it; or in other words of moving the melancholy limits, the significant signs, constantly a little further on, very much as property-marks or staked boundaries are sometimes stealthily shifted at night. He positively cherished in fact, as against the too inveterate gesture of distressfully guarding his eyeballs — so many New York aspects seemed to keep him at it — an ideal of adjusted appreciation, of courageous curiosity, of fairly letting the world about him, a world of constant breathless renewals and merciless substitutions, make its flaring assault on its own inordinate terms. Newness *was* value in the piece — for the acquisitor, or at least sometimes might be, even though the act of 'blowing' hard, the act marking a heated freshness of arrival, or other form of irruption, could never minister to the peace of those already and long on the field; and this if only because maturer tone was after all most appreciable and most consoling when one staggered back to it, wounded, bleeding, blinded, from the riot of the raw — or, to put the whole experience more prettily, no doubt, from excesses of light.

II

If he went in, however, with something of his more or less inevitable scowl, there were really, at the moment, two rather valid reasons for screened observation; the first of these being that the whole place seemed to reflect as never before the lustre of Mrs Worthingham's own polished and prosperous little person — to smile, it struck him, with her smile, to twinkle not only with the gleam of her lovely teeth, but with that of all her rings and brooches and bangles and other gewgaws, to curl and spasmodically cluster as in emulation of her charming complicated yellow tresses, to surround the most animated of pink-and-white, of ruffled and ribboned, of frilled and festooned Dresden china shepherdesses with exactly the right system of rococo curves and convolutions and other flourishes, a perfect bower of painted and gilded and moulded conceits. The second ground of this immediate impression of scenic extravagance, almost as if the curtain rose for him to the first act of some small and expensively mounted comic opera, was that she hadn't, after all, awaited him in fond singleness, but had again just a trifle inconsiderately exposed him to the drawback of having to reckon, for whatever design he might amiably entertain, with the presence of a third and quite superfluous person, a small black insignificant but none the less oppressive stranger. It was odd how, on the instant, the little lady engaged with her did affect him as comparatively black – very much as if that had absolutely, in such a medium, to be the graceless appearance of any item not positively of some fresh shade of a light colour or of some pretty pretension to a charming twist. Any witness of their meeting, his hostess should surely have felt, would have been a false note in the whole rosy glow; but what note so false as that of the dingy little presence that she might actually, by a refinement of her perhaps always too visible study of effect, have provided as a positive contrast or foil? Whose name and intervention, moreover, she appeared to be no more moved to mention and account for than she might have been to 'present' – whether as stretched at her feet or erect upon disciplined haunches – some shaggy old domesticated terrier or poodle.

Extraordinarily, after he had been in the room five minutes – a space of time during which his fellow-visitor had neither budged nor uttered a sound – he had made Mrs Worthingham out as all at once perfectly pleased to see him, completely aware of what he had most in mind, and singularly serene in face of his sense of their impediment. It was as if for all the world she didn't take it for one, the immobility, to say nothing of the seeming equanimity, of their tactless companion; at whom meanwhile indeed our friend himself, after his first ruffled perception, no more adventured a look than if advised by his constitutional kindness that to notice her in any degree would perforce be ungraciously to glower. He talked after a fashion with the woman as to whose power to please and amuse and serve him, as to whose really quite organized and indicated fitness for lighting up his autumn afternoon of life his conviction had lately strained itself so clear; but he was all the while carrying on an intenser exchange with his own spirit and trying to read into the charming creature's behaviour, as he could only call it, some confirmation of his theory that she also had her inward flutter and anxiously counted on him. He found support, happily for the conviction just named, in the idea, at no moment as yet really repugnant to him, the idea bound up in fact with the finer essence of her appeal, that she had her own vision too of her quality and her price, and that the last appearance she would have liked to bristle with was that of being forewarned and eager.

He had, if he came to think of it, scarce definitely warned her, and he probably wouldn't have taken to her so consciously in the first instance without an appreciative sense that, as she was a little person of twenty superficial graces, so she was also a little person with her secret pride. She might just have planted her mangy lion – not to say her muzzled house-dog – there in his path as a symbol that she wasn't cheap and easy; which would be a thing he couldn't possibly wish his future wife to have shown herself in advance, even if to him alone. That she could make him put himself such questions was precisely part of the attaching play of her iridescent surface, the shimmering interfusion of her various aspects; that of her youth with her independence – her pecuniary perhaps in particular, that of her vivacity with her beauty, that of her facility above all with her odd novelty; the high modernity, as people appeared to have come to call it, that made her so much more 'knowing' in some directions than even he, man of the world as he certainly was, could pretend to be, though all on a basis of the most unconscious and instinctive and luxurious assumption. She was 'up' to everything, aware of everything – if one counted from a short enough time back (from week before last, say, and as if quantities of history had burst upon the world within the fortnight); she was likewise surprised at nothing, and in that direction one might reckon as far ahead as the rest of her lifetime, or at any rate as the rest of his, which was all that would concern him: it was as if the suitability of the future to her personal and rather pampered tastes was what she most took for granted, so that he could see her, for all her Dresden-china shoes and her flutter of wondrous befrilled contemporary skirts, skip by the side of the coming age as over the floor of a ballroom, keeping step with its monstrous stride and prepared for every figure of the dance.

Her outlook took form to him suddenly as a great square sunny window that hung in assured fashion over the immensity of life. There rose toward it as from a vast swarming *plaza* a high tide of motion and sound; yet it was at the same time as if even while he looked her light gemmed hand, flashing on him in addition to those other things the perfect polish of the prettiest pink finger-nails in the world, had touched a spring, the most ingenious of recent devices for instant ease, which dropped half across the scene a soft-coloured mechanical blind, a

fluttered fringed awning of charmingly toned silk, such as would make a
bath of cool shade for the favoured friend leaning with her there – that
is for the happy couple itself – on the balcony. The great view would be
the prospect and privilege of the very state he coveted – since didn't he
covet it? – the state of being so securely at her side; while the wash of
privacy, as one might count it, the broad fine brush dipped into clear
umber and passed, full and wet, straight across the strong scheme of
colour, would represent the security itself, all the uplifted inner elegance,
the condition, so ideal, of being shut out from nothing and yet of
having, so gaily and breezily aloft, none of the burden or worry of
anything. Thus, as I say, for our friend, the place itself, while his vivid
impression lasted, portentously opened and spread, and what was before
him took, to his vision, though indeed at so other a crisis, the form of
the 'glimmering square'[1] of the poet; yet, for a still more remarkable
fact, with an incongruous object usurping at a given instant the privilege
of the frame and seeming, even as he looked, to block the view.

The incongruous object was a woman's head, crowned with a little
sparsely feathered black hat, an ornament quite unlike those the women
mostly noticed by White-Mason were now 'wearing,' and that grew
and grew, that came nearer and nearer, while it met his eyes, after the
manner of images in the cinematograph. It had presently loomed so
large that he saw nothing else – not only among the things at a
considerable distance, the things Mrs Worthingham would eventually,
yet unmistakably, introduce him to, but among those of this lady's
various attributes and appurtenances as to which he had been in the very
act of cultivating his consciousness. It was in the course of another
minute the most extraordinary thing in the world: everything had
altered, dropped, darkened, disappeared; his imagination had spread its
wings only to feel them flop all grotesquely at its sides as he recognized
in his hostess's quiet companion, the oppressive alien who hadn't indeed
interfered with his fanciful flight, though she had prevented his immediate declaration and brought about the thud, not to say the felt violent
shock, of his fall to earth, the perfectly plain identity of Cornelia Rasch.
It was she who had remained there at attention; it was she their
companion hadn't introduced; it was she he had forborne to face with
his fear of incivility. He stared at her – everything else went.

'Why, it has been *you* all this time?'

Miss Rasch fairly turned pale. 'I was waiting to see if you'd know me.'

'Ah, my dear Cornelia' – he came straight out with it – 'rather!'

'Well, it isn't,' she returned with a quick change to red now, 'from having taken much time to look at me!'

She smiled, she even laughed, but he could see how she had felt his unconsciousness, poor thing; the acquaintance, quite the friend of his youth, as she had been, the associate of his childhood, of his early manhood, of his middle age in fact, up to a few years back, not more than ten at the most; the associate too of so many of his associates and of almost all of his relations, those of the other time, those who had mainly gone for ever; the person in short whose noted disappearance, though it might have seemed final, had been only of recent seasons. She was present again now, all unexpectedly – he had heard of her having at last, left alone after successive deaths and with scant resources, sought economic salvation in Europe, the promised land of American thrift – she was present as this almost ancient and this oddly unassertive little rotund figure whom one seemed no more obliged to address than if she had been a black satin ottoman 'treated' with buttons and gimp; a class of object as to which the policy of blindness was imperative. He felt the need of some explanatory plea, and before he could think had uttered one at Mrs Worthingham's expense. 'Why, you see we weren't introduced!'

'No – but I didn't suppose I should have to be named to you.'

'Well, my dear woman, you haven't – do me that justice!' He could at least make this point. 'I felt all the while – !' However it would have taken him long to say what he had been feeling; and he was aware now of the pretty projected light of Mrs Worthingham's wonder. She looked as if, out for a walk with her, he had put her to the inconvenience of his stopping to speak to a strange woman in the street.

'I never supposed you knew her!' – it was to him his hostess excused herself.

This made Miss Rasch spring up, distinctly flushed, distinctly strange to behold, but not vulgarly nettled – Cornelia was incapable of that; only rather funnily bridling and laughing, only showing that this was all she had waited for, only saying just the right thing, the thing she could make so clearly a jest. 'Of course if you *had* you'd have presented him.'

Mrs Worthingham looked while answering at White-Mason. 'I didn't want you to go – which you see you do as soon as he speaks to you. But I never dreamed – !'

'That there was anything between us? Ah, there are no end of things!' He, on his side, though addressing the younger and prettier woman, looked at his fellow-guest; to whom he even continued: 'When did you get back? May I come and see you the very first thing?'

Cornelia gasped and wriggled – she practically giggled; she had lost every atom of her little old, her little young, though always unaccountable, prettiness, which used to peep so, on the bare chance of a shot, from behind indefensible features, that it almost made watching her a form of sport. He had heard vaguely of her, it came back to him (for there had been no letters; their later acquaintance, thank goodness, hadn't involved that), as experimenting, for economy, and then as settling, to the same rather dismal end, somewhere in England, at one of those intensely English places, St Leonards, Cheltenham, Bognor, Dawlish – which, awfully, *was* it? – and she now affected him for all the world as some small, squirming, exclaiming, genteelly conversing old maid of a type vaguely associated with the three-volume novels he used to feed on (besides his so often encountering it in 'real life') during a far-away stay of his own at Brighton. Odder than any element of his ex-gossip's identity itself, however, was the fact that she somehow, with it all, rejoiced his sight. Indeed the supreme oddity was that the manner of her reply to his request for leave to call should have absolutely charmed his attention. She didn't look at him; she only, from under her frumpy, crapy, curiously exotic hat, and with her good little near-sighted insinuating glare, expressed to Mrs Worthingham, while she answered him, wonderful arch things, the overdone things of a shy woman. 'Yes, you may call – but only when this dear lovely lady has done with you!' The moment after which she had gone.

III

Forty minutes later he was taking his way back from the queer miscarriage of his adventure; taking it, with no conscious positive felicity, through the very spaces that had witnessed shortly before the considerable serenity of his assurance. He had said to himself then, or had as good as said it, that, since he might do perfectly as he liked, it couldn't fail for him that he must soon retrace those steps, humming, to all intents, the first bars of a wedding march; so beautifully had it cleared up that he was 'going to like' letting Mrs Worthingham accept him. He was to have hummed no wedding-march, as it seemed to be turning out – he had none, up to now, to hum; and yet, extraordinarily, it wasn't in the least because she had refused him. Why then hadn't he liked as much as he had intended to like it putting the pleasant act, the act of not refusing him, in her power? Could it all have come from the awkward minute of his failure to decide sharply, on Cornelia's departure, whether or no he would attend her to the door? He hadn't decided at all – what the deuce had been in him? – but had danced to and fro in the room, thinking better of each impulse and then thinking worse. He had hesitated like an ass erect on absurd hind legs between two bundles of hay; the upshot of which must have been his giving the falsest impression. In what way that was to be for an instant considered had their common past committed him to crazy Cornelia? He repudiated with a whack on the gravel any ghost of an obligation.

What he could get rid of with scanter success, unfortunately, was the peculiar sharpness of his sense that, though mystified by his visible flurry – and yet not mystified enough for a sympathetic question either – his hostess had been, on the whole, even more frankly diverted: which was precisely an example of that newest, freshest, finest freedom in her, the air and the candour of assuming, not 'heartlessly,' not viciously, not even very consciously, but with a bright pampered confidence which would probably end by affecting one's nerves as the most impertinent stroke in the world, that every blest thing coming up for her in any connection was somehow matter for her general recreation. There she was again with the innocent egotism, the gilded and overflowing anarchism, really, of her doubtless quite unwitting but none the less rabid modern note. Her grace of ease was perfect, but it was all grace of ease, not a single shred of it grace of uncertainty or of difficulty – which meant, when you came to see, that, for its happy working, not a grain of provision was left by it to mere manners. This was clearly going to be the music of the future — that if people were but rich enough and furnished enough and fed enough, exercised and sanitated and manicured, and generally advised and advertised and made 'knowing' enough, *avertis* enough, as the term appeared to be nowadays in Paris, all they had to do for civility was to take the amused ironic view of those who might be less initiated. In *his* time, when he was young or even when he was only but a little less middle-aged, the best manners had been the best kindness, and the best kindness had mostly been some art of not insisting on one's luxurious differences, of concealing rather, for common humanity, if not for common decency, a part at least of the intensity or the ferocity with which one might be 'in the know.'

Oh, the 'know' — Mrs Worthingham was in it, all instinctively, inevitably and as a matter of course, up to her eyes; which didn't, however, the least little bit prevent her being as ignorant as a fish of everything that really and intimately and fundamentally concerned *him*, poor dear old White-Mason. She didn't, in the first place, so much as know who he was — by which he meant know who and what it was to *be* a White-Mason, even a poor and a dear and old one, 'anyway.' That indeed — he did her perfect justice — was of the very essence of the newness and freshness and beautiful, brave social irresponsibility by which she had originally dazzled him: just exactly that circumstance of her having no instinct for any old quality or quantity or identity, a single historic or social value, as he might say, of the New York of his already almost legendary past; and that additional one of his, on his side, having, so far as this went, cultivated blankness, cultivated positive prudence, as to her own personal background — the vagueness, at the best, with which all honest gentlefolk, the New Yorkers of his approved stock and conservative generation, were content, as for the most part they were indubitably wise, to surround the origins and antecedents and queer unimaginable early influences of persons swimming into their ken from those parts of the country that quite necessarily and naturally figured to their view as 'God-forsaken' and generally impossible.

The few scattered surviving representatives of a society once 'good' — *rari nantes in gurgite vasto*[2] — were liable, at the pass things had come to, to meet, and even amid old shades once sacred, or what was left of such,

every form of social impossibility, and, more irresistibly still, to find
these apparitions often carry themselves (often at least in the case of the
women) with a wondrous wild gallantry, equally imperturbable and
inimitable, the sort of thing that reached its maximum in Mrs Worthingham. Beyond that who ever wanted to look up their annals, to
reconstruct their steps and stages, to dot their i's in fine, or to 'go
behind' anything that was theirs? One wouldn't do that for the world –
a rudimentary discretion forbade it; and yet this check from elementary
undiscussable taste quite consorted with a due respect for them, or at
any rate with a due respect for oneself in connection with them; as was
just exemplified in what would be his own, what would be poor dear
old White-Mason's, insurmountable aversion to having, on any pretext,
the doubtless very queer spectre of the late Mr Worthingham presented
to him. No question had he asked, or would he ever ask, should his life
– that is should the success of his courtship – even intimately depend on
it, either about that obscure agent of his mistress's actual affluence or
about the happy headspring itself, and the apparently copious tributaries,
of the golden stream.

From all which marked anomalies, at any rate, what was the moral to
draw? He dropped into a Park chair again with that question, he lost
himself in the wonder of why he had come away with his homage so
very much unpaid. Yet it didn't seem at all, actually, as if he could say
or conclude, as if he could do anything but keep on worrying – just in
conformity with his being a person who, whether or no familiar with
the need to make his conduct square with his conscience and his taste
was never wholly exempt from that of making his taste and his conscience square with his conduct. To this latter occupation he further
abandoned himself, and it didn't release him from his second brooding
session till the sweet spring sunset had begun to gather and he had more
or less cleared up, in the deepening dusk, the effective relation between
the various parts of his ridiculously agitating experience. There were
vital facts he seemed thus to catch, to seize, with a nervous hand, and the
twilight helping, by their vaguely-whisked tails; unquiet truths that
swarmed out after the fashion of creatures bold only at eventide,
creatures that hovered and circled, that verily brushed his nose, in spite
of their shyness. Yes, he had practically just sat on with his 'mistress' –

heaven save the mark! – as if *not* to come to the point; as if it had absolutely come up that there would be something rather vulgar and awful in doing so. The whole stretch of his stay after Cornelia's withdrawal had been consumed by his almost ostentatiously treating himself to the opportunity of which he was to make nothing. It was as if he had sat and watched himself – that came back to him: Shall I now or shan't I? Will I now or won't I? Say within the next three minutes, say by a quarter past six, or by twenty minutes past, at the furthest – always if nothing more comes up to prevent.

What had already come up to prevent was, in the strangest and drollest, or at least in the most preposterous, way in the world, that not Cornelia's presence, but her very absence, with its distraction of his thoughts, the thoughts that lumbered after her, had made the difference; and without his being the least able to tell why and how. He put it to himself after a fashion by the image that, this distraction once created, his working round to his hostess again, his reverting to the matter of his errand, began suddenly to represent a return from so far. That was simply all – or rather a little less than all; for something else had contributed. 'I never dreamed you knew her,' and 'I never dreamed *you* did,' was inevitably what had been exchanged between them – supplemented by Mrs Worthingham's mere scrap of an explanation: 'Oh, yes – to the small extent you see. Two years ago in Switzerland when I was at a high place for an "aftercure," during twenty days of incessant rain, she was the only person in an hotel of roaring, gorging, smoking Germans with whom I couldn't have a word of talk. She and I were the only speakers of English, and were thrown together like castaways on a desert island and in a raging storm. She was ill besides, and she had no maid, and mine looked after her, and she was very grateful – writing to me later on and saying she should certainly come to see me if she ever returned to New York. She *has* returned, you see – and there she was, poor little creature!' Such was Mrs Worthingham's tribute – to which even his asking her if Miss Rasch had ever happened to speak of him caused her practically to add nothing. Visibly she had never thought again of anyone Miss Rasch had spoken of or anything Miss Rasch had said; right as she was, naturally, about her being a little clever queer creature. This was perfectly true, and yet it was probably – by being *all* she could dream of about her – what had paralysed his proper gallantry. Its effect had been not in what it simply stated, but in what, under his secretly disintegrating criticism, it almost luridly symbolized.

He had quitted his seat in the Louis Quinze drawing-room without having, as he would have described it, done anything but give the lady of the scene a superior chance not to betray a defeated hope – not, that is, to fail of the famous 'pride' mostly supposed to prop even the most infatuated women at such junctures; by which chance, to do her justice, she had thoroughly seemed to profit. But he finally rose from his later station with a feeling of better success. He had by a happy turn of his hand got hold of the most precious, the least obscure of the flitting, circling things that brushed his ears. What he wanted – as justifying for him a little further consideration – was there before him from the moment he could put it that Mrs Worthingham had no data. He almost hugged that word – it suddenly came to mean so much to him. No data, he felt, for a conception of the sort of thing the New York of 'his time' had been in his personal life – the New York so unexpectedly, so vividly, and, as he might say, so perversely called back to all his senses by its identity with that of poor Cornelia's time: since even she had had a time, small show as it was likely to make now, and his time and hers had been the same. Cornelia figured to him while he walked away as by contrast and opposition a massive little bundle of data; his impatience to go to see her sharpened as he thought of this: so certainly should he find out that wherever he might touch her, with a gentle though firm pressure, he would, as the fond visitor of old houses taps and fingers a disfeatured, over-papered wall with the conviction of a wainscot-edge beneath, recognize some small extrusion of history.

IV

There would have been a wonder for us meanwhile in his continued use, as it were, of his happy formula – brought out to Cornelia Rasch within ten minutes, or perhaps only within twenty, of his having settled into the quite comfortable chair that, two days later, she indicated to him by her fireside. He had arrived at her address through the fortunate chance of his having noticed her card, as he went out, deposited, in the good old New York fashion, on one of the rococo tables of Mrs Worthingham's hall. His eye had been caught by the pencilled indication that was to affect him, the next instant, as fairly placed there for his sake. This had really been his luck, for he shouldn't have liked to write to Mrs Worthingham for guidance – *that* he felt, though too impatient just now to analyse the reluctance. There was nobody else he could have approached for a clue, and with this reflection he was already aware of how it testified to their rare little position, his and Cornelia's – position as conscious, ironic, pathetic survivors together of a dead and buried society – that there would have been, in all the town, under such stress, not a member of their old circle left to turn to. Mrs Worthingham had practically, even if accidentally, helped him to knowledge; the last nail in the coffin of the poor dear extinct past had been planted for him by his having thus to reach his antique contemporary through perforation of the newest newness. The note of this particular recognition was in fact the more prescribed to him that the ground of Cornelia's return to a scene swept so bare of the associational charm was certainly inconspicuous. What had she then come back for? – he had asked himself that; with the effect of deciding that it probably would have been, a little, to 'look after' her remnant of property. Perhaps she had come to save what little might still remain of that shrivelled interest; perhaps she had been, by those who took care of it for her, further swindled and despoiled, so that she wished to get at the facts. Perhaps on the other hand – it was a more cheerful chance – her investments, decently administered, were making larger returns, so that the rigorous thrift of Bognor could be finally relaxed.

He had little to learn about the attraction of Europe, and rather expected that in the event of his union with Mrs Worthingham he should find himself pleading for it with the competence of one more in the 'know' about Paris and Rome, about Venice and Florence, than even she could be. He could have lived on in *his* New York, that is in the sentimental, the spiritual, the more or less romantic visitation of it; but had it been positive for him that he could live on in hers? – unless indeed the possibility of this had been just (like the famous *vertige de l'abîme*, like the solicitation of danger, or otherwise of the dreadful) the very hinge of his whole dream. However that might be, his curiosity was occupied rather with the conceivable hinge of poor Cornelia's: it was perhaps thinkable that even Mrs Worthingham's New York, once it should have become possible again at all, might have put forth to this lone exile a plea that wouldn't be in the chords of Bognor. For himself, after all, too, the attraction had been much more of the Europe over which one might move at one's ease, and which therefore could but cost, and cost much, right and left, than of the Europe adapted to scrimping. He saw himself on the whole scrimping with more zest even in Mrs Worthingham's New York than under the inspiration of Bognor. Apart from which it was yet again odd, not to say perceptibly pleasing to him, to note where the emphasis of his interest fell in this fumble of fancy over such felt oppositions as the new, the latest, the luridest power of money and the ancient reserves and moderations and mediocrities. These last struck him as showing by contrast the old brown surface and tone as of velvet rubbed and worn, shabby, and even a bit dingy, but all soft and subtle and still velvety – which meant still dignified; whereas the angular facts of current finance were as harsh and metallic and bewildering as some stacked 'exhibit' of ugly patented inventions, things his medieval mind forbade his taking in. He had, for instance, the sense of knowing the pleasant little old Rasch fortune – pleasant as far as it went; blurred memories and impressions of what it had been and what it hadn't, of how it had grown and how languished and how melted; they came back to him and put on such vividness that he could almost have figured himself testify for them before a bland and encouraging Board. The idea of taking the field in any manner on the subject of Mrs Worthingham's resources would have affected him on the other hand as an odious ordeal, some glare of embarrassment and exposure in a circle of hard unhelpful attention, of converging, derisive, unsuggestive eyes.

In Cornelia's small and quite cynically modern flat – the house had a grotesque name, 'The Gainsborough,' but at least wasn't an awful boarding-house, as he had feared, and she could receive him quite honourably, which was so much to the good – he would have been ready to use at once to her the greatest freedom of friendly allusion: 'Have you still your old "family interest" in those two houses in Seventh Avenue? – one of which was next to a corner grocery, don't you know? and was occupied as to its lower part by a candy-shop where the proportion of the stock of suspectedly stale popcorn to that of rarer and stickier joys betrayed perhaps a modest capital on the part of your father's, your grandfather's or whoever's tenant, but out of which I nevertheless remember once to have come as out of a bath of sweets, with my very garments, and even the separate hairs of my head, glued together. The other of the pair, a tobacconist's, further down, had before it a wonderful huge Indian who thrust out wooden cigars at an indifferent world – you could buy candy cigars too at the popcorn shop, and I greatly preferred them to the wooden; I remember well how I used to gape in fascination at the Indian and wonder if the last of the Mohicans was like him; besides admiring so the resources of a family whose "property" was in such forms. I haven't been round there lately – we must go round together; but don't tell me the forms have utterly perished!' It was after *that* fashion he might easily have been moved, and with almost no transition, to break out to Cornelia – quite as if taking up some old talk, some old community of gossip, just where they had left it; even with the consciousness perhaps of overdoing a little, of putting at its maximum, for the present harmony, recovery, recapture (what should he call it?) the pitch and quantity of what the past had held for them.

He didn't in fact, no doubt, dart straight off to Seventh Avenue, there being too many other old things and much nearer and long subsequent; the point was only that for everything they spoke of after he had fairly begun to lean back and stretch his legs, and after she had let him, above all, light the first of a succession of cigarettes – for everything they spoke of he positively cultivated extravagance and excess, piling up the crackling twigs as on the very altar of memory; and that by the end of half an hour she had lent herself, all gallantly, to their game. It was the game of feeding the beautiful iridescent flame, ruddy and green and gold, blue and pink and amber and silver, with anything they could pick up, anything that would burn and flicker. Thick-strown with such gleanings the occasion seemed indeed, in spite of the truth that they perhaps wouldn't have proved, under cross-examination, to have rubbed shoulders in the other life so very hard. Casual contacts, qualified communities enough, there had doubtless been, but not particular 'passages,' nothing that counted, as he might think of it, for their 'very own' together, for nobody's else at all. These shades of historic exactitude didn't signify; the more and the less that there had been made perfect terms – and just by his being there and by her rejoicing in it – with their present need to have *had* all their past could be made to appear to have given them. It was to this tune they proceeded, the least little bit as if they knowingly pretended – he giving her the example and setting her the pace of it, and she, poor dear, after a first inevitable shyness, an uncertainty of wonder, a breathlessness of courage, falling into step and going whatever length he would.

She showed herself ready for it, grasping gladly at the perception of what he must mean; and if she didn't immediately and completely fall in – not in the first half-hour, not even in the three or four others that his visit, even whenever he consulted his watch, still made nothing of – she yet understood enough as soon as she understood that, if their finer economy hadn't so beautifully served, he might have been conveying this, that and the other incoherent and easy thing by the comparatively clumsy method of sound and statement. 'No, I never made love to you; it would in fact have been absurd, and I don't care – though I almost know, in the sense of almost remembering! – who did and who didn't; but you were always about, and so was I, and, little as you may yourself care who *I* did it to, I daresay you remember (in the sense of having known of it!) any old appearances that told. But we can't afford at this time of day not to help each other to have had – well, everything there was, since there's no more of it now, nor anyway of coming by it *except so*; and therefore let us *make* together, let us make over and recreate, our lost world; for which we have after all and at the worst such a lot of material. You were in particular my poor dear sisters' friend – they thought you the funniest little brown thing possible; so isn't that again to the good? You were mine only to the extent that you were so much in and out of the house – as how much, if we come to that, wasn't one in and out, south of Thirtieth Street and north of Washington Square, in those days, those spacious, sociable, Arcadian days, that we flattered ourselves we filled with the modern fever, but that were so different from any of *these* arrangements of pretended hourly Time that dash themselves forever to pieces as from the fiftieth floors of sky-scrapers.'

This was the kind of thing that was in the air, whether he said it or not, and that could hang there even with such quite other things as more crudely came out; came in spite of its being perhaps calculated to strike us that these last would have been rather and most the unspoken and the indirect. They were Cornelia's contribution, and as soon as she had begun to talk of Mrs Worthingham – *he* didn't begin it! – they had taken their place bravely in the centre of the circle. There they made, the while, their considerable little figure, but all within the ring formed by fifty other allusions, fitful but really intenser irruptions that hovered and wavered and came and went, joining hands at moments and whirling round as in chorus, only then again to dash at the slightly huddled centre with a free twitch or peck or push or other taken liberty, after the fashion of irregular frolic motions in a country dance or a Christmas game.

'You're so in love with her and want to marry her!' – she said it all sympathetically and yearningly, poor crapy Cornelia; as if it were to be quite taken for granted that she knew all about it. And then when he had asked how she knew – why she took so informed a tone about it; all on the wonder of her seeming so much more 'in' it just at that hour than he himself quite felt he could figure for: 'Ah, how but from the dear lovely thing herself? Don't you suppose *she* knows it?'

'Oh, she absolutely "knows" it, does she?' – he fairly heard himself ask that; and with the oddest sense at once of sharply wanting the certitude and yet of seeing the question, of hearing himself say the words, through several thicknesses of some wrong medium. He came back to it from a distance; as he would have had to come back (this was again vivid to him) should he have got round again to his ripe intention three days before – after his now present but then absent friend, that is, had left him planted before his now absent but then present one for the purpose. 'Do you mean she – at all confidently! – expects?' he went on, not much minding if it couldn't but sound foolish; the time being given it for him meanwhile by the sigh, the wondering gasp, all charged with the unutterable, that the tone of his appeal set in motion. He saw his companion look at him, but it might have been with the eyes of thirty years ago; when – very likely! – he had put her some such question about some girl long since dead. Dimly at first, then more distinctly, didn't it surge back on him for the very strangeness that there had been some such passage as this between them – yes, about Mary Cardew! – in the autumn of '68?

'Why, don't you realize your situation?' Miss Rasch struck him as quite beautifully wailing – above all to such an effect of deep interest, that is, on her own part and in him.

'My situation?' – he echoed, he considered; but reminded afresh, by the note of the detached, the far-projected in it, of what he had last remembered of his sentient state on his once taking ether at the dentist's.

'Yours and hers – the situation of her adoring you. I suppose you at least know it,' Cornelia smiled.

Yes, it was like the other time and yet it wasn't. *She* was like – poor Cornelia was – everything that used to be; that somehow was most definite to him. Still he could quite reply, 'Do you call it – her adoring me – *my* situation?'

'Well, it's a part of yours, surely – if you're in love with her.'

'Am I, ridiculous old person! in love with her?' White-Mason asked.

'I may be a ridiculous old person,' Cornelia returned – 'and, for that matter, of course I *am*! But she's young and lovely and rich and clever: so what could be more natural?'

'Oh, I was applying that opprobrious epithet – !' He didn't finish, though he meant he had applied it to himself. He had got up from his seat; he turned about and, taking in, as his eyes also roamed, several objects in the room, serene and sturdy, not a bit cheap-looking, little old New York objects of '68, he made, with an inner art, as if to recognize them – made so, that is, for himself; had quite the sense for the moment of asking them, of imploring them, to recognize *him*, to be for him things of his own past. Which they truly were, he could have the next instant cried out; for it meant that if three or four of them, small sallow carte-de-visite photographs, faithfully framed but spectrally faded, hadn't in every particular, frames and balloon skirts and false 'property' balustrades of unimaginable terraces and all, the tone of time, the secret for warding and easing off the perpetual imminent ache of one's protective scowl, one would verily but have to let the scowl stiffen or to take up seriously the question of blue goggles, during what might remain of life.

V

What he actually took up from a little old Twelfth-Street table that
piously preserved the plain mahogany circle, with never a curl nor a
crook nor a hint of a brazen flourish, what he paused there a moment
for commerce with, his back presented to crapy Cornelia, who sat
taking that view of him, during this opportunity, very protrusively and
frankly and fondly, was one of the wasted mementoes just mentioned,
over which he both uttered and suppressed a small comprehensive cry.
He stood there another minute to look at it, and when he turned about
still kept it in his hand, only holding it now a little behind him. 'You
must have come back to stay – with all your beautiful things. What else
does it mean?'

'"Beautiful?"' his old friend commented with her brow all wrinkled
and her lips thrust out in expressive dispraise. They might at that rate
have been scarce more beautiful than she herself. 'Oh, don't talk so –
after Mrs Worthingham's! *They're* wonderful, if you will: such things,
such things! But one's own poor relics and odds and ends are one's own
at least; and one *has* – yes – come back to them. They're all I have in the
world to come back to. They were stored, and what I was paying – !'
Miss Rasch woefully added.

He had possession of the small old picture; he hovered there; he put
his eyes again to it intently; then again held it a little behind him as if it
might have been snatched away or the very feel of it, pressed against
him, was good to his palm. 'Mrs Worthingham's things? You think
them beautiful?'

Cornelia did now, if ever, show an odd face. 'Why, certainly,
prodigious, or whatever. Isn't that conceded?'

'No doubt every horror, at the pass we've come to, is conceded.
That's just what I complain of.'

'Do you *complain*?' – she drew it out as for surprise: she couldn't have
imagined such a thing.

'To me her things are awful. They're the newest of the new.'

'Ah, but the old forms!'

'Those are the most blatant. I mean the swaggering reproductions.'

'Oh, but,' she pleaded, 'we can't all be *really* old.'

'No, we can't, Cornelia. But *you* can – !' said White-Mason with the frankest appreciation.

She looked up at him from where she sat as he could imagine her looking up at the curate at Bognor. 'Thank you, sir! If that's all you want – !'

'It *is*,' he said, 'all I want – or almost.'

'Then no wonder such a creature as that,' she lightly moralized, 'won't suit you!'

He bent upon her, for all the weight of his question, his smoothest stare. 'You hold she certainly won't suit me?'

'Why, what can I tell about it? Haven't you by this time found out?'

'No, but I think I'm finding.' With which he began again to explore.

Miss Rasch immensely wondered. 'You mean you don't expect to come to an understanding with her?' And then, as even to this straight challenge he made at first no answer: 'Do you mean you give it up?'

He waited some instants more, but not meeting her eyes – only looking again about the room. 'What do you think of my chance?'

'Oh,' his companion cried, 'what has what I think to do with it? How can I think anything but that she must like you?'

'Yes – of course. But how much?'

'Then don't you really know?' Cornelia asked.

He kept up his walk, oddly preoccupied and still not looking at her. 'Do you, my dear?'

She waited a little. 'If you haven't really put it to her I don't suppose she knows.'

This at last arrested him again. 'My dear Cornelia, she doesn't know – !'

He had paused as for the desperate tone, or at least the large emphasis of it, so that she took him up. 'The more reason then to help her to find it out.'

'I mean,' he explained, 'that she doesn't know anything.'

'Anything?'

'Anything else, I mean – even if she does know *that*.'

Cornelia considered of it. 'But what else need she – in particular – know? Isn't that the principal thing?'

'Well' – and he resumed his circuit – 'she doesn't know anything that *we* know. But nothing,' he re-emphasized – 'nothing whatever!'

'Well, can't she do without that?'

'Evidently she can — and evidently she does, beautifully. But the question is whether *I* can !'

He had paused once more with his point — but she glared, poor Cornelia, with her wonder. 'Surely if you know for yourself — !'

'Ah, it doesn't seem enough for me to know for myself! One wants a woman,' he argued — but still, in his prolonged tour, quite without his scowl — 'to know *for* one, to know *with* one. That's what you do now,' he candidly put to her.

It made her again gape. 'Do you mean you want to marry *me*?'

He was so full of what he did mean, however, that he failed even to notice it. 'She doesn't in the least know, for instance, how old I am.'

'That's because you're so young!'

'Ah, there you are!' — and he turned off afresh and as if almost in disgust. It left her visibly perplexed — though even the perplexed Cornelia was still the exceedingly pointed; but he had come to her aid after another turn. 'Remember, please, that I'm pretty well as old as you.'

She had all her point at least, while she bridled and blinked, for this. 'You're exactly a year and ten months older.'

It checked him there for delight. 'You remember my birthday?'

She twinkled indeed like some far-off light of home. 'I remember everyone's. It's a little way I've always had — and that I've never lost.'

He looked at her accomplishment, across the room, as at some striking, some charming phenomenon. 'Well, *that's* the sort of thing I want!' All the ripe candour of his eyes confirmed it.

What could she do therefore, she seemed to ask him, but repeat her question of a moment before? — which indeed, presently she made up her mind to. 'Do you want to marry *me*?'

It had this time better success — if the term may be felt in any degree to apply. All his candour, or more of it at least, was in his slow, mild, kind, considering head-shake. 'No, Cornelia — not to *marry* you.'

His discrimination was a wonder; but since she was clearly treating him now as if everything about him was, so she could as exquisitely meet it. 'Not at least,' she convulsively smiled, 'until you've honourably tried Mrs Worthingham. Don't you really *mean* to?' she gallantly insisted.

He waited again a little; then he brought out: 'I'll tell you presently.' He came back, and as by still another mere glance over the room, to what seemed to him so much nearer. 'That table *was* old Twelfth-Street?'

'Everything here was.'

'Oh, the pure blessings! With you, ah, with you, I haven't to wear a green shade.' And he had retained meanwhile his small photograph, which he again showed himself. 'Didn't we talk of Mary Cardew?'

'Why, do you remember it?' – she marvelled to extravagance.

'You make me. You connect me with it. You connect it with *me*.' He liked to display to her this excellent use she thus had, the service she rendered. 'There are so many connections – there will *be* so many. I feel how, with you, they must all come up again for me: in fact you're bringing them out already, just while I look at you, as fast as ever you can. The fact that you knew every one – !' he went on; yet as if there were more in that too than he could quite trust himself about.

'Yes, I knew every one,' said Cornelia Rasch; but this time with perfect simplicity. 'I knew, I imagine, more than you do – or more than you did.'

It kept him there, it made him wonder with his eyes on her. 'Things about *them* – our people?'

'Our people. Ours only now.'

Ah, such an interest as he felt in this – taking from her while, so far from scowling, he almost gaped, all it might mean! 'Ours indeed – and it's awfully good they are; or that we're still here for them! Nobody else is – nobody but you: not a cat!'

'Well, I *am* a cat!' Cornelia grinned.

'Do you mean you can tell me things – ?' It was too beautiful to believe.

'About what really *was*?' She artfully considered, holding him immensely now. 'Well, unless they've come to you with time; unless you've learned – or found out.'

'Oh,' he reassuringly cried – reassuringly, it most seemed, for himself – 'nothing has come to me with time, everything has gone from me. How I find out now! What creature has an idea – ?'

She threw up her hands with the shrug of old days – the sharp little

245

shrug his sisters used to imitate and that she hadn't had to go to Europe for. The only thing was that he blessed her for bringing it back. 'Ah, the ideas of people now — !'

'Yes, their ideas are certainly not about *us*.' But he ruefully faced it. 'We've none the less, however, to live with them.'

'With their ideas — ?' Cornelia questioned.

'With *them* — these modern wonders; such as they are!' Then he went on: 'It must have been to help me you've come back.'

She said nothing for an instant about that, only nodding instead at his photograph. 'What has become of yours? I mean of *her*.'

This time it made him turn pale. 'You remember I *have* one?'

She kept her eyes on him. 'In a "pork-pie" hat, with her hair in a long net. That was so "smart" then; especially with one's skirt looped up, over one's hooped magenta petticoat, in little festoons, and a row of very big onyx beads over one's braided velveteen sack — braided quite plain and very broad, don't you know?'

He smiled for her extraordinary possession of these things — she was as prompt as if she had had them before her. 'Oh, rather — "don't I know?" You wore brown velveteen, and, on those remarkably small hands, funny gauntlets — like mine.'

'Oh, do *you* remember? But like yours?' she wondered.

'I mean like hers in my photograph.' But he came back to the present picture. 'This is better, however, for really showing her lovely head.'

'Mary's head was a perfection!' Cornelia testified.

'Yes — it was better than her heart.'

'Ah, don't say that!' she pleaded. 'You weren't fair.'

'Don't you think I was fair?' It interested him immensely — and the more that he indeed mightn't have been; which he seemed somehow almost to hope.

'She didn't think so — to the very end.'

'She didn't?' — ah, the right things Cornelia said to him! But before she could answer he was studying again closely the small faded face. 'No, she doesn't, she doesn't. Oh, her charming sad eyes and the way they *say* that, across the years, straight into mine! But I don't know, I don't know!' White-Mason quite comfortably sighed.

His companion appeared to appreciate this effect. 'That's just the way you used to flirt with her, poor thing. Wouldn't you like to have it?' she asked.

'This – for my very own?' He looked up delighted. 'I really may?'

'Well, if you'll give me yours. We'll exchange.'

'That's a charming idea. We'll exchange. But you must come and get it at my rooms – where you'll see my things.'

For a little she made no answer – as if for some feeling. Then she said: 'You asked me just now why I've come back.'

He stared as for the connection; after which with a smile: 'Not to do *that* – ?'

She waited briefly again, but with a queer little look. 'I can do those things now; and – yes! – that's in a manner why. I came,' she then said, 'because I knew of a sudden one day – knew as never before – that I was old.'

'I see. I see.' He quite understood – she had notes that so struck him. 'And how did you like it?'

She hesitated – she decided. 'Well, if I liked it, it was on the principle perhaps on which some people like high game!'

'High game – that's good!' he laughed. 'Ah, my dear, we're "high!"'

She shook her head. 'No – not you – yet. I at any rate didn't want any more adventures,' Cornelia said.

He showed their small relic again with assurance. 'You wanted *us*. Then here we are. Oh, how we can talk! – with all those things you know! You *are* an invention. And you'll see there are things *I* know. I shall turn up here – well, daily.'

She took it in, but after a moment only answered. 'There was something you said just now you'd tell me. Don't you mean to try – ?'

'Mrs Worthingham?' He drew from within his coat his pocket-book and carefully found a place in it for Mary Cardew's carte-de-visite, folding it together with deliberation over which he put it back. Finally he spoke. 'No – I've decided. I can't – I don't want to.'

Cornelia marvelled – or looked as if she did. 'Not for all she has?'

'Yes – I know all she has. But I also know all she hasn't. And, as I told you, she herself doesn't – hasn't a glimmer of a suspicion of it; and never will have.'

Cornelia magnanimously thought. 'No – but she knows other things.'

He shook his head as at the portentous heap of them. 'Too many – too many. And other indeed – *so* other. Do you know,' he went on, 'that it's as if *you* – by turning up for me – had brought that home to me?'

'For you,' she candidly considered. 'But what – since you can't marry me! – can you do with me?'

Well, he seemed to have it all. 'Everything. I can live with you – just this way.' To illustrate which he dropped into the other chair by her fire; where, leaning back, he gazed at the flame. 'I can't give you up. It's very curious. It has come over me as it did over you when you renounced Bognor. That's it – I know it at last, and I see one can like it. I'm "high." You needn't deny it. That's my taste. I'm old.' And in spite of the considerable glow there of her little household altar he said it without the scowl.

THE BENCH OF DESOLATION

I

SHE had practically, he believed, conveyed the intimation, the horrid, brutal, vulgar menace, in the course of their last dreadful conversation, when, for whatever was left him of pluck or confidence – confidence in what he would fain have called a little more aggressively the strength of his position – he had judged best not to take it up. But this time there was no question of not understanding, or of pretending he didn't; the ugly, the awful words, ruthlessly formed by her lips, were like the fingers of a hand that she might have thrust into her pocket for extraction of the monstrous object that would serve best for – what should he call it? – a gage of battle.

'If I haven't a very different answer from you within the next three days I shall put the matter into the hands of my solicitor, whom it may interest you to know I've already seen. I shall bring an action for "breach" against you, Herbert Dodd, as sure as my name's Kate Cookham.'

There it was, straight and strong – yet he felt he could say for himself, when once it had come, or even, already just as it was coming, that it turned on, as if she had moved an electric switch, the very brightest light of his own very reasons. There *she* was, in all the grossness of her native indelicacy, in all her essential excess of will and destitution of scruple; and it was the woman capable of that ignoble threat who, his sharper sense of her quality having become so quite deterrent, was now making for him a crime of it that he shouldn't wish to tie himself to her for life. The vivid, lurid thing was the reality, all unmistakable, of her purpose; she had thought her case well out; had measured its odious, specious presentability; had taken, he might be sure, the very best advice obtainable at Properley, where there was always a first-rate promptitude of everything fourth-rate; it was disgustingly certain, in short, that she'd proceed. She was sharp and adroit, moreover – distinctly in certain ways a masterhand; how otherwise, with her so limited mere attractiveness, should she have entangled him? He couldn't shut his eyes to the very probable truth that if she should try it she'd pull it off. She *knew* she would – precisely; and her assurance was thus the very proof of her cruelty. That she had pretended she loved him was comparatively nothing; other women had pretended it, and other women too had really done it; but that she had pretended he could possibly have been right and safe and blest in loving *her*, a creature of the kind who could sniff that squalor of the law-court, of claimed damages and brazen lies and published kisses, of love-letters read amid obscene guffaws, as a positive tonic to resentment, as a high incentive to her course – this was what put him so beautifully in the right. It was what might signify in a woman all through, he said to himself, the mere imagination of such machinery. Truly what a devilish conception and what an appalling nature!

But there was no doubt, luckily, either, that he *could* plant his feet the firmer for his now intensified sense of these things. He was to live, it appeared, abominably worried, he was to live consciously rueful, he was to live perhaps even what a scoffing world would call abjectly exposed; but at least he was to live saved. In spite of his clutch of which steadying truth, however, and in spite of his declaring to her, with many other angry protests and pleas, that the line of conduct she announced was worthy of a vindictive barmaid, a lurking fear in him, too deep to counsel mere defiance, made him appear to keep open a little, till he could somehow turn round again, the door of possible composition. He had scoffed at her claim, at her threat, at her thinking she could hustle and bully him – 'Such a way, my eye, to call back to life a dead love!' – yet his instinct was ever, prudentially but helplessly, for gaining time, even if time only more woefully to quake, and he gained it now by not absolutely giving for his ultimatum that he wouldn't think of coming round. He didn't in the smallest degree mean to come round, but it was characteristic of him that he could for three or four days breathe a little easier by having left her under the impression that he perhaps might. At the same time he couldn't not have said – what had conduced to bring out, in retort, her own last word, the word on which they had parted – 'Do you mean to say you yourself would now be *willing* to marry and live with a man of whom you could feel, the thing done, that he'd be all the while thinking of you in the light of a hideous coercion?' 'Never you mind about *my* willingness,' Kate had answered; 'you've known what that has been for the last six months. Leave that to me, my willingness – I'll take care of it all right; and just see what conclusion you can come to about your own.'

He was to remember afterward how he had wondered whether, turned upon her in silence while her odious lucidity reigned unchecked, his face had shown her anything like the quantity of hate he felt. Probably not at all; no man's face *could* express that immense amount; especially the fair, refined, intellectual, gentleman-like face which had had – and by her own more than once repeated avowal – so much to do with the enormous fancy she had originally taken to him. 'Which – frankly now – would you personally *rather* I should do,' he had at any rate asked her with an intention of supreme irony: 'just sordidly marry you on top of this, or leave you the pleasure of your lovely appearance in court and of your so assured (since that's how you feel it) big haul of damages? Shan't you be awfully disappointed, in fact, if I don't let you get something better out of me than a poor plain ten-shilling gold ring and the rest of the blasphemous rubbish, as we should make it between us, pronounced at the altar? I take it, of course,' he had swaggered on, 'that your pretension wouldn't be for a moment that I should – after the act of profanity – take up my life with you.'

'It's just as much my dream as it ever was, Herbert Dodd, to take up mine with *you*! Remember for me that I can do with it, my dear, that my idea is for even as much as that of you!' she had cried; 'remember that for me, Herbert Dodd; remember, remember!'

It was on this she had left him – left him frankly under a mortal chill. There might have been the last ring of an appeal or a show of persistent and perverse tenderness in it, however preposterous any such matter; but in point of fact her large, clean, plain brown face – so much too big for her head, he now more than ever felt it to be, just as her head was so much too big for her body, and just as her hats had an irritating way of appearing to decline choice and conformity in respect to *any* of her dimensions – presented itself with about as much expression as his own shop-window when the broad, blank, sallow blind was down. He was fond of his shop-window with some good show on; he had a fancy for a good show and was master of twenty different schemes of taking arrangement for the old books and prints, 'high-class rarities' his modest catalogue called them, in which he dealt and which his maternal uncle, David Geddes, had, as he liked to say, 'handed down' to him. His widowed mother had screwed the whole thing, the stock and the connection and the rather bad little house in the rather bad little street, out of the ancient worthy, shortly before his death, in the name of the youngest and most interesting, the 'delicate' one and the literary of her five scattered and struggling children. He could enjoy his happiest collocations and contrasts and effects, his harmonies and varieties of toned and faded leather and cloth, his sought colour-notes and the high clearnesses, here and there, of his white and beautifully figured price-labels, which pleased him enough in themselves almost to console him for not oftener having to break, on a customer's insistence, into the balanced composition. But the dropped expanse of time-soiled canvas, the thing of Sundays and holidays, with just his name, 'Herbert Dodd, Successor,' painted on below his uncle's antique style, the feeble penlike flourishes already quite archaic – this ugly vacant mask, which might so easily be taken for the mask of failure, somehow always gave him a chill.

That had been just the sort of chill – the analogy was complete – of Kate Cookham's last look. He supposed people doing an awfully good and sure and steady business, in whatever line, could see a whole front turned to vacancy that way, and merely think of the hours off represented by it. Only for this – nervously to bear it, in other words, and Herbert Dodd, quite with the literary temperament himself, was capable of that amount of play of fancy, or even of morbid analysis – you had to be on some footing, you had to feel some confidence, pretty different from his own up to now. He had never *not* enjoyed passing his show on the other side of the street and taking it in thence with a casual obliquity; but he had never held optical commerce with the drawn blind for a moment longer than he could help. It *always* looked horribly final and as if it never would come up again. Big and bare, with his name staring at him from the middle, it thus offered in its grimness a term of comparison for Miss Cookham's ominous visage. She never wore pretty, dotty, transparent veils, as Nan Drury did, and the words 'Herbert Dodd' – save that she had sounded them at him there two or three times more like a Meg Merrilies[1] or the bold bad woman in one of the melodramas of high life given during the fine season in the pavilion at the end of Properley Pier – were dreadfully, were permanently, seated on her lips. *She* was grim, no mistake.

That evening, alone in the back room above the shop, he saw so little what he could do that, consciously demoralized for the hour, he gave way to tears about it. Her taking a stand so incredibly 'low,' that was what he couldn't get over. The particular bitterness of his cup was his having let himself in for a struggle on such terms – the use, on her side, of the vulgarest process known to the law: the vulgarest, the vulgarest, he kept repeating that, clinging to the help rendered him by his imputation to his terrorist of the vice he sincerely believed he had ever, among difficulties (for oh, he recognized the difficulties!) sought to keep most alien to him. He knew what he was, in a dismal, down-trodden sphere enough – the lean young proprietor of an old business that had itself rather shrivelled with age than ever grown fat, the purchase and sale of second-hand books and prints, with the back street of a long-fronted south-coast watering-place (Old Town by good luck) for the dusky field of his life. But he had gone in for all the education he could get – his educated customers would often hang about for more talk by the half-hour at a time, he actually feeling himself, and almost with a scruple, hold them there; which meant that he had had (he couldn't be blind to that) natural taste and had lovingly cultivated and formed it. Thus, from as far back as he could remember, there had been things all round him that he suffered from when other people didn't; and he had kept most of his suffering to himself – which had taught him, in a manner, *how* to suffer, and how almost to like to.

So, at any rate, he had never let go his sense of certain differences, he had done everything he could to keep it up – whereby everything that was vulgar was on the wrong side of his line. He had believed, for a series of strange, oppressed months, that Kate Cookham's manners and tone were on the right side; she had been governess – for young children – in two very good private families, and now had classes in literature and history for bigger girls who were sometimes brought by their mammas; in fact, coming in one day to look over his collection of students' manuals, and drawing it out, as so many did, for the evident sake of his conversation, she had appealed to him that very first time by her apparently pronounced intellectual side – goodness knew she didn't even then by the physical! – which she had artfully kept in view till she had entangled him past undoing. And it had all been but the cheapest of traps – when he came to take the pieces apart a bit – laid over a brazen avidity. What he now collapsed for, none the less – what he sank down on a chair at a table and nursed his weak, scared sobs in his resting arms for – was the fact that, whatever the trap, it held him as with the grip of sharp, murderous steel. There he was, there he was; alone in the brown summer dusk – brown through *his* windows – he cried and he cried. He shouldn't get out without losing a limb. The only question was which of his limbs it should be.

Before he went out, late on – for he at last felt the need to – he could, however, but seek to remove from his face and his betraying eyes, over his wash-stand, the traces of his want of fortitude. He brushed himself up; with which, catching his stricken image a bit spectrally in an old dim toilet-glass, he knew again, in a flash, the glow of righteous resentment. Who should be assured against coarse usage if a man of his really elegant, perhaps in fact a trifle over-refined or 'effete' appearance, his absolutely gentlemanlike type, couldn't be? He never went so far as to rate himself, with exaggeration, a gentleman; but he would have maintained against all comers, with perfect candour and as claiming a high advantage, that he was, in spite of that liability to blubber, 'like' one; which he *was* no doubt, for that matter, at several points. Like what lady then, who could ever possibly have been taken for one, was Kate Cookham, and therefore how could one have anything – anything of the intimate and private order – out with her fairly and on the plane, the only possible one, of common equality? He might find himself crippled for life; he believed verily, the more he thought, that that was what was before him. But he ended by seeing this doom in the almost redeeming light of the fact that it would all have been because he was, comparatively, too aristocratic. Yes, a man in his station couldn't afford to carry that so far – it must sooner or later, in one way or another, spell ruin. Never mind – it was the only thing he could be. Of course he should exquisitely suffer – but when hadn't he exquisitely suffered? How was he going to get through life by *any* arrangement without that? No wonder such a woman as Kate Cookham had been keen to annex so rare a value. The right thing would have been that the highest price should be paid for it – by such a different sort of logic from this nightmare of *his* having to pay.

II

Which was the way, of course, he talked to Nan Drury – as he had felt the immediate wild need to do; for he should perhaps be able to bear it all somehow or other with *her* – while they sat together, when time and freedom served, on one of the very last, the far westward benches of the interminable sea-front. It wasn't everyone who walked so far, especially at that flat season – the only ghost of a bustle now, save for the gregarious, the obstreperous haunters of the fluttering, far-shining Pier, being reserved for the sunny Parade of mid-winter. It wasn't everyone who cared for the sunsets (which you got awfully well from there, and which were a particular strong point of the lower, the more 'sympathetic' as Herbert Dodd liked to call it, Properley horizon) as he had always intensely cared, and as he had found Nan Drury care; to say nothing of his having also observed how little they directly spoke to Miss Cookham. He had taught this oppressive companion to notice them a bit, as he had taught her plenty of other things, but that was a different matter; for the reason that the 'land's end' (stretching a point it carried off that name) had been, and had had to be by their lack of more sequestered resorts and conveniences, the scene of so much of what she styled their wooing-time – or, to put it more properly, of the time during which she had made the straightest and most unabashed love to *him*: just as it could henceforth but render possible, under an equal rigour, that he should enjoy there periods of consolation from beautiful, gentle, tender-souled Nan, to whom he was now at last, after the

255

wonderful way they had helped each other to behave, going to make love, absolutely unreserved and abandoned, absolutely reckless and romantic love, a refuge from poisonous reality, as hard as ever he might.

The league-long, paved, lighted, garden-plotted, seated, and refuged Marina renounced its more or less celebrated attractions to break off short here; and an inward curve of the kindly westward shore almost made a wide-armed bay, with all the ugliness between town and country, and the further casual fringe of the coast, turning, as the day waned, to rich afternoon blooms of grey and brown and distant – it might fairly have been beautiful Hampshire – blue. Here it was that all that blighted summer, with Nan – from the dreadful May-day on – he gave himself up to the reaction of intimacy with the *kind* of woman, at least, that he liked; even if of everything else that might make life possible he was to be, by what he could make out, for ever starved. Here it was that – as well as on whatever other scraps of occasions they could manage – Nan began to take off and fold up and put away in her pocket her pretty, dotty, becoming veil; as under the logic of his having so tremendously ceased, in the shake of his dark storm-gust, to be engaged to another woman. Her removal of that obstacle to a trusted friend's assuring himself whether the peachlike bloom of her finer facial curves bore the test of such further inquiry into their cool sweetness as might reinforce a mere baffled gaze – her momentous, complete surrender of so much of her charm, let us say, both marked the change in the situation of the pair and established the record of their perfect observance of every propriety for so long before. They afterward in fact could have dated it, their full clutch of their freedom and the bliss of their having so little henceforth to consider save their impotence, their poverty, their ruin; dated it from the hour of his recital to her of the – at the first blush – quite appalling upshot of his second and conclusive 'scene of violence' with the mistress of his fortune, when the dire terms of his release had had to be formally, and oh! so abjectly, acceded to. She 'compromised,' the cruel brute, for Four Hundred Pounds down – for not a farthing less would she stay her strength from 'proceedings.' No jury in the land but would give her six, on the nail ('Oh, she knew quite where she was, thank you!'), and he might feel lucky to get off with so whole a skin. This was the sum, then, for which he had grovellingly compounded – under an agreement sealed by a supreme exchange of remarks.

' "Where in the name of lifelong ruin are you to *find* Four Hundred?" ' Miss Cookham had mockingly repeated after him while he gasped as from the twist of her grip on his collar. 'That's *your* look-out, and I should have thought you'd have made sure you knew before you decided on your base perfidy.' And then she had mouthed and minced, with ever so false a gentility, her consistent, her sickening conclusion. 'Of course – I may mention again – if you too distinctly object to the trouble of looking, you know where to find *me*.'

'I had rather starve to death than ever go within a mile of you!' Herbert described himself as having sweetly answered; and that was accordingly where *they* devotedly but desperately were – he and she, penniless Nan Drury. Her father, of Drury & Dean, was like so far too many other of the anxious characters who peered through the dull window-glass of dusty offices at Properley, an Estate and House Agent, Surveyor, Valuer and Auctioneer; she was the prettiest of six, with two brothers, neither of the least use, but, thanks to the manner in which their main natural protector appeared to languish under the accumulation of his attributes, they couldn't be said very particularly or positively to live. Their continued collective existence was a good deal of a miracle even to themselves, though they had fallen into the way of not unnecessarily, or too nervously, exchanging remarks upon it, and had even in a sort, from year to year, got used to it. Nan's brooding pinkness when he talked to her, her so very parted lips, considering her pretty teeth, her so very parted eyelids, considering her pretty eyes, all of which might have been those of some waxen image of uncritical faith, cooled the heat of his helplessness very much as if he were laying his head on a tense silk pillow. She had, it was true, forms of speech, familiar watchwords, that affected him as small scratchy perforations of the smooth surface from within; but his pleasure in her and need of her were independent of such things and really almost altogether determined by the fact of the happy, even if all so lonely, forms and instincts in her which claimed kinship with his own. With her natural elegance stamped on her as by a die, with her dim and disinherited individual refinement

of grace, which would have made anyone wonder who she was anywhere – hat and veil and feather-boa and smart umbrella-knob and all –
with her regular God-given distinction of type, in fine, she couldn't
abide vulgarity much more than he could.

Therefore it didn't seem to him, under his stress, to matter particularly, for instance, if she *would* keep on referring so many things to
the time, as she called it, when she came into his life – his own great
insistence and contention being that she hadn't in the least entered there
till his mind was wholly made up to eliminate his other friend. What
that methodical fury was so fierce to bring home to him was the falsity
to herself involved in the later acquaintance; whereas just his precious
right to hold up his head to everything – before himself at least – sprang
from the fact that she couldn't make dates fit anyhow. He hadn't so
much as heard of his true beauty's existence (she had come back but a
few weeks before from her two years with her terrible trying deceased
aunt at Swindon, previous to which absence she had been an unnotice-
able chit) till days and days, ever so many, upon his honour, after he had
struck for freedom by his great first backing-out letter – the precious
document, the treat for a British jury, in which, by itself, Miss Cookham's firm instructed her to recognize the prospect of a fortune. The
way the ruffians had been 'her' ruffians – it appeared as if she had posted
them behind her from the first of her beginning her game! – and the
way 'instructions' bounced out, with it, at a touch, larger than life, as if
she had arrived with her pocket full of them! The date of the letter,
taken with its other connections, and the date of *her* first give-away for
himself, his seeing her get out of the Brighton train with Bill Frankle
that day he had gone to make the row at the Station parcels' office
about the miscarriage of the box from Wales – those were the facts it
sufficed him to point to, as he had pointed to them for Nan Drury's
benefit, goodness knew, often and often enough. If he didn't seek
occasion to do so for anyone else's – in open court as they said – that
was his own affair, or at least his and Nan's.

It little mattered, meanwhile, if on their bench of desolation, all that
summer – and it may be added for summers and summers, to say
nothing of winters, there and elsewhere, to come – she did give way to
her artless habit of not contradicting him enough, which led to her

often trailing up and down before him, too complacently, the untimely shreds and patches of his own glooms and desperations. 'Well, I'm glad I *am* in your life, terrible as it is, however or whenever I did come in!' and '*Of course* you'd rather have starved – and it seems pretty well as if we shall, doesn't it? – than have bought her off by a false, abhorrent love, wouldn't you?' and 'It isn't as if she hadn't made up to you the way she did before you had so much as looked at her, is it? or as if you hadn't shown her what you felt her really to be before you had so much as looked at *me*, is it either?' and 'Yes, how on earth, pawning the shoes on your feet, you're going to raise another shilling – *that's* what you want to know, poor darling, don't you?'

III

His creditor, at the hour it suited her, transferred her base of operations to town, to which impenetrable scene she had also herself retired; and his raising of the first Two Hundred, during five exasperated and miserable months, and then of another Seventy piece-meal, bleedingly, after long delays and under the epistolary whiplash cracked by the London solicitor in his wretched ear even to an effect of the very report of Miss Cookham's tongue – these melancholy efforts formed a scramble up an arduous steep where steps were planted and missed, and bared knees were excoriated, and clutches at wayside tufts succeeded and failed, on a system to which poor Nan could have intelligently entered only if she had been somehow less ladylike. She kept putting into his mouth the sick quaver of where he should find the rest, the always inextinguishable rest, long after he had in silent rage fallen away from any further payment at all – at first, he had but too blackly felt, for himself, to the still quite possible non-exclusion of some penetrating ray of 'exposure'. He didn't care a tuppenny damn now, and in point of fact, after he had by hook and by crook succeeded in being able to unload to the tune of Two-Hundred-and-Seventy, and then simply returned the newest reminder of his outstanding obligation unopened, this latter belated but real sign of fight, the first he had risked, remarkably caused nothing at all to happen; nothing at least but his being moved to quite tragically rueful wonder as to whether exactly some such demonstration mightn't have served his turn at an earlier stage.

He could by this time at any rate measure his ruin – with three fantastic mortgages on his house, his shop, his stock, and a burden of interest to carry under which his business simply stretched itself inanimate, without strength for a protesting kick, without breath for an appealing groan. Customers lingering for further enjoyment of the tasteful remarks he had cultivated the unobtrusive art of throwing in, would at this crisis have found plenty to repay them, might his wit have strayed a little more widely still, toward a circuitous egotistical outbreak, from the immediate question of the merits of this and that author or of the condition of this and that volume. He had come to be conscious through it all of strangely glaring at people when they tried to haggle – and not, as formerly, with the glare of derisive comment on their overdone humour, but with that of fairly idiotized surrender; as if they were much mistaken in supposing, for the sake of conversation, that he might take himself for saveable by the difference between sevenpence and ninepence. He watched everything impossible and deplorable happen, as in an endless prolongation of his nightmare; watched himself proceed, that is, with the finest, richest incoherence to the due preparation of his catastrophe. Everything came to seem *equally* part of this – in complete defiance of proportion; even his final command of detachment, on the bench of desolation (where each successive fact of his dire case regularly cut itself out black, yet of senseless silhouette, against the red west) in respect to poor Nan's flat infelicities, which for the most part kept no pace with the years or with change, but only shook like hard peas in a child's rattle, the same peas always, of course, so long as the rattle didn't split open with usage or from somebody's act of irritation. They represented, or they had long done so, her contribution to the more superficial of the two branches of intimacy – the intellectual alternative, the one that didn't merely consist in her preparing herself for his putting his arm round her waist.

There were to have been moments, nevertheless, all the first couple of years, when she did touch in him, though to his actively dissimulating it, a more or less sensitive nerve – moments as they were too, to do her justice, when she treated him not to his own wisdom, or even folly, served up cold, but to a certain small bitter fruit of her personal, her unnatural, plucking. 'I wonder that since *she* took legal advice so freely, to come down on you, you didn't take it yourself, a little, before being so sure you stood no chance. Perhaps *your* people would have been sure of something quite different – *perhaps*, I only say, you know.' She 'only' said it, but she said it, none the less, in the early time, about once a fortnight. In the later, and especially after their marriage, it had a way of coming up again to the exclusion, as it seemed to him, of almost everything else; in fact during the most dismal years, the three of the loss of their two children, the long stretch of sordid embarrassment ending in her death, he was afterward to think of her as having generally said it several times a day. He was then also to remember that his answer, before she had learnt to discount it, had been inveterately at hand: 'What would any solicitor have done or wanted to do but drag me just into the hideous public arena' – he had always so put it – 'that it has been at any rate my pride and my honour, the one rag of self-respect covering my nakedness, to have loathed and avoided from every point of view?'

That had disposed of it so long as he cared, and by the time he had ceased to care for anything it had also lost itself in the rest of the vain babble of home. After his wife's death, during his year of mortal solitude, it awoke again as an echo of far-off things – far-off, very far-off, because he felt then not ten but twenty years older. That was by reason simply of the dead weight with which his load of debt had settled – the persistence of his misery dragging itself out. With all that had come and gone the bench of desolation was still there, just as the immortal flush of the westward sky kept hanging its indestructible curtain. He had never got away – everything had left him, but he himself had been able to turn his back on nothing – and now, his day's labour before a dirty desk at the Gas Works ended, he more often than not, almost any season at temperate Properley serving his turn, took his slow, straight way to the Land's End and, collapsing there to rest, sat often for an hour at a time staring before him. He might in these sessions, with his eyes on the grey-green sea, have been counting again and still recounting the beads, almost all worn smooth, of his rosary of pain – which had for the fingers of memory and the recurrences of wonder the same felt break of the smaller ones by the larger that would have aided a pious mumble in some dusky altar-chapel.

If it has been said of him that when once full submersion, as from far back, had visibly begun to await him, he watched himself, in a cold lucidity, *do* punctually and necessarily each of the deplorable things that were inconsistent with his keeping afloat, so at present again he might have been held agaze just by the presented grotesqueness of that vigil. Such ghosts of dead seasons were all he *had* now to watch – such a recaptured sense for instance as that of the dismal unavailing awareness that had attended his act of marriage. He had let submersion final and absolute become the signal for it – a mere minor determinant having been the more or less contemporaneously unfavourable effect on the business of Drury & Dean of the sudden disappearance of Mr Dean with the single small tin box into which the certificates of the firm's credit had been found to be compressible. That had been his only form – or had at any rate seemed his only one. He couldn't not have married, no doubt, just as he couldn't not have suffered the last degree of humiliation and almost of want, or just as his wife and children couldn't not have died of the little he was able, under dire reiterated pinches, to do for them; but it *was* 'rum,' for final solitary brooding, that he hadn't appeared to see his way definitely to undertake the support of a family till the last scrap of his little low-browed, high-toned business and the last figment of 'property' in the old tiled and timbered shell that housed it had been sacrificed to creditors mustering six rows deep.

Of course what had counted too in the odd order was that even at the end of the two or three years he had 'allowed' her, Kate Cookham, gorged with his unholy tribute, had become the subject of no successful siege on the part either of Bill Frankle or, by what he could make out, of anyone else. She had judged decent – he could do her that justice – to take herself personally out of his world, as he called it, for good and all, as soon as he had begun regularly to bleed; and, to whatever lucrative practice she might be devoting her great talents in London or elsewhere, he felt his conscious curiosity about her as cold, with time, as the passion of vain protest that she had originally left him to. He could recall but two direct echoes of her in all the bitter years – both communicated by Bill Frankle, disappointed and exposed and at last quite remarkably ingenuous sneak, who had also, from far back taken to roaming the world, but who, during a period, used fitfully and ruefully to reappear.

Herbert Dodd had quickly seen, at their first meeting – everyone met everyone sooner or later at Properley, if meeting it could always be called, either in the glare or the gloom of the explodedly attractive Embankment – that no silver stream of which he himself had been the remoter source could have played over the career of this all but re-pudiated acquaintance. That hadn't fitted with his first, his quite primi-tive raw vision of the probabilities, and he had further been puzzled when, much later on, it had come to him in a round-about way that Miss Cookham was supposed to be, or to have been, among them for a few days 'on the quiet,' and that Frankle, who had seen her and who claimed to know more about it than he said, was cited as authority for the fact. But he hadn't himself at this juncture seen Frankle; he had only wondered, and a degree of mystification had even remained.

That memory referred itself to the dark days of old Drury's smash, the few weeks between his partner's dastardly flight and Herbert's own comment on it in the form of his standing up with Nan for the nuptial benediction of the Vicar of St Bernard's on a very cold, bleak December morning and amid a circle of seven or eight long-faced, red-nosed, and altogether dowdy persons. Poor Nan herself had come to affect him as scarce other than red-nosed and dowdy by that time, but this only added, in his then, and indeed in his lasting view, to his general and his particular morbid bravery. He had cultivated ignorance, there were small inward immaterial luxuries he could scrappily cherish even among other, and the harshest, destitutions; and one of them was represented by this easy refusal of his mind to render to certain passages of his experience, to various ugly images, names, associations, the homage of continued attention. That served him, that helped him; but what happened when, a dozen dismal years having worn themselves away, he sat single and scraped bare again, as if his long wave of misfortune had washed him far beyond everything and then conspicuously retreated, was that, thus stranded by tidal action, deposited in the lonely hollow of his fate, he felt even sustaining pride turn to nought and heard no challenge from it when old mystifications, stealing forth in the dusk of the day's work done, scratched at the door of speculation and hung about, through the idle hours, for irritated notice.

The evenings of his squalid clerkship were all leisure now, but there was nothing at all near home, on the other hand, for his imagination, numb and stiff from its long chill, to begin to play with. Voices from far off would quaver to him therefore in the stillness; where he knew for the most recurrent, little by little, the faint wail of his wife. He had become deaf to it in life, but at present, after so great an interval, he listened again, listened and listened, and seemed to hear it sound as by the pressure of some weak broken spring. It phrased for his ear her perpetual question, the one she had come to at the last as under the obsession of a discovered and resented wrong, a wrong withal that had its source much more in his own action than anywhere else. 'That you didn't make *sure* she could have done anything, that you didn't make sure and that you were too afraid!' – this commemoration had ended by playing such a part of Nan's finally quite contracted consciousness as to exclude everything else.

At the time, somehow, he had made his terms with it; he had then more urgent questions to meet than that of the poor creature's taste in worrying pain; but actually it struck him – not the question, but the fact ·itself of the taste – as the one thing left over from all that had come and gone. So it was; nothing remained to him in the world, on the bench of desolation, but the option of taking up that echo – together with an abundance of free time for doing so. That he hadn't made sure of what might and what mightn't have been done to him, that he had been too afraid – had the proposition a possible bearing on his present apprehension of things? To reply indeed he would have had to be able to say what his present apprehension of things, left to itself, amounted to; an uninspiring effort indeed he judged it, sunk to so poor a pitch was his material of thought – though it might at last have been the feat he sought to perform as he stared at the grey-green sea.

IV

It was seldom he was disturbed in any form of sequestered speculation, or that at his times of predilection, especially that of the long autumn blankness between the season of trippers and the season of Bath-chairs, there were westward stragglers enough to jar upon his settled sense of priority. For himself his seat, the term of his walk, was consecrated; it had figured to him for years as the last (though there were others, not immediately near it, and differently disposed, that might have aspired to the title); so that he could invidiously distinguish as he approached, make out from a distance any accident of occupation, and never draw nearer while that unpleasantness lasted. What he disliked was to compromise on his tradition, whether for a man, a woman, or a connoodling couple; it was to idiots of this last composition he most objected, he having sat there, in the past, alone, having sat there interminably with Nan, having sat there with – well, with other women when women, at hours of ease, could still care or count for him, but having never shared the place with any shuffling or snuffling strangers.

It was a world of fidgets and starts, however, the world of his present dreariness; he alone possessed in it, he seemed to make out, the secret of the dignity of sitting still with one's fate; so that if he took a turn about or rested briefly elsewhere even foolish philanderers – though this would never have been his and Nan's way – ended soon by some adjournment as visibly pointless as their sprawl. Then, their backs turned, he would drop down on it, the bench of desolation – which was what he, and he only, made it, by sad adoption; where, for that matter, moreover, once he had settled at his end, it was marked that nobody else ever came to sit. He saw people, along the Marina, take this liberty with other resting presences; but his own struck them perhaps in general as either of too grim or just of too dingy a vicinage. He might have affected the fellow-lounger as a man evil, unsociable, possibly engaged in working out the idea of a crime; or otherwise, more probably – for on the whole he surely looked harmless – devoted to the worship of some absolutely unpractical remorse.

On a certain October Saturday he had got off as usual, early; but the afternoon light, his pilgrimage drawing to its aim, could still show him, at long range, the rare case of an established usurper. His impulse was then, as by custom, to deviate a little and wait, all the more that the occupant of the bench was a lady, and that ladies, when alone, were – at that austere end of the varied frontal stretch – markedly discontinuous; but he kept on at sight of this person's rising, while he was still fifty yards off, and proceeding, her back turned, to the edge of the broad terrace, the outer line of which followed the interspaced succession of seats and was guarded by an iron rail from the abruptly lower level of the beach. Here she stood before the sea, while our friend on his side, recognizing no reason to the contrary, sank into the place she had quitted. There were other benches, eastward and off by the course of the drive, for vague ladies. The lady indeed thus thrust upon Herbert's vision might have struck an observer either as not quite vague or as vague with a perverse intensity suggesting design.

Not that our own observer at once thought of these things; he only took in, and with no great interest, that the obtruded presence was a 'real' lady; that she was dressed — he noticed such matters — with a certain elegance of propriety or intention of harmony; and that she remained perfectly still for a good many minutes; so many in fact that he presently ceased to heed her, and that as she wasn't straight before him, but as far to the left as was consistent with his missing her profile, he had turned himself to one of his sunsets again (though it wasn't quite one of his best) and let it hold him for a time that enabled her to alter her attitude and present a fuller view. Without other movement, but her back now to the sea and her face to the odd person who had appropriated her corner, she had taken a sustained look at him before he was aware she had stirred. On that apprehension, however, he became also promptly aware of her direct, her applied observation. As his sense of this quickly increased he wondered who she was and what she wanted — what, as it were, was the matter with her; it suggested to him, the next thing, that she had, under some strange idea, actually been waiting for him. Any idea about him to-day on the part of any one could only be strange.

Yes, she stood there with the ample width of the Marina between them, but turned to him, for all the world, as to show frankly that she was concerned with him. And she *was* — oh, yes — a real lady: a middle-aged person, of good appearance and of the best condition, in quiet but 'handsome' black, save for very fresh white kid gloves, and with a pretty, dotty, becoming veil, predominantly white, adjusted to her countenance; which through it somehow, even to his imperfect sight, showed strong fine black brows and what he would have called on the spot character. But she was pale; her black brows were the blacker behind the flattering tissue; she still kept a hand, for support, on the terrace-rail, while the other, at the end of an extended arm that had an effect of rigidity, clearly pressed hard on the knob of a small and shining umbrella, the lower extremity of whose stick was equally, was sustainingly, firm on the walk. So this mature, qualified, important person stood and looked at the limp, undistinguished – oh, his values of aspect now! – shabby man on the bench.

It was extraordinary, but the fact of her interest, by immensely surprising, by immediately agitating him, blinded him at first to her identity and, for the space of his long stare, diverted him from it; with which even then, when recognition did break, the sense of the shock, striking inward, simply consumed itself in gaping stillness. He sat there motionless and weak, fairly faint with surprise, and there was no instant in all the succession of so many, at which Kate Cookham could have caught the special sign of his intelligence. Yet that she did catch something he saw – for he saw her steady herself, by her two supported hands, to meet it; while, after she had done so, a very wonderful thing happened, of which he could scarce, later on, have made a clear statement, though he was to think it over again and again. She moved toward him, she reached him, she stood there, she sat down near him, he merely passive and wonderstruck, unresentfully 'impressed,' gaping and taking it in – and all as with an open allowance on the part of each, so that they positively and quite intimately met in it, of the impertinence for their case, this case that brought them again, after horrible years, face to face, of the vanity, the profanity, the impossibility, of anything between them but silence.

Nearer to him, beside him at a considerable interval (oh, she was immensely considerate!) she presented him, in the sharp terms of her transformed state – but thus the more amply, formally, ceremoniously – with the reasons that would serve him best for not having precipitately known her. She was simply another and a totally different person, and the exhibition of it to which she had proceeded with this solemn anxiety was all, obviously, for his benefit – once he had, as he appeared to be doing, provisionally accepted her approach. He had remembered her as inclined to the massive and disowned by the graceful; but this was a spare, fine, worn, almost wasted lady – who had repaired waste, it was true, however, with something he could only appreciate as a rich accumulation of manner. She was strangely older, so far as that went – marked by experience and as if many things had happened to her; her face had suffered, to its improvement, contraction and concentration; and if he had granted, of old and from the first, that her eyes were remarkable, had they yet ever had for him this sombre glow? Withal, something said, she had flourished – he felt it, wincing at it, as that; she had had a life, a career, a history, something that her present waiting air and nervous consciousness couldn't prevent his noting there as a deeply latent assurance. She had flourished, she had flourished – though to learn it after this fashion was somehow at the same time not to feel she flaunted it. It wasn't thus execration that she revived in him; she made in fact, exhibitively, as he could only have put it, the matter of long ago irrelevant, and these extraordinary minutes of their re-constituted relation – how many? how few? – addressed themselves altogether to new possibilities.

Still it after a little awoke in him as with the throb of a touched nerve that his own very attitude was supplying a connection; he knew presently that he wouldn't have had her go, *couldn't* have made a sign to her for it – which was what she had been uncertain of – without speaking to him; and that therefore he was, as at the other, the hideous time, passive to whatever she might do. She was even yet, she was always, in possession of him; she had known how and where to find him and had appointed that he should see her, and, though he had never dreamed it was again to happen to him, he was meeting it already as if it might have been the only thing that the least humanly *could*. Yes, he had come back there to flop, by long custom, upon the bench of desolation *as* the man in the whole place, precisely, to whom nothing worth more than tuppence could happen; whereupon, in the grey desert of his consciousness, the very earth had suddenly opened and flamed. With this, further, it came over him that he hadn't been prepared and that his wretched appearance must show it. He wasn't fit to receive a visit – any visit; a flush for his felt misery, in the light of her opulence, broke out in his lean cheeks. But if he coloured he sat as he was – she should at least, as a visitor, be satisfied. His eyes only, at last, turned from her and resumed a little their gaze at the sea. That, however, didn't relieve him, and he perpetrated in the course of another moment the odd desperate gesture of raising both his hands to his face and letting them, while he pressed it to them, cover and guard it. It was as he held them there that she at last spoke.

'I'll go away if you wish me to.' And then she waited a moment. 'I mean now – now that you've seen I'm here. I wanted you to know it, and I thought of writing – I was afraid of our meeting accidentally. Then I was afraid that if I wrote you might refuse. So I thought of this way – as I knew you must come out here.' She went on with pauses, giving him a chance to make a sign. 'I've waited several days. But I'll do what you wish. Only I should like in that case to come back.' Again she stopped; but strange was it to him that he wouldn't have made her break off. She held him in boundless wonder. 'I came down – I mean I came from town – on purpose. I'm staying on still, and I've a great patience and will give you time. Only may I say it's important? Now that I do see you,' she brought out in the same way, 'I see how inevitable it was – I mean that I should have wanted to come. But you must feel about it as you can,' she wound up – 'till you get used to the idea.'

She spoke so for accommodation, for discretion, for some ulterior view already expressed in her manner, that, after taking well in, from behind his hands, that this was her very voice – oh, ladylike! – heard, and heard in deprecation of displeasure, after long years again, he uncovered his face and freshly met her eyes. More than ever he couldn't have known her. Less and less remained of the figure all the facts of which had long ago so hardened for him. She was a handsome, grave, authoritative, but refined and, as it were, physically rearranged person – she, the outrageous vulgarity of whose prime assault had kept him shuddering so long as a shudder was in him. That atrocity in her was what everything had been built on, but somehow, all strangely, it was slipping from him; so that, after the oddest fashion conceivable, when he felt he mustn't let her go, it was as if he were putting out his hand to *save* the past, the hideous, real, unalterable past, exactly as she had been the cause of its being and the cause of his undergoing it. He should have been too awfully 'sold' if he wasn't going to have been right about her.

'I don't mind,' he heard himself at last say. Not to mind had seemed for the instant the length he was prepared to go; but he was afterward aware of how soon he must have added: 'You've come on purpose to see me?' He was on the point of putting to her further: 'What then do you want of me?' But he would keep – yes, in time – from appearing to show he cared. If he showed he cared, where then would be his revenge? So he was already, within five minutes, thinking his revenge uncomfortably over instead of just comfortably knowing it. What came to him, at any rate, as they actually fell to talk, was that, with such precautions, considerations, reduplications of consciousness, almost avowed feelings of her way on her own part, and light fingerings of his chords of sensibility, she was understanding, she *had* understood, more things than all the years, up to this strange eventide, had given him an inkling of. They talked, they went on – he hadn't let her retreat, to whatever it committed him and however abjectly it did so; yet keeping off and off, dealing with such surface facts as involved ancient acquaintance but kept abominations at bay. The recognition, the attestation that she *had* come down for him, that there would be reasons, that she had even hovered and watched, assured herself a little of his habits (which she managed to speak of as if, on their present ampler development, they were much to be deferred to), held them long enough to make vivid how, listen as stiffly or as serenely as he might, she sat there in fear, just as she had so stood there at first, and that her fear had really to do with her calculation of some sort of chance with him. What chance could it possibly be? Whatever it might have done, on this prodigious showing, with Kate Cookham, it made the present witness to the state of his fortunes simply exquisite: he ground his teeth secretly together as he saw he should have to take *that*. For what did it mean but that she would have liked to pity him if she could have done it with safety? Ah, however, he must give her no measure of safety!

By the time he had remarked, with that idea, that she probably saw few changes about them there that weren't for the worse – the place was going down, down and down, so fast that goodness knew where it would stop – and had also mentioned that in spite of this he himself remained faithful, with all its faults loving it still; by the time he had, after that fashion, superficially indulged her, adding a few further light and just sufficiently dry reflections on local matters, the disappearance of landmarks and important persons, the frequency of gales, the low policy of the Town Council in playing down to cheap excursionists: by the time he had so acquitted himself, and she had observed, of her own motion, that she was staying at the Royal, which he knew for the time-honoured, the conservative, and exclusive hotel, he had made out for himself one thing at least, the amazing fact that he had been landed by his troubles, at the end of time, in a 'social relation,' of all things in the world, and how of that luxury he was now having unprecedented experience. He had but once in his life had his nose in the Royal, on the occasion of his himself delivering a parcel during some hiatus in his succession of impossible small boys and meeting in the hall the lady who had bought of him, in the morning, a set of Crabbe; largely, he flattered himself, under the artful persuasion of his acute remarks on that author, gracefully associated by him, in this colloquy, he remembered, with a glance at Charles Lamb as well, and who went off, in a day or two, without settling, though he received her cheque from London three or four months later.

That hadn't been a social relation; and truly, deep within his appeal to himself to be remarkable, to be imperturbable and impenetrable, to be in fact quite incomparable now, throbbed the intense vision of his drawing out and draining dry the sensation he had begun to taste. He would do it, moreover – that would be the refinement of his art – not only without the betraying anxiety of a single question, but just even by seeing her flounder (since she must, in a vagueness deeply disconcerting to her) as to her real effect on him. She was distinctly floundering by the time he had brought her – it had taken ten minutes – down to a consciousness of absurd and twaddling topics, to the reported precarious state, for instance, of the syndicate running the Bijou Theatre at the Pierhead – all as an admonition that she might want him to want to know why she was thus waiting on him, might want it for all she was worth, before he had ceased to be so remarkable as not to ask her. He didn't – and this assuredly was wondrous enough – want to do anything worse to her than let her flounder; but he was willing to do that so long as it mightn't prevent his seeing at least where *he* was. He seemed still to see where he was even at the minute that followed her final break-off, clearly intended to be resolute, from make-believe talk.

'I wonder if I might prevail on you to come to tea with me tomorrow at five.'

He didn't so much as answer it – though he could scarcely believe his ears. Tomorrow was Sunday, and the proposal referred, clearly, to the custom of 'five-o'clock' tea, known to him only by the contemporary novel of manners and the catchy advertisements of table linen. He had never in his life been present at any such luxurious rite, but he was offering practical indifference to it as a false mark of his sense that his social relation had already risen to his chin. 'I gave up my very modest, but rather interesting little old book business, perhaps you know, ever so long ago.'

She floundered so that she could say nothing – meet *that* with no possible word; all the less too that his tone, casual and colourless, wholly defied any apprehension of it as a reverse. Silence only came; but after a moment she returned to her effort. 'If you *can* come I shall be at home. To see you otherwise than thus was, in fact, what, as I tell you, I came down for. But I leave it,' she returned, 'to your feeling.'

He had at this, it struck him, an inspiration; which he required however a minute or two to decide to carry out; a minute or two during which the shake of his foot over his knee became an intensity of fidget. 'Of course I know I still owe you a large sum of money. If it's about *that* you wish to see me,' he went on, 'I may as well tell you just here that I shall be able to meet my full obligation in the future as little as I've met it in the past. I can never,' said Herbert Dodd, 'pay up that balance.'

He had looked at her while he spoke, but on finishing looked off at the sea again and continued to agitate his foot. He knew now what he had done, and why; and the sense of her fixed dark eyes on him during his speech and after didn't alter his small contentment. Yet even when she still said nothing he didn't turn round; he simply kept his corner as if *that* were his point made, should it even be the last word between them. It might have been, for that matter, from the way in which she presently rose, gathering herself, her fine umbrella and her very small reticule, in the construction of which shining gilt much figured, well together, and, after standing another instant, moved across to the rail of the terrace as she had done before and remained, as before, with her back to him, though this time, it well might be, under a different fear. A quarter of an hour ago she hadn't tried him, and had had that anxiety;

now that she had tried him it wasn't easier – but she was thinking what she still could do. He left her to think – nothing in fact more interesting than the way she might decide had ever happened to him; but it was a part of this also that as she turned round and came nearer again he didn't rise, he gave her no help. If she got any, at least, from his looking up at her only, meeting her fixed eyes once more in silence, that was her own affair. 'You must think,' she said – 'you must take all your time, but I shall be at home.' She left it to him thus – she insisted, with her idea, on leaving him somewhere too. And on her side as well she showed an art – which resulted, after another instant, in his having to rise to his feet. He flushed afresh as he did it – it exposed him so shabbily the more; and now if she took him in, with each of his seedy items, from head to foot, he didn't and couldn't and wouldn't know it, attaching his eyes hard and straight to something quite away from them.

It stuck in his throat to say he'd come, but she had so curious a way with her that he still less could say he wouldn't, and in a moment had taken refuge in something that was neither. 'Are you married?' – he put it to her with that plainness, though it had seemed before he said it to do more for him than while she waited before replying.

'No, I'm not married,' she said: and then had another wait that might have amounted to a question of what this had to do with it.

He surely couldn't have told her; so that he had recourse, a little poorly as he felt, but to an 'Oh!' that still left them opposed. He turned away for it – that is for the poorness, which, lingering in the air, had almost a vulgar platitude; and when he presently again wheeled about she had fallen off as for quitting him, only with a pause, once more, for a last look. It was all a bit awkward, but he had another happy thought, which consisted in his silently raising his hat as for a sign of dignified dismissal. He had cultivated of old, for the occasions of life, the right, the discriminated bow, and now, out of the grey limbo of the time when he could care for such things, this flicker of propriety leaped and worked. She might, for that matter, herself have liked it; since, receding further, only with her white face toward him, she paid it the homage of submission. He remained dignified, and she almost humbly went.

V

Nothing in the world, on the Sunday afternoon, could have prevented him from going; he was not after all destitute of three or four such articles of clothing as, if they wouldn't particularly grace the occasion, wouldn't positively dishonour it. That deficiency might have kept him away, but no voice of the spirit, no consideration of pride. It sweetened his impatience, in fact – for he fairly felt it a long time to wait – that his pride would really most find its account in his acceptance of these conciliatory steps. From the moment he could put it in that way – that he couldn't refuse to hear what she might have, so very elaborately, to say for herself – he ought certainly to be at his ease; in illustration of which he whistled odd snatches to himself as he hung about on that cloud-dappled autumn Sunday, a mild private minstrelsy that his lips hadn't known since when? The interval of the twenty-four hours, made longer by a night of many more revivals than oblivions, had in fact dragged not a little; in spite of which, however, our extremely brushed-up and trimmed and polished friend knew an unprecedented flutter as he was ushered, at the Royal Hotel, into Miss Cookham's sitting-room. Yes, it was an adventure, and he had never had an adventure in his life; the term, for him, was essentially a term of high appreciation – such as disqualified for that figure, under due criticism, every single passage of his past career.

What struck him at the moment as qualifying in the highest degree this actual passage was the fact that at no great distance from his hostess in the luxurious room, as he apprehended it, in which the close of day had begun to hang a few shadows, sat a gentleman who rose as she rose, and whose name she at once mentioned to him. He had for Herbert Dodd all the air of a swell, the gentleman – rather red-faced and bald-headed, but moustachioed, waistcoated, necktied to the highest pitch, with an effect of chains and rings, of shining teeth in a glassily monocular smile; a wondrous apparition to have been asked to 'meet' him, as in contemporary fiction, or for him to have been asked to meet. 'Captain Roper, Mr Herbert Dodd' – their entertainer introduced them, yes; but with a sequel immediately afterward more disconcerting apparently to Captain Roper himself even than to her second and more breathless visitor; a 'Well then, good-bye till the next time,' with a hand thrust straight out, which allowed the personage so addressed no alternative but to lay aside his teacup, even though Herbert saw there was a good deal left in it, and glare about him for his hat. Miss Cookham had had her tea-tray on a small table before her, she had served Captain Roper while waiting for Mr Dodd; but she simply dismissed him now, with a high sweet unmistakable decision, a knowledge of what she was about, as our hero would have called it, which enlarged at a stroke the latter's view of the number of different things and sorts of things, in the sphere of the manners and ways of those living at their ease, that a social relation would put before one. Captain Roper would have liked to remain, would have liked more tea, but Kate signified in this direct fashion that she had had enough of him. Herbert had seen things, in his walk of life – rough things, plenty; but never things smoothed with that especial smoothness, carried out as it were by the fine form of Captain Roper's own retreat, which included even a bright convulsed leave-taking cognisance of the plain, vague individual, of no lustre at all and with the very low-class guard of an old silver watch buttoned away under an ill-made coat, to whom he was sacrificed.

It came to Herbert as he left the place a shade less remarkable – though there was still wonder enough and to spare – that he had been even publicly and designedly sacrificed; exactly so that, as the door closed behind him, Kate Cookham, standing there to wait for it, could seem to say, across the room, to the friend of her youth, only by the expression of her fine eyes: 'There – see what I do for you!' 'For' him – that was the extraordinary thing, and not less so that he was already, within three minutes, after this fashion, taking it in as by the intensity of a new light; a light that was one somehow with this rich inner air of the plush-draped and much-mirrored hotel, where the firelight and the approach of evening confirmed together the privacy and the loose curtains at the wide window were parted for a command of his old lifelong Parade – the field of life so familiar to him from below and in the wind and the wet, but which he had never in all the long years hung over at this vantage.

'He's an acquaintance, but a bore,' his hostess explained in respect to Captain Roper. 'He turned up yesterday, but I didn't invite him, and I had said to him before you came in that I was expecting a gentleman with whom I should wish to be alone. I go quite straight at my idea that way, as a rule; but you know,' she now strikingly went on, 'how straight I go. And he had had,' she added, 'his tea.'

Dodd had been looking all round – had taken in, with the rest, the brightness, the distinguished elegance, as he supposed it, of the tea-service with which she was dealing and the variously tinted appeal of certain savoury edibles on plates. 'Oh, but he *hadn't* had his tea!' he heard himself the next moment earnestly reply; which speech had at once betrayed, he was then quickly aware, the candour of his interest, the unsophisticated state that had survived so many troubles. If he was so interested how could he be proud, and if he was proud how could he be so interested?

He had made her at any rate laugh outright, and was further conscious, for this, both that it was the first time of that since their new meeting, and that it didn't affect him as harsh. It affected him, however, as free, for she replied at once, still smiling and as a part of it: 'Oh, I think we shall get on!'

This told him he had made some difference for her, shown her the way, or something like it, that she hadn't been sure of yesterday; which moreover wasn't what he had intended – he had come armed for showing her nothing; so that after she had gone on, with the same gain of gaiety, 'You must at any rate comfortably have yours,' there was but one answer for him to make.

His eyes played again over the tea-things – they seemed strangely to help him; but he didn't sit down. 'I've come, as you see – but I've come, please, to understand; and if you require to be alone with me, and if I break bread with you, it seems to me I should first know exactly where I am and to what you suppose I so commit myself.' He had thought it out and over and over, particularly the turn about breaking bread; though perhaps he didn't give it, in her presence – this was impossible, her presence altered so many things – quite the full sound or the weight he had planned.

But it had none the less come to his aid – it had made her perfectly grave. 'You commit yourself to nothing. You're perfectly free. It's only I who commit myself.'

On which, while she stood there as if all handsomely and deferentially waiting for him to consider and decide, he would have been naturally moved to ask her what she committed herself then *to* – so moved, that is, if he hadn't, before saying it, thought more sharply still of something better. 'Oh, that's another thing.'

'Yes, that's another thing,' Kate Cookham returned. To which she added, 'So *now* won't you sit down?' He sank with deliberation into the seat from which Captain Roper had risen; she went back to her own, and while she did so spoke again. 'I'm *not* free. At least,' she said over her tea-tray, 'I'm free only for this.'

Everything was there before them and around them, everything massive and shining, so that he had instinctively fallen back in his chair as for the wondering, the resigned acceptance of it; where her last words stirred in him a sense of odd depreciation. Only for 'that'? 'That' was everything, at this moment, to his long inanition, and the effect, as if she had suddenly and perversely mocked him, was to press the spring of a protest. 'Isn't "this" then riches?'

'Riches?' she smiled over, handing him his cup – for she had triumphed in having struck from him a question.

'I mean haven't you a lot of money?' He didn't care now that it was out; his cup was in his hand, and what was that but proved interest? He had succumbed to the social relation.

'Yes, I've money. Of course you wonder – but I've wanted you to wonder. It was to make you take that in that I came. So now you know,' she said, leaning back where she faced him, but in a straighter chair and with her arms closely folded, after a fashion characteristic of her, as for some control of her nerves.

'You came to show you've money?'

'That's one of the things. Not a lot – not even very much. But enough,' said Kate Cookham.

'Enough? I should think so!' he again couldn't help a bit crudely exhaling.

'Enough for what I wanted. I don't always live like this – not at all. But I came to the best hotel on purpose. I wanted to show you I could. Now,' she asked, 'do you understand?'

'Understand?' He only gaped.

She threw up her loosed arms, which dropped again beside her. 'I did it *for* you — I did it *for* you!'

'"For" me — ?'

'What I did — what I did here of old.'

He stared, trying to see it. 'When you made me pay you?'

'The Two-Hundred-and-Seventy — all I could get from you, as you reminded me yesterday, so that I had to give up the rest. It was my idea,' she went on — 'it was my idea.'

'To bleed me quite to death?' Oh, his ice was broken now!

'To make you raise money — since you could, you *could*. You did, you did — so what better proof?'

His hands fell from what he had touched; he could only stare — her own manner for it was different now too. 'I did. I did indeed — !' And the woeful weak simplicity of it, which seemed somehow all that was left him, fell even on his own ear.

'Well then, here it is — it isn't lost!' she returned with a graver face.

'"Here" it is,' he gasped, 'my poor agonized old money — my blood?'

'Oh, it's *my* blood too, you must know now!' She held up her head as not before — as for her right to speak of the thing today most precious to her. 'I took it, but this — my being here this way — is what I've made of it! That was the idea I had!'

Her 'ideas,' as things to boast of, staggered him. 'To have everything in the world, like this, at my wretched expense?'

She had folded her arms back again — grasping each elbow she sat firm; she knew he could see, and had known well from the first, what she had wanted to say, difficult, monstrous though it might be. 'No more than at my own — but to do something with your money that you'd never do yourself.'

'Myself, myself?' he wonderingly wailed. 'Do you know — or don't you? — what my life has been?'

She waited, and for an instant, though the light in the room had failed a little more and would soon be mainly that of the flaring lamps on the windy Parade, he caught from her dark eye a silver gleam of impatience. 'You've suffered and you've worked — which, God knows, is what I've done! *Of course* you've suffered,' she said — 'you inevitably had to! We have to,' she went on, 'to do or to be or to get anything.'

'And pray what have I done or been or got?' Herbert Dodd found it almost desolately natural to demand.

It made her cover him again as with all she was thinking of. 'Can you imagine nothing, or can't you conceive – ?' And then as her challenge struck deeper in, deeper down than it had yet reached and with the effect of a rush of the blood to his face, 'It was *for* you, it was *for* you!' she again broke out – 'and for what or whom else could it have been?'

He saw things to a tune now that made him answer straight: 'I thought at one time it might be for Bill Frankle.'

'Yes – that was the way you treated me,' Miss Cookham as plainly replied.

But he let this pass; his thought had already got away from it. 'What good then – its having been for me – has that ever done me?'

'Doesn't it do you any good *now*?' his friend returned. To which she added, with another dim play of her tormented brightness, before he could speak: 'But if you won't even have your tea – !'

He had in fact touched nothing, and if he could have explained, would have pleaded very veraciously that his appetite, keen when he came in, had somehow suddenly failed. It was beyond eating or drinking, what she seemed to want him to take from her. So if he looked, before him, over the array, it was to say, very grave and graceless: 'Am I to understand that you offer to repay me?'

'I offer to repay you with interest, Herbert Dodd' – and her emphasis of the great word was wonderful.

It held him in his place a minute, and held his eyes upon her; after which, agitated too sharply to sit still, he pushed back his chair and stood up. It was as if mere distress or dismay at first worked in him, and was in fact a wave of deep and irresistible emotion which made him, on his feet, sway as in a great trouble and then, to correct it, throw himself stiffly toward the window, where he stood and looked out unseeing. The road, the wide terrace beyond, the seats, the eternal sea beyond that, the lighted lamps now flaring in the October night-wind, with the few dispersed people abroad at the tea-hour; these things, meeting and melting into the firelit hospitality at his elbow – or was it that portentous amenity that melted into *them*? – seemed to form round him and to put before him, all together, the strangest of circles and the newest of experiences, in which the unforgettable and the unimaginable were confoundingly mixed. 'Oh, oh, oh!' – he could only almost howl for it.

And then, while a thick blur for some moments mantled everything, he knew she had got up, that she stood watching him, allowing for everything, again all 'cleverly' patient with him, and he heard her speak again as with studied quietness and clearness. 'I wanted to take care of you – it was what I first wanted – and what you first consented to. I'd have done it, oh, I'd have done it, I'd have loved you and helped you and guarded you, and you'd have had no trouble, no bad blighting ruin, in all your easy, yes, just your quite jolly and comfortable life. I showed you and proved to you this – I brought it home to you, as I fondly fancied, and it made me briefly happy. You swore you cared for me, you wrote it and made me believe it – you pledged me your honour and your faith. Then you turned and changed suddenly, from one day to another; everything altered, you broke your vows, you as good as told me you only wanted it off. You faced me with dislike, and in fact tried not to face me at all; you behaved as if you hated me – you had seen a girl, of great beauty, I admit, who made me a fright and a bore.'

This brought him straight round. 'No, Kate Cookham.'

'Yes, Herbert Dodd.' She but shook her head, calmly and nobly, in the now gathered dusk, and her memories and her cause and her character – or was it only her arch-subtlety, her line and her 'idea'? – gave her an extraordinary large assurance.

She had touched, however, the treasure of his own case – his terrible own case that began to live again at once by the force of her talking of hers, and which could always all cluster about his great asseveration. 'No, no, never, never; I had never seen her then and didn't dream of her; so that when you yourself began to be harsh and sharp with me, and to seem to want to quarrel, I could have but one idea – which was an appearance you didn't in the least, as I saw it then, account for or disprove.'

'An appearance – ?' Kate desired, as with high astonishment, to know which one.

'How *shouldn't* I have supposed you really to care for Bill Frankle? – as, thoroughly believing the motive of your claim for my money to be its help to your marrying him, since you couldn't marry me. I was only

THE BENCH OF DESOLATION

surprised when, time passing, I made out that that hadn't happened; and perhaps,' he added the next instant, with something of a conscious lapse from the finer style, 'hadn't been in question.'

She had listened to this only staring, and she was silent after he had said it, so silent for some instants that while he considered her something seemed to fail him, much as if he had thrown out his foot for a step and not found the place to rest it. He jerked round to the window again, and then she answered, but without passion, unless it was that of her weariness for something stupid and forgiven in him, 'Oh, the blind, the pitiful folly!' – to which, as it might perfectly have applied to her own behaviour, he returned nothing. She had moreover at once gone on. 'Put it then that there wasn't much to do – between your finding that you loathed me for another woman, or discovering only, when it came to the point, that you loathed me quite enough for myself.'

Which, offered him in that immensely effective fashion, he recognized that he must just unprotestingly and not so very awkwardly – not so *very*! – take from her; since, whatever he had thus come to her for, it wasn't to perjure himself with any pretence that, 'another woman' or no other woman, he hadn't, for years and years, abhorred her. Now he was taking tea with her – or rather, literally, seemed not to be; but this made no difference, and he let her express it as she would while he distinguished a man he knew, Charley Coote, outside on the Parade, under favour of the empty hour and one of the flaring lamps, making up to a young woman with whom (it stuck out grotesquely in his manner) he had never before conversed. Dodd's own position was that of acquiescing in this recall of what had so bitterly been – but he hadn't come back to her, of himself, to stir up, to recall or to recriminate, and for *her* it could but be the very lesson of her whole present act that if she touched anything she touched everything. Soon enough she was indeed, and all overwhelmingly, touching everything – with a hand of which the boldness grew.

'But I didn't let *that*, even, make a difference in what I wanted – which was all,' she said, 'and had only and passionately been, to take care of you. I had *no* money whatever – nothing then of my own, not a penny to come by anyhow; so it wasn't with mine I could do it. But I could do it with yours,' she amazingly wound up – 'if I could once get yours out of you.'

He faced straight about again – his eyebrows higher than they had ever been in his life. 'Mine? What penny of it was mine? What scrap beyond a bare, mean little living had I ever pretended to have?'

She held herself still a minute, visibly with force; only her eyes consciously attached to the seat of a chair the back of which her hands, making it tilt toward her a little, grasped as for support. 'You pretended to have enough to marry me – and that was all I afterwards claimed of you when you wouldn't.' He was on the point of retorting that he had absolutely pretended nothing – least of all to the primary desire that such a way of putting it fastened on him; he was on the point for ten seconds of giving her full in the face: 'I never *had* any such dream till you yourself – infatuated with me as, frankly, you on the whole appeared to be – got round me and muddled me up and made me behave as if in a way that went against the evidence of my senses.' But he was to feel as quickly that, whatever the ugly, the spent, the irrecoverable truth, he might better have bitten his tongue off: there beat on him there this strange and other, this so prodigiously different beautiful and dreadful truth that no far remembrance and no abiding ache of his own could wholly falsify, and that was indeed all out with her next words. 'That – *using* it for you and using you yourself for your own future – was my motive. I've led my life, which has been an affair, I assure you; and, as I've told you without your quite seeming to understand, I've brought everything fivefold back to you.'

The perspiration broke out on his forehead. 'Everything's mine?' he quavered as for the deep piercing pain of it.

'Everything!' said Kate Cookham.

So it told him how she had loved him – but with the tremendous effect at once of its only glaring out at him from the whole thing that it was verily she, a thousand times over, who, in the exposure of his youth and his vanity, had, on the bench of desolation, the scene of yesterday's own renewal, left for him no forward step to take. It hung there for him tragically vivid again, the hour she had first found him sequestered and accessible after making his acquaintance at his shop. And from this, by a succession of links that fairly clicked to his ear as with their perfect fitting, the fate and the pain and the payment of others stood together in a great grim order. Everything there then was *his* – to make him ask

what had been Nan's, poor Nan's of the constant question of whether
he need have collapsed. She was before him, she was between them, his
little dead dissatisfied wife; across all whose final woe and whose lowly
grave he was to reach out, it appeared, to take gifts. He saw them too,
the gifts; saw them – she bristled with them – in his actual companion's
brave and sincere and authoritative figure, her strangest of demon-
strations. But the other appearance was intenser, as if their ghost had
waved wild arms; so that half a minute hadn't passed before the one
poor thing that remained of Nan, and that yet thus became a quite
mighty and momentous poor thing, was sitting on his lips as for its sole
opportunity.

'Can you give me your word of honour that I mightn't, under decent
advice, have defied you?'

It made her turn very white; but now that she had said what she *had*
said she could still hold up her head. 'Certainly you might have defied
me, Herbert Dodd.'

'They would have told me you had no legal case?'

Well, if she was pale she was bold. 'You talk of decent advice –!' She
broke off, there was too much to say, and all needless. What she said
instead was: 'They would have told you I had nothing.'

'I didn't so much as ask,' her sad visitor remarked.

'Of course you didn't so much as ask.'

'I couldn't be so outrageously vulgar,' he went on.

'*I* could, by God's help!' said Kate Cookham.

'Thank you.' He had found at his command a tone that made him
feel more gentlemanlike than he had ever felt in his life or should
doubtless ever feel again. It might have been enough – but somehow as
they stood there with this immense clearance between them it wasn't.
The clearance was like a sudden gap or great bleak opening through
which there blew upon them a deadly chill. Too many things had fallen
away, too many new rolled up and over him, and they made something
within shake him to his base. It upset the full vessel, and though she kept
her eyes on him he let that consequence come, bursting into tears,
weakly crying there before her even as he had cried to himself in the
hour of his youth when she had made him groundlessly fear. She turned
away then – *that* she couldn't watch, and had presently flung herself on

283

the sofa and, all responsively wailing, buried her own face on the cushioned arm. So for a minute their smothered sobs only filled the room. But he made out, through this disorder, where he had put down his hat; his stick and his new tan-coloured gloves — they had cost two-and-thruppence and would have represented sacrifices — were on the chair beside it. He picked these articles up and all silently and softly — gasping, that is, but quite on tiptoe — reached the door and let himself out.

VI

Off there on the bench of desolation a week later she made him a more particular statement, which it had taken the remarkably tense interval to render possible. After leaving her at the hotel that last Sunday he had gone forth in his reaggravated trouble and walked straight before him, in the teeth of the west wind, close to the iron rails of the stretched Marina and with his tell-tale face turned from persons occasionally met and towards the surging sea. At the land's end, even in the confirmed darkness and the perhaps imminent big blow, his immemorial nook, small shelter as it yielded, had again received him; and it was in the course of this heedless session, no doubt, where the agitated air had nothing to add to the commotion within him, that he began to look his extraordinary fortune a bit straighter in the face and see it confess itself at once a fairy-tale and a nightmare. That, visibly, confoundingly, she was still attached to him (attached in fact was a mild word!) and that the unquestionable proof of it was in this offered pecuniary salve, of the thickest composition, for his wounds and sores and shames — these things were the fantastic fable, the tale of money in handfuls, that he seemed to have only to stand there and swallow and digest and feel himself full-fed by; but the whole of the rest was nightmare, and most of all nightmare his having thus to thank one through whom Nan and his little girls had known torture.

He didn't care for himself now, and this unextinguished and apparently inextinguishable charm by which he had held her was a fact incredibly romantic; but he gazed with a longer face than he had ever had for anything in the world at his potential acceptance of a great bouncing benefit from the person he intimately, if even in a manner indirectly, associated with the conditions to which his lovely wife and his little girls (who would have been so lovely too) had pitifully succumbed. He had accepted the social relation – which meant he had taken even that on trial – without knowing what it so dazzlingly masked; for a social relation it had become with a vengeance when it drove him about the place as now at his hours of freedom (and he actually and recklessly took, all demoralized and unstrung and unfit either for work or for anything else, other liberties that would get him into trouble) under this queer torment of irreconcilable things, a be-wildered consciousness of tenderness and patience and cruelty, of great evident mystifying facts that were as little to be questioned as to be conceived or explained, and that were yet least, withal, to be lost sight of.

On that Sunday night he had wandered wild, incoherently ranging and throbbing, but this became the law of his next days as well, since he lacked more than ever all other resort or refuge and had nowhere to carry, to deposit, or contractedly let loose and lock up, as it were, his swollen consciousness, which fairly split in twain the raw shell of his sordid little boarding-place. The arch of the sky and the spread of sea and shore alone gave him space; he could roam with himself anywhere, in short, far or near – he could only never take himself back. That certitude – that this was impossible to him even should she wait there among her plushes and bronzes ten years – was the thing he kept closest clutch of; it did wonders for what he would have called his self-respect. Exactly as he had left her so he would stand off – even though at moments when he pulled up sharp somewhere to put himself an intensest question his heart almost stood still. The days of the week went by, and as he had left her she stayed; to the extent, that is, of his having neither sight nor sound of her, and of the failure of every sign. It took nerve, he said, not to return to her, even for curiosity – since how, after all, in the name of wonder, had she invested the fruits of her extortion to such advantage, there being no chapter of all the obscurity of the years to beat that for queerness? But he dropped, tired to death, on benches, half a dozen times an evening – exactly on purpose to recognize that the nerve required was just the nerve he had.

As the days without a token from her multiplied he came in as well for hours – and these indeed mainly on the bench of desolation – of sitting stiff and stark in presence of the probability that he had lost everything for ever. When he passed the Royal he never turned an eyelash, and when he met Captain Roper on the Front, three days after having been introduced to him, he 'cut him dead' – another privileged consequence of a social relation – rather than seem to himself to make the remotest approach to the question of whether Miss Cookham had left Properley. He had cut people in the days of his life before, just as he had come to being himself cut – since there had been no time for him wholly without one or other face of that necessity – but had never affected such a severance as of this rare connection, which helped to give him thus the measure of his really precious sincerity. If he had lost what had hovered before him he had lost it, his only tribute to which proposition was to grind his teeth with one of those 'scrunches,' as he would have said, of which the violence fairly reached his ear. It wouldn't make him lift a finger, and in fact if Kate had simply taken herself off on the Tuesday or the Wednesday she would have been reabsorbed again into the darkness from which she had emerged – and no lifting of fingers, the unspeakable chapter closed, would evermore avail. That at any rate was the kind of man he still was – even after all that had come and gone, and even if for a few dazed hours certain things had seemed pleasant. The dazed hours had passed, the surge of the old bitterness had dished him (shouldn't he have been shamed if it hadn't?) and he might sit there as before, as always, with nothing at all on earth to look to. He had therefore wrongfully believed himself to be degraded; and the last word about him would be that he *couldn't* then, it appeared, sink to vulgarity as he had tried to let his miseries make him.

And yet on the next Sunday morning, face to face with him again at the land's end, what she very soon came to was: 'As if I believed you didn't *know* by what cord you hold me!' Absolutely, too, and just that morning in fact, above all, he wouldn't, he quite couldn't have taken his solemn oath that he hadn't a sneaking remnant, as he might have put it to himself – a remnant of faith in tremendous things still to come of their interview. The day was sunny and breezy, the sea of a cold purple; he wouldn't go to church as he mostly went of Sunday mornings, that being in its way too a social relation — and not least when two-and-thruppenny tan-coloured gloves were new; which indeed he had the art of keeping them for ages. Yet he would dress himself as he scarce mustered resources for even to figure on the fringe of Society, local and transient, at St Bernard's and in this trim he took his way westward; occupied largely, as he went, it might have seemed to any person pursuing the same course and happening to observe him, in a fascinated study of the motions of his shadow, the more or less grotesque shape projected, in front of him and mostly a bit to the right, over the blanched asphalt of the Parade and dangling and dancing at such a rate, shooting out and then contracting, that, viewed in themselves, its eccentricities might have formed the basis of an interesting challenge: 'Find the state of mind, guess the nature of the agitation, possessing the person so remarkably represented!' Herbert Dodd, for that matter, might have been himself attempting to make by the sun's sharp aid some approach to his immediate horoscope.

It had at any rate been thus put before him that the dandling and dancing of his image occasionally gave way to perfect immobility, when he stopped and kept his eyes on it. 'Suppose she should come, suppose she *should*!' it is revealed at least to ourselves that he had at these moments audibly breathed — breathed with the intensity of an arrest between hope and fear. It had glimmered upon him from early, with the look of the day, that, given all else that could happen, this would be rather, as he put it, in her line; and the possibility lived for him, as he proceeded, to the tune of a suspense almost sickening. It was, from one small stage of his pilgrimage to another, the 'For ever, never!' of the sentimental case the playmates of his youth used to pretend to settle by plucking the petals of a daisy. But it came to his truly turning faint — so 'queer' he felt — when, at the gained point of the long stretch from which he could always tell, he arrived within positive sight of his immemorial goal. His seat was taken and she was keeping it for him — it could only be *she* there in possession; whereby it shone out for Herbert Dodd that if he hadn't been quite sure of her recurrence she had at least been quite sure of his. *That* pulled him up to some purpose where recognition began for them — or to the effect, in other words, of his pausing to judge if he could bear, for the sharpest note of their

THE BENCH OF DESOLATION

intercourse, this inveterate demonstration of her making him do what she liked. What settled the question for him then — and just while they avowedly watched each other, over the long interval, before closing, as if, on either side, for the major advantage — what settled it was this very fact that what she liked she liked so terribly. If it were simply to 'use' him, as she had said the last time, and no matter to the profit of which of them she called it, one might let it go for that; since it could make her wait over, day after day, in that fashion, and with such a spending of money, on the hazard of their meeting again. How could she be the least sure he would ever again consent to it after the proved action on him, a week ago, of her last monstrous honesty? It was indeed positively as if he were now himself putting this influence — and for their common edification — to the supreme, to the finest test. He had a sublime, an ideal flight, which lasted about a minute. 'Suppose, now that I see her there and what she has taken so characteristically for granted, suppose I just show her that she *hasn't* only confidently to wait or whistle for me, and that the length of my leash is greater than she measures, and that everything's impossible always? — show it by turning my back on her now and walking straight away. She won't be able not to understand *that!*'

Nothing had passed, across their distance, but the mute apprehension of each on the part of each; the whole expanse, at the church hour, was void of other life (he had scarce met a creature on his way from end to end) and the sun-seasoned gusts kept brushing the air and all the larger prospect clean. It was through this beautiful lucidity that he watched her watch him, as it were — watch him for what he would do. Neither moved at this high tension; Kate Cookham, her face fixed on him, only waited with a stiff appearance of leaving him, not for dignity but — to an effect of even deeper perversity — for kindness, free to choose. It yet somehow affected him at present, this attitude, as a gage of her *knowing too* — knowing, that is, that he wasn't really free, that this was the thinnest of vain parades, the poorest of hollow heroics, that his need, his solitude, his suffered wrong, his exhausted rancour, his foredoomed submission to any shown interest, all hung together too heavy on him to let the weak wings of his pride do more than vaguely tremble. They couldn't, they didn't carry him a single beat further away; according to which he stood rooted, neither retreating nor advancing, but presently correcting his own share of their bleak exchange by looking off at the sea. Deeply conscious of the awkwardness this posture gave him, he yet clung to it as the last shred of his honour, to the clear argument that it was one thing for him to have felt beneath all others, the previous days, that she was to be counted on, but quite a different for her to have felt that *he* was. His checked approach, arriving thus at no term, could in these odd conditions have established that he wasn't only if Kate Cookham had, as either of them might have said, taken it so – if she had given up the game at last by rising, by walking away and adding to the distance between them, and he had then definitely let her vanish into space. It became a fact that when she did finally rise – though after how long our record scarce takes on itself to say – it was not to confirm their separation but to put an end to it; and this by slowly approaching him till she had come within earshot. He had wondered, once aware of it in spite of his averted face, what she would say and on what note, as it were, she would break their week's silence; so that he had to recognize anew, her voice reaching him, that remarkable quality in her which again and again came up for him as her art.

'There are twelve hundred and sixty pounds,[2] to be definite, but I have it all down for you – and you've only to draw.'

They lost themselves, these words, rare and exquisite, in the wide bright genial medium and the Sunday stillness, but even while that occurred and he was gaping for it she was herself there, in her battered ladylike truth, to answer for them, to represent them, and, if a further grace than their simple syllabled beauty were conceivable, almost embarrassingly to cause them to materialize. Yes, she let her smart and tight little reticule hang as if it bulged, beneath its clasp, with the whole portentous sum, and he felt himself glare again at this vividest of her attested claims. She might have been ready, on the spot, to open the store to the plunge of his hand, or, with the situation otherwise conceived, to impose on his pauperized state an acceptance of alms on a scale unprecedented in the annals of street charity. Nothing so much counted for him, however, neither grave numeral nor elegant fraction, as the short, rich, rounded word that the breeze had picked up as it dropped and seemed now to blow about between them. 'To draw – to draw?' Yes, he gaped it as if it had no sense; the fact being that even while he did so he was reading into her use of the term more romance than any word in the language had ever had for him. He, Herbert Dodd, was to live to 'draw,' like people, scarce hampered by the conditions of earth, whom he had remotely and circuitously heard about, and in fact when he walked back with her to where she had been sitting it was very much, for his strained nerves, as if the very bench of desolation itself were to be the scene of that exploit and he mightn't really live till he reached it.

When they had sat down together she did press the spring of her reticule, extracting from it, not a handful of gold nor a packet of crisp notes, but an oblong sealed letter, which she had thus waited on him, she remarked, on purpose to deliver, and which would certify, with sundry particulars, to the credit she had opened for him at a London bank. He took it from her without looking at it, and held it, in the same manner, conspicuous and unassimilated, for most of the rest of the immediate time, appearing embarrassed with it, nervously twisting and flapping it, yet thus publicly retaining it even while aware, beneath everything, of the strange, the quite dreadful, wouldn't it be? engagement that such inaction practically stood for. He could accept money to that amount, yes — but not for nothing in return. For what then in return? He kept asking himself for what, while she said other things and made above all, in her high, shrewd, successful way, the point that, no, he needn't pretend that his conviction of her continued personal interest in him wouldn't have tided him over any question besetting him since their separation. She put it to him that the deep instinct of where he should at last find her must confidently have worked for him, since she confessed to her instinct of where she should find *him*; which meant — oh, it came home to him as he fingered his sealed treasure! — neither more nor less than that she had now created between them an equality of experience. He wasn't to have done all the suffering, *she* was to have 'been through' things he couldn't even guess at; and, since he was bargaining away his right ever again to allude to the unforgettable, so much there was of it, what her tacit proposition came to was that they were 'square' and might start afresh.

He didn't take up her charge, as his so compromised 'pride' yet in a manner prompted him, that he had enjoyed all the week all those elements of ease about her; the most he achieved for that was to declare, with an ingenuity contributing to float him no small distance further, that of course he had turned up at their old place of tryst, which had been, through the years, the haunt of his solitude and the goal of his walk any Sunday morning that seemed too beautiful for church; but that he hadn't in the least built on her presence there – since that supposition gave him, she would understand, wouldn't she? the air, disagreeable to him, of having come in search of her. Her quest of himself, once he had been seated there, would have been another matter – but in short, 'Of course after all you did come to me, just now, didn't you?' He felt himself, too, lamely and gracelessly grin, as for the final kick of his honour, in confirmation of the record that he had then yielded but to her humility. Her humility became for him at this hour and to this tune, on the bench of desolation, a quantity more prodigious and even more mysterious than that other guaranteed quantity the finger-tips of his left hand could feel the tap of by the action of his right; though what was in especial extraordinary was the manner in which she could keep making him such allowances and yet meet him again, at some turn, as with her residuum for her clever self so great.

'Come to you, Herbert Dodd?' she imperturbably echoed. 'I've been coming to you for the last ten years!'

There had been for him just before this sixty supreme seconds of intensest aspiration – a minute of his keeping his certificate poised for a sharp thrust back at her, the thrust of the wild freedom of his saying: 'No, no, I *can't* give them up; I can't simply sink them deep down in my soul for ever, with no cross in all my future to mark *that* burial; so that if this is what our arrangement means I must decline to have anything to do with it.' The words none the less hadn't come, and when she had herself, a couple of minutes later, spoken those others, the blood rose to his face as if, given his stiffness and her extravagance, he had just indeed saved himself.

Everything in fact stopped, even his fidget with his paper; she imposed a hush, she imposed at any rate the conscious decent form of one, and he couldn't afterward have told how long, at this juncture, he must have sat simply gazing before him. It was so long, at any rate, that

Kate herself got up – and quite indeed, presently, as if her own forms were now at an end. He had returned her nothing – so what was she waiting for? She had been on the two other occasions momentarily at a loss, but never so much so, no doubt, as was thus testified to by her leaving the bench and moving over once more to the rail of the terrace. She could carry it off, in a manner, with her resources, that she was waiting with so little to wait for; she could face him again, after looking off at the sea, as if this slightly stiff delay, not wholly exempt from awkwardness, had been but a fine scruple of her courtesy. She had gathered herself in; after giving him time to appeal she could take it that he had decided and that nothing was left for her to do. 'Well then,' she clearly launched at him across the broad walk – 'well then, good-bye.'

She had come nearer with it, as if he might rise for some show of express separation; but he only leaned back motionless, his eyes on her now – he kept her a moment before him. 'Do you mean that we don't – that we don't?' But he broke down.

'Do I "mean" – ?' She remained as for questions he might ask, but it was well-nigh as if there played through her dotty veil an irrepressible irony for that particular one. 'I've meant, for long years, I think, all I'm capable of meaning. I've meant so much that I can't mean more. So there it is.'

'But if you go,' he appealed – and with a sense as of final flatness, however he arranged it, for his own attitude – 'but if you go shan't I see you again?'

She waited a little and it was strangely for him now as if – though at last so much more gorged with her tribute than she had ever been with his – something still depended on her. 'Do you *like* to see me?' she very simply asked.

At this he did get up; that was easier than to say – at least with responsive simplicity; and again for a little he looked hard and in silence at his letter; which, at last, however, raising his eyes to her own for the act, while he masked their conscious ruefulness, to his utmost, in some air of assurance, he slipped into the inner pocket of his coat, letting it settle there securely. 'You're too wonderful.' But he frowned at her with it as never in his life. 'Where does it all come from?'

'The wonder of poor me?' Kate Cookham said. 'It comes from *you*.'

He shook his head slowly – feeling, with his letter there against his heart, such a new agility, almost such a new range of interest. 'I mean so *much* money – so extraordinarily much.'

Well, she held him a while blank. 'Does it seem to you extraordinarily much – twelve-hundred-and-sixty? Because, you know,' she added, 'it's all.'

'It's enough!' he returned with a slight thoughtful droop of his head to the right and his eyes attached to the far horizon as through a shade of shyness for what he was saying. He felt all her own lingering nearness somehow on his cheek.

'It's enough? Thank you then!' she rather oddly went on.

He shifted a little his posture. 'It was more than a hundred a year – for you to get together.'

'Yes,' she assented, 'that was what year by year I tried for.'

'But that you could live all the while and have that – !' Yes, he was at liberty, as he hadn't been, quite pleasantly to marvel. All his wonderments in life had been hitherto unanswered – and didn't the change mean that here again was the social relation?

'Ah, I didn't live as you saw me the other day.'

'Yes,' he answered – and didn't he the next instant feel he must fairly have smiled with it? – 'the other day you *were* going it!'

'For once in my life,' said Kate Cookham. 'I've left the hotel,' she after a moment added.

'Ah, you're in – a – lodgings?' he found himself inquiring as for positive sociability.

She had apparently a slight shade of hesitation, but in an instant it was all right; as what he showed he wanted to know she seemed mostly to give him. 'Yes – but far of course from here. Up on the hill.' To which, after another instant, 'At The Mount, Castle Terrace,' she subjoined.

'Oh, I *know* The Mount. And Castle Terrace is awfully sunny and nice.'

'Awfully sunny and nice,' Kate Cookham took from him.

'So that if it isn't,' he pursued, 'like the Royal, why, you're at least comfortable.'

'I shall be comfortable anywhere now,' she replied with a certain dryness.

It was astonishing, however, what had become of his own. 'Because I've accepted – ?'

'Call it that!' she dimly smiled.

'I hope then at any rate,' he returned, 'you can now thoroughly rest.' He spoke as for a cheerful conclusion and moved again also to smile, though as with a poor grimace, no doubt; since what he seemed most clearly to feel was that since he 'accepted' he mustn't, for his last note, have accepted in sulkiness or gloom. With that, at the same time, he couldn't but know, in all his fibres, that with such a still-watching face as the dotty veil didn't disguise for him there was no possible concluding, at least on his part. On hers, on hers it was – as he had so often for a week had reflectively to pronounce things – another affair. Ah, some-how, both formidably and helpfully, her face concluded – yet in a sense so strangely enshrouded in things she didn't tell him. What *must* she, what mustn't she, have done? What she had said – she had really told him nothing – was no account of her life; in the midst of which conflict of opposed recognitions, at any rate, it was as if, for all he could do, he himself now considerably floundered. 'But I can't think – I can't think – !'

'You can't think I can have made so much money in the time and been honest?'

'Oh, you've been *honest*!' Herbert Dodd distinctly allowed.

It moved her stillness to a gesture – which, however, she had as promptly checked; and she went on the next instant as for further generosity to his failure of thought. 'Everything was possible, under my stress, with my hatred.'

'Your hatred – ?' For she had paused as if it were after all too difficult.

'Of what I should for so long have been doing to you.'

With this, for all his failures, a greater light than any yet shone upon him. 'It made you think of ways – ?'

'It made me think of everything. It made me work,' said Kate Cookham. She added, however, the next moment: 'But that's my story.'

'And I mayn't hear it?'

'No – because I mayn't hear yours.'

'Oh, mine – !' he said with the strangest, saddest yet after all most resigned sense of surrender of it; which he tried to make sound as if he couldn't have told it, for its splendour of sacrifice and of misery, even if he would.

It seemed to move in her a little, exactly, that sense of the invidious. 'Ah, mine too, I assure you – !'

He rallied at once to the interest. 'Oh, we *can* talk then?'

'Never,' she most oddly replied. 'Never,' said Kate Cookham.

They remained so, face to face; the effect of which for him was that he had after a little understood why. That was fundamental. 'Well, I see.'

Thus confronted they stayed; and then, as he saw with a contentment that came up from deeper still, it was indeed she who, with her worn fine face, would conclude. 'But I can take care of you.'

'You *have*!' he said as with nothing left of him but a beautiful appreciative candour.

'Oh, but you'll want it now in a way – !' she responsibly answered.

He waited a moment, dropping again on the seat. So, while she still stood, he looked up at her; with the sense somehow that there were too many things and that they were all together, terribly, irresistibly, doubtless blessedly, in her eyes and her whole person; which thus affected him for the moment as more than he could bear. He leaned forward, dropping his elbows to his knees and pressing his head on his hands. So he stayed, saying nothing; only, with the sense of her own sustained, renewed and wonderful action, knowing that an arm had passed round him and that he was held. She was beside him on the bench of desolation.

NOTE ON THE TEXTS

Maqbool Aziz is producing what may perhaps eventually be a full scholarly edition of *The Tales of Henry James*, Oxford, 1973– (Vol. 3, 1875–1879, is the latest [1989]) using what he calls, in his discussion of the recension, the B texts, i.e. their 'first published' 'serial' versions. But in his *The Complete Tales of Henry James* (London, 1962–4) Leon Edel prints the 'original book form of the story where there was one' (the D text for Aziz). I have followed this astute practice, making only a few mainly silent corrections, for it provides what is likely to be the most responsible and readable text. In these late tales revisions from magazine publication, where there was one, are naturally not extensive even where the work was incorporated into the 'New York' edition.

The details of publication *before* Edel's *Complete Tales* are as follows (for full details see *A Bibliography of Henry James* by Leon Edel and Dan H. Laurence, London, 1957; revised edition, assisted by James Rambeau, 1982).

'THE THIRD PERSON'

(a) Not in a magazine.
(b) *The Soft Side*, London, 1900.
(c) Not in the 'New York' edition, but reprinted in Percy Lubbock's 'New and Complete Edition' (CE), London 1921–3; 1949.
(d) Translated into Italian.

'BROKEN WINGS'

(a) *Century Magazine*, December 1900.
(b) *The Better Sort*, London, 1903.

(c) Reprinted in the 'New York' edition (Vol. XVI), 1907–9; CE; 1956(?).
(d) Translated into German.

'THE BEAST IN THE JUNGLE'

(a) Not in a magazine.
(b) *The Better Sort*, London, 1903.
(c) Reprinted in the 'New York' edition (Vol. XVII); *The Uniform Tales of Henry James*, London, 1915 (UT); CE; 1949.
(d) Translated into Danish, French, German, and Italian (*La Tigra* . . .).

This must be one of James's most widely anthologized tales – and indeed is not possible to resist. It and 'The Jolly Corner' appear in the 'Norton Critical' *Tales of Henry James* ed. Christof Wegelin (New York and London, 1984) with material from James's prefaces and Notebooks, and both are in *Henry James: Selected Tales*, ed. Peter Messent and Tom Paulin, London, 1982, which also has 'The Bench of Desolation' and, unusually, 'The Birthplace'.

'THE BIRTHPLACE'

(a) Not in a magazine.
(b) *The Better Sort*, London, 1903.
(c) Reprinted in the 'New York' edition (Vol. XVII); CE.
(d) Translated into Danish.

'THE JOLLY CORNER'

(a) *English Review*, December 1908.
(b) No book publication before: –
(c) Reprinted in the 'New York' edition (Vol. XVII); UT; CE; 1947; 1949.
(d) Translated into German, Italian, and Spanish.

'THE VELVET GLOVE'

(a) *English Review*, March 1909.

(b) *The Finer Grain*, New York and London, 1910.
(c) Reprinted in CE.
(d) Translated into Italian and Spanish.

'CRAPY CORNELIA'

(a) *Harper's Magazine*, October 1909.
(b) *The Finer Grain*, New York and London, 1910.
(c) Reprinted in CE; 1947.

'THE BENCH OF DESOLATION'

(a) *Putnam's Magazine*, October–December 1909, January 1910.
(b) *The Finer Grain*, New York and London, 1910.
(c) Reprinted in CE.
(d) Translated into Italian.

NOTES

James addressed his stories at first to an educated audience, and I think it patronizing to modern readers to assume that they know much less or much differently from their forebears. 'Notes are often necessary, but they are necessary evils' says Dr Johnson in his *Preface to Shakespeare*. The real trouble with them when applied to the prose of art, as opposed to merely expository prose, is that they interrupt the flow and rhythm actually *more* than the absence of a piece of information – or even a translation – would do. They blunder in with more or less relevant matter, the essential point of which can in nearly every case be understood or gleaned from its context. An interruption is felt, whether the attention is diverted to the small print at the foot of the page or to the back of the book. The same is true of an editor's failure to resist the – considerable – temptation to intrude a petty critical commentary *via* the notes. I have in mind certain paperback editions of James's novels where interpretations of a ruthless mediocrity are forced upon one's conscientious but unwilling eyes.

The notes to this edition are therefore selective. What to include is a matter of tact in regard to the stories and guesswork as to a reader's ordinary fund of information. Everyone knows, for example, what a 'kodak' is, or that Diana and Artemis are different names for the same goddess. It is only when the references are recondite or foreign phrases not very familiar that I have disturbed James's prose with little numbers – and then often reluctantly. And there is a short comment on a famous conjectural 'source' necessary at the end of 'The Velvet Glove'.

It is probably mere coincidence that the two finest of the tales, 'The Beast in the Jungle' and 'The Jolly Corner', have required no annotation.

For the same reasons as those above the, in any case very slight, textual variants have not been included or discussed. For questions pertinent to these, see Aziz, *op. cit.* – although his edition has got nowhere near this late period as yet (1989).

'THE THIRD PERSON'

1. (p. 15) *Tauchnitz*. The continental reprints of British and American authors by Bernhard Tauchnitz, Leipzig, were very popular with travellers. Up to this date fourteen titles by James (mainly of the earlier novels and stories) had been included, and there were to be two more. I have a copy of *Washington Square* in a characteristic cream paper binding with dark pink and black lettering dated 1953 – but it comes, post-War, from Stuttgart. James approved of Baron Tauchnitz because he paid author's royalties, though not legally obliged to do so.

   George Bishop has a coy conjecture that the Tauchnitz at the end of this story is implied to be a work of James's (*When the Master Relents: The Neglected Short Fictions of Henry James*, Ann Arbor and London, 1988).

'BROKEN WINGS'

1. (p. 53) *The New Girl*. James's sardonic tone about this is no doubt partly accounted for by his own disappointments with writing for the theatre, particularly the bitter failure of *Guy Domville* in 1895, and by the comparisons he therefore felt compelled to make. Of *Lady Windermere's Fan* he had remarked (in a letter to Mrs Hugh Bell in February 1892) that 'Oscar's play . . . strikes me as a mixture that will run (I feel as if I were talking to a laundress), though infantine to my sense, both in subject and form. As a drama it is of a candid and primitive simplicity . . . absolutely no characterization and all the people talk equally strained Oscar – but there is a "situation" . . .' Perhaps he had something like this in mind?
2. (p. 56) *For the fee*. This, and what immediately follows, recalls an episode in 1876 when James explained to Whitelaw Reid, the editor of *The New York Tribune*, that his comparable letters – thought too intellectual – 'are the poorest I can do, especially for the money'. But in 1897 he – wonderful he – had again contributed (excellent) 'London Notes' to *Harper's Weekly*.
3. (p. 63) *Les lauriers sont coupés*. This is an old nursery rhyme used by the Parnassian poet Théodore de Banville (1823–91) in *'Les Cariatides, Les Stalactites'*. It seems similar in mood to Byron's 'So, we'll go no more a-roving'.

NOTES

'THE BIRTHPLACE'

1. (p. 127) *There were*. Both *The Better Sort* (1903, p. 196) and Edel in the *Collected Tales* read 'There are'. But this is an obvious error, corrected in the 'New York' edition and hence in CE.
2. (p. 135) *like a thief at night*. In 1 Thessalonians 5:2 'the day of the Lord so cometh as a thief in the night' (referring primarily to Matthew 25:13 and the Second Coming). In my opinion this, like all the religious overtones in this tale: — 'Him', his having 'covered His tracks as no other human being has done', 'pilgrims', 'They kill Him every day', the birthplace as a 'temple', etc. — is to be taken as a familiar kind of serious humour. But experience of literary critics suggests that such a potentially fruitful vein for allegorization may not always be left as quiet as Shakespeare's bones: and if not poor Gedge of course ends up as an anti-clerical priest.

'THE VELVET GLOVE'

1. (p. 195) *Gloriani's*. Gloriani is one of James's few repeated, motif figures. He is a sculptor who represents the artist as a worldly success — and is thus by implication not quite of the highest stature as an artist though wonderful as a man of the world. He appears previously in *Roderick Hudson* (1875) and *The Ambassadors* (1903).
2. (p. 199) *hand mailed in silver*. This version of the Emperor Charles V's iron hand within a velvet glove refers to the tenor's voice. But it is impossible to say what 'number' from either *Tristan und Isolde* or *Parsifal* the (unmusical) James could have had in mind, since there are no such numbers.
3. (p. 207) *been prompted by*. As the mis-titling of *The Winter's Tale* suggests, these evocations are meant to be vague. The magically still and lambent landscapes of Claude Lórraine (1600–82) are a different kind of pastoral from the actually rather rumbustious 'train of peasants' in Shakespeare. However I suppose the juxtaposition of the very modern with the timeless and unknown ('kodaks' and 'unvisited seas') in the following paragraph might be the result of James having written on *The Tempest* shortly before (1907).
4. (p. 208) *Astarte*. The Phoenician Aphrodite, called Ishtar in Babylon, and Amy Evans is mixing up both periods and myths in coupling her with Phidias, Pericles' sculptor in fifth-century Athens.
5. (p. 209) *'go behind' (don't you say?)*. James indeed did say this, but it is one of his terms of art for describing an author's possible entry into the mind of one

301

of his characters, and this is thus an excruciating and pretentious (and very amusing to those who know) misuse.

6. (p. 210) *crânerie*. Pluck – cavalier courage.

7. (p. 211) *high lawn of Mount Ida*. 'High lawn' is Milton's poetical way of referring to the dawn glades near Cambridge ('Lycidas', l.25), and it is possible that James's association is by way of *Paradise Lost* and the epical. For Mount Ida is, crucially, the location of the seduction of Zeus by Hera (beguiling his attention from the supervision of the Trojan War) amid fresh Spring grass and on a bed of clover, saffron and hyacinth in *Iliad*, XIV.

8. (p. 218) *supped to my fill*. cf. *Macbeth* V.v.13: 'I have supp'd full with horrors'. Shakespeare is behind the English novel in the most beneficially creative way. But one sometimes feels that what Edmund Bertram says in *Mansfield Park* – 'His celebrated passages are quoted by every body; they are in half the books we open, and we all talk Shakespeare, use his similies, and describe with his descriptions; but this is totally distinct from giving his sense . . .' – is too true. Here I feel the implication to be roughly as apt as Maria Edgeworth's in her brilliant *Helen* (1834) where the heroine, faced with a problem of *politesse* 'felt as if thrown into a sea of doubts, and she was not clear that she could, even by opposing, end them'.

9. (p. 220) (For elaboration of the literary references in this tale see Adeline R. Tintner – that mistress of the occasionally illuminating parallel – in 'James's Mock-Epic: "The Velvet Glove", Edith Wharton and Other Tales' in *Modern Fiction Studies*, 17, 1971–2, 483–99.)

For more ideas about the 'source' having been Edith Wharton, a belief which seems to have gained a fairly wide credence, see also the same author's 'The Metamorphoses of Edith Wharton in Henry James's *The Finer Grain*', *Twentieth Century Literature*, 21, 1975, 355–79. The facts are that James had rather ironically agreed to 'dedicate a few remarks to the mystery of your [Edith Wharton's] genius' at the request of a New York editor and apropos of her novel *The Fruit of the Tree* (cf. the Princess's *The Top of the Tree*) in 1907. But, she having denied that she was behind this request and he having read the novel and been disappointed, he thought better of the idea. Then, in response to her as usual generous praise of the story, he (while recording that two American periodicals had declined to print it) admitted that '*bien assurement* the whole thing *reeks* of you – and with Cook' (her chauffeur) – see *Henry James: Letters*, Vol. IV, ed. Leon Edel, Cambridge, Mass., and London, 1984, 521 (and xxviii, 461, 504). But obviously, *pace* Edel and Adeline R. Tintner, this modelling on Mrs Wharton (let alone further speculation by them that the very different Mrs Worthingham in 'Crapy

Cornelia' is also a portrait) needs to be taken with tact and a *good deal* of salt. Edith Wharton was rich and had a 'chariot of fire' (= car – but not James's rhyming slang). But she was not young, not beautiful in the way of the Princess, and could not possibly have written anything remotely so bad as to be justly parodied by the excerpt from *The Top of the Tree*. More definitely it seems odd that these scholars should want to imply that she was lying in her own, freely offered, account in *A Backward Glance* (New York, 1934):

> The tale – perhaps the most beautiful of his later short stories – called *The Velvet Glove* ... was suggested by the fact that a very beautiful young Englishwoman of great position, and unappeased literary ambitions had once tried to beguile him into contributing an introduction to a novel she was writing – or else into reviewing the book; I forget which. She had sought from him, at any rate, a literary 'boost' which all his admiration and liking for her could not, he thought, justify his giving; and they parted, though still friends, with evidences on her part of visible disappointment – and surprise (308–9).

This may be pure motiveless self-justifying fantasy – Adeline R. Tintner feels that it is a 'claim' dependent on having 'suppressed any memory of being' a model, which sorts oddly with her further argument that Edith Wharton 'replied' to James by implication in her own work of the period; and Edel (*Life of Henry James*, Vol. V, 'The Master', London, 1972, 352–3) thinks the passage 'perhaps a way of throwing dust in the reader's eyes'. (See also Millicent Bell, *Edith Wharton and Henry James*, New York, 1965.) But in both cases it is unclear why the perfectly sane and very affectionate (to the memory of James) Edith Wharton should wish to do, or be, like this. Actually I see no problem: James, like most creative writers, habitually transmutes his material into something quite other – a subject on which he is eloquent in his preface to *The Spoils of Poynton*, and of which it is disablingly naïve to be innocent.

'CRAPY CORNELIA'

1. (p. 228) *glimmering square*. James quite often refers to Tennyson. This –

> The casement slowly grows a glimmering square;
> So sad, so strange, the days that are no more.

– is from 'Tears, idle tears' in *The Princess*, IV (lyrics added to the third edition, 1853). The point is that White-Mason's rosy vision through *his* window is the precise opposite of the famous nostalgic lament.

2. (p. 232) *rari nantes in gurgite vasto*. '*Apparent rari nantes in gurgite vasto*', Virgil, *Aeneid*, I, 118: 'Here and there in the wastes of the ocean a swimmer was seen'. This is after the shipwreck, engineered by Juno, which drives Aeneas and the remnant of the Trojan fugitives to the Libyan shore – to Dido in Carthage, and thus to a tragic love which is a diversion from the imperial mission. But, as often, one doubts whether James meant, or would have tolerated, so detailed an application of his reference.

'THE BENCH OF DESOLATION'

1. (p. 253) *Meg Merrilies*. The formidable, outspoken – though benign – old gypsy woman in Sir Walter Scott's *Guy Mannering* (1815).

2. (p. 289) *twelve hundred and sixty pounds*. James is usually very sparing of specific, hard, facts like this – his holding back of the nature of the manufactures at the Newsome factory at Woollett, Mass., which puts the money into *The Ambassadors* is an important and popular joke. So he must intend something quite definite here, and at first sight the sum seems incommensurate with anything like the sacrifices involved in raising it. It is not vast. We should reflect, however, that – extremely difficult as it is to compare the money values of one period with those of another because of the varying relative prices of commodities – the national average weekly wage at this time (my figure is for 1903–4) was 21s. 8d. (i.e. £56.2s.8d p.a.) for a fifty-five hour week, on which it was supposed possible to support a family of five.

FOR THE BEST IN PAPERBACKS, LOOK FOR THE

In every corner of the world, on every subject under the sun, Penguin represents quality and variety – the very best in publishing today.

For complete information about books available from Penguin – including Puffins, Penguin Classics and Arkana – and how to order them, write to us at the appropriate address below. Please note that for copyright reasons the selection of books varies from country to country.

In the United Kingdom: Please write to *Dept E.P., Penguin Books Ltd, Harmondsworth, Middlesex, UB7 0DA.*

If you have any difficulty in obtaining a title, please send your order with the correct money, plus ten per cent for postage and packaging, to *PO Box No 11, West Drayton, Middlesex*

In the United States: Please write to *Dept BA, Penguin, 299 Murray Hill Parkway, East Rutherford, New Jersey 07073*

In Canada: Please write to *Penguin Books Canada Ltd, 2801 John Street, Markham, Ontario L3R 1B4*

In Australia: Please write to the *Marketing Department, Penguin Books Australia Ltd, P.O. Box 257, Ringwood, Victoria 3134*

In New Zealand: Please write to the *Marketing Department, Penguin Books (NZ) Ltd, Private Bag, Takapuna, Auckland 9*

In India: Please write to *Penguin Overseas Ltd, 706 Eros Apartments, 56 Nehru Place, New Delhi, 110019*

In the Netherlands: Please write to *Penguin Books Netherlands B.V., Postbus 195, NL–1380AD Weesp*

In West Germany: Please write to *Penguin Books Ltd, Friedrichstrasse 10–12, D–6000 Frankfurt/Main 1*

In Spain: Please write to *Longman Penguin España, Calle San Nicolas 15, E–28013 Madrid*

In Italy: Please write to *Penguin Italia s.r.l., Via Como 4, I-20096 Pioltello (Milano)*

In France: Please write to *Penguin Books Ltd, 39 Rue de Montmorency, F-75003 Paris*

In Japan: Please write to *Longman Penguin Japan Co Ltd, Yamaguchi Building, 2–12–9 Kanda Jimbocho, Chiyoda-Ku, Tokyo 101*

PENGUIN CLASSICS

Matthew Arnold	**Selected Prose**
Jane Austen	**Emma**
	Lady Susan, The Watsons, Sanditon
	Mansfield Park
	Northanger Abbey
	Persuasion
	Pride and Prejudice
	Sense and Sensibility
Anne Brontë	**Agnes Grey**
	The Tenant of Wildfell Hall
Charlotte Brontë	**Jane Eyre**
	Shirley
	Villette
Emily Brontë	**Wuthering Heights**
Samuel Butler	**Erewhon**
	The Way of All Flesh
Thomas Carlyle	**Selected Writings**
Wilkie Collins	**The Moonstone**
	The Woman in White
Charles Darwin	**The Origin of Species**
	The Voyage of the Beagle
Benjamin Disraeli	**Sybil**
George Eliot	**Adam Bede**
	Daniel Deronda
	Felix Holt
	Middlemarch
	The Mill on the Floss
	Romola
	Scenes of Clerical Life
	Silas Marner
Elizabeth Gaskell	**Cranford and Cousin Phillis**
	The Life of Charlotte Brontë
	Mary Barton
	North and South
	Wives and Daughters

PENGUIN CLASSICS

William James	**Varieties of Religious Experience**
Jack London	**The Call of the Wild and Other Stories**
	Martin Eden
Henry Wadsworth Longfellow	**Selected Poems**
Herman Melville	**Billy Budd, Sailor and Other Stories**
	Moby-Dick
	Redburn
	Typee
Thomas Paine	**Common Sense**
Edgar Allan Poe	**The Narrative of Arthur Gordon Pym of Nantucket**
	The Other Poe
	The Science Fiction of Edgar Allan Poe
	Selected Writings
Harriet Beecher Stowe	**Uncle Tom's Cabin**
Henry David Thoreau	**Walden and Civil Disobedience**
Mark Twain	**The Adventures of Huckleberry Finn**
	A Connecticut Yankee at King Arthur's Court
	Life on the Mississippi
	Pudd'nhead Wilson
	Roughing It
Owen Wister	**The Virginian**

FOR THE BEST IN PAPERBACKS, LOOK FOR THE 🐧

PENGUIN CLASSICS

Arnold Bennett	The Old Wives' Tale
Joseph Conrad	Heart of Darkness
	Nostromo
	The Secret Agent
	The Shadow-Line
	Twixt Land and Sea
	Under Western Eyes
E. M. Forster	Howard's End
	The Longest Journey
	A Passage to India
	A Room With a View
	Where Angels Fear to Tread
Henry James	The Aspern Papers and The Turn of the Screw
	The Bostonians
	Daisy Miller
	The Europeans
	The Golden Bowl
	Portrait of a Lady
	Roderick Hudson
	Washington Square
	What Maisie Knew
	The Wings of the Dove
Rudyard Kipling	The Day's Work
	The Light That Failed
	Wee Willie Winkie
D. H. Lawrence	The Plumed Serpent
	The Rainbow
	Selected Short Stories
	Sons and Lovers
	The White Peacock
	Women in Love